CASSIE MILES

IN THE
MANOR
WITH THE
MILLIONAIRE

Harlequin
Mills & Boon™

INTRIGUE™

First Published 2008
First Australian Paperback Edition 2008
ISBN 978 0 733 58885 3

IN THE MANOR WITH THE MILLIONAIRE © 2008 by Harlequin Books S.A.
Special thanks and acknowledgment to Cassie Miles
for her contribution to The Curse of Raven's Cliff miniseries.
Philippine Copyright 2008
Australian Copyright 2008
New Zealand Copyright 2008

Published by
Harlequin Mills & Boon®
Level 5
15 Help Street
CHATSWOOD NSW 2067
AUSTRALIA

Printed and bound in Australia by
McPherson's Printing Group

ABOUT THE AUTHOR

For Cassie Miles, the best part about writing a story set in Eagle County near the Vail ski area is the ready-made excuse to head into the mountains for research. Though the winter snows are great for skiing, her favourite season is fall when the aspens turn gold.

The rest of the time, Cassie lives in Denver where she takes urban hikes around Cheesman Park, reads a ton and critiques often. Her current plans include a Vespa and a road trip, despite eye-rolling objections from her adult children.

CAST OF CHARACTERS

Blake Monroe—This world-famous architect has been hired to oversee the renovations of Beacon Manor and the lighthouse. A widower, he still mourns the death of his wife, Kathleen.

Madeline Douglas—A proper schoolteacher from Boston, she's hired to be the live-in tutor for Blake's son. She comes to Raven's Cliff with secrets of her own.

Duncan Monroe—Blake's six-year-old son has been diagnosed with high-functioning autism.

Alma Eisen—The Beacon Manor housekeeper was once a foster mother for Madeline.

Dr. Teddy Fisher—The Beacon Manor owner whose scientific experiments might have caused an epidemic.

Helen Fisher—A librarian, this old maid resents the wealth of her brother, Teddy.

Perry Wells—Mayor of Raven's Cliff who lost his daughter on her wedding day.

Beatrice Wells—The Mayor's wife.

Grant Bridges—The ambitious Assistant District Attorney also coaches the local T-ball team.

Detective Andrei Lagios—Homicide investigator.

Sofia Lagios—Sister of Andrei, recently murdered by the Seaside Strangler.

Detective Joe Curtis—Newly transferred from the LAPD, he works with Lagios.

Alex Gibson—A local fisherman.

Marty Todd—Madeline's ne'er-do-well brother.

Chapter One

"One, two, three…" Duncan Monroe counted the steps as he climbed the stairs, not touching the banister or the wall. "…four, five, six."

That was how old he was. Six years old.

"Seven, eight, nine."

Here was where the staircase made a corner, and he could see to the top. Daddy had turned on the light in his bedroom, but there were shadows. Dark, scary shadows. Outside the rain came down and rattled against the windows.

Duncan shivered. Even though this was the middle of summertime, he felt cold on the inside. So cold it made his tummy hurt. Sometimes, when he touched people or things, he got creepy feelings like spider legs running up and down his arms. And he saw stuff. Bad stuff.

But he wasn't touching anything. His feet were in sneakers. He had on jeans and a long-sleeved T-shirt. He shouldn't be scared.

"Duncan." His dad called to him. "Are you getting ready for bed?"

"No." He hadn't meant to yell. His voice was too loud.

He covered his open mouth with both hands. His fingers pushed hard, holding back an even louder yell. His skin tasted like salt. Usually he wore gloves to keep from feeling things.

"Duncan, are you all right?"

His dad hated when Duncan was inappropriate. That's what his teacher used to call it. *Inappropriate behavior*. The doctors had other words for him. *Trauma. Autism. Hyper-something*. They all meant the same thing. He was a freak.

He yanked his hands down to his sides. "I'm okay."

"Get into your pajamas, buddy. I'll be there in a minute."

The shadow at the top of the stairs was as big as a T-Rex with giant, pointy teeth. Duncan wasn't going there. He turned around on the stairs and quietly counted backward. "Nine, eight, seven…"

He was at the front door of the big house they had just moved into. Though he didn't like touching doorknobs, he grabbed it and pulled.

Outside, the rain wasn't too bad. Big, fat drops splashed on the flat stones leading up to the front door. He stuck out his hand to catch them.

He walked out into it. Five steps. Then ten.

The light by the front door didn't reach very far into the dark. The thunder went boom. He heard the ocean smashing on the rocks at the bottom of the cliff.

He turned around and stared at the big house. On the first floor were four windows and one door, exactly in the middle. Five windows, all exactly the same size, on top. All exactly balanced. He liked that. What he didn't like was the big, old, wrecked-up tower that Daddy said used to be a lighthouse.

He looked toward it and saw a girl in a long dress and a red cape. She skipped toward the trees in the forest.

She giggled. Not the kind of mean laugh that kids used when they pointed at his gloves and called him Dunk the Skunk. She waved to him as though she wanted to play.

He heard her singing. "She sells seashells by the sea-shore."

MADELINE DOUGLAS gripped the steering wheel with both hands and squinted through her glasses at the narrow road winding through the thick Maine forest. Her headlights barely penetrated the rain and fog that had turned the summer night into a dense black shroud.

She opened her window to disperse the condensation on her windshield; the defroster in her ancient Volkswagen station wagon had quit working. This cranky old rattletrap always chose the worst possible moment to be temperamental. If the skies had been clear—the way normal weather in July ought to be—the defrost would have been fine.

How much farther? The man at the service station in Raven's Cliff where she'd spent her last ten bucks on gas told her that this road led to Beacon Manor. "Can't miss it," he'd said.

"We'll see about that," she muttered. Thus far, everything about her drive from Boston to this remote fishing village in Maine had gone wrong. An accident with a logging truck had clogged the highway. Then, she'd missed the turnoff and had to backtrack several miles. Then, her cell phone died. And now, the weather from hell.

At five minutes past eight o'clock, she was more than

half an hour late for her interview with world-famous architect Blake Monroe. Not to mention that she was a mess. Her green-patterned blouse didn't go with the bright red cardigan she'd dragged out of her suitcase when the rain started. Her khaki skirt was creased with wrinkles. Her black hair, pulled up in a knot on top of her head, had to be a frizz mop.

Somehow, she had to pull herself together and convince Blake Monroe to hire her as a tutor for his six-year-old son, Duncan, who had been diagnosed with a form of high-functioning autism. Though she had no formal training in handling kids with special needs, Madeline had been a substitute teacher for the past two years in Boston's inner-city schools. She had first-hand experience with a wide range of behaviors.

She'd convince him. *She had to.*

If Blake Monroe didn't hire her, she had a serious problem. With her meager supply of cash spent and her credit cards maxed, she couldn't even afford a cheap motel room for tonight. Sleeping in her car would be difficult; she'd crammed all her earthly belongings in here, including the potted ficus that sat beside her on the passenger seat.

The rain died down, replaced by gusts of fog that slapped against her windshield like tattered curtains. The tired old engine coughed on the verge of a breakdown as she emerged from the forest.

In the distance, perhaps a half mile away, she saw the glimmer of lights. Beacon Manor. Huge as a fortress, the mansion loomed in the foreboding darkness.

She maneuvered around a sharp curve that circled a stand of trees. On the opposite side, the shoulder of the road vanished into nothingness at the edge of a cliff. A dangerous precipice with no guard rail.

Her headlights shone on a dark-colored SUV parked smack in the middle of the road. His lights were off. There was no way around him.

She cranked the steering wheel hard left—away from the cliff—and slammed on the brake. Though she couldn't have been going more than twenty miles an hour, her tires skidded on the wet asphalt.

In slow motion, she saw the inevitable collision coming closer, inch by inch. Her brakes screeched. The fog whirled. Her headlights wavered.

Her right fender dinged the rear bumper of the SUV, and she jolted against her seat belt. Though the impact felt minor, the passenger-side airbag deployed against the ficus. Great! Her plant was protected from whiplash.

But not herself. The driver's-side airbag stayed in place. Like everything else in her life, it was broken.

She slumped over the steering wheel. A nasty, metallic stink from the engine gushed through her open window. A car wreck would have been disaster, and she ought to be grateful that her car wasn't a crumpled mass. Instead, hot tears burned the insides of her eyelids. In spite of a lifetime of careful plans and hard work, in spite of her best intentions…

A hand reached through the window and grabbed her upper arm. "What's wrong with you? Didn't you see me?"

Startled, she stared into the stark face of a smallish man with a goatee. A sheen of moisture accented the hollows beneath his eyes and his angry, distorted snarl.

He shook her. "Don't think you can run away. You'll pay for this damage."

Enough! She shoved open her door, forcing him back.

Justified rage shot through her as she leaped from the car into the drizzle. "You're the one at fault. Look where you're parked. There's no way I could get around you."

"You're trespassing." With his left hand, he pulled his collar tight around his throat. His right arm hung loosely at his side. "This is my property."

Her hopes sank. "Blake Monroe?"

"Monroe? He's the architect I hired to fix this place up." His skinny neck craned. Even so, he wasn't as tall as her own five feet, ten inches. "I own Beacon Manor. I'm Theodore Fisher. *Doctor* Fisher."

He announced himself as if she should be impressed, but she'd never heard of him. "All right, *Doctor*. Let's take a look at the damage."

The deep gouge on her fender blended with other scrapes and nicks. Dr. Fisher glanced at the scratch on his SUV, then turned his back on her. Clearly agitated, he walked wide of the two vehicles with tense, jerky steps. His brow furrowed as he peered into the darkness at the edge of the cliff. Watching for something? For someone? As he paced, he muttered under his breath. Though she couldn't make out the words, he sounded furious.

Madeline didn't want that crazy anger turned in her direction. Speaking with the measured voice she used to calm a classroom full of second-graders, she said, "We should exchange insurance information."

"Not necessary," he snapped.

"I agree." She wouldn't bother with this repair, couldn't afford to have her insurance premiums go up. "I'm willing to forget about this if you are."

His head swiveled on his neck. He focused intently on her. "Not trying to pull a fast one, are you?"

"Certainly not." She removed her rain-splattered glasses. His face blurred.

"Why are you here?" he demanded.

"I'm applying for a job as a tutor for Blake Monroe's son."

"So you'll be staying at the Manor. At my house." Very deliberately, he approached her. "I'll always know where to find you."

The wind wailed through the trees, and she heard something else. A voice? Dr. Fisher turned toward the sound. His arm raised. In his right hand, he held an automatic pistol.

SHE SELLS seashells…

In her long dress, she was the prettiest girl Duncan had ever seen. Her hair was golden. Her skin was white. She looked like the marble angel on Mama's gravestone.

"I would like to be your friend," she said. "My name is Temperance Raven."

"That's the name of this town," Duncan said. "Raven's Cliff."

"Named after my father," she said. "Captain Raven."

He knew she was telling a lie. The town was founded in 1794. He remembered that date, just as he remembered all numbers. So what if she fibbed? He liked the way she talked, like an accent. "Where are you from?"

"Dover in England."

They were standing under the trees, and his clothes were soppy. But she hardly seemed wet at all. "Come inside, Temperance. I'll show you my computer games."

Maybe he'd even let her win. Her smile was so pretty. *Seashells, seashells. By the seashore.*

She held up her hand. "I brought a gift for you."

Before he could tell her that he never touched anyone or anything with his bare hands, she placed a glowing white shell on the ground before him. "It's for you, Duncan."

If he didn't pick it up, she'd think he was scared. Then she'd laugh at him and run away. So, he leaned down and grabbed the shell. It burned his hand. He couldn't let go. Shivers ran up his arm. There was a roar inside his head.

"Temperance." He gasped.

"I am here, Duncan. I will always be here for you."

His eyes closed and he fell to the ground. In his mind, he saw a whole different place. A different time: Sunset. He was at the bottom of the cliff, near the rocks that stuck out into the waves.

He moaned and tried to get up. Something very bad had happened in this place and time, something that had to do with the shell....

He saw a pretty lady with curly black hair. Sofia, her name was Sofia. She had on a long white dress, kind of like the one Temperance wore, and she was lying on the rocks. Duncan felt her fear. Inside his head, he heard her silent screams for help, but she was too weak to move. Couldn't even lift a finger.

Someone else chanted. In a low voice, he sang about the sea. The dangers of the sea. The curse of the sea.

Duncan couldn't see his face. But he knew. This man was very bad. Very strong. Very mean. He put a necklace of seashells over Sofia's head.

"No," Duncan cried out. "Stop him. No."

The bad man pulled the necklace tighter and tighter. He twisted hard. Duncan felt the shells bite into his own throat. He couldn't breathe.

Lying on the wet grasses, he shook and shook. He was crying. He heard grunts and whimpers, and he knew the sounds were coming from him.

His eyes opened.

There was a lady kneeling beside him. She wore glasses. Her hair was pulled back, but some had got loose. It was black and curly. She looked kind of like Sofia. He whispered the name. "Sofia?"

"My name is Madeline," she said, reaching toward him. "Are you—"

"Don't," he yelled. "Don't touch me. Never touch."

She held up both hands. "Okay. Whatever you say. You're Duncan, right?"

He sat up and looked around for Temperance. She was gone. But he still held the shell in his hand. It was a warning. Temperance had warned him about the bad man.

He scrambled to his feet. Where was Temperance? Where was his friend? "She sells seashells…"

"By the seashore." The lady smiled and stood beside him. She was tall for a girl. "She sells seashells."

"By the seashore," he said.

She pointed. "Do you see that light over there? I'll bet that's your father's flashlight."

"He's going to be mad. I was inappropriate."

Madeline looked down at the sopping-wet boy in his jeans and T-shirt. A terrible sadness emanated from this child. She longed to cuddle him in her arms and reassure him, but she'd promised not to touch.

"There's nothing wrong with being inappropriate," she said. "I've often been that way myself."

He stared up at her. "Are you a freak?"

"Absolutely." She took off her glasses, tried wiping the

lenses on her damp shirt and gave up, stowing them in the pocket of her skirt. "It takes someone courageous to be different. I think you're very brave, Duncan."

The hint of a smile curved his mouth. "You do?"

"Very brave indeed." She bobbed her head. "Let's find your father."

When the boy took off running toward the flashlight's beacon, Madeline had a hard time keeping up. The two-inch heels on the beige leather pumps she'd worn to create a professional appearance for her interview made divots in the rain-soaked earth.

The flashlight's beam wavered, then charged in their direction. In seconds, a tall man in a hooded rain poncho was upon them. He held out his arms to Duncan, but the boy stopped a few yards away and folded his arms across his skinny torso. "I'm okay, Daddy."

"Thank God," his father murmured. "I was worried."

"I'm okay," Duncan shouted.

Blake Monroe dropped to one knee. He reached toward his son. Without touching the boy, he caressed the air around him with such poignancy that Madeline's heart ached.

Before she'd set out on this journey, she'd taken a couple of minutes to check out Blake Monroe on the Internet. An internationally renowned architect and designer, he'd worked in Berlin, Paris and all over the United States, most notably on historic renovations and exclusive boutique hotels. His international fame was somewhat intimidating, but right now he was a frightened parent whose only concern was the safety of his child.

Blake stood, whipped off his poncho and dropped it around his son's shoulders.

When he turned toward her, a flash of lightning illuminated his high cheekbones and the sharp line of his jaw. Even without her glasses, she realized that he was one of the most handsome men she'd ever seen.

The rain started up with renewed fury, lashing against his broad shoulders, but he didn't cower the way she did. His powerful presence suggested a strength that could match the raging storm. His fiery gaze met her eyes, and a sizzle penetrated her cold, wet body.

"Who are you?"

"Madeline Douglas. I'm here about the teaching position."

"What were you doing out here with my son?"

There was an unmistakable accusation in his question. He blamed her? Did he think she'd lured Duncan out of the house in this storm?

Fumbling in her pocket, she found her glasses and stuck them onto her nose, wishing she had a ten-inch-thick shield of bulletproof glass to protect herself from his hostility. "I was driving along the road, just coming out of the forest. And I had a bit of an accident with Dr. Fisher."

"The owner of the Manor," Blake said. "Nice move."

Though Madeline had done nothing wrong, she felt defensive. "We decided that the damage was too minor to report. Then we heard something from the forest. Voices." With Duncan standing here, she decided not to mention Dr. Fisher's gun. "I followed the sound of Duncan's voice. Found him at the edge of the trees."

"She did," Duncan said. "She's pretty. I thought she was Sofia."

Blake tensed. He hunkered down so his eyes were level with his son's. "What name did you say?"

"Poor, poor Sofia. She's with Mama and the angels."

"Did you see something, Duncan?"

"No," he shouted. "No, no, no."

"Let's go inside," Blake said.

Duncan spun in a circle. "Where's Temperance? She's my friend."

"Time for bed, son. Back to the house. You can count the steps."

The boy walked toward the front door in a perfectly straight line, counting each step aloud.

Without saying another word to her, Blake walked beside him.

"Hey," she called after them. "Should I bring my car around to the front?"

"I don't give a damn what you do."

A scream of sheer frustration crawled up the back of her throat. This trip was cursed. Every instinct warned her to give up, to turn back, find another way.

But she was desperate.

Through the driving rain, she heard Duncan counting and singing. "She sells seashells…"

Chapter Two

Gathering up the remnants of her shredded self-respect, Madeline chased after Blake and his son. If she didn't follow them into the house, she was certain that the door would be locked against her. Not only did she need this job, but she wanted it. She'd connected with Duncan. In him, she saw a reflection of her own childhood. She knew what it was like to be called a freak. Always to be an outsider.

As the daughter of a drug-addicted mother and an absent father, she'd been shuffled from one foster home to another until she was finally adopted by the Douglases when she was twelve. In spite of their kindness and warmth, Madeline still hadn't fitted in with other kids. Her adopted family was poor, and she grew too fast. Her secondhand clothing never fitted properly on her long, gangly frame. And then there were the glasses she'd worn since first grade.

Most of the time, her childhood was best forgotten. But, oddly, her past had brought her here. Standing in the doorway of Beacon Manor, Madeline saw someone she had once lived with. Alma Eisen.

Eighteen years ago, Alma had been a foster parent for Madeline and her older brother, Marty. They'd stayed with her for a year—a dark and terrible year during which Alma had decided to divorce her abusive husband. Unlike the other fosters, Alma had stayed in touch with Christmas cards and birthday greetings, which Madeline had dutifully responded to.

It was Alma—now employed as Blake's housekeeper and cook—who had told Madeline about the tutoring position. At the door to the manor, she greeted Madeline with a smile but held her at arm's length, not wanting to get wet. "What on earth happened to you?"

"Long story."

The years had been kind to Alma Eisen. Her hair was still blond and elaborately styled with spit curls at the cheeks. Her makeup, including blue eye shadow, almost disguised the wrinkles. Madeline figured that this petite woman had to be in her fifties. "You look terrific."

"Thanks, hon. Wish I could say the same for you."

Blake had followed his son—who was still counting aloud—to the top of the staircase.

Madeline called to him. "Mr. Monroe?"

He glared. "What is it?"

"I came all this way, sir. At the very least, I'd like to have an interview."

"After I get my son to bed, I'll deal with you."

He turned away. Though Madeline wasn't a betting woman, she guessed that her odds of being hired were about a thousand to one. A shiver trembled through her.

"You need to get out of those wet clothes," Alma said, "before you catch your death of cold."

"I don't have anything to change into. My car is parked way down the road."

"Come with me, hon. I'll take care of you."

Though Alma had stayed in touch, Madeline didn't remember her as a particularly nurturing woman. Her phone call about this job had been a huge surprise, and Madeline couldn't help wondering about Alma's motives. What could she hope to gain from having Madeline working here?

She trailed the small woman up the grand staircase and looked back down at the graceful oval of the foyer. She couldn't see into any of the other rooms. Doors were closed, and plastic sheeting hung across the arched entry to what must have been a drawing room. Signs of disrepair marred the grandeur of the manor, but the design showed a certain civility and elegance, like a dowager duchess who had fallen on hard times.

Alma hustled her past Duncan's bedroom to the far end of the long, wainscoted hallway with wallpaper peeling in the corners. She opened the door farthest from the staircase and hustled Madeline inside.

The center light reflected off the crystals of a delicate little chandelier. With dark wood furnishings, somewhat worn, and a four-poster bed with a faded gray silk duvet, this bedroom was the essence of "shabby chic."

"Guest room," Alma said as she rummaged through the drawers of a bureau. "This is where you'll be staying after you're hired."

"Hired?" She scoffed. "I doubt it. Blake Monroe can't stand me."

"In any case, you're staying here tonight. It's not safe for you to be out." She tossed a pair of sweatpants and a T-shirt toward her. "These ought to fit. They were left behind by one of Blake's friends who spent the night."

Madeline picked up the ratty gray sweatpants. "I really appreciate this, Alma."

"Don't thank me yet." She lowered her voice. "This little town, Raven's Cliff, comes with a curse."

"Superstitions," Madeline said.

"Don't be so sure. There's a serial killer on the loose. A couple of weeks ago, he murdered two girls on the eve of their senior prom. One of them was the sister of a local cop. Sofia Lagios."

Sofia. Duncan had looked at Madeline and spoken that name. "What did she look like?"

"I've only seen photographs. But she was a bit like you. Long, curly black hair."

Duncan must have heard people talking about the serial killer. But why would a six-year-old remember the name of a murder victim?

"Get changed," Alma said. "I'll tell Blake that you're too pooped to talk tonight. In the morning, you can have a nice, professional interview."

"Great." She dropped her car keys on top of the bureau. "Nothing sounds better right now than a good night's sleep."

BLAKE LINGERED in the doorway of his son's bedroom, gazing with all the love he possessed at Duncan's angelic little face. So beautiful. So like his mother. Often, when Blake looked into his son's bright blue eyes, he saw Kathleen staring back at him. On those rare occasions when Duncan laughed, he heard echoes of her own joy, and he remembered the good times. Only three years ago, cancer had taken her away from him forever.

"Time for sleep, Duncan."

As usual, no response.

To get an answer, Blake used the rhyming repetition that his son enjoyed. "Nighty-night. Sleep tight…"

"And don't let the bedbugs bite," Duncan said.

Sometimes, the kid scared the hell out of him. Tonight, when he'd disappeared, Blake had feared disaster. A fall from the precipitous cliffs near the lighthouse. An attack by wild dogs or animals. Worse, a confrontation with a serial killer. Why had Duncan spoken the name of one of the victims? The boy must have known that Sofia Lagios was dead because he said she was with the angels. But how? How had he known?

Life would be a lot easier if Blake could ask a simple question and get a simple answer, but his son's brain didn't work that way.

Duncan stared up at the fluorescent stars Blake had attached to the ceiling in a precise geometric pattern. "I have a friend," he said. "She sells seashells."

"That's great, buddy." It had to be an imaginary friend. He hadn't been around any other children. "What's her name?"

"Temperance Raven. She wears a red cape." His tiny fingers laced together, then pulled apart. He repeated the action three times. "I like French fries."

"Where did you meet Temperance?"

"By the lighthouse. She wanted me to play with her."

Blake didn't like the sound of this. The lighthouse was under construction, dangerous. "Was Temperance outside? In the rain?"

Duncan turned to his side. "Seashells, seashells, sea-shells…"

"Goodnight, son."

Blake left the door to his son's bedroom ajar. Duncan wanted it that way.

Blake wanted to find out what had happened tonight,

and there was one person who could tell him. He'd seen Alma escorting that very wet young woman down the hall toward the guest room. What was her name? Madeline? She might be able to give him information about Duncan's supposed new friend. Blake tapped on her door.

"Alma?" she called out. "Come on in."

Blake strode inside. "We need to talk."

Wearing baggy sweatpants and an oversize T-shirt, she stood in front of the mirror above the antique dressing table. Her long black hair fell past her shoulders in a mass of damp tangles. As soon as she spotted him, she grabbed her black-framed glasses and stuck them on the end of her straight, patrician nose. "Mr. Monroe. I thought we might have our interview tomorrow."

He'd almost forgotten that she was here to apply for a job as his son's tutor. "I need to know what happened tonight. Duncan mentioned someone named Temperance."

"I didn't see anyone else," she said. "There aren't any other houses nearby, are there?"

"We're isolated."

"That could be a problem." She pushed the heavy mane away from her face. Her complexion was fresh, with rosy tints on her cheeks and the tip of her nose. Behind those glasses, black lashes outlined her eyes. An unusual color. Aquamarine.

"Problem?" he asked.

"Not having neighbors." She gave him a prim smile. "Surely, you'll want Duncan to have playmates."

"He doesn't do well with other children."

"I know," she said. "He told me."

Like hell he did. His son's conversations were limited to discussions of simple activities, like brushing his teeth. Or repetitions. Or numbers.

She continued, "He was worried that you'd be angry because he was…how did he say it? Inappropriate."

That sounded like Duncan. "His teachers said his behavior was inappropriate. The word stuck in his mind."

"Everybody's like that. We all tend to remember the words that hurt. To let criticism soak in."

His son wasn't like everybody else. Far from it. But he appreciated the way she phrased her comments, and Duncan seemed to like her. Maybe Madeline Douglas would be a suitable tutor, after all.

He crossed the room and took a seat in a carved wooden rocking chair, one of several handmade pieces in the manor. "Show me your résumé and recommendations."

When she gestured toward the window, the graceful motion of her wrist contrasted the baggy black T-shirt. "All my papers are in my car, which is still down the road."

"Where you ran into Teddy Fisher."

"I didn't want to mention this in front of Duncan," she said, "but Dr. Fisher had a handgun."

Not good news. He hated to hear that the local loons were armed. Fisher had tons of money and a decent reputation as a scientist with his own laboratories in Raven's Cliff. He came from a good family; his father had been a Nobel Prize winner. But Teddy's behavior went beyond eccentric into borderline insanity.

The main reason Blake had taken this job—a step down from his typically high-profile architectural assignments— was because he wanted to get Duncan out of the city into a small-town environment where the pace was slow and distractions were minimal.

"Teddy Fisher owns the Manor," he said. "But he's not supposed to visit without notifying me. I'll remind him."

She gave a brisk nod. "If you like, I can tell you about my qualifications."

"Do it."

She started by rattling off her educational achievements, special recognitions and a bachelor's degree from an undistinguished college which had taken six years because she'd been holding down a job while going to school. For two years, she'd taught second grade at a parochial school. "Then I started substitute teaching in some of Boston's inner-city schools."

He held up his hand, signaling a stop. "Why did you leave a full-time position to be a sub?"

"Alma might have mentioned that I grew up in the foster-care system."

Vaguely, he recalled some comment. "She might have."

"I was a throwaway kid. No one expected me to amount to much. But I had a teacher in third grade...a wonderful teacher. She wouldn't let me shirk on my assignments, made me work hard and kept after me to do better. She noticed me."

Behind her glasses, her eyes teared up. "She changed my life. By working in inner-city schools, I felt like I might make that kind of difference."

He liked her earnest compassion. She sure as hell had the empathy needed to work with his son. But did she have the training? Blake wasn't accustomed to settling for second best. "How much do you know about autism?"

She picked up a straight-back wooden chair and moved it close to his rocker. When she sat, she leaned forward. "What can you tell me about Duncan's behavior?"

"On the behavioral range of autism, he's considered to be high-functioning." Blake had taken his son to a cadre of doctors and therapists. "Initially, we tried drug therapy, but Duncan didn't respond well. The specialists call his condition a form of hypersensitivity."

"Which is why he doesn't like to be touched."

"When he touches someone, he says that he knows what they're thinking."

"Like a psychic."

"Don't go there," he warned. It was difficult enough to manage Duncan's illness without the extra burden of some harebrained, paranormal philosophy.

"I'm trying to understand," she said. "When I found Duncan in the woods, we had a coherent communication. More important, he reacted to me. He looked me in the eye, and he smiled. That behavior isn't consistent with what I know about autism."

Her presumption ticked him off. For the past three years, since his wife had died, he'd struggled with his son's condition. They'd gone through brain scans, blood tests, physical and psychological diagnostics…. He rose from the rocking chair. "Are you an expert?"

"No, but I can see the obvious." Instead of cowering, she stood to confront him. "Duncan is smart. And he cares about what you think. He wants you to love him."

Her words were a slap in the face. Tight-lipped, he said, "This interview is over."

WITH THE ECHO of the door slamming behind Blake still ringing in her ears, Madeline collapsed onto the bed. Disaster! She'd infuriated Blake and blown her chance at this job. Truly a shame because she thought she might work well with Duncan, and she found herself drawn to his father. What red-blooded woman wouldn't be? Blake was gorgeous and intense. Unfortunately, he despised her.

She shifted around on the bed. Before she went to sleep, she needed to use the facilities.

Since there was no adjoining bathroom with this bedroom, she had to go into the hallway. Poking her head out the door, she checked to make sure Blake was nowhere in sight. One doorway stood ajar and light spilled into the corridor. Duncan's room. She tiptoed past.

"Madeline?"

Peeking into his room, she said, "You remembered my name. Hi, Duncan."

"Will I see my friend again?"

She had no right to be here, no justifiable reason to talk with Blake's son. But she couldn't turn away from this troubled child. Slipping into his room, she pulled a rocking chair near his bed. "Is her name Temperance?"

"Temperance Raven."

"Like the town," Madeline said. "Raven's Cliff."

"Temperance lied to me about the town being named after her daddy in 1794. But I don't care. Lots of people lie. Liar, liar, pants on fire."

"Hang them up on a telephone wire," she responded. "You like rhymes."

"Temperance gave me a present." He rolled over on his bed and picked up a smooth, white shell.

Madeline grinned. "She sells seashells."

"By the seashore," Duncan concluded.

Though their conversation scattered in several directions, they were communicating. Instead of telling him that she liked his room, she pointed up at the ceiling and recited, "Starlight, star bright. First star I see tonight."

He watched her with an intensity that reminded her of his father. "Finish the rhyme."

"Wish I may, wish I might, have the wish I wish tonight."

He parroted the rhyme back to her perfectly. Not once, but three times. Then he laughed.

Hearing a sound near the door, she glanced over her shoulder and saw Blake standing in the hallway. He stepped away too quickly for her to decide if he was angry about her talking to Duncan. And, frankly, she didn't care. This wasn't about him.

"Duncan," she said, "I know a very long rhyme. A poem about baseball."

He nodded for her to continue.

"You'd like baseball. It's all about numbers." She drew a diamond in the air as she talked about the bases and the pitcher and the batter. "Four balls and three strikes."

"Three strikes and you're out," he said.

"You're right," she said. "This poem is called 'Casey at the Bat.'"

He lay back on his pillow to listen while she recited the poem she'd memorized in fifth grade. The rhyming cadence lulled him, and Duncan's eyelids began to droop.

When she had finished, he roused himself. "Again."

She started over. By the time she finished, he was sound asleep.

Leaving his door ajar, exactly the way she'd found it, she went down the hallway to the bathroom. Like every other part of the house she'd seen, the room was sorely in need of fresh paint. But it seemed clean and had an old-fashioned claw-footed tub. Fantastic! One of her favorite pastimes was a long, hot soak. And why not? It wasn't as if she could make Blake Monroe dislike her even more. Besides, she didn't know when or if she'd ever have the chance to luxuriate in a tub again.

As she filled the tub, fears about her uncertain future arose. No money. No job. No home. She had only enough gas to get back to Raven's Cliff. That would have to be where she started her new life, maybe working as a waitress or a short-order cook. She had experience at both from when she was putting herself through college.

Stripping off the sweatpants and T-shirt, she eased into the hot, steamy water.

Damn it, Marty. This is all your fault. Her brother had popped back into her life just long enough to wreck everything. When he'd showed up, she should have thrown him out on his handsome butt. Should have, but didn't. Water under the bridge.

After a nice, long soak, she climbed out of the tub, somewhat refreshed, and padded down the hallway to her "shabby chic" room.

The door was open, just the way she'd left it. But something was different. At the foot of her bed was the canvas suitcase that had been in the back of her car. Had Alma trudged all the way down the road to get it? She opened the flap and took out a nightgown.

"Madeline Douglas."

She turned and saw Blake standing in the doorway. He tossed the keys to her car to the center of the bed. "You shouldn't leave these lying around."

"I didn't." The keys had been on top of the bureau in her room. *Inside her room!* Even if the door was open, he shouldn't have barged in uninvited.

"You're hired," he said without smiling. "We'll talk in the morning."

The door closed behind him.

Chapter Three

The next morning, the skies outside Madeline's bedroom window were clear, washed clean by the rain. And she tried to focus on the sunny side. She had a job and a place to live. Working with Duncan provided an interesting challenge. For now, she was safe.

The dark cloud on her emotional horizon was Blake Monroe. A volatile man. She didn't know why he had changed his mind about hiring her and decided it was best not to ask too many questions. He didn't seem like the type of man who bothered to explain himself.

Entering the high-ceilinged kitchen, she smiled at Alma, who sat at the table, drinking coffee and keeping company with a morning television chat program on a small flat-screen.

"I'm hired," Madeline announced. "I can't thank you enough for telling me about this job."

"Congrats." Using the remote, Alma turned down the volume. "How about lending me a hand with breakfast?"

"Sure."

She turned and confronted a mountain of dirty dishes, glasses, pots and crusted skillets that spread across the countertop like a culinary apocalypse. It appeared that Alma hadn't wiped a single plate since they'd moved into this house.

How could anyone stand such a mess! Madeline rolled up the sleeves of her daisy-patterned cotton shirt, grabbed an apron that was wadded in the corner of the counter and dug in.

"You haven't changed a bit," Alma said. "Even as a kid, you were good about cleaning up."

Maybe even a teensy bit compulsive. "Is that why you thought of me for this job?"

"I don't mind having a helper." Alma shuffled toward the butcher-block island and leaned against it. Though she was completely dressed with hair and makeup done, she wore fuzzy pink slippers. "Did you sleep well?"

"Took me a while to get accustomed to the creaks and groans in this old house." Once during the night, she'd startled awake, certain that someone had been in the room with her. She'd even imagined that she saw the door closing, which made her wonder. "Does Duncan ever sleepwalk?"

"Not as far as I know, but I wouldn't be surprised by anything that kid does. Or his father, for that matter."

"Is Blake difficult to work for?"

"A real pain in the rear."

Yet, he put up with the mess in the kitchen. "How so?"

"In the past year, he went through two other housekeepers and four nannies."

"Why?"

"His lordship is one of those dark, brooding, artistic types. Real moody. Gets caught up in a project and nothing else matters. He forgets to eat, then blames you for not feeding him." She patted her sculpted blond curls. "It's not part of my job description to keep track of his phone calls, and most of the business contacts go through his office in New York. But if I forget a phone call, he blows a gasket."

"He yells at you?" Madeline was beginning to feel more and more trepidation about this job.

"Never raises his voice," Alma said. "He growls. Real low. Like an angry lion."

With Blake's overgrown dark blond mane and intense hazel eyes, a lion was an apt comparison. As Madeline rinsed glasses and loaded them into the dishwasher, she said, "I looked Blake up on the Internet. He does amazing restorations. There were interior photos of this gorgeous hotel in Paris."

"Paris." Alma sighed. "That's what I expected when I signed on as a housekeeper four months ago. Trips to Europe. Fancy places. Fancy people. La-di-dah."

"Sounds like a lovely adventure."

"So far, I've been at the brownstone in Manhattan and here—Maine. I mean, Maine? The whole state is about as glamorous as a lumberjack's plaid shirt." She paused to sip her coffee. "Let's hear about you, hon. How's your big brother, Marty?"

At the mention of her brother's name, Madeline almost dropped the plate she was scrubbing in the sink. "We've kind of lost touch."

"Good-looking kid. A bit devilish, though. Didn't he get into some kind of trouble with the law?"

She heard Duncan counting his steps as he came down the hall to the kitchen and assumed his father wasn't far behind. "I'd rather not talk about Marty."

"It's okay." Alma patted her arm. "I won't say a word."

Duncan preceded his father into the kitchen. His clothing was the same as last night: a long-sleeved, striped T-shirt and jeans. At the table, he climbed into his chair and sat, staring straight ahead.

Alma went into action. She measured oat-bran cereal into a clear glass bowl, then measured the milk. She placed them in front of Duncan, then fetched a pre-chilled glass of OJ from the fridge.

Neither she nor Blake said a word.

Madeline assumed this was some sort of ritual and didn't interfere until Duncan had taken his first bite of cereal. Then she took a seat opposite him and watched as he chewed carefully before swallowing. She smiled. "Good morning, Duncan."

He said nothing, didn't acknowledge her presence in any way.

Blake cleared his throat. When she looked at him, he shook his head, warning her not to rock the boat. She rose from her seat and went toward him. Seeing him in the morning light, she noticed the lightly etched crow's feet at the corners of his eyes and the unshaven stubble on his chin. He dragged his fingers through his unruly dark blond hair. His careless grooming and apparent disarray reminded her of an unmade bed that had been torn apart in a night of wild, sexual abandon.

She intended to discuss her plans for Duncan's lessons. After his interest in the "Casey at the Bat" poem, she'd decided to use baseball as a learning tool. There were other things she needed to ask Blake about, such as her salary, rules of the household and teaching supplies. But being near him left her tongue-tied.

She pushed her glasses up on her nose and said, "Do you have a baseball?"

"I can find one."

Her cheeks were warm with embarrassment. Seldom was she so inarticulate. "Other supplies? Pencils and paper?"

"Everything you'll need is in a room at the end of this hallway. It was once a conservatory so there's a whole wall of windows. Until the renovations are done, we're using it as a family room. Alma can show you."

She stammered. "I-is there, um, some kind of schedule?"

He lifted an eyebrow; his expression changed from arrogant to vaguely amused. He stretched out his arm and pointed to the wall beside her. "How's this?"

Right in front of her nose was a three-foot-by-two-foot poster board with a heading in letters five inches high: Duncan's Schedule. The entire day was plotted in detail.

"I've found," he said, "that Duncan does best when we stick to a consistent routine."

She pointed to the slot after breakfast. "Quiet Time in Family Room. What does that mean?"

"Exactly what it says. Duncan likes to spend time by himself, and all his toys are in the family room. Usually he plays computer games."

The next slot said Lessons. "How do I know where to start?"

"Duncan's last tutor left a log that detailed her teaching plans and Duncan's progress. She wasn't a live-in, and I can't say that I was happy with her results." He glanced toward the housekeeper. "Is that coffee hot?"

"Piping."

He went to the coffeemaker and filled a mug. "Well, Alma, it's nice to see that you're finally cleaning up in here."

"I aim to please," she said. "Breakfast in your studio?"

"Eggs over easy, wheat toast and bacon."

With a nod to Madeline, he left the kitchen.

Though his back was turned, she made a "bye-bye" motion with her hand. Oh, good grief. Could she possibly be more of a dork?

Alma chuckled. "Got a little crush on his lordship?"

"Of course not."

"He's a handsome thing. And he's even taller than you are. Probably six foot two or three."

"I hadn't noticed."

She returned to the sink and dug into the stack of dirty dishes with renewed vigor. After she'd cleaned up the kitchen and grabbed an energy bar for breakfast, she trailed Duncan into the family room. He spoke not a word, went directly to his computer and turned it on.

Like the kitchen, this room was a mess. Sunlight gushed through a wall of windows, illuminating a cluttered worktable where Duncan sat at his computer. Though the wall had a neat row of storage bins and shelves, everything had been heaped on the floor—played with and then discarded.

The chaos didn't make sense. Every hour of Duncan's day was regimented, but here—in the place where he was supposed to learn—he was surrounded by disarray.

Obviously, she needed to put things in order. One of the earliest lessons taught in grade school was "Putting Things Away." Getting Duncan to participate in the clean-up would have been good, but she didn't want to disrupt his schedule. This hour was for quiet time.

While he fiddled with his computer, she picked up a plush blue pony and placed it on the shelf labeled Stuffed Animals. Then another stuffed toy. Blocks in the bin.

Crayons back in their box. Trucks and cars on another labeled shelf.

Eventually, she found a place for everything. "All done," she said. "I'm going out to my car to bring a few things inside."

He didn't even glance in her direction. No communication whatsoever. A cone of isolation surrounded him. No one was allowed to touch.

After running up to her bedroom to grab her car keys, she stepped outside into the sunny warmth of a July day. Her beat-up Volkswagen station wagon with the brand-new dent from her collision with Dr. Fisher was parked just outside the front door. When she unlocked the back, she noticed that the flaps on a couple of boxes were open. She hadn't put them in here like that. Everything had been sealed with tape or had the flaps tucked in. Had someone been tampering with her things? When Blake got her suitcase, did he also search her belongings?

Before she built up a full-blown anger at him about his callous intrusion into her privacy, a more ominous thought occurred. What if it was someone else?

Last night, she'd sensed that someone was in her bedroom. She hadn't actually seen anyone; it was just a fleeting impression. But what if it were true? Dr. Fisher had said that he'd "always know where to find her." He owned this house. Surely he had a key. But why would he look through her things?

"Need some help?" Alma called from the doorway.

Madeline slammed the rear door. "I'll worry about this stuff later. But I need to get the ficus out of the front seat before it wilts."

She unlocked the passenger-side door and liberated

the plant. The ficus itself wasn't anything special, but the fluted porcelain pot painted with rosebuds was one of her favorite things.

"Heavy," she muttered as she kicked the car door closed and lurched toward the house, not stopping until she reached her second-floor bedroom where she set the plant near the window. The delicately painted pot looked as though it belonged here—more than she did.

Had someone crept into her room last night? There was no way to prove she'd had an intruder unless she contacted the police and had them take fingerprints. Even then, Dr. Fisher had a right to be in the house; he owned the place. If not Fisher, who? The serial killer. His last victim, Sofia, had looked like her.

Madeline plucked off her glasses and wiped the lenses. She didn't want to raise an alarm about a prowler unless she had tangible evidence. Tonight, before she went to bed, she'd push the ficus against the door so no one could enter without making a lot of noise.

She hurried down the staircase toward the family room. In the doorway, she came to an abrupt halt. The room she had so carefully cleaned was ransacked. Stuffed animals had been flung in every direction. Books spilled across the floor. The toy trucks and cars looked like a major highway collision. Little Duncan stood in the midst of it, oblivious to her presence.

Either she could laugh or cry. She chose the former, letting out her frustration in a chuckle. Now she knew why the room had been a mess.

Duncan paced toward her. When he held out his hand, she saw that he was wearing latex gloves. In the center of his palm was the white seashell he'd shown her last night.

"Temperance," she said.

He marched past her into the corridor that led to the front door. His clear intention was to go outside. And how could she stop him? From the information she had on autistic kids, she knew that corporal punishment often led to tantrums. Arguments were futile.

The key, she decided, was to gain his trust. Maybe she could impart a few bits of knowledge along the way.

At the front door, she stepped ahead of him, blocking his way and creating the illusion that she was in control. "We're going to take a walk. Across the yard to the forest. And we'll gather pinecones. Six pinecones."

"Ten," he said.

"Ten is good."

Outside, he started counting his steps. "One, two, three…"

"*Uno, dos, tres.* Those are Spanish numbers."

He repeated the words back to her. She took him up to ten in Spanish, then started over. At least he was learning something.

Halfway across the grassy stretch leading to the forested area, Blake jogged up beside them.

"It's such a beautiful day," she said. "We decided to do our lesson outdoors."

"Couldn't stand the mess in the family room?"

"I might be a bit of a neat freak," she admitted. "Anyway, we're learning numbers in Spanish."

He fell into step beside her, and she surreptitiously peeked up at him. Definitely taller than she, he moved with a casual, athletic grace.

Near the woods, Duncan scampered ahead of them.

"It's good for him to be outside," Blake said. "Gives him a chance to work on his coordination."

"His fine motor skills are okay. He didn't seem to be having any problem with the computer."

"It's the big stuff that gives him problems. Running, skipping, playing catch."

Duncan had entered the trees but was still clearly visible. She glanced over her shoulder at the house. In daylight, the two-story, beige-brick building with four tall chimneys looked elegant and imposing. "What are your plans for the Manor?"

He was taken aback by her question. "How much do you know about historic restoration?"

"Very little. But I looked up some of your other architectural projects on the Web. Many seemed more modern than traditional."

"That's one reason why this project appealed to me. I plan to restore the American Federalist style while totally updating with new wiring, plumbing and insulation. I want to go green—make it ecological."

"Solar panels?"

"Too clumsy," he said. "The challenge in this project," he said, "is to maintain the original exterior design and restore the decorative flourishes of the interior. At the same time, I'm planning modern upgrades. Maybe a sauna and gym in the basement."

As he talked about architecture, she caught a glimpse of a different Blake Monroe—a man who was passionate about his work. Still intense, but focused. And eager to have an adult conversation.

She liked this side of his personality. Liked him a lot.

"SHE SELLS SEASHELLS…" Duncan repeated the rhyme again and again. "Temperance, where are you?"

"Here I am."

She stood with her back against a tree. He could see her, but his daddy and Madeline couldn't. And that was good. He didn't want to share his new friend.

He held out the shell. "You gave me this to warn me about the bad man."

She bent down and picked up a pinecone. Her shiny golden hair fell across her face. "There is something dangerous in the Manor."

"What?"

"Perhaps the basement. I cannot enter the Manor."

"You don't have to be scared, Temperance. I won't let anybody hurt you."

She placed a pinecone into his gloved hand. "You need ten of these. For your teacher."

He was happy to have a friend who didn't tease about his gloves. "I'm very brave. Madeline said so."

"Duncan, you must not forget the danger."

"Danger," he repeated.

Chapter Four

Half an hour before the scheduled time for lunch, Madeline was pleased with their progress. She and Duncan had arranged the ten pinecones for an afternoon art project. And they'd read an entire book about trains.

Her initial assessment of his skills matched the reports from his previous tutor. Exceptional mathematic ability. Reading and writing skills were poor.

Duncan jumped to his feet. "I want to explore."

"So do I," she said. "We could get your father to give us a tour. He knows a lot about the Manor."

"No," he shouted. "No."

His loud, strident voice had an edge to it. She hadn't figured out how to deal with disagreements, but it couldn't be good to continually back down to his demands. She replied with a statement, not a question. "We'll explore one room."

"Basement," he said.

Not what she was hoping for. She should have been more specific, should have told him that they would explore his father's studio, which would give her a chance to spend a bit more time with Blake. Unfortunately, she hadn't specified a room, and she needed to be unambiguous with Duncan. "The basement it is."

The door leading to the basement was off the kitchen where Alma should have been preparing lunch. She was nowhere in sight.

Madeline turned on the light, revealing a wooden staircase that descended straight down. "I'll go first," she said. "You need to hold tight to the railing."

Duncan followed behind her, counting each step aloud.

A series of bare bulbs lit the huge space that was divided with heavy support pillars and walls. The ceiling was only eight feet high. Like most unfinished basements, it was used for storage. There were stacks of old boxes, discarded furniture and tools. A series of notched shelves suggested that the basement had at one time been a wine cellar.

A damp, musty smell coiled around them, and she shuddered, thinking of rats and spiders. As far as she could tell, there were no windows.

"I've seen enough," she said.

Duncan reached out and touched a concrete wall with his gloved hand. "Danger," he said.

The word startled her.

He zigzagged from the walls to the stairs and back. In spite of her rising trepidation, Madeline noticed a geometric pattern in his movements. If she could have traced his steps, the pattern would form a perfect isosceles triangle. Under his breath, Duncan repeated, "Danger."

She took the warning to heart; his father said that he sensed things. And Alma had mentioned a curse on the town. "Danger means we should leave. Right now."

He ran away from her and disappeared behind a concrete wall.

She started after him. "Duncan, listen to me."

"Danger," came a louder shout.

The door at the top of the stairs slammed with a heavy thud. Fear shot through her. She spun around, staring toward the stairs. Though she saw no one, her sense of being stalked became palpable. That door hadn't blown shut by accident.

The lights blinked out. Darkness consumed her. Not the faintest glimmer penetrated this windowless tomb. Trapped. She thought of Teddy Fisher. Of the serial killer who liked women with long black hair.

Terror stole her breath. Where were the stairs? To her right? Her left? Her hands thrust forward, groping in empty space.

If she'd been here by herself, Madeline would have screamed for help. But Duncan was with her, and she didn't want to frighten him. "Duncan? Where are you?"

"Right here." He didn't sound scared. "Thirty-six steps from the stairs."

"Don't move." She listened hard, trying to discern if anyone else was here with them. The silence filled with dark portent. She moved forward with hesitant steps. Her shin bumped against a cardboard box. Her outstretched hands felt the cold that emanated from the walls. She pivoted and took another step. Was she going the wrong way? "Duncan, can you find the stairs?"

Instead of answering, he started counting backward from thirty-six. His strange habit came in handy; the boy seemed to know his exact location while she was utterly disoriented.

She bit back a sob. Even with her eyes accustomed to the dark, she couldn't see a thing.

"I'm at the stairs," Duncan announced.

She took a step toward his voice and stumbled. Falling forward to her hands and knees, she let out a yip.

"I'm okay," she said, though Duncan hadn't inquired. The only way she'd find the stairs was for him to keep talking. "Can you say the poem about starlight?"

Instead, he chanted, "She sells seashells…"

Crouched low, she inched toward the sound. When her hand connected with the stair rail, she latched on, desperately needing an anchor, something solid in the dark.

"Danger," he shouted.

Shivers chased up and down her spine. She had to get a grip, had to get them to safety. "I'm going up the stairs, Duncan. I'll open the door so we have enough light to see. Then I'll come back down for you."

"I can go. I'm very brave."

"Yes, you are." But she didn't want to take a chance on having him slip and fall on the stairs. "That's why you can stay right here. Very still."

As she stumbled up the steps in the pitch-dark, the staircase seemed ten miles long. By the time she reached the door, a clammy sweat coated her forehead. Her fingers closed around the round brass doorknob. It didn't move.

She jiggled and twisted. It was locked.

Panic flashed inside her head. A faint shimmer of daylight came around the edge of the door, and she clawed at the light as if she could pry this heavy door open.

Drawing back her fists, she hammered against the door. "Alma. Help. We're trapped in the basement. Help."

Behind her, she heard Duncan start up the stairs. She couldn't allow him to climb. In the darkness, balance was precarious, and Duncan wasn't like other kids. She couldn't hold his arm and keep him from falling, couldn't touch him at all.

"Wait," she said. "I'm coming back down."

Quickly, she descended. They'd just have to wait until they were found. Not much of a plan, but it was all she had. She sat beside Duncan on the second step from the bottom. "Here's what we're going to do. I'll count to five and you call for help. Then you count for me. Start now."

He yelled at the top of his lungs.

Then it was her turn. Screaming felt good. Her tension loosened. After she caught her breath, she said, "Now, we wait. Somebody will find us."

"My mama is already here," he said quietly. "She takes care of me. Whenever I get in trouble, my mama is close. She promised. She's always close."

His childlike faith touched her heart. "Your mama must be a very good woman. Can you tell me about her?"

"Soft and pretty. Even when she was crying, she smiled at me."

"She loved you," Madeline said. "And your daddy loves you, too."

"So do you," he said confidently. "From the first time you saw me."

In spite of her fear, Madeline breathed more easily. She should have been the one comforting him. Instead, this young boy lightened the weight of the terrible darkness with his surprising optimism. "You're very lovable."

"And brave."

"Let's yell again. Go."

At the end of his five seconds of shouting, the door at the top of the staircase opened. Daylight poured down with blinding, wonderful brilliance. Silhouetted in that light was the powerful masculine form of Blake Monroe.

"What the hell is going on?" he growled.

"Danger," Duncan yelled.

She heard Blake flick the light switch. "What's wrong with the lights?"

Duncan scrambled up the wooden staircase, and she followed. Stepping into the kitchen, she inhaled the light and warmth. This must be how it felt to escape from being buried alive. As she stepped away from the basement door, she wiped the clammy sweat from her forehead with the back of her hand. She and Duncan were free. No harm done.

When she saw the expression on Blake's face, her sense of relief vanished like seeds on the wind. The friendly camaraderie of this morning had been replaced by tight-lipped anger. "I want an explanation," he said.

She pushed her glasses up on her nose and cleared her throat. "Duncan and I decided to explore one room of the house before lunchtime."

"And you chose the basement." His hazel eyes flared. "There's all kinds of crap down there. Damn it, Madeline. What the hell were you thinking?"

She wouldn't blame this dreadful excursion on Duncan's insistence that they go to the basement. She was the person in charge. "We were fine until the door slammed shut. It was locked."

His brows arched in disbelief. He went down a step to test the doorknob, and the horrible darkness crawled up his leg. She was tempted, like Duncan, to warn him. To shout the word *danger* until her lungs burst.

Blake jiggled the knob. "It's sticking but not locked. You must have twisted it the wrong way."

She hadn't turned the knob wrong. That door had been locked. "Then the lights went out."

"There's a rational explanation. I have a crew of electricians working today."

She glanced toward Duncan, who stood silently, staring down at the toes of his sneakers. She didn't want to frighten the boy with her suspicions about Dr. Fisher or being stalked by the serial killer, but they hadn't been trapped by accident.

Blake yanked the door shut with a resounding slam and took a step toward her. Anger rolled off him in hot, turbulent waves.

Frankly, she couldn't blame him. It appeared that she'd made an irresponsible decision. When he spoke, his voice was low and ominous, like the rumble of an approaching freight train. And she was tied to the tracks. "You're supposed to be teaching my son. Not leading him into a potentially dangerous situation."

"All of life is potentially risky," she said in her defense. "Children need to explore and grow. New experiences are—"

"Stop." He held up a hand to halt her flow of words. "I don't need a lecture."

"Perhaps I'm not explaining well."

"You're fired, Madeline."

"What?" She took a step backward. Perhaps she deserved a reprimand, but not this.

He reached into his back pocket and pulled out a wallet. Peeling off a hundred-dollar bill, he slapped it down on the counter. "This should cover your expenses. Pack your things and get out."

Looking past his right shoulder, she saw Alma enter

through the back door with a couple of grocery bags in her arms. The housekeeper wouldn't be happy about Madeline being fired. Nor would Duncan.

But Blake was the boss. And his attitude showed no willingness to negotiate.

Though she would have liked to refuse his money, pride was not an option. She was too broke. With a weak sigh, she reached for the bill.

"Daddy, no." Duncan rushed across the kitchen and wrapped his skinny arms around his father's waist. "I like Madeline. I want her to stay."

Blake's eyes widened in surprise, and she knew that her own expression mirrored his. They were both stunned by this minor miracle. Duncan was touching his father, clinging to him.

As Blake stroked his son's shoulders with an amazing tenderness, she wondered how long it had been since Duncan had allowed him to come close.

The boy looked up at him. "Please, Daddy."

Blake squatted down to his son's level. Though Duncan's eyes were bright blue and his hair was a lighter shade of blond, the physical resemblance between father and son resonated.

Blake asked, "Do you want Madeline to stay?"

The hint of a smile touched Duncan's mouth. He reached toward his father's face with his gloved hand and patted Blake's cheek. "I like her."

With the slow, careful, deliberate motions used to approach a feral creature, Blake enclosed his son in a yearning embrace. A moment ago, he'd been all arrogance and hostility. Now, he exuded pure love.

Empathy brought Madeline close to tears. Her hand

covered her mouth. Staying at Beacon Manor was like
riding an emotional roller coaster. In the basement, she'd
been terrified. Facing Blake's rage, she was defensive and
intimidated. As she watched the tenderness between father
and son, her heart swelled.

The front doorbell rang.

"Get the door," Blake said to her.

Hadn't she just been fired? "I don't—"

"You're not fired. You're still Duncan's teacher. Now,
answer the door."

Not much of an apology, but she'd take it. She needed
this job. Straightening her shoulders, she walked down the
corridor to the front door.

Standing at the entryway were two women. A cheerful
smile fitted naturally on the attractive face of a slender lady
in a stylish ivory suit with gray-blue piping that matched
the color of her eyes. Her short, tawny hair whisked neatly
in the breeze. Confidently, she introduced herself. "I'm
Beatrice Wells, the mayor's wife."

Madeline opened the door wider to invite them inside.
"I'm Madeline Douglas. Duncan's teacher."

When she held out her hand, she noticed the smears of
dirt from crawling around in the basement and quickly
pulled her hand back. "I should wait to shake your hand
until I've had a chance to wash up."

"It's not a problem, dear." Beatrice gave her hand a
squeeze, then turned toward her companion. "I'd like you
to meet Helen Fisher."

As in Teddy Fisher? Madeline couldn't imagine that
creep had a wife. "Are you related to Dr. Fisher?"

The frowning, angular woman gave a disgusted snort.
"Teddy is my brother."

She stalked through the open door in her practical oxblood loafers. Her nostrils pinched and the frown deepened as she set a battered briefcase on the floor. She folded her arms below her chest, causing a wrinkle in her midcalf dress and brown cardigan. Though the month was July and the weather was sunny, Helen Fisher reminded Madeline of the drab days at the end of autumn. Everything about her said "old maid." Madeline suppressed a shudder. For the past couple of years, she'd feared that "old maid" would be her own destiny. If she stayed at this job long enough to put some money aside, she really ought to invest in something pretty and sexy. A red dress.

Beatrice Wells twinkled as if to counterbalance her companion's grumpy attitude. "Helen is our town librarian, and we're here to talk with Blake about the renovations."

"Beacon Manor is a historic landmark," Helen said. "The designs have to be approved by the historical committee."

"I really don't know anything about the house. My job is Duncan." She looked toward Beatrice. "I wondered if there was a baseball team in town. Something I could take Duncan to watch."

"We have an excellent parks and recreation program. There's even a T-ball program for the children."

Though Madeline wasn't sure if Duncan could handle a team sport, T-ball might be worth a try. "I'll certainly look into it."

When Blake came down the corridor toward them, he seemed like a different man. An easy grin lightened his features. He looked five years younger…and incredibly handsome. Even Helen was not immune to his masculine

charms. She perked up when he warmly shook her hand.
A girlish giggle twisted through her dour lips.

Given half a chance, Blake Monroe could charm the fish
from the sea.

Chapter Five

As Blake escorted Beatrice Wells and Helen Fisher into the formal dining room with the ornate ceiling mural, he listened with half an ear to their commentary about the historical significance of Beacon Manor. In their eyes, the painting of cherubs and harvest vegetables rivaled the Sistine Chapel.

His thoughts were elsewhere. When he'd held Duncan in his arms, his blood had stirred. His son had smiled, actually smiled, and responded to a direct question. For the first time in years, Blake had seen a spark in his son's eyes.

Then Duncan had turned away from him and marched to his seat at the kitchen table for his usual silent lunch.

For today, one hug was enough. Maybe tomorrow…

Helen placed her fat leather briefcase on the dropcloth covering the carved cherrywood table and pulled out a stack of photographs. "These pictures were taken in the 1940s during an earlier restoration. Perhaps they'll be useful in recreating the ceiling mural."

"I've already ordered the paint," Blake said, "including the gold leaf. There's an artist in New York who specializes in historical restorations."

"Sounds expensive," Helen said archly. "I don't suppose my brother has set any sort of prudent financial limits."

Blake had submitted a detailed budget. Not that the expenditure was any of Helen's business. "You'll have to talk to Teddy about that."

As they moved to another room, he heard Madeline talking to Alma in the kitchen. How had she made such a difference with Duncan in such a short time? She lacked the expertise of the autism specialists he'd consulted. She wasn't a psychologist or a behaviorist. Just a schoolteacher.

For some unknown reason, his son connected with her. Was it her appearance? At first glance, he hadn't noticed anything remarkable about her, except for those incredibly long legs. When she took her glasses off, her aquamarine eyes glowed like the mysterious depths below the ocean waves. Was she magical? Hell, no. Madeline was down-to-earth. Definitely not an enchantress. And yet there was something about her that even he had to admit was intriguing.

He climbed the sweeping front staircase behind the two ladies from town. At the landing, Beatrice paused to catch her breath and said, "Duncan's teacher mentioned that you might be interested in signing your son up for one of the T-ball teams."

"Did she?" A baseball team? What was she thinking?

"Raven's Cliff might not have all the cultural advantages of a big city, but there's nowhere like a small town for raising children."

If Duncan did well here, Blake was ready to move in a heartbeat. "How's the real estate market?"

"Quite good." Beatrice warmed to him. "In fact, my husband and I are considering selling a lovely three-bedroom on the waterfront. Should I have Perry talk to you about it?"

"Sure."

He imagined himself living in this Maine backwater, planting a vegetable garden while Duncan played in the yard behind a white picket fence. Maybe his son could find friends his own age. Maybe a dog. Blake imagined a two-story slate-blue house with white shutters. The back door would open, and Madeline would step through, carrying a plate of cookies. Yeah, sure. Then they could all travel in their time machine back to the 1950s when life seemed pure and simple.

After he showed the ladies the one bedroom that had been repainted and refurbished with velvet drapes, they went back down the staircase to the first floor. Without being rude, he guided them toward the exit.

Standing at the doorway, Beatrice said, "Be sure to tell that nice young woman, Madeline, that the person to contact about the T-ball team is Grant Bridges. He's an assistant District Attorney. A fine young man."

He noticed a tremor in her voice. "Are you feeling all right, Beatrice?"

"Grant was almost my son-in-law," she said softly. "It's difficult to think of him without remembering my beautiful daughter. Camille."

He'd heard this tragic story before. It was part of the curse of Raven's Cliff. "I'm sorry for your loss."

They stepped onto the porch below the Palladian window just as Teddy Fisher's forest-green SUV screeched to a halt at the entrance. Blake remembered what Madeline had said about Fisher carrying a handgun and stepped protectively in front of the women.

Teddy sprang from the driver's-side door like a Jack-in-the-box with a goatee. With a fastidious twitch, he straightened the lapels of his tweed jacket. Every time Blake had dealt with Teddy, he'd been well-mannered, but he seemed distracted, unhinged. His small face twisted with strong emotion that might be anger. Or it might be fear.

Helen shoved past Blake and confronted her brother with fists on her skinny hips. "Well, well. If it isn't the mad scientist."

"We haven't spoken in months, Helen. At least try to be civil."

"Don't bother holding out an olive branch to me," she snapped. "You don't deserve my forgiveness."

"Your forgiveness?" His eyebrows arched. "I don't recall apologizing to you."

When he lifted his chin, Blake noticed that Teddy's shirt collar was loose. He'd been losing weight, had been under stress. Blake had heard stories about how Teddy's latest "scientific breakthrough"—a nutrient for fish—had caused a recent epidemic in Raven's Cliff.

"Bastard!" Oddly, Helen's facial expression mirrored that of her brother. "You ought to be in jail."

"At least I'm trying to do something with my life, working to enhance the Fisher name, like our grandfather."

"Grandfather won the Nobel Prize for science." Her voice rang with pride. "You're the booby prize."

"And I suppose it's better to play it safe like you? The town librarian? A manless crone who grows older and more dried up every day?"

"How dare you." She turned toward Beatrice, who watched with horrified eyes. "Your husband never should have allowed Teddy to buy the Manor."

Beatrice shifted uncomfortably. "There wasn't much choice, Helen. The abandoned property belonged to the town. After the hurricane, Raven's Cliff needed the revenue from the sale."

Frankly, Blake was glad that the Manor had only one owner. If he'd been forced to get approval from some kind of township committee, the restoration of the Manor and lighthouse would have been impossible.

Helen went on the attack again. "Damn you, Teddy. You hoarded your share of the family inheritance."

"And you frittered yours away."

"I invested in you," she said with hoarse loathing.

He gave a smug little grin. "Someday you'll get your investment back. I'm on the verge of a discovery."

She poked at him with a long finger. "The only way I'll ever be paid back is when you're dead."

Blake stepped in before this brother-and-sister reunion erupted into a physical fight. He grasped Teddy's arm and guided him away from Helen with a brisk, "Please excuse us, ladies."

Teddy walked a few paces before he shook Blake's hand off. "I'm sorry you had to witness that outburst. My sister has always been hot-tempered."

Blake glanced over his shoulder at the plain, thin woman whose angular face had gone white with rage. "Yeah, she's a real spitfire."

"She never believed in me. Not really."

"Was there something you wanted to talk to me about, Teddy?"

"I saw Beatrice and Helen arrive, and I just wanted to remind you that you're working for me. Not some idiotic historical society."

"I'm clear on who's paying the tab," Blake said.

"Well, good."

In his architectural redesign business, Blake came into contact with a number of eccentrics. He had to draw clear boundaries and didn't like the idea that Teddy had been watching the manor. "You know, Teddy, anytime you want to see the progress on the restoration, I'll try to accommodate you."

"Of course." The little man pulled a white handkerchief from his jacket pocket and dabbed nervously at his forehead. His beady little eyes darted. "It's my house, after all."

"However," Blake said, "while my family is in residence, you need an appointment to set foot inside. Otherwise, you're trespassing. And I don't deal kindly with trespassers."

"Is that a threat?"

"A friendly warning," Blake said.

Beacon Manor was only a job. Duncan's safety took precedence.

THAT NIGHT, after Duncan had gone to bed, Madeline finished unpacking in her bedroom. She'd found a place for all her clothing, set up her laptop and placed a few precious knickknacks around the room. There wasn't space for her books, so she'd left three full boxes in the back of her station wagon. All her other belongings had either been sold or given to charity, which was no great loss. Her apartment had been mostly furnished with hand-me-downs and inexpensive necessities.

At least, that was what she told herself. She ought to be glad to get rid of that worthless clutter, but her foster-home upbringing made her into a bit of a security junkie. She tended to hoard things for no other reason than to have them. That had to change. She needed to embrace the fact that she was unencumbered, free to pick up and leave at a moment's notice…the next time Blake fired her.

That man was an enigma. At times, he seemed to be the archetype of a dark, brooding genius who was passionate about his work. But he was also a loving father who clearly adored his son. When he was around Duncan, his barriers dropped, and she saw genuine warmth. Otherwise, he was arrogant, demanding. Sophisticated, but not much of a conversationalist.

Earlier this afternoon, he'd pulled her aside to offer a rational explanation for what had happened when she and Duncan were trapped in the basement. The door at the top of the staircase must have blown shut in a gust of wind. He pointed out that several windows had been left open to let in the warm July weather. One of the electricians working on the renovations had tripped the breaker switch, causing the lights to go out. Blake had insisted that the basement door wasn't locked.

She wanted to believe him, to accept the possibility that being trapped in the basement was nothing more than an unfortunate accident. Yet, she had sensed the danger that Duncan identified in shouts, and she fully intended to shove her potted ficus in front of the bedroom door before she fell asleep.

When she heard a tap on her bedroom door, she pulled it open. Blake stood there. He was dressed for the outdoors in a denim jacket and jeans. No matter what else she thought of him, Madeline couldn't deny the obvious. He was intensely handsome.

However, seeing him at her door, she assumed the worst. "Is something wrong? Does Duncan need something?"

"He fell asleep as soon as his head hit the pillow." A tender smile lit his features. "He let me kiss his forehead and tuck him in."

She couldn't take credit for his son's change of habit. The workings of Duncan's mind were a mystery to her. "He truly cares about you."

"It occurred to me," he said, "that it's a pleasant night. Would you like to take a walk on the grounds?"

"In the dark?"

"It might be better to do this while Duncan is asleep. There are several places I'd prefer he didn't explore."

His rationale made sense; she ought to be aware of the boundaries. "Let me grab a jacket."

She pulled a lightweight blue sweatshirt over her cotton blouse and khaki slacks. Since she was already wearing sneakers, she was appropriately dressed for a trek. Stepping into the hallway, she said, "Lead the way."

Outside, in the moonlight, she appreciated the pristine isolation and beauty of their surroundings. In last night's storm, the rugged forests had loomed and threatened. Tonight, the tall pines formed a protective boundary at the western edge of the property. A sea-scented breeze whispered through the high branches as they stretched toward the canopy of stars.

With his hands clasped behind his back, Blake walked along the road leading toward the lighthouse ruins. Moonlight cast mysterious shadows on the charred, tumbled-down tower.

"How was the lighthouse destroyed?" she asked.

"A fire and a freak category-five hurricane. It was about five years ago. That storm also did a lot of damage to the Manor that was never properly repaired."

"I can understand why someone would want to restore the Manor. It's a beautiful house. But why bother with the lighthouse? With GPS satellite navigational systems, nobody needs these old lighthouses anymore."

"Both the Manor and lighthouse are part of the legacy of the town. If you're interested, Helen Fisher dropped off a booklet about the history of Raven's Cliff."

"And the curse?"

"A legend that started when the town was founded. It's good for tourists. Everybody loves a ghost story."

"I suppose so."

"By the way, the lighthouse is off-limits to Duncan. Especially after the scaffolding goes up and reconstruction gets under way."

Obviously, a construction site was no place for a child. Nor was a basement. She never should have allowed Duncan to go down there. The echo of his voice rang in her mind. *Danger. Danger. Danger.* "What about the serial killer? The Seaside Strangler. Is he part of the curse?"

"He's real. Abducts young women, dresses them in white gowns, like brides, and drapes them in seaweed before he kills them."

A shiver ripped down her spine. The first time Duncan had seen her, he'd identified her with one of the victims. "That doesn't seem like a story that would draw visitors."

"Which is why the locals play it down. Tourism is the second most important industry in Raven's Cliff. Mostly, this is a fishing village."

He directed her toward the rocky edge of the cliff. Across the bay, the lights of the town glimmered. Fishing boats and other sailing crafts bobbed in the harbor. She saw the spire of a church and a few other tall buildings but nothing that resembled a skyscraper. Though she'd expected to find average dwellings and stores in Raven's Cliff, this picturesque view could have come from another century. "When was Raven's Cliff founded?"

"Late 1700s." He glanced down at her. "You're going to keep asking questions until I tell you the whole story, aren't you?"

She couldn't tell if he was irritated or amused. "I'll read Helen Fisher's booklet later. Just give me the short version."

"Captain Earl Raven owned the land. When he brought his wife and two small children over from England, his boat was shipwrecked on those rocks." He pointed toward a treacherous shoal. Even in this pleasant July night, the dark waves crashed and plumed against the rugged outcropping. "His wife and children were washed away and their bodies never found."

"Sounds like the town started with a curse."

"Could be. Captain Raven was involved in some shady dealings," he said. "Stricken with grief, he settled here and commissioned the building of the lighthouse with a powerful beacon. One night a year, on the anniversary of his family's death, he focused the beam on those rocks. His apprentice claimed that on that dark and scary night he saw Raven take a sailboat out to the rocks where he was joined by the ghosts of his family."

Pushing her glasses up on her nose, she peered down at the rugged coastline. Relentless waves crashed against the dark, jagged rocks. "A family of ghosts. What happened next?"

"After Raven passed away, the apprentice inherited the Manor. The town prospered and grew."

He went silent, and she turned toward him. His expression was utterly unreadable. She wondered if he was thinking of his personal ghost—his wife who had passed away only a few years ago.

"The townsfolk kept up the old traditions," he said. "Even after the lighthouse was no longer in use, the lighthouse keeper fired up the beacon every year on the anniversary. Until five years ago."

"The start of the curse."

He nodded. "The beacon wasn't lit at the appointed time. Somebody screwed up. Then came the fire that claimed the lives of the elderly lighthouse keeper and his grandson, Nicholas Sterling. The hurricane not only damaged the manor but destroyed a lot of other property in the town. Since then, Raven's Cliff has been plagued by bad luck."

"More than the serial killer?"

"Deaths at sea. Fishermen losing their boats. Strange disappearances. Recently there was a weird genetic mutation in the fish that caused an epidemic. And a couple of months ago, the daughter of the mayor was swept off the edge of the cliff in a gale-force wind. It happened on her wedding day."

"The daughter of Beatrice Wells?" Madeline remembered the determinedly perky smile of the mayor's wife. Beatrice didn't look like someone who had lost her daughter so recently. Either she was amazingly resilient or firmly in denial.

"There are rumors that the daughter, Camille, is still alive." He raised a skeptical eyebrow. "That ought to be enough story-telling to satisfy your curiosity."

"Perhaps."

When he started walking at the edge of the cliff, she chose the inward side to walk beside him. Though not afraid of heights, she was thinking about the bride who was whisked over the edge by a gust of wind. "These local legends are interesting. I could make the history of Raven's Cliff into a lesson for Duncan."

"I'd rather you didn't. I don't want him worrying about the curse. He's already picked up something he must have heard about Sofia Lagios."

"Which indicates an interest," she said. "Something I could use to focus his reading and writing skills."

"No serial killers," he repeated firmly. "Duncan has already had enough tragedy in his life."

She pressed her lips together to keep from arguing, but she didn't agree. Blake couldn't pretend that the death of Duncan's mother had never happened, especially since the boy talked to her ghost every day.

Chapter Six

Following the moonlit path at the edge of the cliff, Blake led her to the weathered, wooden staircase that descended forty feet to the rugged private beach. He hadn't decided how he felt about Duncan being allowed to explore in this hazard-filled area. Swimming was, of course, out of the question in these frigid northern Atlantic waters. Not to mention these treacherous currents.

He paused at the top of the staircase and watched as Madeline tentatively stepped onto the landing and peeked over the railing. Tendrils of her black hair had escaped the tight ponytail on top of her head and formed delicate curls against her pale cheeks.

The real reason he'd wanted to take this walk with her was to express his gratitude for whatever she'd done to cause Duncan to open up. Her work impressed him, but he didn't want to give the impression that she had free rein with her lesson plans. Left to her own devices, she'd probably be teaching his six-year-old son how to spell *homicide* and *strangulation*.

He needed to get a handle on this tall, slender school-teacher who had made such a huge impression on his son.

Who was Madeline Douglas? Her reticent nature made her almost invisible. She seemed organized, almost fastidious. And yet—by her own admission—she'd shown up on his doorstep without a penny to her name.

It shouldn't be so hard for him to figure her out. She was only an employee—another in the seemingly endless parade of tutors, teachers and nannies. But he knew she was different. Duncan cared about her; that made her special.

As she leaned out over the railing, he noticed the flare of her hips and the rounded curve of her bottom. She sure as hell didn't dress to show off her shape. Not in those prim little cotton blouses and baggy sweatshirts. Right now, the only skin visible was that on her trim ankles above her sneakers. His gaze swept the length of her legs. Too easily, he could imagine those legs entwined with his.

When she faced him, her eyes widened behind her glasses. "Where do the stairs lead?"

"To a private beach and several caves." He stepped in front of her. "I'll go first. If you slip, I can catch you. Hang on tight to the railing."

The wood-plank staircase, firmly anchored to the wall of the cliff, zigzagged like a fire escape. At the bottom was a cove of jagged rock that surrounded less than a mile of dark, wet sand. Moonlight shone on the churning waves, and the roar of the surf echoed against rock walls. Even on a temperate night like this, the rugged beach was lashed by wind and sea. The power of these untamed elements aroused his artistic nature, reminding him of life's fragility. The buildings he designed and restored—even skyscrapers and cathedrals—were frail shells compared to the timeless ocean.

She walked across the sand, leaving footprints, until she

stood at the edge of the foaming surf. "The water looks cold."

"And the undertow is deadly."

"I wonder," she said, "if there's any way I could bring Duncan down here. It's so beautiful."

"The problem with introducing Duncan to this area is that he might try to come here alone. Sometimes, he sticks to the rules. And other times…"

"He's headstrong," she said.

Her plain-spoken description amused him. His son's autistic behavior had been studied by teams of specialists who stated their theories in polysyllabic profusion: *Pervasive developmental disorder. Hypersensitivity. Asperger's Syndrome*.

She called it headstrong. If only life were so simple.

"For now," Blake said, "let's keep this area off-limits to Duncan."

"For now."

As she nodded, he studied the sharp outline of her jaw. Her features were too angular to be pretty, but her face had character. An interesting face. Appealing.

When she met his gaze, she seemed startled to find him watching her. Quickly, she looked down. Shyness? Or was she hiding something?

"Madeline, there's something I need to tell you."

"You're not going to fire me again, are you?"

"Hell, no. Why would you think that?"

"Because I've only been at the Manor for twenty-four hours, and you've already ordered me to get out twice."

Damn it, she made him sound like a total bastard. He pushed away his irritation. "I wanted to thank you. It's been months since Duncan has allowed me to hold him in my arms, to kiss his forehead, to tuck him under the covers. Thank you for this precious gift."

She darted a glance in his direction. "You're welcome."

"I want to build on this foundation. Tell me how you got my son to open up?"

She shrugged. "I haven't been following any special program. Mostly, I just treat him like a regular kid."

Not what he wanted to hear. In the back of his mind, Blake had been hoping for a teaching technique—a set of rules he could follow.

He strode across the sand. "This way to the caves."

"Of course," Madeline said, though she wasn't sure she wanted to go spelunking in the dark.

Carefully picking her way across the narrow strip of dark sand toward the wild shrubs near the cliff wall, she followed his lead. His expression of gratitude surprised her. Though he'd been visibly moved when he held Duncan in his arms, she never thought he'd attribute his son's openness to her.

At the inward side of the cove, craggy granite formations sloped down to the sea, like the arms of a giant reaching for the surf. Blake stepped onto the ledge and held out his hand to assist her. When her fingers linked with his, a powerful surge raced up her arm. His intensity frightened her while his strength drew her closer.

He helped her onto the ledge and steadied her by holding her other arm. Their position was almost an embrace. She met his gaze and saw starlight reflected in his hazel eyes. On this rocky promontory jutting into the sea, Blake was in his element, braced firmly against the wind and salt spray from crashing waves.

For a moment, she wished his touch meant something

more intimate. She wished for his affection, wished that this dynamic, talented man could care for her.

Releasing her arm, he pointed upward. "There's a shallow cave there. We'll have to climb."

"I see the opening." She had no desire to test her balance on these slippery rocks. "But let's not go there."

"I thought you were curious, ready for an adventure."

"Not if it means breaking my leg when I slip and fall." If she hadn't been firmly anchored to his hand, she might have stumbled right here. "Let me get my bearings. Where are we in terms of the lighthouse and the manor?"

He looked skyward as if he could discern their location by the position of the stars. "Do you see the trees up there? We're almost directly across from the entrance to the manor."

She hadn't realized that the cliff's edge was so close to the forest. No wonder he insisted on having Duncan accompanied on his outdoor excursions.

"The largest cavern is back on the beach."

"No climbing?"

"Not a bit."

"Let's check it out."

He helped her down from the ledge and crossed the sand to a gaping maw the size of a double-wide garage. A few standing rocks, taller than her head, shielded the entrance from view. "I can't believe I didn't see this giant hole before."

"It's the shape of the rocks and the shadows," he said. "Even in daylight, you might not notice the cave."

As soon as she stepped inside, the cold stone walls shielded her from the wind. An impermeable curtain of darkness hung before her. They had entered a place of eerie secrets. A dragon's lair.

"It's huge." Her voice dropped to a whisper. "Did smugglers and pirates once use these caves?"

"You'll have to read Helen Fisher's history of the town to learn the local superstitions."

Though she didn't consider herself psychic, she felt a deep foreboding. Bad things had happened in this cave—murders and intrigues by seafaring renegades. Or perhaps something had happened not too long ago. The curse of Raven's Cliff.

After a few steps into the darkness, she scooted back into the moonlight. Her memory of being trapped in the windowless basement was still too fresh. She had no desire to go deeper. "This is enough for me."

"Scared of the ghosts?" he teased.

"Not all ghosts are frightening, you know." Though she hated to risk making him angry, she felt it was important for him to know about Duncan's connection to his deceased mother. "Duncan has spoken to me about his mother."

"Kathleen."

When he whispered her name, a pall of sadness slipped over him. In the moonlight, she saw a haunted expression in his eyes. "Can you tell me about her?"

He raked his fingers through his dark blond hair. A nervous habit. "She was beautiful. Blond hair. Laughing eyes. She loved to dance. And she was a gourmet chef."

The combination of wistful sorrow in his voice and the strange atmosphere of the cave was almost too heavy for her to bear. Still, she wanted to know more. "Why did you and your wife choose to name your son Duncan?"

"Family name. I used to tease Kathleen that she'd named our boy after the cake mix."

"A major insult for someone who cooked from scratch."

"I guess so." He shook his head as if to clear the cobwebs on these buried memories. "When she didn't like one of my architectural designs, she called me Frank Lloyd Wrong."

"She had a good sense of humor."

"Kathleen was good at everything."

It was obvious that he still treasured her memory, still loved her. She doubted anyone would ever measure up to his deceased wife. "Before she passed away, was she aware of Duncan's disability?"

"She was spared that pain. Duncan was only three, almost four, when she died. He was always a goofy kid. A trickster. Loved to play games." His eyebrows lifted. "I never thought of this before. It was Kathleen who started his habit of counting his steps. When they came out the door of our brownstone, they counted the stairs. Up and down. Up and down the stairs."

Madeline wondered if the boy heard the echo of his mother's voice when he measured his steps. "She sounds like a good mother."

"A lot better at parenting than I was." He winced as if in physical pain. "I was building my career. Spent a lot of time away from home on different restoration projects. Always thought there'd be more time with Kathleen. Then, the cancer. I didn't know our days were limited."

Acting on an instinct to comfort him, she placed her hand on his arm. His muscles tensed, hard as granite. "You couldn't predict the future, Blake."

"After she died, I was even more of a workaholic. Couldn't stand being in the house where we'd been so happy. I sold it. We moved. I took every project that came my way. I was running day and night, running away from my sorrow, so caught up in my own pain that I lost track

of Duncan. I was a damn selfish fool. I should have been
there for Duncan. Should have…"

His voice trailed off in the wind.

There was nothing she could say to heal his grief and
soothe his regrets. Her concern was his son. For his sake,
she had to speak. "When Duncan and I were trapped in the
basement, he told me that I didn't need to be afraid because
his mother was watching over us. She's always there for
him. He talks to her. She's a very real presence in his life."

"Like a ghost?" he asked angrily.

"An angel."

Anguish deepened the lines in his face. For a moment,
she thought he might erupt. By poking into the past, she
might have overstepped the bounds of propriety. He had a
right to his privacy, his personal hell.

"An angel," he whispered. "I like that."

His tension seemed to ebb as he strode across the wind-
swept sands. At the foot of the weathered wooden staircase,
he turned toward her.

Nervously, she met his gaze, preparing herself for the
worst. The man was so mercurial that she didn't know
what to expect. He was capable of ferocious anger. And
even greater love, like the abiding love for his wife.

The merest hint of a smile played at the corner of his
mouth. "I'm glad you told me."

"Oh." She exhaled in a whoosh. "Not fired?"

His smile spread. When he rested his hand on her
shoulder, she felt the warmth of connection. A warmth that
sent her heart soaring. What would it be like to experience
the force of his passion? To be swept away?

"You'll always have a place with me, Madeline."

This was where she belonged. With him. And Duncan.

Chapter Seven

After a few days with no major disasters, Madeline began
to believe that she really was part of this odd little family.
Duncan's carefully charted daily routine gave a rhythm to
each day in spite of the arrival of roofers and bricklayers who
were repairing the chimneys. The workmen kept Blake busy;
she'd hardly been alone with him since their walk on the
beach.

He'd been friendly—at least, what passed for friendly
with this brooding architectural genius—and she couldn't
complain about the way he treated her. Still, Madeline had
hopes for something more. A real friendship, perhaps. Who
was she kidding? Her fantasies about Blake skipped down
a far more sensual path—one that was totally inappropriate.

While Duncan ate his solitary lunch, counting each
chew before he swallowed, she delivered a lunch tray to
Blake's studio on the first floor. Originally, this room had
been a formal library, and one wall was still floor-to-ceiling
books. The antiques that would one day occupy this space
had been removed for expert refinishing, and Blake used
a purely functional, L-shaped desk and black metal file

cabinets. His computer, phones and fax machine rested amid stacks of papers, invoices and research materials.

His back was toward her as he stared at blueprints taped onto a slanted drafting table near the west-facing window. Without turning, he said, "Just leave the lunch on the table. Thanks, Alma."

"It's me," she said quietly, not wanting to disturb his concentration but wanting him to notice her.

He pivoted. His unguarded gaze sent a bolt of heat in her direction. "Hello, Madeline."

Those two simple words unleashed an earthquake of awareness through her body. She placed the lunch tray on his desk before she dropped it. He'd shaved today. The sharp line of his jaw was softened by a dimple at the left corner of his mouth.

Pushing her glasses up on her nose, she broached the topic she'd wanted to discuss. "I was wondering if I could possibly get an advance on my paycheck. There were a few things I wanted to purchase. For Duncan."

"I'd be happy to pay for anything my son needs."

"These aren't teaching supplies." His prior teachers had compiled an excellent selection of books, educational materials and computer programs. "It's other stuff."

He came around the desk. "What kind of stuff?"

She hated asking for money, even though she had a good reason. Avoiding his direct gaze, she mumbled, "Baseball equipment. Duncan and I have been playing catch in the afternoon and I—"

"Catch? You and Duncan?"

"After his regular lessons are finished," she assured him. "We've gotten to the point where we can throw the ball back and forth five times without either of us dropping it."

"Five catches? That's better than Duncan has ever done before. Why didn't you tell me?"

"You've been so busy with the work crews arriving."

"I'm never too busy for my son. I made that mistake once already, and I won't make it again. Duncan is my number-one concern. The whole reason I took this job in Raven's Cliff was so I could spend more time with him in a relaxed, stress-free atmosphere."

She couldn't imagine a situation involving Blake that would be without stress. The air surrounding him crackled with electricity. "Of course, you're welcome to join us."

He sat on the edge of his desk with his arms folded across his broad chest. "I've tried physical activities with Duncan before. It's never turned out well."

"Playing with me is no challenge because—as Duncan is delighted to point out—I'm just a girl. There's more pressure with you."

"Why?"

She shrugged. "He doesn't want to disappoint you. He can play catch, but he's no Roger Clemens or Wade Boggs."

"Clemens and Boggs. Legendary Red Sox players."

"I'm from Boston."

"Uh-huh." He nodded slowly. "It's high time for me to get involved in this baseball teaching plan of yours. Can't have you raising my boy to be a Sox fan. This family roots for the Cubs."

She drew the obvious conclusion. "You're from Chicago."

"Born and bred in the 'burbs. One sister, one brother and a German shepherd named Rex." He went behind his desk, opened a drawer and pulled out a checkbook. "No problem with an advance, Madeline. You've made excellent progress with Duncan. He's still letting me hug him and touch him."

The boy hadn't yet extended that invitation to her. Nor had his father, she thought ruefully.

Blake handed the check to her. Reading the amount, her eyes popped. Five hundred dollars. "This is too much."

"And I'll be paying for his sports equipment out of my own pocket. Getting my son his own glove, his own bat. Damn. That's every father's dream. Give me an hour to make sure everything here is running smoothly. Then we'll all go into town. You and me and Duncan."

"We'll be ready." A trip into Raven's Cliff sounded like an adventure. She hadn't left the Manor since she'd arrived and was beginning to feel cloistered.

She returned to the kitchen just as Duncan set down his spoon. Without a word, he hopped down from his chair and marched toward the family room. His schedule called for quiet time, which usually meant he sat at his computer.

Since Alma was nowhere in sight, Madeline cleaned up the dishes and loaded them in the dishwasher. For the past couple of days, she'd been using this after-lunch lull as her own personal time to read or fiddle around on her laptop. Today, she was too excited to sit still.

She climbed the staircase to her bedroom and tucked Blake's check into her wallet. With this money, she'd open a bank account and start rebuilding the chaos of her life. As if to underline her thoughts of reconstruction, she heard hammering from the roofers overhead. Progress, she thought. Progress in many directions.

With a bounce in her step, she returned to the family room where Duncan sat on the floor amid a clutter of toy trucks. Instead of following her regular pattern of relent-lessly tidying up the mess, she pushed aside a couple of books on the large sectional sofa, grabbed the remote from the top of the television and sat facing the screen.

Duncan cast a curious glance in her direction. He seldom asked what she was doing. Planning ahead wasn't part of his behavior, and she was careful not to make that sort of demand. Instead, she announced, "I'm going to watch a baseball game on TV. You're welcome to join me."

She tuned in to a Boston station on cable. The game hadn't yet started, and a local news program was on. The smoothly coiffed anchorman glanced down at his notes, and she caught the words *diamond heist* and *estimated loss of over seven hundred thousand dollars*. Quite a haul. She couldn't even imagine what seven hundred thousand dollars' worth of diamonds looked like.

A mug shot of her brother appeared on the screen. "A suspect is in custody."

Oh my God, Marty. What have you done?

The anchorman's words hit her like a hail of bullets. "The jewels have not been recovered. Police are looking for an accomplice."

Her thumb hit the off button and the TV went blank.

"Where's the game?" Duncan looked up at her. "I want to watch the baseball."

"In a minute."

Her gut clenched. The ache spread through her body. She wanted to bury her face in her hands and sob, but she didn't want Duncan to be alarmed. Or, even worse, to start asking questions. *Damn it.* She'd known that Marty was up to no good.

A few months ago, he'd shown up on her doorstep. Miserable and broke, he'd told her that he wanted to go straight but owed a lot of money. He had to pay it back or he'd be hurt, maybe even killed. How could she turn him away? He was her brother.

Fearing the worst, she'd emptied her bank account and savings to give him the cash he needed. Instead of thanks, he ran her credit card up to the max. She had no way to pay rent or any of her other bills.

Maybe she could have worked things out, but Marty got into a knock-down, drag-out argument with her landlord. She had to move. There was always the option of going home to live with the Douglases, but she'd been too humiliated. They'd always told her she couldn't trust Marty. Even as a child, he'd been a liar and a thief. But pulling off a diamond heist?

Damn you, Marty. Two weeks ago when she'd confronted him, he put on a cool, smug attitude and told her not to worry because he was coming into a lot of money. From a debt that was owed to him. Hah! She should have suspected the worst. But she'd purposely closed her eyes, wanting to believe that maybe, just maybe, her brother was telling the truth.

When she got the call from Alma about the teaching position with Duncan, it had seemed like a godsend. At least Madeline would have employment and a place to live. Being far away from Marty in Maine seemed prudent.

The night before she left, he'd showed up at her apartment. Instead of his usual smooth talk, he'd been agitated and sweaty. Had he just stolen those diamonds? He'd collapsed on the floor in her empty apartment and slept like a log. The next morning, he was gone but had left a note that said: "The police might come around asking about me. Don't tell them anything."

That should have been her cue to go directly to the police. But she didn't have anything to tell them. She didn't know what her brother had done. Until now.

Looking up, she saw Duncan standing only a few feet away from her, watching her curiously, almost as though he could read all the dark thoughts swirling inside her head.

Were the Boston police looking for her? The TV anchorman had mentioned an accomplice. Would the authorities think she'd aided and abetted in the jewel heist? Would she end up in jail for no other reason than her brother was a criminal?

No, she wouldn't allow Marty to destroy her life any more than he had already.

No, she wouldn't talk to the police. She had no useful information for an investigator.

No, no, no. This wasn't happening.

If she kept her mouth shut, she'd be safe. *Don't make trouble. Stay in the background.* As a child in foster care, she'd learned those lessons well.

Forcing a smile, she looked at Duncan. "The baseball game should be on now."

He climbed onto the sofa, and she turned on the television. A wide-angle shot of Fenway Park appeared on the screen.

Duncan pointed and said, "Ninety feet from base to base. It's a square."

"But they call it a diamond," she said, cringing at the word. Over seventy thousand dollars' worth of diamonds.

When the national anthem was played, she stood on shaky legs. "Every game starts with that song about our country. We stand and place our hand over our heart to show respect."

Duncan pointed to the flag on the screen. "Fifty stars for fifty states."

She looked down at his smooth blond hair as he stood at attention. The innocence of this troubled boy soothed her own fears. If she concentrated solely on Duncan, she might be able to forget her own problems.

As the Red Sox took the field, she ran through all the numbers that would appeal to him. First base, second and third. Nine players on a team. Distance from the pitcher's mound to home plate was sixty and a half feet.

"When we play catch," he asked, "how far apart are we?"

"I don't know. We'll have to measure."

"Good."

Duncan leaned forward. He seemed to be completely caught up in the game. As they counted balls and strikes together, her fears lessened. The symmetry of the game comforted her. All of life was about balance. Ups and downs. She and her brother had always been at opposite ends of the spectrum.

Suddenly, Duncan jumped off the sofa. He ran close to the television, then back to the sofa. He was breathing fast, almost hyperventilating.

"You want to show me something," she guessed. "Something on the television. What is it?"

At that moment, Blake sauntered into the room.

Duncan's skinny arm pumped back and forth like a metronome at the television screen. "Gloves," he said.

"That's right," his father said. "Baseball players in the field need to wear a glove to catch the ball."

"Not them." Duncan shook his head. "The man with the bat. The batter. He has gloves."

And so he did. The man at the plate wore leather gloves on both hands. Madeline hadn't even thought of this advantage. When Duncan played baseball with other kids, he could wear gloves and not be considered strange at all.

"Batting gloves," Blake said with a wide smile. "Do you want to get some batting gloves?"

"Yes." Duncan's blue eyes actually seemed to sparkle. "I want to be a baseball player when I grow up."

Wearing gloves was a simple solution, allowing him to be around other children without touching. She wished that her own problems could be so easily solved.

Chapter Eight

The central business district in Raven's Cliff clung desperately to its heritage as a historic New England village. Tourists enjoyed the ambience. Blake didn't.

As a general rule, he disdained any shop with "Ye Olde" in the name. Still, he preferred shopping in the village to visiting a superstore with drab neutral walls and overstuffed rows of undifferentiated merchandise. He appreciated that most of these businesses—even those that were self-consciously cutesy—were mom-and-pop operations that had been in the family for years.

He parked on the street opposite the Cliffside Inn, a three-story bed-and-breakfast with genuinely interesting features, including a two-story tower with cornice and a cone-shaped roof.

"Charming," Madeline said as she peered through the windshield at the house. "Look at the roses. Those gardens are brilliant."

"I stayed at the Inn on my first visit to Raven's Cliff," he said. "The interior has nicely maintained Victorian antiques and some very good art, but the real draw is the proprietor, Hazel Baker. She's a character."

When he stepped out of the SUV and held the back door open for Duncan, he spotted Hazel in the front yard with a garden hose. Her long, rainbow-colored skirt caught the July breeze and swirled around her sturdy legs as she waved vigorously and called out, "Good afternoon, Blake. Lovely weather, eh?"

"Nice to see you, Hazel."

He liked that they knew each other's name. This sort of small-town atmosphere was exactly what he wanted for Duncan. In a place where people looked out for each other, a kid like Duncan had a shot at being accepted.

Though he would have liked to cross the street and introduce Madeline to kooky Hazel, who declared herself to be Wiccan, Duncan was tugging on his arm. "Hurry, Daddy. We have to get my gloves."

"Sure thing, buddy."

He linked his hand with his son's. Though he knew from experience that Duncan could, at any moment, pitch a tantrum or go stiff as a board, he savored this moment. Having a kid who was excited about baseball was so damn normal. Once again, he had Madeline to thank for this phenomenon.

As she strolled along the wide sidewalk on the other side of Duncan, she smiled at every person they met—tourists and residents alike. Straightforward and direct, this woman had nothing to hide. Behind her glasses, her gaze scanned constantly, taking in all the details of the neatly painted storefronts and the various eateries, most of which were off-limits to Duncan because of his dietary restrictions. No sugar. No wheat. No salt.

Madeline was quick to point out a sign in the bakery window. "Gluten-free, sugar-free muffins."

"This is where Alma picks up our bread."

"Maybe later, we could get a treat."

Duncan yanked his hand. "First, my gloves."

They crossed the street to enter the general store—a large, high-ceilinged space with an array of tourist products up front. A tall, barrel-chested man with curly red hair and a beard to match approached them. "Hey, now. Aren't you that architect fella working up at the Manor?"

"That's me." Blake shook his hand. "I'm Blake Monroe. This is my son, Duncan. And his teacher, Madeline Douglas."

"I'm Stuart Chapman. What can I do you for?"

"Sporting equipment," Blake said.

When Stuart reached up to scratch his head, Blake noticed the tattoos on his forearms. Inside a heart with bluebirds on each side was the name *Dorothy*. "I don't have a whole lot of stock, but I can order anything you need."

"It's for Duncan," Madeline explained. "He'd like to start playing T-ball."

"You're in luck," Stuart boomed as he lumbered toward the rear of the store. "We've got a T-ball league for the youngsters, and I carry all the equipment. Hats, balls, gloves."

"Gloves," Duncan said loudly.

Blake knew that tone of voice. A signal of tension building inside his son. A warning.

Hoping to avoid an outburst, Blake went directly to the batting gloves and selected one that ought to fit his son. Opening the package, he held it out. "Try this."

As soon as Duncan slipped the leather-backed glove onto his right hand, he beamed. Finally, this was a glove he could wear without being teased.

"The other hand," he said.

"Well, now," Stuart said. "Most batters just use the one. No need for two."

"Not really," Madeline said. "All the major leaguers wear gloves on both hands."

"Eh, yup. You're right about that." Stuart chuckled. "Duncan could be the next Wade Boggs."

"Boggs," Blake muttered. "Another Red Sox fan."

They picked out another glove, which Duncan insisted on wearing, then selected mitts for each of them, bats and a tee for practicing. All things considered, this was one of the most blissfully normal shopping trips he'd ever had with his son.

He eyed the bases. "I'm thinking we might go all the way and set up our own practice field at the Manor."

Stuart chuckled again. "I'd like to see the look on Helen Fisher's face if you do."

"True," Madeline said. "I doubt they ever had a baseball field at the Manor."

Stuart shrugged his heavy shoulders. "That Helen. She's a stickler for historical accuracy."

The hell with Helen Fisher and the good folks of Raven's Cliff Historical Preservation Committee. This was his son. "We'll take the bases. And a couple of duffel bags to carry everything."

"Good for you." Stuart clapped Blake on the shoulder. "When my four boys were young, I'd have chosen them over historical accuracy any day of the week. Building the athletes of tomorrow. Ain't that right, Duncan?"

"Yes."

Before Blake could stop him, Stuart reached down and ruffled the hair on Duncan's head. Then he turned away to gather up their equipment.

Duncan's reaction to physical contact with a stranger was immediate. His lips pressed together in a tight, white line. His eyes went blank. He seemed to stop breathing.

Dreading the worst, Blake squatted down to his son's eye level. "Are you okay, buddy?"

Madeline was also leaning down. She whispered, "Tell your daddy what you saw."

Duncan's chest jerked as he inhaled. "That man is very sad. Dorothy is sick. His wife. Must be brave. Must hope for the best."

"Thank you for telling us," Madeline said.

Duncan's eyes flickered to his father's face. His breathing returned to a more normal rhythm. He licked his lips, blinked, then he held up both hands. "Gloves."

Blake studied his son's face. The signs of tension had already faded. He ran to the front of the store where Stuart was ringing up their total expenditure on an old-fashioned cash register.

Crisis averted.

Madeline stepped up beside him. "Do you think Duncan really saw something? That he sensed what Stuart was feeling?"

"No," he said curtly. Dealing with an autistic child was difficult enough. He damn well refused to start worrying about his son being a psychic weirdo. Leave that nonsense to the kooks like Hazel at the Cliffside Inn.

While Stuart was tallying up their haul, Blake thought he recognized the mayor walking past the front window. "Is that Perry Wells?"

"Yup." Stuart frowned. "I'm surprised he's got the nerve to show his face."

"Why?" Madeline asked.

"There's been letters in the newspaper about corruption in the mayor's office." He ran the back of his fingers across his beard. "Anonymous letters."

"A cowardly way to make accusations," Madeline said. "How can you believe someone who won't sign their—"

"Excuse me," Blake said. He handed his wallet to Madeline. "Pay for this. I'll be right back."

His reason for talking to Mayor Perry Wells had nothing to do with accusations or political corruption. A few days ago, when the mayor's wife had come to the Manor, she'd mentioned the possibility of a house for sale. A beachfront three-bedroom. It was worth taking a look.

On the sidewalk, he called out, "Mayor Wells."

The tall man in a khaki-colored suit came to an abrupt halt and darted a nervous glance over his shoulder as if expecting someone to throw a pie in his face.

Blake strode toward him. "Good afternoon, sir. I'm not sure if you remember me. Blake Monroe."

"Of course. Call me Perry." His practiced politician's smile lifted the corners of his mouth.

When he shook Blake's hand, his fingers trembled. Those anonymous letters must be having an effect, which made Blake wonder about the validity of the charges. "I'm enjoying my time in Raven's Cliff."

"And you're doing important work at the Manor. Vital to our town."

"Nice to be appreciated," Blake said, "but I'm just doing my job. Teddy Fisher is paying me very well."

At the mention of Teddy's name, the mayor's elegant features tensed, but he was quick to recover his poise and launch into what sounded like a prepared speech. "When the restoration of the Manor and the lighthouse are complete, when the beacon shines forth across the sea, it will signal a new era of prosperity for Raven's Cliff. A full recovery from our tragedies. A lifting of the curse."

Blake couldn't let that remark pass. "Surely a man such as yourself doesn't believe in a curse."

"It's symbolic. On that dark day when the lighthouse was destroyed, the hearts and minds of the citizens in Raven's Cliff were poisoned."

"You must be pleased that Teddy has taken on the responsibility of restoring the lighthouse."

"Why do you keep mentioning him? Teddy isn't…" He paused, visibly shaken. What had Teddy Fisher done to this man to provoke such a response?

Blake dropped the topic, which was really none of his concern. "A few days ago, your wife visited the Manor and mentioned a house you might have for sale."

"Are you thinking of settling in our town?"

"Considering it."

Perry reached into his tailored jacket and took out a polished gold case. He handed his card to Blake. "Call my office, and we'll make an appointment. I'd be happy to have you as one of my constituents."

Pocketing the card, Blake returned to the general store to gather up their purchases. Two duffel bags full.

After they'd dragged the baseball equipment back to the car, he was ready to head back to the Manor. So far, this had been a pleasant outing. He didn't want to push their luck.

When he unlocked his driver's-side door, Madeline objected. "Wait. I had a few things I wanted to do. A stop at the bank. And I noticed a dress in one of the store windows."

He glanced over at Duncan, who paced in a circle around a streetlamp. "What do you think, buddy? I say we hang around while Madeline goes shopping."

Duncan stopped in front of his father. With an expression typical of any other six-year-old, he rolled his eyes. "I guess."

"We can watch the fishing boats."

"Yes," he shouted.

"It's settled," Blake said. "We'll wait for you at the docks. On the bench outside the Coastal Fish Shop."

"Thanks, boys."

As she hurried down the street ahead of them, he was struck by the feline gracefulness of her walk. Most of the time, she looked like a drab little house cat, but when she moved with a purpose, her long legs stretched and strode like a more exotic creature. Maybe a cheetah.

He and Duncan took their time going back into town. They stopped in the bakery for a gluten-free, sugar-free cookie and a couple of bottled waters. Then they went to watch the boats.

Beyond the end of the commercial district, the street sloped down to the fishing docks. Not many tourists came to this fishy-smelling area where hardworking crews off-loaded the day's catch from boats that had been battered by years at sea. They were coarse men, scarred and weathered from their heavy, sometimes dangerous labor. Blake admired their grit and determination.

Drinking their bottled water, he and Duncan sat on a bench outside Coastal Fish—a business that had almost gone under during the recent epidemic that had been traced to genetically altered fish.

Across the cove, the ruins of the lighthouse seemed picturesque. He pointed it out to Duncan. "There's where we live."

"I don't see our house."

"It's behind the trees. But there's the lighthouse."

He stood and craned forward for a better view. "I'm not supposed to go to the lighthouse."

"You got that right."

He counted four steps forward, then four steps back, then forward again. His gaze stuck on a group of fishermen. Two grizzled older men smoked and laughed. The third was younger, more refined in his features. He turned toward Duncan and stared for a long moment.

"Four, three, two, one." Duncan was back at his side. He pressed his face against Blake's arm. Under his breath, he mumbled unintelligible words.

"I can't hear you," Blake said.

"She sells seashells," Duncan said. "Seashells by the seashore. Seashells."

He was tired. After a full afternoon, he needed to get back to the Manor. They needed to go. Now.

Fortunately, Madeline appeared on the docks with a bag from the dress shop hanging from her arm.

When Blake looked back toward the fishermen, the younger man had vanished.

Chapter Nine

After they returned to the Manor, Madeline left Blake and Duncan to sort out the new baseball equipment while she went up to her room. Kicking off her sneakers and socks, she stretched out on the duvet. A sea-scented breeze through the open window stirred the dangling teardrop crystals on the quaint little chandelier, causing bits of reflected light to dance against the walls like a swarm of fireflies.

She closed her eyes, thinking she might catch a nap, but there were too many other worries. At the bank in Raven's Cliff, she'd cashed the check from Blake but hadn't opened an account, fearing that her location might be traced by the Boston police. As if withholding her name from a bank account would hide her whereabouts. She had to file a change of address form to make sure her creditors knew her location. She couldn't just disappear. If the police wanted to find her, they would.

And she couldn't keep her brother's crime a secret, certainly not from Blake. Alma knew Marty. It was only a matter of time before Alma heard about the diamond heist and said something. It would be a hundred times better if Blake heard about Marty from her own lips.

She left the downy-soft bed and went to the window overlooking the grounds at the front of the house. It was after five o'clock; the roofers and other workmen had knocked off for the day. The scheduled dinnertime was in less than an hour. For now, Blake and Duncan were playing catch.

Her own games with Duncan had been casual, tossing the ball and reciting rhymes while pausing to pick wild-flowers. With his father in charge, catch took on the aspect of a male-bonding ritual. Not only did he throw the ball back and forth, but also straight up in the air and bouncing wildly across the grass. Blake chased after one of those grounders, scooped it up and rolled across the ground in a somersault and lay there. Duncan ran to him and pounced on his chest. Both were laughing.

So normal. So sweet.

Stepping away from the window, she took the red dress from the bag and prepared to hang it in her closet. The silky fabric glided through her fingers. Never in her life had she purchased anything so blatantly flirty.

She tore off her everyday outfit and slipped the dress over her head. The sleeveless bodice criss-crossed over her breasts and nipped in at the waist, giving her an hourglass shape. The skirt floated gracefully over her hips and ended at her knees. The clerk in the store had complimented the hem length, which would have been too long on a shorter woman.

The clerk had also given her another bit of information that she needed to share with Blake, even though he probably wouldn't want to hear it.

On tiptoe, she twirled in front of the antique mirror above the dressing table. A red dress. Definitely not the sort of outfit for an old-maid schoolteacher.

A bit of jewelry at the throat might be nice. She tried on various lockets and pearls. None of her accessories seemed chic enough for the dress. The same was true for her clunky, practical shoes.

She reached up on top of her head and unfastened the clip holding her hair in place. The heavy black curls tumbled around her neck and shoulders. Still watching herself in the mirror, she went to the bed and sat on the edge, crossing her legs. When she leaned forward, the plunging neckline showed a nice bit of cleavage.

Tonight she would tell Blake about Marty and the diamond heist. Why shouldn't she? Her brother might be a crook, but she had nothing to hide.

A tap on her bedroom door startled her, and she bolted to her feet. "Who is it?"

"Blake."

She snatched her other outfit from the bed where she'd discarded it. She ought to change clothes, slip back into her teacher persona. But why? If she ever intended to wear this red dress outside the confines of her own bedroom, she ought to get a second opinion from Blake.

Tossing her other clothes into the closet, she straightened her shoulders. "Come in."

The instant he saw her, his eyes lit up. "Wow."

His appreciative grin was worth every penny she'd paid for the dress. "I wanted to try it on," she said. "To see if it looked as good here as in the shop."

He came forward, took her hand and raised it to his lips for a light kiss that sent a tingle up her arm. He murmured, "You're beautiful."

"Thank you." She dropped a small curtsy and reclaimed her hand. Unaccustomed to such outright admiration from the opposite sex, she experienced a nervous flutter in her tummy. He wasn't lying. He really liked the dress.

"Turn around," he said.

She twirled on her bare toes, and the fabric floated away from her legs.

"I need shoes," she said. "I don't have a single pair that looks right with the dress."

"I like your bare feet," he said as he came closer.

She was about to complain about the size of her feet, something that made her nearly as self-conscious as her height, but the glow from his hazel eyes mesmerized her. She froze where she stood, watching with almost detached curiosity as he reached toward her.

His fingers glided through her hair as he removed her glasses. "The color of your eyes is striking. Aquamarine."

He stood close enough that she could see him clearly without her glasses. His lips parted.

She tilted her chin upward, waiting to accept whatever he offered. Gently, he kissed her forehead just above her eyes. She wanted so much more.

When his hand clasped her waist, she responded. Leaning toward him, the tips of her breasts grazed his broad chest. She reached up and caressed the firm line of his clean-shaven jaw.

Then he kissed her for real. His mouth pressed hard against hers. A fierce heat blazed in her chest, stealing her breath. She clung to him, caught up in this magical moment, lost in a red-dress fantasy. The most handsome man she'd ever seen was kissing her. Her? Tall, gawky Madeline? It didn't seem possible. Somehow, in a moment, she'd transformed into a swan.

His tongue slid across the surface of her teeth and

plunged into her mouth. She responded with a passion she'd never known existed within the boundaries of her humdrum life. She was spinning and dizzy, yet utterly aware of every incredible sensation.

When they separated, she was gasping. She wanted him close where she could see him. Wanted many more kisses. A thousand or so.

AFTER DINNER, Duncan knew he shouldn't be outside. But there was still a little bit of sun in the sky, and the stars weren't out. He wanted to set up the bases so he and Daddy could play real baseball.

He carried one of the flat, white rubber bases into the yard and dropped it. "Home plate," he said.

First base was ninety feet away. How many steps was that? He picked up another base from the duffel bag and turned toward the forest. He counted his steps all the way to fifty, then fifty again, then backward ten. This wasn't right. Too far.

Then he heard her voice, high and pretty, singing the seashell song.

"Temperance," he called out.

He dropped the base and ran toward the sound. He wanted to show her his new batting gloves and tell her about the trip to Raven's Cliff.

Where was she? He looked around the tree trunks but didn't see her white dress and long gold hair.

"Don't play hide-and-seek." He turned around in a circle, looking everywhere. "That's a baby game."

There were so many shadows in the forest. He heard the waves at the bottom of the cliff. He was never, ever supposed to go near the cliff alone. But he wasn't by himself. Temperance was here.

She stepped out from behind a tree trunk. "Hide-and-seek is not a baby game."

"I play baseball." He reached into his pocket and pulled out his new gloves. "This is what baseball players wear."

She turned up her nose. "Can girls play?"

"Mostly not. Madeline tries, but she's not as good as my daddy."

"I dislike baseball." Temperance stamped her foot. "How should I like a game I cannot play?"

"Don't be mad." He hid his gloves behind his back. "You're my friend, Temperance. I'll teach you how to play."

"Really?"

"I'm making a diamond." He remembered how she said she could never go into the Manor. "It's outdoors."

She wrinkled her brow. "There is danger in the Manor. In the basement."

Danger. The basement was dark and scary, but nobody had hurt him when he got trapped with Madeline. "I'm not afraid."

"Come with me." She laughed. "There is something I must show you."

He followed her through the trees to the very edge of the cliff. She was standing way too close. The wind blew her dress and her red cape. "Come back, Temperance."

She pointed along the ledge. "Do you see that man?"

He squinted through the gloom. The sun was gone. Night was coming. "I can't see him."

"Step out here by me."

This was wrong. His daddy would be very angry if he found out. Taking very careful baby steps, he left the shelter of the trees. The wind blew right in his face, but he didn't run away. He wasn't a scaredy-cat.

Far away along the cliffside, he saw the man. "Who is he?"

"The lighthouse keeper's grandson. Nicholas."

"Is he the bad man? The one who hurt Sofia?"

"Goodness, no." Her mouth made a pretty little bow. "He is very unhappy, as well he should be. He caused the fire in the lighthouse and brought the curse on Raven's Cliff."

Duncan didn't know much about curses. But starting a fire was bad. "I want to go back to the yard."

"Come play with me." She twirled on her tiptoes at the edge. "You are my best friend."

He had never been anybody's best friend. He wanted to please Temperance. He took one more step forward. The waves roared. The noise filled up his head and made him dizzy.

Temperance sang, "She sells seashells."

"By the seashore," he responded. "I want to go back."

"And so we shall." She darted into the forest.

Duncan turned to follow, but he couldn't move. His feet seemed to be stuck at the rocky edge of the cliff. He looked out at the waves and saw a boat coming. Danger. The boat could run into the rocks. Danger.

The wind pushed him closer to the edge.

Someone grabbed him. He couldn't see the person, but he felt skeleton fingers close tightly around his arm and shake him until his teeth rattled.

Black darkness rolled over him. Hate-filled darkness.

Chapter Ten

"Alma, have you seen Duncan?"

"Sorry, boss."

Blake left the kitchen and headed upstairs. He'd only left Duncan alone for a moment while he went into his studio to tidy up the details of the day's work. Now he couldn't find the boy. He checked the bedroom. The bathroom. Maybe he was with Madeline.

Blake paused outside her bedroom door. Only a few hours ago, a simple knock on this door had introduced him to a vision in red and the most incredible kisses. Her slender body had fitted so perfectly in his arms that she seemed to be made for him—created to fulfill his exact specifications. The subtle fragrance of her hair had enticed him. Her lips had been soft and sweet. He hadn't wanted to stop. His instincts told him to seize the moment, to make love to her—this amazing, feminine creature with the mesmerizing eyes, cascading black hair and long legs.

A thin leash of propriety had held him back. She was Duncan's teacher and doing a damn good job with his son. Blake would be a fool to jeopardize that relationship by taking Madeline to bed.

He tapped on the door.

She opened. Her glasses were perched on her nose. Her hair was twisted up on top of her head, and she wore loose-fitting jeans and a baggy T-shirt. In reverse metamorphosis, she'd gone from a butterfly to a plain caterpillar.

"What's wrong?" she asked.

"I can't find Duncan."

Twin frown lines furrowed her brow. "Do you think he went outside?"

"I sure as hell hope not. I've told him a hundred times that he's not to go outside after dark." Apparently, a hundred wasn't enough. "Damn it. Every time I start thinking that he's like other kids, he pulls something."

"Seems to me that a little boy wanting to play outside is the least strange thing in the world." She stepped into the hallway and closed the door behind her. "Let's go find him."

She made everything sound so simple. As they descended the staircase, he said, "You understand, don't you? Duncan isn't like other kids?"

"He's special." In the foyer, she turned to him. "When I was in town, buying my dress—"

"Your red dress." He couldn't help grinning as he thought of that silky fabric sliding over her body.

Behind her glasses, she gave him a wink. "I talked to the clerk about Dorothy. Do you remember Dorothy? She's the wife of Stuart, the man who owns the general store. When Stuart touched Duncan, he said Dorothy was sick."

Blake remembered. He'd seen the Dorothy tattoo on Stuart's beefy forearm. "And?"

"Dorothy is battling MS. Duncan sensed that from touching her husband."

He didn't like where this conversation was headed. "Let's not get started on the psychic crap."

"Duncan might be an empath. Someone who can sense the emotions of others with just a touch. Don't you see, Blake? That's good news."

He didn't see anything positive about having his son take on yet another abnormality. "Why good?"

"I'm not an expert," she said, "but empathy seems to be somewhat the opposite of autism. Instead of being trapped in his own little world, Duncan might be supersensitive to the moods and feelings of others."

"And that's good?"

"Difficult," she admitted. "Can you imagine what it must be like to know what other people are feeling?"

If anyone but Madeline had suggested this theory, he would have scoffed. But she'd been right before.

And his beloved Kathleen had been sensitive. Always talking about feelings, she seemed to know who he could trust and who he should avoid. Her first impressions were always on target. Autism was supposed to have a basis in genetics. What if the same were true for empathy? What if Duncan inherited that ability from his mother?

Blake's gaze dropped to the patterned tile floor in the foyer. Near the door were the duffel bags holding the baseball equipment. One was missing. Duncan must have taken it.

He was probably outside right now, setting up the baseball diamond. "Let's go find my son."

Outside, the dusk had settled into night. He strode across the unkempt grassy area until he saw the glow of moonlight on home plate. Duncan had been out here.

Madeline pointed to another base that was nearer the trees. His son was nowhere in sight.

"Duncan," he called out. "Duncan, where are you?"

Anxiously, he looked toward the lighthouse. The charred, jagged tower held a dark foreboding. For a young boy, danger was everywhere. Climbing around on that lighthouse presented formidable hazards. Not to mention the cliffs with their fierce winds and uncertain footing.

Even more than the natural perils, Blake feared the human danger. Until now, the Seaside Strangler had only attacked young women. But Duncan had known the name of Sofia Lagios. He might have witnessed something suspicious, might be a threat to this predator.

From the corner of his eye, Blake caught a flash of movement. Heart pounding, he raced toward the trees. "Duncan."

Madeline was close beside him. When he looked into her face, he saw a reflection of his own panic. They were near the cliffs. The wind howling through the branches sounded like a cry for help.

As he stepped closer to the edge, he looked down and saw the gloves on the ground. Duncan's batting gloves. Oh God, no. He knelt and picked up the limp little gloves.

How could this be happening? Blake couldn't lose Duncan. He couldn't. Not his son. Not his precious child.

Fear paralyzed him. His heart stopped.

He couldn't bring himself to look over the edge, couldn't bear the thought of seeing Duncan's small body crumpled on the rocks below, his blue eyes staring sightless into the dark.

"Back this way," Madeline said. She tugged on his arm. "Come on, Blake."

"What?"

"I heard something. A shout. Back toward the house."

Desperately hoping that she was right, he fought his way through the low-hanging branches until they were back at the yard.

He saw Duncan stumbling toward the house.

Frantic, Blake dashed toward him, gathered the child up in his arms and held on tightly. "Are you all right? Are you hurt?"

Duncan's small body trembled. Over and over, he mumbled, "Danger, danger, danger."

"It's okay," Blake assured him. Waves of relief rushed through him. His cheeks were wet with tears. "It's okay, Duncan. I've got you. You're safe."

He carried the boy back to the manor. Inside, in the light, he could examine his son for possible injuries. In the kitchen, he sat Duncan on the countertop.

Alma poked her head around the corner. "Heavens, what's going on?"

"Get the first-aid kit," Blake ordered. He stared into his son's pale face. There was a smear of mud on his cheek, but Blake didn't see blood, thank God. "Duncan, can you hear me?"

"Yes."

"Are you hurt?"

The boy grabbed his own arm below the shoulder. "He held on to me here. And he shook me. He hates everybody. They don't treat him right."

"Who did this to you?" Blake immediately thought of Dr. Fisher and how he was always lurking around the grounds. If that bastard had laid a hand on his son…

"What did he look like?"

Duncan's eyelids drooped. His shoulders sagged forward. "Danger. Don't go in the basement. Danger."

Alma placed the first-aid kit on the countertop beside Blake and stepped back. Madeline stood on the other side. Blake was only marginally aware of their presence. His entire focus was on his son. "Who shook you, Duncan?"

"I don't know." He leaned forward, almost toppling from the counter. "Bedtime."

"He's exhausted," Madeline said. "Maybe in the morning, he'll remember more."

Not likely. Duncan's attention span was short-lived. By tomorrow, he would have forgotten this entire incident. "Why were you near the cliff? I've told you again and again how dangerous that is. You're not ever to go—"

A sharp jab in his ribs stopped his tirade. Madeline glared at him. "Bedtime," she said.

Duncan had scared him half to death with this escapade, and the boy knew better. "He needs to hear this."

"He needs you."

Her steady gaze grounded him. Blake had every right to be angry, but more than that, he was thankful and relieved. Now wasn't the time for scolding. He kissed the boy on the top of his head. "I love you, Duncan. I'm so glad. So glad that you're safe."

"Nicholas," Duncan said. "I saw Nicholas."

"Is that who grabbed your arm?"

Duncan frowned. "Nicholas. The lighthouse keeper's grandson."

That wasn't the answer Blake wanted to hear. Nicholas Sterling the Third had died five years ago when the lighthouse was destroyed.

AFTER DUNCAN went to bed, Madeline joined Blake in the studio downstairs. They needed to discuss what had happened to his son. Someone had frightened Duncan. A predator. "In my opinion," she said, "we should report this Nicholas person to the police."

"I don't think so."

"Why not?"

"Nicholas Sterling is dead."

She sank into the chair opposite the desk. "But Duncan saw him. Was he a ghost?"

"Obviously not." Blake stood in front of his drafting table where several blueprints were taped. "The only way my son would know that name and the fact that Nicholas Sterling was the lighthouse keeper's grandson is if someone told him. That same person must have mentioned the name of Sofia Lagios."

She couldn't imagine anyone so depraved. Telling stories about curses and murder victims to an innocent child? "Who would do that? Why?"

Blake picked up a T-square and held it against the blue-print. "Could be Helen Fisher, who is obsessed with the history of Raven's Cliff. Could be her nutball brother."

"Teddy." She'd despised that nasty little man since she'd bumped his car. "Sometimes he wanders around on the grounds."

"It's his property."

"That certainly doesn't excuse him. Why would he grab Duncan and scare him?"

Blake stared intently at the blueprints. "Both times when Duncan got himself lost in the night, he was warned about danger in the basement. Whoever keeps frightening him doesn't want him to go down there."

When she and Duncan had disobeyed that warning, they'd been trapped. No matter how many times Blake gave her a logical explanation for what had happened, she knew better. Maybe someone had been trying to scare them. "You might be onto something."

He tapped his forefinger against the blueprints. "I've noticed anomalies in the structural measurements regarding the basement. We need to check it out."

Fear rippled around the edges of her consciousness. Go back into that overwhelming darkness? "Maybe we should call the police."

"And tell them what? My son saw a ghost who told him not to go into the basement?"

A little boy's nightmare vision wouldn't be taken seriously. "You're right."

"We should explore now. While Duncan's asleep." He lightly stroked her cheek. "If you want to stay here, it's okay. I'll understand."

Now was her chance to back down. She had nothing to prove, had never claimed to be courageous. But he needed her, and she liked the feeling of being able to help. "I want flashlights. Several flashlights."

The appreciative light from his hazel eyes warmed her heart. "Don't worry, Madeline. I won't let anyone—human or ghost—hurt you."

He crossed the studio to the closet near the door. From the top shelf, he took down a locked box which he placed on the desk while he flipped through a set of keys in the top drawer.

Unlocked, the box revealed an automatic handgun and a holster—lethal protection against any threat that might live in the basement. Knowing they would be armed should have made her feel safer. Instead, her blood ran cold.

Chapter Eleven

They left Alma in Duncan's room, keeping watch over him while he slept. Madeline had a cell phone to call the housekeeper in case of trouble. She stashed the cell in the left back pocket of her jeans. In the other back pocket was a small penlight. In her right hand was a heavy-duty metal flashlight—just in case the electricity malfunctioned again.

Together, she and Blake descended the wooden staircase.

With the lights on, the musty concrete basement didn't appear too frightening, yet the word *danger* echoed inside her head. *Danger, danger, danger.* She looked for spiders on the dusty, broken shelving that leaned drunkenly against one wall. The creaks and groans of the old house made her think of ghosts walking across the floorboards above their head. Oh, she hoped not. There was enough to worry about without bringing in threats from the supernatural.

She followed Blake as he picked his way through the fat, heavy support beams and framed walls that divided the space into haphazard rooms.

Shaking off her sense of foreboding, she asked, "Why aren't there any windows down here?"

"This house was built in the late 1700s. A long time before finished basements." Blake adjusted the blueprints in his hand and turned to his left. "Originally, this was probably a pantry for preserves. Then a wine cellar. In later years, there was a coal chute for the furnace."

"Which means there must be another way out."

"There was." He pointed to the blueprint. "When the furnace and water heater were upgraded, the chute was plastered over."

Despite the lack of windows and doors, the musty air stirred as they walked through it. Motes of dust that hadn't been disturbed for years swirled near her feet. The cold seeped through her sweatshirt to her bones, and she shivered. "Doesn't seem safe to have only one way out."

"I'll need to add another exit if I do upgrades down here."

She followed Blake behind one of the walls. The current furnace and water heater were fairly modern, probably only ten or fifteen years old, housed in the cleanest part of the basement. Behind the next wall was a filthy pen of heavy wood.

"Coal bin," Blake said as he kept moving.

Stacked haphazardly in corners of the makeshift rooms were cardboard cartons, old furniture and discarded odds and ends. Paint cans. A rolled-up sheet of linoleum. Several sheets of paneling.

"Junk," Blake said. "Unfortunately, I can't trash this stuff until I sort through it. There could be something of value."

"Maybe that's why someone warned Duncan to stay away from the basement. A hidden treasure."

"Maybe."

He went around another wall, then pivoted and came back in the opposite direction. His intense concentration on the blueprints reminded her of Duncan's single-mindedness, but Blake wasn't the least bit boyish. Not with those muscular shoulders. Not with the holster fastened to his belt.

She tiptoed behind him. "Could there really be a treasure?"

"Beacon Manor is the real deal, full of valuable antiques. Anything could be stashed down here." At the far eastern end of the basement, he ran his hand along the concrete. "There could be a hidden room."

"Is that why you keep checking the blueprints?"

"There are several discrepancies in the measurements," he said. "Most notable is a difference of eighteen inches between the upstairs floor plan and the basement, which could be explained by poor draftsmanship."

"Or a secret room."

A rising excitement replaced her cold dread. They had embarked on a real-life treasure hunt. She imagined rare artworks, priceless antique silver, a pirate's chest full of gold doubloons.

He pulled a sheet of plywood away from the wall, revealing nothing but more concrete. A daunting pile of clutter stood between them and the last bit of wall. Moving all that junk would be filthy work.

"I have another idea," Blake said.

She followed him as he retraced his steps to the coal bin. Blake climbed over the heavy boards blackened by ancient soot. With some trepidation, she followed. "Now what?"

"When you said the coal bin provided another way out, it got me thinking. All the outer walls are concrete, except for here. This could be a door. A crude door that was built over two hundred years ago."

"I don't see it."

"Look hard." He felt along the rough-hewn boards at the rear wall. His hands were immediately covered with thick black grime. "Do you feel that, Madeline? A breeze."

She heard the anticipation in his voice, but she didn't feel the breeze, didn't see the door. "I don't—"

"Got it." His fingers closed around a ridge in the wood. "A hinge."

In a moment, he'd found the latch and opened the secret door. A whisper of chill air swept over her. Beyond the entrance was nothing but darkness.

She turned on her flashlight and shone the beam into the open space—an earthen tunnel that led straight down. "A secret passageway."

Beaming as though he'd unearthed the treasures of King Tut's tomb, he turned to her. "This is a first for me. I've worked on some really old properties. Ancient. Mysterious. A villa in Milan. A small castle in Tuscany. And I've never discovered a secret passageway before."

She didn't share his enthusiasm. A passageway leading out meant that other people could secretly enter the house, which might explain how some nefarious person could have been sneaking into her room. That person could be lurking down there right now, hidden in the darkness. "Where do you think it goes?"

"There's only one way to know for sure. Bring the flashlight closer."

Instead, she drew back. Her feet rooted to the filthy floor of the coal bin. "What if someone's down there?"

"Then we've found what we're looking for." He drew

his automatic pistol from the holster. "I can carry this if it makes you feel better."

It didn't. The idea of a shoot-out in a dark cave terrified her. "I don't think we should do this. We should come back tomorrow with plenty of lights. And a police escort."

"How many times in your life will you discover a secret passageway? Come on, Madeline. Take a chance."

She'd never been a risk-taker. Those few times in her life when she'd acted against her cautious instincts—like when she'd trusted her brother—had resulted in disaster. But Blake's eyes enticed her. His eagerness to explore would not be denied. "You go first."

"I'll need the flashlight."

Reluctantly, she handed it over while keeping the smaller one for herself. "I'll be right behind you."

He stepped into the darkness. Slowly, he walked through the tunnel that appeared to be carved from the stone. The earth floor slanted down at a steep angle; they descended through bedrock.

The beams of their flashlights barely cut into the thick darkness—so heavy that she felt as though she was suffocating. The sound of her own breathing echoed in her ears. She shivered as an icy draft brushed her cheeks. God, it was cold.

The only way she could keep going forward was to concentrate on Blake's back. She followed him as closely as a shadow.

"The floor seems to be leveling out," he said. "There's a curve ahead. An intersection with another tunnel."

What if this tunnel turned into another? And another. What if they'd entered a labyrinth? She wished Duncan were here to count their steps. They could be lost forever.

When Blake halted, she bumped into him. "What is it?"

"A cave."

Peeking around his shoulder, she watched the beam of his flashlight as it played across a high, craggy ceiling. Massive boulders clumped on the floor like the crude furniture of a giant. His flashlight beam reflected on a small, opaque puddle of water, reminding her that they were near the shore. "Do you think this cave reaches all the way to the beach?"

"Oh, yeah. The tunnel we came through was man-made. This is natural." He pointed his flashlight to the right. "This way. Watch your step. There are lots of loose rocks."

She stumbled along behind him, trying to guess the distance from the manor to the shore. Half a mile? It felt like more, seemed like they were walking forever. Climbing over piles of rock, slipping through odd-shaped spaces as the cave widened and narrowed.

"I can hear the ocean," Blake said.

She heard it, too. The crashing of waves outside the cave. The darkness thinned. The air freshened. Excited that they were almost out, she dodged around him. Then slipped. Then fell.

She landed hard on her backside.

Blake was immediately attentive. He took her hand and pulled her to her feet. "Are you okay?"

"More embarrassed than hurt." She reached into her back pocket and took out the smashed cell phone. "Which is more than I can say for the phone."

He played his flashlight over her hands, then lifted the beam to her face. "We're almost out."

And she was proud of herself for taking the risk. "This isn't like anything I've ever done before. I'm glad I'm here."

"So am I."

He pushed stray wisps of hair off her forehead and gently kissed her lips—a reminder of their passion when she was wearing the red dress.

As they moved forward again, his flashlight shone on a plain, rectangular structure about the size of a trailer. Was someone living down here?

They approached the door, found it unlocked and entered. A switch turned on overhead lights, illuminating an open space with tables lining the walls, two large refrigerators and a desk. The generator that powered the lights must have also activated a fan because she heard the hum of a ventilation system. Stacked near the door were several wooden crates and packing materials. Resting on the tables were microscopes and laboratory equipment.

She examined a large centrifuge and read the label on the side, "Fisher Laboratories."

"Son of a bitch." Blake rummaged through the desk. "Teddy Fisher moved his lab down here."

"No wonder he's always creeping around the Manor."

"Technically, this property belongs to him. The private beach is part of the estate."

"But why? Why would anybody put a laboratory here?" She wished that they had stumbled across a chest of pirate's gold. Nothing good would result from this discovery. "This is all wrong."

INSIDE THE makeshift lab, Blake slammed a desk drawer. He was tempted to rake his arm across the surface of the lab tables, sending beakers and instruments flying. What the hell was Teddy trying to pull? His motive had to be criminal. "The only reason to put a lab here is to keep it secret."

"You said something about Teddy's experiments and an epidemic."

"He was looking for a nutrient to make fish bigger and more prolific."

"Not a bad idea," she said. "Bigger fish. More fish. That sounds like an economic boon for the town."

"Teddy's plan was a hell of a lot bigger than Raven's Cliff." The first time Blake had met the little scientist, Teddy had been bubbling with excitement, patting himself on the back so vigorously that he could have dislocated a shoulder. "The fish experiment was supposed to be his claim to fame. A cure for world hunger."

"But it backfired."

"In a big way." He tried to remember details of the stories he'd heard secondhand. "The fish weren't hurt. But people who ate them fell ill. Some died."

"That's murder," she said. "Why is Teddy walking around free? Why isn't he in jail?"

He'd wondered the same thing. "I looked into the situation. I had to."

"Of course you did. You wouldn't want to be hired by a murderer."

Actually, Blake's ethical concerns were secondary. Most of the wealthy, powerful people he'd worked for weren't Boy Scouts. If he started turning down projects because his clients weren't entirely innocent, he'd soon be left with nothing better to do than charity work for churches.

His main reason for wanting to know about the charges against Teddy was monetary; he didn't want to move to Raven's Cliff if the guy paying the bills was going to prison. "Teddy wasn't charged."

"Why not?"

"The curse."

The corner of her delectable mouth pulled into a frown, and he could tell that she didn't like what she was hearing. Primly, she said, "Please continue."

"A lot of the townspeople and the fishermen themselves blamed the epidemic on the curse. The gods of the sea are angry, and the spirit of Captain Raven is offended." A load of superstitious crap. "The only way to lift the curse is to rebuild the lighthouse and shine the beacon."

"Which made them anxious to have you get started."

He'd been welcomed with open arms. "I was assured that Teddy was in the clear. He voluntarily closed down his laboratory operation."

"Apparently not." She took the damaged cell phone from her pocket and punched the keys. "It's definitely broken."

"What are you doing?"

"We need to inform the proper authorities about Teddy's secret lab. He was clearly up to no good."

If he had ever felt the need for a moral compass, he need look no further. Madeline had the earnest eyes and determined chin of a crusader—a defender of underdogs, losers and endangered species. He usually found those traits to be tedious and incompatible with his creativity. Rules were made to be broken.

After Kathleen died, he'd preferred women who were free and easy, who left before breakfast, who wanted nothing but a one-night stand. Madeline was the opposite; she'd always expect him to do the right thing. "I'll bet you never break the rules."

"I try not to," she said.

"You use the turn signal even when there aren't other cars behind you."

"Yes," she said.

"If a clerk gives you change for a twenty when you gave them a ten, you return the extra."

"And I tip twenty percent, even if the waitress is surly. I don't cheat on my taxes. Don't jaywalk. I follow the recipes exactly when I cook."

"No risks. No adventures."

"I like order." She took a step toward him. Her voice softened to a whisper that made those solid values resonate with a purely sensual undertone. "I'm not a risk-taker. Sorry if that disappoints you."

His arm slipped around her slender waist and pulled her snug against him. "Who says I'm disappointed?"

"Most men are."

He nuzzled her ear and felt her body respond with a quiver. At this moment, he wanted to give her all the stability her heart desired. "I'm not most men."

She kissed him with a passion that seemed at odds with her need for order. Messy and wild. He didn't try to make sense of it. Just leaned into the kiss and enjoyed.

Breaking away from him, she said, "We should get back to the Manor."

To his bed. Making love to her was becoming more and more inevitable. Damn, he was ready.

As they stepped out of Teddy's secret lab, they were blinded by the darkness of the cave. Taking charge, Blake aimed the beam of his flashlight toward the secret passage, then in the opposite direction. "Let's keep heading toward the shore."

"Agreed. I don't want to go back through that passage unless I have to."

He led the way, circling an outcropping of stone that

kept the location of the lab hidden. Through another chamber, then into the final cave where the stone walls were damp with salt spray and the bright moonlight beckoned them toward the roaring surf.

"Wait," she said. Her flashlight pointed at the rocks near the edge of the cave, and she picked up a necklace made of shells. "Duncan has a shell like this."

Before he could respond, he heard a moan. A weak cry for help. Just outside the cave, something was moving. Blake handed his flashlight to Madeline and drew his handgun. "Stay back."

On the rocks outside the cave, Blake saw him. Teddy Fisher. Or what was left of him.

Struggling for every inch, Teddy crawled—dragging himself across the rocks. One of his legs was bent at an unnatural angle. His head was bloody. His eyes swollen shut. His dapper gray suit was torn and smeared with blood.

He'd been beaten by someone who knew how to make it hurt.

Chapter Twelve

Instinct drove Madeline forward. No matter how much she disliked Teddy Fisher, the man was seriously injured and needed help.

Blake caught hold of her arm. "No closer," he warned. "He might be armed."

She shone her flashlight back toward the cave. The person who had beaten Teddy might still be nearby. Might have been following them. Might be biding his time before he lashed out at them. What if there was more than one attacker? What if they were facing an army?

Blake handed her the gun. The heft of it surprised her. She'd never held a firearm before, hated when the kids in her classes pretended to shoot each other. Guns weren't toys.

Blake knelt on the rocks beside the injured man, rolled him onto his back and frisked his clothing.

Teddy's face was grotesque. Inside the neat circle of his goatee, his lips were bruised and bloody. Dark crimson blood streaked across his forehead. Each breath he drew caused him to wince.

He was trying to speak.

"What is it?" Blake asked. "Teddy, who did this?"

The swollen lips moved, but the only sound he made was a guttural moan. He convulsed. His body went limp.

Blake tore open Teddy's shirt.

"What are you doing?" she asked.

"Looking for other wounds. Shine the flashlight down here." He pushed aside the blood-stained white shirt. Using his fingers, he gently probed the harsh, red welts that criss-crossed Teddy's rib cage. "The blood seems to be coming from his head and other abrasions. He wasn't stabbed or shot."

But beaten to within an inch of his life. She turned away, couldn't stand to look. What kind of person could possibly inflict so much damage on another? To what purpose?

Blake stood. "There's got to be internal bleeding. He needs a doctor. Madeline, do you know CPR?"

In a couple of teacher-training sessions, she'd taken lessons. But she had never practiced life-saving techniques on another human being. "Not well enough."

"One of us needs to stay with Teddy. The other has to go to the house and call an ambulance."

Both alternatives sounded equally terrible. Facing un-known dangers on the way to the house? Staying here with the crashing waves and dark cave, watching over a dying man? She didn't know how she could manage to do either. Never in her life had she been heroic.

Blake stood and peeled off his jacket. "We need to move fast. He's fighting for his life."

"You're right." She swallowed hard. "Of course, you're right."

"Stay or go?"

Though she might encounter danger on the way to the

house, she'd be better at running than staying here to help Teddy. If he died under her watch, she couldn't live with that guilt. "I'll go."

"Take the gun," Blake said. "If anyone comes near you, shoot. Don't worry about aiming. The noise should keep them back."

"Okay."

"If I hear a gunshot, I'll come running." He squeezed her shoulder. "You can do this."

Though she didn't share his confidence, she turned on her heel and ran. In one hand, she clutched the flashlight. The other held the gun. Neither comforted her.

Scrambling across the uneven rocks on the shore, she moved faster than she would have thought possible. In minutes, she had reached the staircase. Moonlight shimmered on each stair, but she only saw shadows—formless shapes, threatening outlines.

Her heart pounded against her rib cage. In spite of the night breeze, sweat beaded across her forehead. As she climbed, the muscles in her legs throbbed, more from tension than exertion. Common sense held her back, warned her to be careful. But she had to get to the house, to summon the police. They needed the help of the authorities, and Teddy desperately needed a doctor.

At the top of the staircase, she drew huge gulps of air into her aching lungs. The beam of her flashlight slashed across the tree trunks of the forest that separated her from the Manor. Fierce gusts of wind chased over the edge of the cliff.

Before her fears took solid form, she plunged into the trees and fought her way through, shoving tree branches out of her way, stumbling, falling and rising again. She emerged on the other side. Across the yard, she could see the house. Only one light shone from the windows. The light from her own bedroom.

That could not be. She'd left the light off.

Though she couldn't see clearly from this distance, a shadow passed behind her bedroom curtains. Was it him? The person who attacked Teddy Fisher? He could be in her bedroom. Only a few steps away from Duncan.

The fear she felt for herself was nothing compared to her need to protect the child. She ran full out with her legs churning and arms pumping. She would not, could not allow anyone to hurt Duncan.

At the front door, she stabbed her key into the lock. Barely pausing, she charged up the staircase and down the hall. Into Duncan's room. In the faint glow of a night-light, she saw him sleeping. His lips parted as he breathed steadily, peacefully. A sweet, innocent boy. Protected by his mother, an angel.

Madeline turned back toward the corridor. She leveled the gun. If anyone came near Duncan, she'd have no trouble pulling the trigger.

The hall light went on, and she blinked. Standing near the bathroom was Alma. In her hand, she held a gun. "What's going on?" she demanded.

"Why do you have a gun?"

"Why do you?"

Her chin thrust out. Though Alma's face without her usual makeup showed her age, Madeline caught a hint of a younger woman. A woman she'd known many years ago. Her foster mother. Always yelling, thriving on conflict. Alma hadn't been mean, but angry. So very angry.

She shook away the memory; Madeline wasn't a helpless child. "What were you doing in my room?"

"I heard a noise." Alma looked down at the gun and seemed almost surprised that she was holding it. Immediately, she lowered the muzzle. "Sorry, honey. I was a little scared."

As well she should be. The vicious attack on Teddy Fisher gave validity to all of Madeline's vague fears. It was time to call the police.

As soon as the ambulance and paramedics arrived, Blake raced back to the house where he was greeted by Alma. Though a fresh coat of makeup smeared across her face, she couldn't disguise the tension at the corners of her eyes.

"Is he dead?" she asked.

"Hanging on by a thread." Teddy had never regained consciousness. Every ragged breath he inhaled seemed like his last. The external injuries were horrific, but Blake suspected worse damage had been done to his insides. Ruptured organs. Internal bleeding. "Where's Duncan? Where's Madeline?"

"Family room," Alma said. "Should I make coffee?"

"I'd say so. In a couple of minutes, we'll have a house full of cops."

He ran upstairs to wash the blood from his hands and change into a clean shirt. No need to scare Duncan by looking as though he'd been through a war. The circumstances would be traumatic enough for his overly sensitive son.

The police would have questions for the boy, namely who had grabbed him earlier tonight? If Duncan started talking about the ghost of Nicholas Sterling, things could get complicated.

In the family room, he found Madeline reading a book of rhymes to Duncan, who was still wearing his flannel pajamas. Her voice was low and soothing. Though her hair was a mass of tangles, she managed to appear calm.

Not the way she'd been when they'd found Teddy outside the cave. Then she'd been terror-stricken. Her delicate face had turned as white as ivory. Every muscle in her body had trembled, and she'd looked as if she was on the verge of fainting. It had taken a lot of courage for her to make it back to the house and call 911.

Duncan looked up, saw Blake and vaulted off the sofa. He ran to his father, who hoisted him into his arms and held him close.

"It's going to be okay, buddy." Blake stroked his son's fine blond hair. "Everything is going to be okay."

"What happened, Daddy? Madeline said you'd tell me."

"A man was badly hurt." The fewer details, the better. "Pretty soon, the police are going to come here and ask us some questions."

Duncan pulled back so he could look into his father's face. "Real policemen?"

"That's right."

The boy considered for a moment, digesting this information. Then he shrugged. "Okay."

"When we talk to the real policemen, we have to tell the truth. Isn't that right, Madeline?"

"You bet." The color had returned to her cheeks. The smudges of soot on her chin and forehead would have been cute if the expression in her aquamarine eyes hadn't been so solemn and serious.

His own feelings were more akin to euphoria. They'd been in a dire situation and had escaped intact. He'd been lucky as hell that whoever attacked Teddy hadn't stayed around to finish the job.

Apparently, Madeline took the wider view. A man had been brutally beaten. There was a dangerous person on the loose. Primly, she said, "Before the police arrive, I should change clothes."

Still holding his son, he held out his other arm toward her, pulled her close and gave her a hug. "You did good," he said.

"The night isn't over yet."

As she left the family room, he carried Duncan into the kitchen where he smelled the aroma of fresh brewed coffee. Alma had also laid out mugs, plates and napkins. She slid a tray of frozen baked goods into the oven.

Blake made a mental note. If he wanted Alma to perform in the kitchen, all he needed to do was to promise a houseful of handsome young cops.

The short end of the rectangular kitchen table fitted up against the wall, and Blake seated Duncan in the chair nearest the wall where he'd be protected from accidental touches from the police. After providing his son with bottled water to drink and a coloring book to keep him occupied, he left Alma watching Duncan as he went to answer the doorbell.

Two uniformed cops arrived first. The taller officer had red hair like the proprietor of the general store, and the metal name tag pinned above his front pocket said Chapman.

Blake shook hands. "Is Stuart Chapman your father?"

"That's right. All four of us Chapman boys are on the force." His proud grin and the sprinkle of freckles across his nose made him look more like a choirboy than an officer of the law. His eyes widened as he scanned the entryway. "I haven't been inside Beacon Manor since I was a kid singing Christmas carols."

"Most of the rooms are under construction. You'll need to watch your step."

"I'll do that, sir." He cleared his throat and tried to look official. "Can you tell me how many people are currently living at the house?"

"Myself, the housekeeper, my six-year-old son and his teacher." Blake glanced down the hallway toward the kitchen and lowered his voice so Duncan couldn't possibly overhear. "We never saw the person who attacked Dr. Fisher. In case he's still hanging around, I'd appreciate it if your officers could search the house and the grounds."

"He was found at the bottom of the cliff. What makes you think his attacker might be in the house?"

"In the basement, there's a passage that leads down to the caves by the shore."

"A secret passageway?" Chapman nudged his partner. "We gotta check that out."

Another squad car pulled up with lights flashing. Then two more unmarked vehicles. Though Blake hadn't expected such a large response, he was glad to see the cops converging on his front door. He'd meant what he said about a thorough search.

The man in charge wore a dark suit, white shirt and dark necktie. His hair was jet-black and curly. His ebony eyes held the haunted sadness of someone who had experienced recent tragedy. After he conferred briefly with Chapman, he introduced the plainclothes cop who was with him. "This is Detective Joe Curtis. I understand you have some concerns about an intruder."

"Yeah, I'm concerned." Blake shook hands with Curtis, a thick-necked man with a short-cropped, military haircut and shoulders like a bull. "I'm worried that whoever attacked Dr. Fisher is still here."

"Detective Curtis will be in charge of organizing a sweep of the house and the grounds." He held out his hand. "I'm Detective Andrei Lagios. Homicide."

Blake winced. "Is Dr. Fisher dead?"

"DOA at the nearest hospital."

"I'm sorry to hear that."

"Were you a close friend?"

Blake shook his head. "Hardly knew the man."

Teddy Fisher was, however, the person paying the bills for this restoration. Though Blake drew his necessary funds from an escrow account, Teddy's death would have an impact on what happened to the Manor and the lighthouse.

Those were worries for tomorrow. For right now, Blake had something else on his mind. He pulled Lagios aside. "Before you start taking statements, I need you to be aware of one thing. My son, Duncan, is autistic. I'm never sure how he'll react to strangers."

"I'll keep that in mind." His gaze sharpened. "Is there a reason I should talk to the boy?"

Blake considered lying to protect his son, but he was fairly sure that Lagios would see through any deception. Unlike the boyish Chapman, the homicide detective was intense. Tough. Professional. Though Andrei Lagios worked on a small-town police force, he sure as hell wasn't a hick.

"Earlier tonight," Blake said, "Duncan was outside playing. He was upset. Said a man grabbed his arm."

"The man who attacked Dr. Fisher?"

"Could be." That was truth. "Duncan said he didn't get a good look at the guy. Sometimes, he imagines things."

The detective gave a quick nod. "I'll try not to upset the boy. Why don't I talk to him first so he can go to bed?"

As if Duncan would fall asleep with all this commotion in the house. Blake led the way to the kitchen where he sat beside Duncan at the table, shielding him. His son concentrated intently on the coloring book, staying precisely within the lines.

When Lagios sat opposite them, Blake said, "Duncan, this is Detective Lagios."

Without looking up, Duncan said, "We tell the truth to the policemen."

Blake prompted, "Earlier today, you went outside to measure the yard for a baseball diamond. Then something happened. Tell us about it."

"Temperance was in the forest. She's my very, very best friend. She went close to the cliff. I'm not supposed to go there. Inappropriate behavior." He fell silent. The crayon in his hand poised above the page.

Blake guessed that Duncan had also gone to the edge of the cliff when he knew damn well he shouldn't. "It's okay, buddy. I'm not angry."

"I understand," Lagios said in a voice so gentle that it was almost musical. "Temperance went near the cliff. Then what?"

Duncan threw down the crayon. His fingers balled into tight little fists. "He grabbed me. And shook me. A bad man. He's very bad."

"What did he look like?"

"I don't know."

"It's okay," Lagios soothed. "Does he have a name?"

Duncan shouted. "Don't know."

Blake recognized the signs of an oncoming tantrum and

was glad when Madeline joined them. Her presence seemed to brighten the room and defuse the rising tension. She was so blessedly normal and grounded.

She introduced a clean-cut guy wearing a polo shirt and a sweater knotted around his neck, preppy-style. He looked familiar. "This is Grant Bridges, Assistant District Attorney. He's in charge of the T-ball program for the kids in town."

Bridges offered an affable grin as he shook hands with Blake. "I believe we've met. When you were staying at the Cliffside Inn."

"Of course." Blake recalled that Grant Bridges lived at the Inn. "Are you here in an official capacity?"

"I like to get in early on the investigation. This is going to be a high-profile homicide."

Blake recognized ambition when he saw it. Bridges was hoping to be assigned as prosecutor on this crime. "The detective had a few questions for my son."

"Madeline tells me that Duncan is interested in playing T-ball." He leaned toward the boy. "Is that right?"

Through pinched lips, Duncan said, "Yes."

"We'd be happy to have you on the team."

"I have gloves," Duncan said, too loudly.

"That's terrific." He glanced at Blake. "I'll make sure Madeline has our schedule."

When he looked back at her, his smile was warm and appreciative...too appreciative. His eyes twinkled.

Blake was pretty sure he didn't like Grant Bridges, and he had the sense that Lagios felt the same antipathy. Though the detective had acknowledged Bridges's presence, he retreated into stoic silence, waiting for the assistant DA to move aside so his investigation could proceed.

It was Madeline who provided the next distraction. To Duncan, she said, "Hey, I have a surprise for you."

He looked up at her. "Why?"

"Because I like you." She pulled her hand out of her pocket. Dangling from her fingertips was the shell necklace she'd found. "I thought you'd like this."

Lagios reacted. He stood so quickly that his chair crashed backward onto the floor. "Where did you find that?"

"In the caves." Her gaze stayed on Duncan. "You have that other shell that's exactly like these."

"From Temperance." Instead of reaching for the necklace, he plunged his hands into his lap. "Don't want to touch it."

"May I?" Lagios took the necklace from Madeline, handling it carefully by the string as if he didn't want to leave fingerprints.

"What is it?" Blake asked.

Instead of answering, Lagios spoke to Duncan. "Do you have another shell like these?"

The boy nodded.

"I'd like to see it."

"Fine," Madeline said. "Duncan, we'll go to your bedroom and find the shell."

Duncan climbed down from his chair. He walked close to Madeline without touching her. Under his breath, he counted every step as they left the kitchen.

As soon as they were gone, Blake confronted Lagios. "What is it? What's the deal with that necklace?"

"I've seen another exactly like this." His dark eyes turned as hard as anthracite. "The Seaside Strangler uses these necklaces to kill his victims."

Chapter Thirteen

Duncan went to find his seashell for the policeman with the sad, dark eyes. Madeline came with him, and he stayed close to her. Up the stairs to his bedroom. "One, two, three…"

These policemen were very loud. Some of them were mean. "…seven, eight…"

He put his hands over his ears so he couldn't hear the noise. He stared at the floor so he couldn't see, but the inside of his tummy hurt. There was something bad in the house. Something that could hurt him.

Inside his bedroom, Madeline closed the door. "They're making a lot of noise. Even more than the workmen on the roof. Does it bother you?"

"Some."

"They're searching the whole house to make sure we're safe. They're on this floor right now. With those heavy boots, it sounds like there are fifty of them."

"Not fifty." Fifty was half a hundred. Really a lot.

"Maybe five," she said.

In here with Madeline, he felt safe. Duncan ran across the floor and jumped into the center of his bed. The covers were soft and puffy. He wanted everybody to go away.

Madeline sat in the rocking chair beside his bed. "It's lucky that Mr. Bridges came here. He could be your baseball coach."

"I'm going to be a baseball player. Like Wade Boggs."

"Exactly like Wade Boggs." She rocked back and forth. He counted six times before she talked again. "Detective Lagios really wants to see your shell."

"He misses Sofia." Pretty Sofia in her long white dress. "He's unhappy."

"He might want to take the shell with him."

Inside his head, Duncan heard Temperance's voice. *She sells seashells…* "Danger."

"Where is the danger?"

"Basement." Like Temperance always said.

"Anywhere else?"

"Don't know." But he could feel it. All creepy and dark, it was coming closer. "I want my daddy."

"We can go back downstairs."

"No." His voice wasn't too loud. "I want him here."

Madeline frowned, but he knew she wasn't mad at him. She made that face when she was thinking. "I can get him, but I'd have to leave you here by yourself."

"Yes. I want him here. Here, here, here."

"Okay, I'll take the shell."

"No." He was louder. "I want Daddy."

"Stay right here. I'll be back in a flash."

When she left the room, he dove under the covers and curled up in a ball. Outside his room, he heard lots of feet walking. Policeman feet.

He couldn't hide under a blanket. That was dumb. And he didn't want to be a scaredy-cat. He was a baseball player. And he was brave.

He ran to his bedroom door and pulled it open. He charged into the hallway and ran smack into a big man in a suit.

"Hey, kid. Watch where you're going."

"You watch."

"Careful there. You're going to fall down."

Duncan turned away. He slipped.

The big man grabbed his hand. His skin was rough like a tree trunk. His breath was cold. Ice-cold.

"No." Duncan gasped. He couldn't breathe.

The big face came closer and closer. He had sharp, pointy teeth, and they were dripping with blood. Instead of arms, he had big heavy hammers.

They were in a dark, wet place. The hammer came down hard. "Don't hit me," he yelled.

He felt as if his bones were cracking.

Another thud from the hammer. He pulled his arms up over his head. "No, no, no. Help. Danger."

"What the hell is wrong with you, kid?"

He was a bully. A bad man.

Duncan fell to his knees. Thud, thud, thud. His eyes squeezed shut.

BLAKE HEARD his son's frantic cries and raced up the stairs to find Duncan curled up on the floor with Detective Curtis kneeling beside him. His beefy hand rested at Duncan's throat, feeling for a pulse.

He was touching Duncan. Damn it! Blake should have been more specific when he informed Lagios about his son's autism, should have warned him about touching.

He shoved Curtis's shoulder. "Get back."

The big cop looked up and shook his head in confusion.

"I don't know what happened. The kid came busting out of his room and ran right into me. I tried to steady him so he wouldn't fall down."

"Get away from him," Blake snapped.

He scooped Duncan off the floor and carried his limp body into his bedroom. Sitting on the bed, he held his son close. Duncan coughed. A sob convulsed his skinny chest and he clung tightly to his father.

"The bad man." Duncan choked out the words. "Hammer arms. And blood."

Blake looked past Duncan's shoulder to the doorway where Joe Curtis stood, watching and waiting. Though obviously nervous about what had happened, there was something menacing about the man. The way his fingers flexed then tightened into fists. The set of his heavy shoulders.

When Madeline touched Curtis's arm, he pivoted so quickly to face her that she took a step backward. He wasn't much taller than she, but his bulk loomed over her as she said, "It's best if you leave."

"What's wrong with the kid?" he asked.

Madeline stiffened her shoulders. As Blake well knew, she hated any suggestion that there was something wrong with his son. "Forget it, Detective. You wouldn't understand."

"I didn't do anything." He looked out toward the hall where a couple of other uniformed cops had gathered. "I swear. I didn't do a damn thing. The kid was just—"

"Frightened." Madeline's voice took on an authoritative teacherly tone as she defended his son. "Quite frankly, I can't blame Duncan. Not a bit. You're a big, rough man, Detective Curtis. In the eyes of a little boy, you must look as terrifying as a T-Rex."

There were guffaws from the cops in the hall.

Madeline silenced them with a glare. "Step back, gentlemen. We'll handle this."

When she again touched Curtis's arm to push him out of the way, he balked. In that physical contact, Blake saw a battle of wills. A stare-down. Behind her glasses, Madeline's eyes flared with determination.

Curtis met her gaze with an instant of unguarded hostility. Then he shrugged and stepped aside as Madeline closed the door to Duncan's bedroom and came toward them.

If Blake hadn't already been attracted to her, this moment would have convinced him that she was the right woman for him. She'd defended his son fiercely.

HOURS LATER, Madeline kicked off her slippers and dove under the bedcovers. The coolness of the sheets did little to quench her rising anxiety. Her mind raced. She remembered the impenetrable dark of the cave, the mangled body of Dr. Fisher, the clawing branches of trees as she ran through the forest toward the house. Most of all, she thought of Duncan.

The boy had been terrified after his encounter with Detective Curtis, and she knew in her heart that Duncan had sensed something. What was it? What did he see?

After Duncan had calmed down, Blake had stayed with him in his room, leaving her and Alma to deal with the herd of cops who centered their search on the passageway which definitely wasn't a secret anymore.

The police were reassuring, especially Detective Lagios. He seemed certain that the murder of Teddy Fisher was unrelated to the Manor. Teddy had a lot of enemies—one of whom he had driven over the edge.

Supposedly, they were safe. Madeline wasn't sure that she believed that logic. Any person capable of murder was dangerous. They might strike again.

She took off her glasses and reached to turn off her bedside lamp, then hesitated. Sleep wouldn't come easily tonight, not while her nerves vibrated with tension. Even though the Manor was locked up tightly, including the door from the basement leading into the house, and she had shoved her potted ficus against her bedroom door, she was still afraid.

She glanced at the novel on her bedside table—a thriller with a tough heroine who pulverized evil-doers with karate kicks. Nothing could be further from Madeline's reality. In her own way, she was tough. Growing up in foster care meant learning survival skills. But she'd never been a fighter.

There was a tap on the door. Blake whispered, "Madeline, are you awake?"

"Just a minute."

She leaped from the bed, dragged the ficus away from the door and opened it.

Exhaustion deepened the lines at the corners of his lips, but his hazel eyes burned with intensity. His gaze skimmed the outline of her body under her blue cotton nightgown. "I wanted to make sure you were all right," he said.

"I'm fine," she lied. "How's Duncan?"

"He seems okay. I'll never understand what goes on in that little head of his." He exhaled a weary sigh. "I've been watching him sleep for the past half hour."

Feeling exposed, she folded her arms across her breasts. For a moment, she considered grabbing her robe from the closet and covering up. Then she remembered his kiss, and she purposely lowered her arms to her sides. *Let him look. Let him come closer.* A night in his strong arms would be the perfect antidote to her fears.

She cleared her throat and asked, "Did Duncan tell you what he saw when he touched Detective Curtis?"

"A big, bad man with bloody teeth and hammer fists. Then, being Duncan, he started counting in Spanish and showed me how the hands on a clock move." He stepped inside her room, closed the door and glanced at the ficus. "Odd place to put a plant."

Not wanting to tell him that she'd been using her ficus to barricade the door, she ignored his observation. "I know you don't believe in psychic abilities, but we really must consider the possibility that Duncan sensed danger from Detective Curtis."

"Must we?" He raised an eyebrow. "Why?"

"Because Teddy Fisher was beaten to death."

"You think Curtis killed him?" He considered for a moment, then shook his head. "He's a cop, Madeline. His job involves danger. I'm not surprised that he gives off that vibe."

"Nobody knows Curtis well. Detective Lagios said he recently transferred here from Los Angeles."

"The LAPD? That's a tough place to work. A violent place. That's got to be what Duncan sensed."

She wasn't willing to dismiss Duncan's premonition so quickly. The boy had been right when Stuart Chapman had touched him and he had sensed that Stuart's wife was gravely ill. "What if Duncan is right? What if Curtis is dangerous?"

A smile curved his lips. "I get it, Madeline. You believe in Duncan."

"Of course I do."

"I appreciated the way you defended him when Curtis said there was something wrong with the kid." He reached toward her. With the back of his hand, he stroked the line of her chin. "But facts are facts. Duncan is autistic. He sometimes says things that don't make sense. He isn't like other kids."

In her mind, that was a positive attribute. Duncan was smarter than most. And more sensitive. "Being normal is highly overrated."

He came closer to her. "Are you speaking from experience?"

His voice had dropped to a low, intimate level. Even without her glasses, she could clearly see his intentions and she welcomed them. "I know what it's like to be an outsider."

"So do I."

She didn't believe for a moment that this tall, gorgeous, confident man had ever been the butt of jokes. Yet, he was diffident and cool. "Were you a bit of a lone wolf?"

"Even as a kid, I spent a lot of time by myself, imagining castles in the air."

She leaned toward him. The tips of her breasts were inches from his chest. "As an architect, you've been able to turn your daydreams into reality."

His arm slipped around her waist and pulled her close. "I usually get what I want."

Apparently, he wanted her. And she was glad, truly glad, because she wanted him, too. Willingly, she allowed herself to be overwhelmed by the force of his embrace and the wonderful pressure of his lips against hers. Joyfully, she savored the taste of him.

Behind her closed eyelids, starbursts exploded. Sensation flooded her body, rushing through her veins as his hand closed over her breast. His hard body pressed against hers. His thigh parted her legs.

An excited gasp escaped her lips. In her admittedly limited experience of lovemaking there had usually been a great deal of fumbling around. Not with Blake. He knew what he wanted. Even better, he knew what *she* wanted. Every murmur, every kiss, every caress aroused her more.

He was a fierce lover. Strong and demanding. How could she ever resist him? Why would she? Swept away by a roaring passion, she disregarded the small, logical voice in the back of her mind that told her this could never work, could never be a real relationship. They had no future. They were from different worlds. He was her employer. The bottom line she couldn't ignore: he was still in love with his late wife.

This might be a one-night stand. But what a night!

She tore at the buttons on his shirt. In a frenzy, their clothing peeled away. Naked, their bodies joined, and the impact stunned her. Her skin was on fire.

Every cell in her body throbbed with aching desire as he lowered her to the bed. His fingers tangled in her long hair, and he kissed her hard.

She clawed at his back, pulling him closer, needing him inside her. In the momentary pause while he sheathed himself in a condom, she couldn't keep her hands off him. His muscular arms. The crisp hair on his chest. The sharp angle of his jaw.

His gaze became tender. With an expression she'd never seen from him before, he looked deep, seeing her in a different way. Momentarily gentle, he stroked her cheek. "Your eyes are the most amazing color. Aquamarine."

He lightly tasted her lips. "I love your long hair."

He arranged her curls on the pillow, framing her face. Then he leaned down and kissed her again. The time for talk was over.

Chapter Fourteen

The next morning, Blake got out of his bed at the same time as usual. He followed his regular routine, got Duncan up and dressed. All the while, he knew that today was different—not because of the secret passageway in the basement or the police investigation or even the murder of Teddy Fisher. Today was different because of Madeline.

As he followed his son down the staircase, Blake had a bounce in his step. He couldn't wait to see her. His fingers twitched as he recalled the feel of her curly, silky black hair and the satin-softness of her ivory skin. The amazing color of her eyes made him think of deep, clear waters.

The intensity of her passion had surprised the hell out of him. Last night, Madeline had been a wild woman—an untamed, tempestuous force of nature. When he saw her this morning, he halfway expected her to growl. Or pounce. Oh yeah, that would be good.

As he stepped into the kitchen, his gaze went directly to her. Washing dishes at the sink, she had her back to him. Her luxurious hair was pulled into a tidy knot at the top of her head. Not one single, flirty tendril escaped. She'd covered her pastel-patterned cotton blouse and loose-fitting khaki slacks with a blue apron. On her feet were practical loafers, a little worn down at the heel. Definitely not the type of outfit worn by a wild woman. He'd been hoping for a topless sarong.

When she turned and faced him, her expression behind her black-rimmed glasses showed nothing more than the usual friendliness. Likewise, her smile was annoyingly calm.

"Good morning, Blake." She nodded to his son. "Hi, Duncan."

"Good morning," Blake said as Duncan climbed into his seat and began his silent breakfast-eating procedure.

Alma stalked toward him on four-inch heels. "Here's the deal, Blake. I know you hate when I make plans for you, but I had to set this appointment." With her pouffy hair, tight slacks and makeup, she was making ten times the effort to be attractive that Madeline put forth. She continued, "Detective Lagios will be here in about half an hour. He wants to finish the conversation you started last night."

"Fine," Blake said. His gaze returned to Madeline. Oddly enough, her prim exterior aroused him even more than if she'd been flaunting herself.

"I'll make fresh coffee for the detective," Alma said. "Maybe some sweet rolls. Would that be okay for your breakfast, Blake?"

"Whatever." Food was the last thing on his mind.

Alma turned to Madeline. "Did you know that Detective Lagios is single?"

"I wasn't aware," Madeline said.

"So is Grant Bridges. He's not a bad-looking guy and seems to have recovered from the tragedy of losing his bride on their wedding day."

"Must have been terrible," Madeline said.

Blake realized that she was avoiding his gaze, keeping herself so tightly wrapped that not even Alma suspected what had happened last night.

"I'll take breakfast in my studio," he said as he grabbed a mug of coffee. He needed to put some distance between himself and Madeline before he lost control.

In the studio, he sank into the chair behind his desk and quickly sorted through the progress reports of various crews and today's schedule. Concentrating on his work usually provided an orderly solution for life's other problems. No matter what else happened, he could see real progress in the completion of tasks.

Not today. He was distracted by Madeline's transformation. Today, she gave every appearance of propriety. Cool and distant. Nothing wanton about her. Was she playing games with him? Acting out a role? Was this prissy-proper attitude supposed to be a variation on the naughty-secretary fantasy?

He didn't think so. She wasn't a gamer. Madeline was just being herself, keeping her passions in check. But if he teased her, how would she react? Blake sipped his coffee. If he kissed her?

Lagios arrived before Blake's breakfast. After a brisk handshake, he took the chair opposite the desk. From his inner jacket pocket, he produced a small notebook. "I have a few more questions," he said.

"So do I." This conversation didn't need to be a confrontation; they were both on the same page. All the same, he would have appreciated an apology from Lagios for upsetting Duncan. "Starting with Detective Joe Curtis. I understand he's new in town."

"He's from LA. His experience has been useful on the Seaside Strangler investigation."

Blake thought of Madeline's concerns last night and her belief that Duncan had sensed a threat from Curtis. That suspicion could be easily erased if Curtis had an alibi for last night.

Blake tried to be subtle. "My son thought he recognized Curtis, but I don't recall meeting him. Has he ever been at the Manor before?"

"I don't know."

"What about last night? Was Curtis at the Manor last night or was he on duty?"

Lagios frowned. "What are you implying?"

So much for subtlety. "Does he have an alibi for the time of the murder?"

The detective's dark eyes flared with temper. "I don't keep track of the men I work with. When they're off duty, their time is their own. If you have questions about Curtis, I suggest you talk directly to him."

"I'll do that."

The door to the study opened, and Alma minced across the hardwood floor on her high heels. She carried a tray piled high with sweet rolls, bagels and a mug of coffee for Lagios. Her attempt at flirting with the detective fell flat as a water balloon dropped from a ten-story balcony.

Lagios didn't waste time with small-town charm. As soon as Alma left the room, he asked, "Have you noticed anyone unusual on the grounds of the Manor?"

"You'll have to be more specific," Blake said.

"You know what I mean."

Blake matched the detective's brusque manner with his own sarcasm. "If you're asking if I've seen obvious homicidal maniacs, the answer is no. But there are lots of people on the grounds, every day. I have several crews of workmen. Roofers. Carpenters. Painters."

"I'll need a list of names."

"Everything is taken care of through subcontractors. They hire their own men and pay them." He took a duplicate sheet from a folder inside his desk drawer. "These are the companies I'm working with."

"Did anyone have contact with Dr. Fisher?"

"I don't keep track of my crew." Blake lobbed Lagios's comment about Curtis back at him. "Off duty, their time is their own."

"How was your relationship with Fisher?"

"You suspect me? Seriously?" Blake's mood was moving rapidly from irritated to angry. "I have no motive for hurting Teddy Fisher. He's the guy who hired me—the man with the wallet. Plus, I have an alibi for last night."

"I had to ask." Without backing down, Lagios reached into his pocket and placed Duncan's shell on the desktop. "Your son can have this back."

"Did it match the necklace?"

Lagios nodded. "Necklaces similar to the one Madeline found were used by the Seaside Strangler."

The detective's sister, Sofia, had been one of the Strangler's victims. As Blake retrieved the shell and slipped it into his pocket, he adjusted his attitude and cut Lagios some slack. It must be hell to investigate the murder of a close family member. "Do you have any leads on the Strangler?"

"Not much." He glanced down at the notebook in his hand. "I brought my family here from New York to escape violence. I thought we'd be safe. Secure."

When he looked up, his abrupt manner was replaced by a haunted expression that Blake knew well. They had both suffered the loss of a loved one. They shared that pain.

"I feel the same way about Raven's Cliff," Blake said. "It seems like a good place for my son. Maybe here, in a small town, he won't be teased. The pace is slower. There's room to grow."

"Instead, you have a murder on your doorstep." Lagios frowned. "Then somebody like Curtis implies that there's something wrong with your boy. I'm sorry."

"Thanks." The air between them cleared. "The best way I can help your investigation is through Duncan. The person who grabbed him last night on the cliffs might be your murderer. Do you think it was the Strangler?"

"Not likely. The profile for Teddy's murder and the others is completely different."

"Unfortunately, Duncan doesn't respond to direct questions. And he has an active imagination." He decided against telling Lagios about his son's mention of Sofia. "Last night, he said that he saw Nicholas Sterling."

"The lighthouse keeper's grandson." Lagios sat up straighter. "Sterling has been dead for years."

And Blake sure as hell didn't want to start a rumor that his boy saw dead people. "I thought Duncan might have identified Nicholas Sterling from family portraits in the Manor. He might have noticed a resemblance."

"This is helpful. Gives us a starting place for a physical description." Lagios made a note. "Is there anything else Duncan mentioned?"

"Hammer hands," Blake said. "He kept talking about a man with pointy teeth and arms that were hammers."

The detective reached for his coffee mug and raised it

to his lips. He seemed to be struggling with a decision about how much to say and how much to leave blank. "I want to be able to trust you."

"We both want the same thing, Detective Lagios. To keep our families safe."

"I have the preliminary autopsy results." He looked directly into Blake's eyes, hiding nothing. "Teddy Fisher was beaten to death with a hammer."

DURING THE morning lessons with Duncan, Madeline tried to get him to open up about what he'd seen after touching Detective Joe Curtis, but the boy's thoughts scattered in a wild flurry, jumping from numbers to rhymes to simple repetitive motions. Nothing held his interest.

For the first time since she'd been at the Manor, she understood why Duncan had been diagnosed as autistic. He made no connection with her or anything she said. While she measured out geometrical shapes that usually fascinated him, Duncan hummed to himself and kicked his heel against the leg of his chair. He seemed lost in his own little world, unwilling to communicate.

She dropped her pencil. "It's much too nice a day to stay inside. Let's set out that baseball diamond."

He snapped to attention. "Outside."

"Yes, Duncan. We'll go outside. On the grass."

He whipped his baseball gloves from his pocket and made a beeline for the front door, counting every step.

Before leaving the house, she grabbed the duffel bag holding the bases and the measuring tape that Blake had provided for setting up a proper baseball field. As she trailed behind the small, determined boy, she couldn't help worrying about how she'd control him. If Duncan marched into the forest and approached the dangerous cliffs, she couldn't force him to stop, couldn't even touch him.

She dropped the duffel bag and loudly proclaimed, "Here is where we start with home plate."

Duncan halted, still facing the forest. In a singsong voice, he said, "She sells seashells."

"By the seashore," Madeline responded, hoping he'd turn around and come back toward her. "Duncan, come here. I need your help."

Slowly, he walked backward until he was beside her. "I want to play baseball."

"Let's set up the diamond."

"Really a square," he said.

For the next half hour, they measured and placed the bases, more or less in the right position. As long as she kept focus on the task, Duncan cooperated. But she was glad when Blake joined them.

Hearing his deep voice and seeing him stride toward them provoked a response much deeper than relief. Her stomach clenched. Her heartbeat accelerated. Though she was doing her best to maintain a proper attitude—as Duncan would say, appropriate behavior—she could barely control her raging hormones. She was willing to accept their lovemaking as a one-night stand, but she wanted so much more.

But she couldn't let her passion show. Not until she had a better idea of what their relationship—if it could even be called a relationship—entailed. Fortunately, she had a lifetime of experience in practicing restraint, never saying what she wanted, never complaining.

She was happy for the respite when he took control of their outdoor project, allowing her to step aside and watch as he and Duncan set up the bases and walked around them. First. Second. Third. Home.

"Again," Duncan shouted.

They walked again. Then jogged. Duncan's motor skills had improved tremendously.

Sitting on the duffel bag so she wouldn't get grass stains on her beige slacks, she admired Blake's easygoing attitude with his son. Male bonding, she thought. Athletics seemed to be a natural arena for fathers and sons.

With no tasks of her own, she was free to admire Blake himself. His long-legged gait. His masculine shoulders. His habit of pushing his overlong hair off his forehead. So incredibly handsome, he wasn't the type of man who usually gave her a second glance. She could hardly believe they'd made love last night with a passion as fiery as a supernova. Just thinking about it made her perspire.

Flapping her hand by her cheek, she fanned herself as she gazed up into the clear July sky. It was a warm day with the sun beating down. Several of the workmen hammering away at the Manor's rooftop had taken off their shirts.

Blake did the same. The sight of his bare chest and lean torso took her breath away. She had to make love to him again. There had to be at least one more night.

Her passionate reverie was interrupted by a car pulling up to the front door of the Manor. When she saw Detective Curtis emerge from the driver's side, she rose quickly and hurried toward him, hoping that she could handle this situation without disturbing Duncan and Blake.

Grant Bridges—dressed in a nicely tailored suit with a striped silk tie—stepped out of the passenger side and waved to her. "Hello, Madeline. Beautiful weather today."

She returned his friendly greeting. "How can I help you gentlemen?"

Curtis scowled, giving the impression that he was here under duress. "I wanted to check on the kid. Make sure he was okay."

"As well as can be expected," she said. "It's rather disruptive to have a murder so close to home."

His thick neck swiveled as he squinted toward the baseball diamond. He wore a blazer, probably to cover his shoulder holster, and a tie. Too many clothes for such a warm day. His forehead glistened with sweat. "Did the boy ever say anything? About why he got so freaked out?"

"What would you expect him to say?"

"Don't know." He stared at the field. "I should talk to him. Let him know that policemen aren't scary."

"Not today." She planted herself in front of him, ready to tackle him if he made a move toward Duncan. "Leave him alone."

"Good advice," Grant said. "Duncan seems to be doing okay. I hope you'll bring him to T-ball practice tomorrow. It'd be good for him to have other kids to play with."

"I couldn't agree more," Madeline said.

The smooth, charming Grant Bridges was the direct opposite of the thuggish policeman. With an easy grin, he asked, "Will you be coming with Duncan to T-ball practice?"

"Of course."

"Maybe afterward, we could get a cup of coffee."

He was asking her for a date? Amazing! There had been times in her adult life when she'd gone months without any man noticing she existed. Now, she had two very eligible bachelors who were both interested. Obviously, she should have moved to Maine a lot sooner.

But it wasn't right to lead him on. "I'm sorry, Grant. My responsibilities with Duncan are keeping me so busy that I can't make other plans."

"I'd like to be friends." A hint of sadness tugged at his smile. "Sometimes it's hard for me to talk to the locals. They look at me, and they remember the tragedy."

"You have my deepest sympathy." She remembered stories about the accident, in which Grant's bride was swept off the cliff on their wedding day. How could anyone get over such a terrible tragedy? He probably wasn't even asking for a date. Just companionship.

"They never found her. Camille could still be alive." He straightened his shoulders. "I want to move on, but I can't."

She changed the topic. "How's the murder investigation going?"

"I hate to say this, but suspicion seems to be centered on Mayor Wells. He was the last person to see Dr. Fisher alive. And he had motive."

Curtis cleared his throat. "We shouldn't talk about the ongoing investigation."

"No point in trying to keep this a secret. Everybody in town knows what's going on. Perry Wells hated Fisher."

"Why?" she asked.

"You might have heard about anonymous letters to the press about corruption in the mayor's office. Those accusations were written by Teddy Fisher."

She found it hard to believe that the mayor was capable of the violence that had killed Dr. Fisher. His injuries had been brutal. "Political accusations come with the territory for any elected official. They don't seem like a motive for murder."

"The mayor has been under a lot of pressure. He's falling apart. I hardly know him anymore." The smile slipped from his face. "A damned shame. Perry Wells was almost my father-in-law."

Again, she said, "I'm so sorry, Grant."

"Camille was an amazing woman. I miss her. I miss the family we could have had together." His gaze returned to the grassy field. "A son. Like Duncan."

As if sensing Grant's scrutiny, Duncan waved.

"Excuse me," Grant said. "I need to see what the newest member of my T-ball team wants."

He jogged toward Duncan and Blake, leaving her alone with Joe Curtis. When the policeman took a step to follow, she snapped, "Don't."

"Why not? Give me a reason."

Because she didn't want Duncan to be frightened again and she'd lay down her life to protect him. "I don't want you near him."

When he confronted her directly, she realized just how big he was. His shoulders looked massive enough to haul a Volkswagen.

His mouth curled in a sneer. "Why the hell shouldn't I talk to the kid?"

"Because you frighten him." She remembered his earlier question; Curtis was afraid that Duncan had said something about him.

She had no intention of explaining Duncan's abilities to this man. All she wanted was to deflect his focus from the boy. "The boy doesn't know anything, but I do."

She saw a flicker of wariness in his eyes. "Yeah? And what do you know?"

Though she'd never been a good liar, she summoned up all her confidence and nerve. This lie was for a good cause. To protect Duncan.

"I'm a little bit psychic," she said. "I can see your aura. So much violence. So much rage."

Though he scoffed, she could tell that her words made an impact. "You're a violent man, Joe Curtis." Possibly that was why he'd left the LAPD. She continued, "I know why you're here in Raven's Cliff. I'm warning you. Stay away from Duncan. Or I'll tell everything."

"You're bluffing."

"Maybe." She refused to break eye contact. "Maybe not."

Grant jogged up beside her. His earlier sadness vanished behind a brilliant smile. "Duncan is definitely on the team."

Abruptly, Joe Curtis pivoted, ending their face-to-face confrontation. He lumbered around the car to the driver's side and opened the door. Before he got behind the wheel, he cocked his fingers like a gun and aimed it at her. "I'll be seeing you, Madeline."

She wasn't looking forward to the next time.

Chapter Fifteen

Madeline went to bed early that night. During the course of the day, she and Blake had exchanged only a few words. Neither of them had mentioned their previous night of passion. Nor did they speak of what would happen next.

A few times, she'd caught him watching her with what she hoped was longing. Or perhaps, curiosity. She couldn't tell what was going on inside his head. Just like his son, Blake revealed very little of himself. The only thing he'd been adamant about was a restoration project he'd started in one of the upstairs bedrooms that involved some delicate handiwork. Repeatedly, he'd told them that no one was allowed to enter that room.

Though he'd given her no real reason to believe that he might show up at her bedroom door, she dressed in her best pink satin nightshirt with matching panties—a gift to herself from one of the better lingerie shops in Boston. With her long hair brushed to a glossy sheen, she slipped between the sheets and waited.

Duncan had been tucked in half an hour ago, plenty of time for him to be sound asleep. If Blake intended to join her in bed, there should be nothing stopping him.

A glance at the bedside clock told her that it was exactly four minutes since the last time she'd checked the time. She ought to take matters into her own hands. Trot down the hall to his room.

Their passion last night had been spectacular. Of that, she had no doubt. But he might not want a repeat. He might have decided that it was inappropriate to seduce his son's tutor. Or he might be remembering his beloved Kathleen. An angel. How could anyone compete with such a perfect memory?

Another ten minutes ticked slowly by. She exhaled a frustrated sigh. *He wasn't coming.* Might as well shove the ficus against the door and try to sleep.

Then she heard a rap on her bedroom door. She bolted to a sitting posture on the bed and called out, "Come in."

"You come out," Blake responded.

In the ensuing silence, the pounding of her heart was louder than the drum and bugle corps in the St. Patrick's Day Parade. *He wanted her to come to him.*

She floated from the bed to the mirror, put on her glasses to check her reflection, then took them off. Her hazy vision matched her dreamlike mood as she wafted to the door and opened it.

A trail of colorful wildflowers—daisies and bluebells— led down the hallway, marking the way from her bedroom to his. Never had she expected such a sweet gesture. Step by step, she gathered her bouquet, pausing at the slightly opened door to Duncan's bedroom and peeking inside at the soundly sleeping child.

Like a bride to the altar, holding her colorful bouquet, she walked the few paces. No matter what else happened between them, she would always remember this moment. More than passion, he had given her romance.

When she pushed open the door to Blake's room, she found him waiting. He scooped her off her feet and into his arms, neatly closing his door at the same time.

Her flowers scattered across the sheets as he deposited her on his bed. Unlike last night's wild frenzy of passion, tonight was slow. Deliberate. Divine.

She savored his kisses. Pushing aside his unbuttoned shirt, she traced the muscles on his chest. His strong but gentle caresses pulled her so close that they breathed as one being. Their hearts synchronized in perfect harmony.

Through her swirling senses, she heard a cry.

It was Duncan. "Danger," he shouted. "Danger."

INSTANTLY, Blake responded to his son's voice. He leaped from the bed and charged down the hall to Duncan's room. The door was shut when it should have been open. He yanked the knob, flung it open and stormed inside.

His son stood on his bed, cowering against the headboard. As Blake approached, Duncan jumped toward him, into his arms. He was cold, shivering.

"What happened?" Blake asked. "Bad dream?"

"Bad dream. Bad man. Bad dream."

Blake stroked Duncan's fine blond hair. "It's okay, buddy. Nobody is going to hurt you."

"I saw his shadow. Hammer hands."

It had been several months, nearly a year, since Duncan had last been yanked awake by a nightmare. After his mother died, these bad dreams came almost every night, but that behavior was history. Until now.

Blake glanced toward Madeline as she entered the room, wearing that sexy satin nightshirt that showed off her long, curvy legs. Her flushed complexion and disheveled hair contrasted with her calm voice as she asked, "What should I do? Duncan, do you want a glass of water?"

"No," Duncan shouted. "He'll get you. Stay."

Blake sat on the edge of the bed with Duncan on his lap. "The nightmare is gone. We're all safe."

When Madeline sat beside them—carefully not touching his son—her presence felt right. They were a unit. Together, they faced the dark fears in Duncan's mind.

She urged, "Tell us what happened, Duncan. Everything you can remember."

"Noise," he said.

"You heard a noise," she prompted.

"Thump. Big feet. The door opened up. Opened up. Opened up wide. Shadows came inside. A big shadow." He shook his head. "Danger."

"But your door was closed," Blake said.

"He shut it." His shoulders slumped as he began to calm down. "All gone now. All gone."

Blake cradled his son against his bare chest. This sure as hell wasn't the way he had planned to spend this night, but Duncan came first. And he knew Madeline would agree with him. "You've got nothing to worry about, buddy."

Duncan pulled away and looked into his eyes. It was unusual for the boy to make such direct contact. His voice was normal without a hint of agitation. "Daddy, I saw him. I really saw him."

"Who? Who did you see?"

"The man."

"What did he look like?"

"He smelled like the ocean."

Had this been more than a nightmare? It was possible that someone had crept up the staircase and into his son's room. Blake needed to know. "Concentrate, buddy. Tell me about the man. Was he tall?"

Duncan frowned and looked down at his hands. He laced his fingers together, then pulled them apart. After three repetitions of this gesture, he murmured, "She sells seashells."

Last night, Duncan had been approached on the cliff by a stranger—someone had grabbed his shoulder. Duncan was a witness. He might have seen the man who murdered Teddy Fisher. "Duncan, look at me."

The boy clapped his hands together. "All gone."

Damn, this was frustrating. All Blake wanted was an answer to a simple question. "Does the man have a name?"

"Time for sleep, Daddy." He wriggled out of Blake's arms and dove under his covers. "Nighty-night, Madeline. Don't let the bedbugs bite."

Duncan's fears—having been expressed—seemed to disappear. He closed his eyelids. With each calm breath, his skinny chest rose and fell in an untroubled, steady rhythm.

Blake was nowhere near so calm. He whispered to Madeline. "I'm staying here until he's asleep."

"Of course." She left the room.

Settling into the rocking chair beside the bed, Blake fastened the buttons on his shirt. He hoped Duncan's vision had only been a nightmare, but feared otherwise.

What the hell should be done? Trust the cops to take care of things? Though Detective Lagios seemed like a competent officer, his abilities were limited. The only clue Duncan could offer was to say he'd seen a bad man. Or Nicholas Sterling, who had been dead for years.

The Raven's Cliff police force didn't have enough manpower to stand guard over the Manor day and night.

Even if they could, there was no sure protection against a determined assailant. There were dozens of ways into this sprawling house. Windows that were being replaced. Doors that were off the hinges. Installing a security system was a waste of time with all the workmen coming and going. Not to mention the secret passageway that led from the caves into the basement.

If Duncan truly was in danger, they should pack up and leave Raven's Cliff. But Duncan was doing well in this place. Just this afternoon, they'd played baseball like a regular father and son.

Moving carefully so he wouldn't wake Duncan, Blake slipped out of the room into the hallway.

Madeline popped through her bedroom door where she'd obviously been waiting. Wearing her flannel bathrobe with her glasses perched on her nose and her hair tied back at her nape, she gave the clear signal that she wasn't interested in sex.

"Is Duncan okay?" she whispered.

He nodded and pointed toward the staircase. Together, they descended and went into the kitchen.

She went to the cabinets by the sink. "I could really use a cup of tea."

"I was thinking of something stronger." From a top shelf, he took down a bottle of bourbon and poured a couple of shots into a tumbler. "You?"

"I'll stick to chamomile." She placed the teakettle on the burner and turned up the flame.

He took a sip and savored the burn. "Duncan hasn't had a nightmare like this in months."

"I can't blame him for being upset. It's been a rough couple of days." Her gaze rested on the poster board—

Duncan's Schedule. "Being lost in the woods. The murder. His reaction to Joe Curtis."

"He's agitated. Overexcited."

"Of course."

Blake really wanted to believe that his son's nightmare was nothing more than imagination—a disturbing sleep experience. He sank into a chair and took another drink. "What if he really saw someone?"

"It's possible. Very possible." She dove into the chair opposite him and leaned forward on her elbows. Her robe gaped open, giving a glimpse of the pink satin. "Someone could have come into his room."

Fear struck him hard. "A killer in the same room with my son."

Behind her glasses, her eyes shone with purpose and hope. "It's up to us, Blake. We have to find out what Duncan saw."

He agreed, but trying to figure out what was going on in Duncan's brain was like entering a maze. "Got any ideas?"

"There's got to be a way we can get Duncan to identify the person who grabbed him on the cliff."

"Then what?" He inhaled another gulp of bourbon, hoping to deaden the fear that writhed inside his chest. "I won't put my son through the ordeal of testifying. He can hardly stand to be in the same room with other people much less face a judge and jury. Damn it, he's only six years old."

"We need to know the truth, Blake."

"Here's what I need, Madeline. To keep my child safe. I should cancel all the work crews and bar the doors. Better yet, we should leave. Get the hell away from this cursed little town."

On the stove, the teakettle whistled, and she went to prepare her drink. "Is that what you want, Blake? To leave?"

"No." His response was immediate and definite. He was enjoying the restoration of this American Federalist estate, especially the project he'd started in the upstairs bedroom this afternoon. Even more important, Duncan's behavior improved every day by leaps and bounds. "I want my son to have a normal life, to play baseball. I want him to have a chance to be like other kids."

She returned to her seat opposite Blake and placed the flower-sprigged cup and saucer on the tabletop. "That's not too much to hope for."

Ever since the first diagnosis of autism, Blake's life with Duncan had been a series of disappointments. He'd learned not to expect too much. A normal life? "It's an impossible dream."

Reaching across the table, she laced her fingers with his. Her hand was soft and warm from holding her teacup. "Sometimes," she said, "the impossible comes true."

Her sincerity struck a chord inside him. Through his anger and frustration, he felt an echo of her hope. Sometime. Somehow. Someday. His son would be all right.

"I want to believe that."

"You can."

He liked the way her common sense cut through all the complications. She made all things seem possible. In so many ways, she amazed him. Being with Madeline was part of the reason he wanted to stay in Raven's Cliff. Their relationship was still in the early, delicate stages. He needed time to nurture his feelings for her, to see if his heart could ever blossom again.

But Duncan came first. "I've got to protect my son. If he's in danger, we can't stay here."

"As you well know," she said, "I'm Duncan's biggest

advocate. I think he sees things that the rest of us don't. But what happened tonight might have been nothing more than a bad dream."

"True." He could be making too much of a nightmare. "If we stay, we can't leave him alone. Not for a minute."

"But we can't lock him up in his room. Tomorrow, we should go to the T-ball practice in town."

"That's dangerous on so many levels. First, there's the basic problem of having Duncan interact with other kids. Leaving the house. Changing his schedule." A worse thought occurred. "What if he sees the killer?"

"A good thing," she said firmly. "If he identifies the killer, Lagios can arrest him. Duncan will be safe."

She made the process of putting his son in close proximity to a murderer sound rational. "The next thing you'll suggest is that we arrange for a police lineup of the main suspects."

"Probably not," she conceded. "That's too much pressure. I wouldn't want to put Duncan in the position of coming face-to-face with his nightmare man."

With a final squeeze, she withdrew her hand and concentrated on her tea. Her ladylike manner when she lifted the cup to her lips was a definite turn-on. He was tempted to sweep everything off the kitchen table and take her right here.

"Perhaps," she said, "there's a way for Duncan to see the suspects without facing them. We could arrange our own lineup."

"How?"

"Using your cell phone, you could take photos of the various suspects. I believe the police are concentrating on the mayor, Perry Wells."

"I still don't understand what you're talking about."

"We can make it a game. Like a lesson plan. Show Duncan all the photos and watch his reaction."

Once again, she'd come up with a simple solution for a complex problem. Using cell-phone photos, they could create their own photo array for Duncan to use in identification. In that way, his son wouldn't have to face the police. If he recognized the killer, they'd be right there beside him.

Blake turned the idea over in his head, looked at it from several angles. He couldn't find a flaw.

He raised his tumbler to her in toast. "We'll do it. It's a good plan."

"Thank you." She clinked her dainty teacup with his bourbon tumbler.

A very good plan. Maybe even brilliant. If grade-school teachers were running Homeland Security, the terrorists wouldn't stand a chance.

Chapter Sixteen

"First base, second base…" In the back of the car, Duncan counted to himself and punched his batting glove into the big catcher's mitt. Yesterday, Daddy had showed him how to do a high five. "…third base. Home plate. Home run."

He was on a team. A T-ball team. And he knew all the numbers. He leaned forward against his seat belt and stuck out his catching glove toward the front seat. "Madeline. High five."

She turned around and slapped the glove. "High five."

She looked funny in her Red Sox baseball cap with her ponytail hanging out the back. But her teeth were pretty and white, and she smiled a lot. That made him think of his best friend, Temperance, and how it sounded when she laughed. He wished Temperance could see him play baseball.

His Daddy parked and turned around. He smiled, too.

"Hey, buddy."

"Hey, Daddy."

"I'm proud of you, Duncan. Let's play ball."

He jumped out of the car. There was a fence and a green field with bases. Lots of kids. Lots of parents.

Duncan wasn't scared. He knew all the numbers.

STEPPING OUT of the car into a sunny summer day, Madeline tensed. The possibility of running into the person who killed Teddy Fisher was secondary to her concerns for Duncan. More than anything, she wanted him to have a positive experience this afternoon. She walked stiffly at Blake's side—as apprehensive as if she herself were approaching the batter's box in Fenway Park.

The baseball diamond where the kids—aged five to seven—played T-ball was in a park across the street from the high school. A tall chain-link fence formed the backstop. The grass was cut short in the infield, and the paths for base running were marked off with white chalk lines. A simple setup with no dugouts or bleachers. She noticed that some of the other adults had brought along their own lawn chairs.

Grant Bridges sauntered toward them. His casual shorts and T-shirt didn't flatter him nearly as much as his suit and tie. Though he seemed fit, he lacked the athletic grace that came so naturally to Blake.

"Glad you're here," Grant said as he shook hands with Blake and twinkled a grin at Madeline. "With Duncan playing we've got enough kids for two full teams."

"Nine players on a team," Duncan said quickly.

"That's right," Grant said. "Come with me and we'll meet the other kids."

With a wave of his gloved hand, Duncan went forward.

Madeline held her breath. Since she'd never seen Duncan with other children, she didn't really know what to expect. But Blake did. With arms folded across his chest and every muscle in his body clenched, he radiated nervous energy.

They were close enough to overhear the other kids greet

Duncan. He was quickly surrounded by four boys and two girls, all wearing baseball caps.

A stocky, redheaded boy who looked as if he might belong to the Chapman clan said, "You live in that big place near the lighthouse."

"Yes," Duncan said.

"There was a murder there."

The other kids jostled closer, obviously curious. There were comments about scary murders and the curse. One of the boys spat into the dirt.

Madeline noticed that Blake's arms had dropped to his sides and he leaned forward on the balls of his feet as if ready to immediately sprint to his son's aid.

The redheaded kid spoke to Duncan again. "Did you see him? Did you see the dead guy?"

"No."

A skinny little girl with long blond braids started to tremble. "Don't talk about it. I'm scared."

"Geez, Annie," said the other girl. "You're such a big crybaby."

"Am not!"

With his gloved hand, Duncan reached toward Annie and patted her shoulder. "It's okay. The bad man isn't here."

"Aren't you scared?"

"Sometimes." He shrugged. "I don't like T-Rex dinosaurs."

"Me, too," piped up the shortest boy in the group. "And sharks. I hate sharks. They can eat you up in one bite."

Grant stepped in to break up the conversation, assigning them places in the field for practice. Duncan ran to second base and stood on the bag. Though his lips were tight, Madeline detected the beginning of a grin. She beamed back at him. A sense of real pride bubbled up inside her. When Grant lobbed a ball toward him, Duncan managed to scoop it up and throw in the general direction of first base. His playing skills seemed to be no better and no worse than most of the other kids'.

She touched Blake's arm. "He's going to be okay."

"Thanks to you." When he looked at her, his eyes held a special tenderness and intimacy. "You've done so much. Our little family is coming together."

Our family? He seemed to be including her in that unit. "We're a good team."

"You, me and Duncan," he said. "I never imagined my son being able to play baseball."

She held his gaze, not wanting to make too much of the casual way he lumped them together. Being accepted as part of a family—his family—was deeply important to her. She'd always yearned for a family of her own. Not her adoptive parents. Not her addict mother who'd tossed her into the foster-care system. Certainly not her genetic sibling, Marty. Which reminded her that she still hadn't found the right time to tell Blake about the diamond theft. Now was certainly not that moment.

She turned toward the sidelines where the other parents had gathered. "We should introduce ourselves to the parents of Duncan's new friends."

"Friends," he said with obvious satisfaction. "Duncan's friends. That's a hell of a concept."

"Maybe we can set up a couple of playdates."

He took his cell phone from his pocket. "Or snap a

couple of pictures. I'm going to include Grant Bridges in our photo array."

She didn't understand why he'd taken such a dislike to Grant. "Okay."

None of the people they met seemed the least bit suspicious. Average people. Very pleasant. Like the kids on the field, they were all buzzing about the murder of Teddy Fisher. The general opinion seemed to be that Dr. Fisher was an obnoxious person, too rich for his own good, a genuine eccentric.

"And dangerous," said Lucy Tucker in a conspiratorial tone. Her trinket shop—Tidal Treasures—was in the center of town, and Lucy seemed to have her finger on the pulse of Raven's Cliff.

"Why dangerous?" Madeline asked.

The petite strawberry blonde pulled her aside. "You didn't hear this from me, but Dr. Fisher's experiments at his lab caused the epidemic. You know, the dark-line disease that killed people? If it hadn't been for Dr. Peterson, we'd all be dead."

With no encouragement, Lucy rattled on about the lady doctor who had apparently hooked up with a sexy toxicologist and they were getting married. "I mean, he's a babe magnet. And a doctor."

Madeline had never been fond of gossip but wanted to bond with Lucy, who was the aunt of Annie—the little girl with braids whom Duncan had comforted. "About the epidemic," she said. "Weren't there anonymous letters in the paper saying that Mayor Wells was to blame?"

"Lower your voice," Lucy warned as she nodded toward her left. "That skinny guy in the suit is Rick Simpson, the mayor's top aide."

Rick Simpson appeared to be deep in conversation with two other men who looked as if they'd just stepped out of their offices. "Who's with him?"

"A couple of guys who work in the D.A.'s office. You know, lawyers."

Madeline glanced toward the baseball diamond where Grant Bridges was organizing the kids into two teams, then turned back to Lucy. "There are a lot of high-powered people here. Are they all parents?"

"Mostly," Lucy said. "Some of them are here because the mayor's wife supports the baseball program."

Apparently, showing up at a T-ball game was a good way to impress the powers that be. Now Madeline understood why Grant Bridges—a single man with no children of his own—had volunteered to coach the team. This was his way of making contacts. "Why is Beatrice Wells so involved?"

"Raven's Cliff baseball is a whole program—from these little ones to middle school. According to Beatrice, sports are a good way to keep the kids off the street."

These teams of five- to seven-year-olds hardly looked like budding juvenile delinquents, but Madeline liked the idea of children being involved in group sports, especially during the summer when they tended to lose focus. From her years of teaching, she remembered how dreadful the first weeks of school could be.

But she wasn't here to discuss her educational philosophy with Lucy. Madeline returned to the pertinent gossip about the murder. "I've heard that Mayor Wells is a suspect."

"If he killed Teddy Fisher, I say good for him. Fisher was a menace." Her blue eyes brightened as she caught sight of two tough-looking fishermen approaching. "That's my boyfriend, Alex Gibson. Got to run."

Madeline turned her gaze toward the field where Duncan's team sat in a row on the sideline, waiting for their turn to bat. The rules in T-ball were different than regular baseball. Though one of the kids stood on the mound, the pitcher didn't really throw the ball. He just pantomimed the motion. The actual ball rested on a stand, and the batter had unlimited swings in trying to hit it. An inning came to an end when every kid on the team had had a turn at bat.

The theory was to give the kids an idea of how to run bases and field without really keeping score. The atmosphere should have been low-pressure, but Blake was tense as he came up beside her. "Duncan is next."

"He'll do fine," she assured him.

"We haven't practiced much on batting. I showed him how to swing, but that's about it."

The batter before Duncan wound up and unleashed a monster swing that spun him around like a top. He did, however, miss the ball standing on the tee.

"Strike one," his teammates yelled.

His second swing connected for a dribbling little hit that was enough for the boy to run to first base.

It was Duncan's turn. As he walked to the plate, his lips were moving. Madeline knew he was silently counting his steps. His small gloved hands wrapped around the bat, and he took his stance. With serious concentration, he swung. A hit!

"Yes," Blake said with a quiet fist pump. "Okay, son. Now run. Run to first."

Duncan went to first. Then second. That was where he

stopped. Breathing hard, he gave a high five to the second baseman for the other team. Then he waved to his father.

"That's my boy. He hit a double."

While Duncan was on base, Blake concentrated on the field with a mixture of pride and incredulity. He couldn't believe how well Duncan was doing. No outbursts. No signs of rising panic. The batting gloves kept him shielded from unwanted touches, and the mechanics of the game kept his attention occupied. When he crossed home plate, he jumped on it with both feet.

Even more satisfying for Blake was the way Duncan interacted with his teammates. Though his son never laughed, a tiny grin played around the corners of his mouth. Blake overheard Duncan volunteering information, citing statistics about Madeline's beloved Red Sox.

Even that jerk, Grant Bridges, took notice of Duncan's expertise. "You're quite a Sox fan," he said.

"Yes," Duncan replied. "And the Cubbies."

That's my boy!

Blake's paternal reverie ended abruptly when he saw Helen Fisher charging toward him from the street. She was dressed in black from head to toe in apparent mourning for her dead brother. She'd topped the outfit with a big-brimmed straw hat that made her look like a walking lampshade.

She planted her feet in front of him and glared. "I want an accounting of every penny you spend on the restoration of the Manor. And I want it now."

Blake had no intention of being drawn into a business discussion at his son's T-ball game. "My condolences on the loss of your brother."

"Right. Thanks." She spat the words. "Teddy died without a will and has no heirs. That means Beacon Manor now belongs to me."

"That's for the probate courts to decide."

"Don't you dare put me off." Her voice rose to a finger-nails-on-chalkboard vibrato. "I own it."

Madeline stepped in to defuse the situation. "Perhaps we could talk about this another time."

Helen's furious glare swept past her and encompassed the rest of the people gathered at the sidelines. "I own the Manor and the lighthouse. I might just decide to move in and shut down the renovations entirely."

A tough-looking guy growled at her. "You can't do that."

"Don't tell me what I can't do, Alex Gibson."

"The lighthouse has to be repaired," he said. "It's the only way to lift the curse."

"All of you fishermen are so superstitious." Her mouth puckered. "The Manor is a historic landmark. The curse isn't real."

As Alex Gibson rose to his feet, Blake recognized him. He was the fisherman whom Duncan had seen at the docks and reacted to—definitely someone Blake should have in his photo array of suspects.

"Never deny the curse," Alex said darkly.

The little strawberry blonde who owned the trinket shop backed him up. "Helen, please. We're on the right track with repairing the lighthouse."

"How can you say that? Teddy was killed." Amid the crowd who were mostly dressed in summery clothing, her black dress marked her as a harbinger of bad luck. "You'd all better get used to treating me with more respect. I'm a wealthy woman now."

Which sounded to Blake like a damn good motive for

murder. Did Helen have the strength to beat her brother to death with a hammer?

Beatrice Wells hurried toward them, covering the last few yards across the grass with surprising speed for a small, short-legged woman. Gasping for breath, she said, "Helen, dear, you simply must lower your voice. You're upsetting the children."

Was she? Blake glanced back toward the field. None of the kids were watching. Even Duncan appeared to be undisturbed as he stared across the baseball diamond at the far edge of the outfield.

"Of all people," Helen said to Beatrice, "I'd expect you to understand. The money my brother threw away by hiring a world-famous designer could have gone to charity."

Beatrice tossed an apologetic smile toward Blake while Helen continued, "My brother got rich, and I spent my whole life struggling to get by."

"Not much of a struggle," said the trinket-shop owner. "The way I've heard it, you own your house and your bills are paid by a family trust."

Mayor Perry Wells had followed his wife to the sidelines. Though he was obviously ragged around the edges and stressed, his voice rang with the authority of his office. "Everyone calm down. You're distraught, Helen. Which is understandable under the circumstances. But you need to take it easy."

"Or what? What are you going to do, Perry?" She sneered. "Are you going to kill me, too?"

Beatrice gasped. Her small hand flew to cover her mouth. A murmur ripped through the people at the sidelines.

Helen took no notice. She turned on her heel and stalked off.

To his credit, Perry Wells didn't react to Helen's accusation. He pasted a smile on his face. "It's a beautiful day. Beautiful! Play ball."

Though Blake took out his cell phone and started snapping picture of possible suspects, he had to agree with the mayor. A beautiful day!

Raven's Cliff was one hell of a weird little town, but his son was thriving. This T-ball game was as close to normal as Duncan had been in years.

Madeline came up beside him. "How are you doing?"

"Normal." He savored the word. Nothing in the world seemed more beautiful than an ordinary day, watching Duncan at play with other kids. No tantrums. No hysterics. No inappropriate behavior.

"Helen Fisher didn't get to you?"

"Not at all."

It would take more than wild-eyed demands and accusations from Helen Fisher to drive him away. This little town was where Blake intended to stay. In spite of the curse.

Chapter Seventeen

During the four innings of T-Ball, Blake had collected a series of photos on his cell phone which he printed out in his office and spread across his desktop. None of these faces struck him as the visage of a murderer. He glided his hands above the pictures, trying to pick up a vibe, an idea of who among them might be dangerous. He closed his eyes and did it again. Nothing. Not even a tremor.

How did Duncan feel when he sensed danger? Did his pulse accelerate? Were there images? The boy talked about sounds. The thud of a hammer. The slam of the door.

In the past, Blake had dismissed his son's reactions, considering them to be imaginary. Preparing this photo array was the closest he'd come to acknowledging the possibility that his son had some kind of psychic ability. Though Blake wanted to tell himself that the pictures were only a police lineup to jog Duncan's memory, he knew it was more. Duncan saw more than other people; he sensed moods and the past history of people he touched. Was that better or worse than a diagnosis of autism?

Blake sprawled in his desk chair. Tilting back, he stared at the ceiling. A couple of the roofers were still hammering, though it was after five o'clock. Time for Duncan's dinner.

The T-ball game had thrown their schedule off. By damn, that disruption was worth it. The couple of hours they'd spent on the baseball diamond would always be a treasured memory. Duncan's first hit. His first time around the bases. In his batting gloves, Duncan had been part of the group—just like any normal six-year-old. It didn't matter if he was psychic or hypersensitive or autistic. He was happy.

Madeline came through the open door of his office. Her cheeks were slightly sunburned from being outside this afternoon, and she looked particularly vivacious as she scanned the photo array. "This doesn't exactly look like murderer's row, does it?"

"They all seem pretty average," he said. "Where's Duncan?"

"In the kitchen with Alma, having dinner." She picked up the photo of the mayor. "Perry Wells. I hope it's not him. The poor man has gone through enough tragedy. He didn't have time to get over losing his daughter on her wedding day before the epidemic hit Raven's Cliff. Now, he has to deal with anonymous letters to the newspaper, accusations and gossip."

"All of which might have driven him over the edge, turning a basically decent man into a killer."

"Do you think that's possible?" Behind her glasses, her eyes were troubled. "Can a truly good person be driven to commit a terrible crime?"

"There's plenty of times when I've been angry enough or frustrated enough to consider murder."

"But you didn't act on that impulse," she pointed out.

"Thinking violent thoughts is different from carrying them out. I've always been puzzled by the nature versus nurture issue."

"Genetics," he said.

"Is behavior predetermined by DNA?" She frowned. "Is someone born to be bad? Or is that a learned behavior?"

"It sounds like you're thinking of someone specific."

"My brother, Marty."

It was the first time she'd spoken of her family, and he sensed that this was important to her. "Younger brother or older?"

"About two years older than me. He was always very handsome. We don't look much alike, expect that we're both tall and have big, gawky feet."

"There's nothing wrong with your feet." His gaze scanned from her ponytail to the tips of her sneakers. "I like *everything* about your body. Your long legs. Your slim torso. Your—"

"I get it," she said, interrupting his listing of her attributes before he got to the interesting parts. She still insisted on a proper atmosphere during the day. At night, she was a different creature. "We were talking about my brother."

"Go ahead."

"When we were growing up, Marty was always in trouble. He got in fights and stole things. It almost seemed that he preferred lies to the truth. And he was a huge tease."

"Did he steal your Barbie dolls?"

"Worse. He hid my books before I was done reading them."

He imagined her as an adorable little girl with curly black hair and incredible aquamarine eyes. "I bet you were a shy kid."

Her eyebrows arched. "We aren't talking about me."

He couldn't resist teasing. "With your cute little nose always buried in a book."

"After I was adopted," she continued, "I lost touch with Marty. We didn't go to the same schools. I hardly ever saw him."

"Did you miss him?"

"Sometimes." She exhaled a ragged sigh. "I can't help wondering what would have happened if Marty had been the one to be adopted. If he'd been with caring, nurturing parents, he might have turned out better."

Her insistence on talking about her brother made him think that there was more to this story—something more pertinent to her life right now. "Where's Marty now?"

"In jail."

"I'm sorry, Madeline."

"That isn't the worst part." Her slender fingers knotted together. "Marty came to me a couple of weeks ago, needing money. I couldn't refuse. I gave him everything I had, even ran up my credit cards to the max."

Which explained why she'd turned up on his doorstep flat broke and desperate for a job. He had wondered about her circumstances, about how a supposedly well-organized, intelligent woman didn't have a savings account.

Trusting her ne'er-do-well brother might have been foolish, but Blake knew all about family loyalty. He rose from his chair and went toward her. "I understand."

She held up her hand, warding off his approach. "There's more I need to tell you."

What the hell was this about? "Go on."

"I knew Marty was up to something, even when he promised to pay me back with interest. He said that if the police ever came looking for him, I should keep my mouth shut." Her eyes filled with pain. "I swear to you, Blake. I swear. I never suspected that he was talking about a major crime."

"Not murder."

"No, thank God. I didn't know what Marty had done until I got here and saw it on the news from Boston. He's in jail because he's suspected of stealing diamonds worth seven hundred thousand dollars."

"You think he's guilty."

"I don't know. The diamonds still haven't been recovered, and I hope the police will find that someone else is responsible." She clenched her fingers again in an attitude that was almost like prayer. "He's my brother. How could he do this?"

Blake hated this situation. Unwittingly, he'd hired the sister of a major felon to work with his son, to teach Duncan. Damn it. What if Marty's partners in crime came after her? What if she'd brought another form of danger into his house?

"If you'd told me this when you arrived, I wouldn't have hired you."

"You almost didn't hire me," she reminded him. "When I first arrived here, I didn't know what my brother had done. Only that he was in trouble again. That's something I've had to live with since birth."

"Does he know you're here?"

"No. I haven't heard anything from him."

He believed her. Madeline was the most honest person he'd ever known. "I don't blame you for your brother's crime. I'm glad you're here, glad you're part of our family now."

When she stepped into his embrace and rested her head against his shoulder, he realized that this was the first time they'd touched outside the bedroom. Her nearness felt right to him. Part of the family. His family.

He inhaled the fragrance of her thick, curly hair and whispered, "You're a good person, Madeline. You just got caught up in a bad situation."

She swiped the corner of her eye. A relieved smile curved her lips and brightened her face. "Thank you, Blake, for understanding. Being with you and Duncan means everything to me."

Before her gratitude took on an uncomfortable weight, he changed the topic. Gesturing to the photos, he said, "What do you think?"

She leaned over the photos. "You don't have Helen Fisher. According to Lucy Tucker, Helen ought to be considered a suspect in her brother's murder."

Though Blake agreed that Helen's hate-filled attitude could turn violent, he didn't consider her a possibility. "Duncan was clear about one thing. The person who grabbed him was male. A bad man."

Madeline looked up at him. "And you don't have Joe Curtis."

"I didn't see him this afternoon." And he couldn't think of a good excuse to stop by the police station and snap photos. "But I have an idea of how I can get his mug shot."

She cocked her head to one side. "How?"

"I did a restoration project for a Washington, D.C., client who's a hotshot in Homeland Security. He's got access to photos from police departments, and he owes me a favor. He can fax it to me."

"Maybe he can do a background check on Joe Curtis.

Maybe there's something in his past with LAPD that would explain why Duncan had such a strong reaction to him."

"I'll make the call," Blake said. "Tomorrow, we'll do this photo array. Right now, he's too tired."

"He did so well at the T-ball game. Today was wonderful."

And tonight, Blake thought, would be even better.

WITH A clear conscience, Madeline prepared for bed. Telling Blake about Marty had been difficult, but his response had warmed her heart. He thought of her as family, as part of his life. She couldn't hope for more.

She'd barely had a chance to brush her hair when she heard the tap on her bedroom door. "Blake?"

Just like last night, he told her to come out. This time, she opened the door confidently. A trail of votive candles lit her way down the hall to his bed. As she followed the flickering lights, she paused and blew each one out.

Tonight, she noticed, the door to Duncan's room was closed. As soon as she entered Blake's room, he swept her into his arms for a long, deep kiss.

With her senses reeling, she leaned back in his arms and gazed at his oh-so-sexy smile. "Are you worried about leaving Duncan alone?"

"He agreed to have his door locked tonight. He'll be safe." He leaned close and kissed the tip of her nose. "Why did you blow the candles out?"

"Fire hazard," she said.

His low chuckle resonated inside his chest. "Safety first."

"I *am* a schoolteacher."

His hands slid down her back and cupped her bottom,

positioning her firmly against him. "It's a good thing that I never had a teacher as pretty as you. I wouldn't have learned a thing."

"I know your type." She reached up to run her fingers through his disheveled hair. "The second-grade boy who gives me love notes and shares half of his candy bar."

"I'm not the first to have a crush on the teacher."

"Actually," she said, "I was hoping there might be something you could teach me."

"About what?"

"You seem to be an expert in here." Boldly, she gestured toward the bed. In these intimate moments with Blake, her normal inhibitions evaporated like dew on a hot summer morning. "Teach me."

He needed no further encouragement. In seconds, he had her on the bed. Stretched out on his sheets, she experienced a crash course in sensuality. His expert touch aroused her in ways she'd never imagined possible. His kisses left her breathless. Gasping, she asked, "How on earth do you do that thing with your tongue?"

"First lesson," he murmured. "Don't analyze."

"But how will I learn if I don't ask questions?"

"Number two." He nibbled below her earlobe. "Accept the experience."

Trembling sensations raised goose bumps on her arms. "How many lessons are there?"

"Only one more." He straddled her thighs, looked directly into her eyes and said, "Enjoy."

"That," she said, "I can do."

Willingly, she gave herself over to a surging tide of pleasure as he fondled and nibbled and caressed. A clever student, she found her own creative ways of giving back to him. When he finally entered her, her level of excitement was such that she felt as if she might expire from an overdose of sheer ecstasy.

Afterward, she lay beside him on the bed, fully satisfied and blissful. The word *love* popped into her mind. Did she love him?

With a shake of her head on his pillow, she chased that idea away. For now, it was more than enough to make love…rather than *being* in love.

Chapter Eighteen

The next morning, Madeline woke early, still sorting out her emotions and wishing it were as easy as pulling petals from a daisy. *I love him…I love him not.* Not an easy decision.

Instead of pondering all the complications of their relationship, she decided it was time to completely erase her guilt about Marty. Talking to Blake had been the hard part. Now she needed to come clean with Alma.

As usual, the housekeeper sat at the kitchen table, already dressed and coiffed with the puffy blond hairdo that hadn't changed in twenty years. Madeline's typical procedure was to start off the day by wiping down the countertops and sweeping crumbs off the floor. Instead, she poured herself a mug of coffee and took the chair opposite Alma. "There's something I need to tell you."

Using the remote, Alma clicked off the small television she'd been watching. "It's about Marty, isn't it?"

She nodded. "He's gotten himself into a lot of trouble back in Boston."

"I saw it on the news. He stole seven hundred thousand dollars' worth of diamonds." She hoisted a penciled eyebrow. "And the loot still hasn't been recovered."

Madeline eyed her curiously. "You knew but you didn't say anything?"

"I didn't want to mess up this thing you've got going with Blake. You turned out okay, Madeline. I'm proud of you. Twenty-three kids passed through my home, and most of them are doing just fine. But you? You're special."

Though Alma's compliment had the ring of sincerity, Madeline didn't quite trust her. "You stay in touch with all your former fosters?"

"I do my best, hon. It doesn't take much to send a Christmas card or an occasional note."

"I remember those notes." Most of which related to a "great new project" that Alma was selling, like mail-order detergent, homemade jewelry or hypoallergenic makeup. Madeline had purchased some of these things, which undoubtedly kept her on Alma's list.

Her former foster mother had a mercenary side and generally put her own self-interest above all other concerns. But she wasn't a bad person.

"I never had any kids of my own." Her brassy voice softened with a sigh. "Sometimes I think that was a big mistake. I like kids."

"Even Duncan?"

"He's a dickens. But he's not mean, and he's got his father's good looks. Duncan can be as cute as a little angel."

Though this was the first time she'd heard Alma say anything nice about Duncan, the housekeeper was always gentle with Blake's son. The only household chore she took seriously was the preparation of Duncan's meals.

Alma continued, "If your fling with Blake goes anywhere, I want you to remember who's responsible for getting you this job."

Not quite ready to say thank you, Madeline asked, "Did you stay in contact with Marty?"

"I always liked your brother. He's a rogue. But such a handsome young man."

"You've seen him? Recently?"

In her fuzzy slippers, Alma shuffled to the coffee machine for a refill. "Marty always had your best interests at heart."

Madeline seriously doubted that. "Why do you think so?"

"Here's the thing. You weren't topmost in my mind when Blake started looking for a tutor. The real reason I got in touch with you was that Marty called me and said that you needed a job."

Her explanation sounded innocent. Perhaps too innocent. "Why didn't you tell me this before?"

"Must have slipped my mind."

Not likely. Alma had a reason for keeping her conversation with Marty a secret. She was covering something up. Like what? *Like his plan to steal the diamonds?*

That had to be the answer. Alma and Marty were working together. "Oh my God, you're his accomplice."

"Don't be silly, Madeline. I was here in Maine when Marty was robbing that safe."

Her statement was as good as a confession. "How do you know when he was committing the robbery?"

"Just guessing." Her shoulders twitched in another shrug.

"How do you know he robbed a safe?"

"Calm down." She returned to the table and sat. "Let's just take it easy, okay?"

Her eyes darted as if searching for a plausible lie, but it

was too late. Madeline already had a pretty good idea of
what had happened. "You knew what Marty was planning."

"I tried to talk him out of it. I warned him. Told him that
he'd probably get caught. And he did, didn't he?"

Madeline was all too familiar with her brother's machi-
nations and his persuasive skills. "He talked to you because
he wanted something. What was it?"

"He asked me to take care of you. He wanted you to get
out of town and asked me if I could invite you to stay with
me. Since Blake was already looking for a tutor, it seemed
like a perfect fit."

"What did you ask for in return? What was your pay-
off?"

"He promised that he'd make it worth my while. After
the heat died down in Boston, he was going to come up
here and join us."

"Why?"

Her gaze sharpened. "In the last call I had from Marty,
he said the diamonds were with you."

Shocked, Madeline sat back in her chair. "With me?"

"At first, I thought you knew about the jewels, that you
were hiding them." Her tongue slid across her lower lip as
if tasting the sweetness of promised wealth. "If I found
them, I figured that I'd get a reward."

"You searched my things."

"I'm not proud of myself," Alma admitted. "I should
have known that you'd never do anything illegal. You've
always been a good girl."

"It was you." Incredulous, Madeline glared. "You were
the one who kept sneaking into my room and going
through my stuff."

"But no harm done. Now that I've explained, we can

forget about it. There's no need to tell Blake." She tried a smile. "Am I right?"

Anger surged through Madeline, driving her to her feet. "What about the basement? Did you lock me and Duncan in the dark basement so you could search?"

"I needed time to go through all your things."

"How could you?"

"I wasn't thinking straight." Alma stood on the opposite side of the table. She was at least six inches shorter than Madeline. "I didn't plan to trap you down there. But when I saw you both go into the basement, I took advantage of the situation."

"I was scared half to death. Duncan could have been traumatized."

Alma spread her small hands, holding out an invisible olive branch. "I'm sorry. Truly, I'm sorry."

"Why should I believe you?"

"I'd never do anything to hurt that little boy. I might not be the best housekeeper in the world. Or the most upright, honest human being. But I like kids. I really do." Once again, her voice muted. "Poor little Duncan. He's had it rough. I want the best for him."

Though still furious, Madeline believed that voice, that tone as soothing as a lullaby. Though Alma pretended to be tough, she liked kids, wished she had some of her own. But that didn't excuse what she'd done. "What about Marty's accomplice? Is there somebody else coming after these jewels that I don't have?"

"No," Alma said simply. "Marty planned the heist by himself. He'd been working construction at the home of these rich people and somehow got the combination to their safe. He was working alone."

"You believe him?"

"Your brother has never lied to me."

Unlike the way he'd treated her. Marty had looked her straight in the eye and told one lie after another. He'd used her to get what he wanted, what he needed.

"There's one lie," Madeline said. "He never gave the jewels to me."

"I guess not." The air went out of her, and she sank back into her chair. "Are you going to tell Blake?"

"I haven't decided," Madeline said. "But I promise you this. From now on, you're washing the dishes and scrubbing the floors. You're going to do the job you were hired for."

Unable to stand being in the kitchen with Alma for one more second, she stalked down the hallway to the front door and went outside. A misty rain was falling. Through the hazy sky, the morning light spread lightly on the treetops and the grassy yard. From the cliff beyond the forest, she heard the echo of the surf pounding against the rocky shore.

Madeline should have been relieved to know that Alma had been the one who pawed through her things when she first arrived at the Manor. No other person had been entering the house through the secret passageway. It was only Alma. A confused and deceptive woman. But not a murderer.

Through the mist, she saw a shadow moving through the trees. A glimpse of darkness.

And Madeline knew the danger was not yet over.

THE RAINY WEATHER meant Blake's construction crew wouldn't be working today, and he was glad for the break.

He needed some creative time for himself to complete the project he'd been working on in the upstairs front bedroom. He stepped back from the wall mural he'd just completed. A damn fine job, if he said so himself.

The four-poster bed was made, and the curtains were hung. Only a few more details needed to be added. Though the bold color in this design scheme didn't match the American Federalist decor in the rest of the house, he knew that Madeline would love this room.

The only other project on his schedule for the day was the photo array, and he was prepared. His former client at Homeland Security had already faxed a mug shot for Joe Curtis and promised to check further into Curtis's background with LAPD.

He and Madeline planned the photo array for midafternoon—about an hour from now. If Duncan was upset by what he saw or what he sensed, they'd have plenty of time to get him calmed down before bed.

As he adjusted the red velvet curtains, Blake looked through the window and saw headlights cutting through the steady rain. A jolt of tension went down his spine. Who the hell was coming here? He had a bad feeling about this unscheduled visitor.

Leaving the bedroom, he went downstairs and opened the door for Perry Wells. Stepping inside, the mayor brushed droplets from the sleeves of his trench coat. He took off his rain hat and dragged his fingers through his salt-and-pepper hair. The man looked like hell. His complexion was pasty white. "That's a nasty little storm," he said. "I trust you're all well."

"The heating system in the Manor leaves a lot to be desired," Blake said. "The furnace is relatively new, but a lot of ducts are clogged, and the windows aren't properly sealed."

"Your renovations will take care of those problems."

"Hope so." He didn't really think Mayor Wells had come here for an update on the progress of the restoration. "What can I do for you, Perry?"

"You mentioned that you might be interested in purchasing a property I own. I'm willing to drop my asking price to expedite the deal."

"But I haven't even looked at the house."

"We could go right now," he offered.

Blake was tempted. His experience in the housing market told him that the best bargains came when the seller was desperate. And that word described everything about Perry. Desperate.

As a businessman, he ought to take advantage. But he'd be a rotten human being if he exploited this man's fear. "Let me take your coat, Perry. We need to talk."

When Blake entered his office, he turned on the overhead light. On a sunny day, the windows provided enough illumination to see clearly. Today was gray and murky.

He sat behind his desk. "Tell me why you're so anxious to get rid of this property."

"There's nothing wrong with the house. It's a fine little place." Instead of sitting, he paced behind the chair. "I need to improve my cash flow. Immediately."

"To hire a lawyer?" Blake cut to the chase. There was no point in dancing around the issue. "You'll need an experienced attorney to defend you if you're charged with murder."

"What have you heard?"

"I know the evidence against you is mounting."

He braced both hands on the back of the chair opposite Blake's desk. His fingers clenched, white-knuckled. "The police are at my house right now, executing a search warrant."

"What are they going to find?"

"Documents." He peered at Blake through red-rimmed eyes. "Teddy and I had a business arrangement. He needed political favors, and I complied with his wishes. I'm sure you understand. You're a man of the world, a businessman. Sometimes it's necessary to make a deal with the devil."

"What kind of deal?"

"Rebuilding Raven's Cliff after the hurricane has been expensive. Our coffers ran dry months ago. That's when Teddy Fisher stepped up with a supposedly philanthropic offer to help repair the damages. A supposedly generous offer." His tone was bitter. "In exchange for this philanthropy, he asked me to keep the inspectors away from his lab and to issue necessary permits for the purchase of raw materials. It all seemed innocent enough. Just a matter of expediency."

"Then you learned that Teddy's experiments caused the genetically mutated fish, which, in turn, started the epidemic."

"People died." He circled the chair and sat heavily. "With better oversight, those experiments would never have gone forward. I blame myself. For each and every one of those tragic deaths, I blame myself."

His shoulders bowed under the burden of his guilt. Though the mayor's political skills undoubtedly included the ability to look contrite, he wasn't faking this emotion. His grief was too raw.

Blake almost felt sorry for him. Almost. "Why didn't you expose Teddy?"

"I should have. I'm sorry. So terribly sorry."

It was all too easy for politicians to make their heartfelt apologies and throw themselves on the mercy of public opinion. "Don't look to me for forgiveness," Blake said. "Even after you knew what Teddy was doing, you continued to grant him favors. You worked your political magic and made it possible for him to purchase the Manor and to hire me."

"I stand behind that decision." He straightened in the chair. "Teddy promised to restore the lighthouse. To end the curse."

"Come on, Perry. You're a man of the world. You don't believe in superstitions." Blake was losing sympathy fast. "You couldn't turn Teddy over to the police because it made you look bad. You went along with him to save your own hide."

"That's not the only reason."

Perry's face twisted as if he were in physical pain, but Blake wasn't buying these crocodile tears. The mayor had sold his soul to the devilish Teddy Fisher, and now he was reaping the consequences. "Did you know about the lab Teddy set up in the caves? It's likely he was continuing his experiments."

"I didn't know."

"But maybe you figured it out." Blake sensed that he might be treading on dangerous ground. As he continued to talk, he unlocked his desk. His gun was in the lower left drawer within easy reach. "Maybe you knew exactly what Teddy had in mind, and you couldn't let him do it again. You couldn't let other innocent people die."

Perry rose to his feet. "You've got it all wrong."

"Do I?" Blake eased the lower drawer open. If he needed

the gun it was within reach. "I think you finally realized that the only way you could stop Teddy was to kill him."

Perry slammed his fist down hard on the desktop. "I'm not a murderer. Teddy deserved to die, but I couldn't do it. I couldn't."

"Why not?"

"Camille."

His daughter? What did any of this have to do with his daughter? "She's dead, Perry."

"Her body was never found. Teddy said she'd survived. He knew where she was. If I didn't help him, I'd never see Camille again."

Surprised, Blake jolted back in his chair. He sure as hell hadn't seen this coming. "Did you tell the police?"

"I was afraid." He trembled. "If there was any chance that Camille was still alive…"

Blake doubted that possibility. From what he'd heard, the whole town had witnessed Camille's death. More likely, Teddy had been clever enough to use the one threat that he knew would be effective in tying Perry's hands. His love for his daughter.

From down the hallway, he heard voices and the clamor of footsteps. Detective Lagios entered the study.

After a nod to Blake, he confronted the mayor and said, "Perry Wells, you're under arrest for the murder of Teddy Fisher. You have the right to remain silent…"

Chapter Nineteen

"Rain, rain, go away. Come again another day." Duncan stared through the window in the family room. He wanted to be outside. "Rain, rain, go away…"

"Hey, buddy." His daddy picked him up off his feet and spun around in a circle. "Madeline and I have a new game for you."

"Don't want a new game. I want baseball."

"We can't do that in the house. There's not enough room for the bases."

"Ninety feet from home to first." Duncan shook his head. "Not enough room."

Daddy set him down, and they went to the table where he did art projects. This morning, he'd drawn a picture of a baseball diamond and his new friend Annie. She was funny. Some of the other kids called her Annie Banana, but he didn't.

"Here's what I want you to do," Daddy said. "I want you to try to remember the man who grabbed you on the cliff."

"Geez Louise." He slapped his forehead the way he'd seen kids do at T-ball. "I told you before, Daddy. I didn't see his face."

"I know. But maybe if we show you some pictures, you'll remember."

"How many pictures?"

"Seven," Madeline said. "You take a look, then tell us if you remember anything. Let's start with this one."

She set a picture down on the table.

"That's Coach Grant." He whisked the picture off the table onto the floor. "Ready for number two."

Two, three and four were men he had seen. But they didn't mean anything. He shoved their pictures away. Number five was different. He looked real close with his nose right down by the paper. "This man came to our house today. And he left with the policeman."

He shoved the picture aside, but his Daddy put it back in front of him. "I want you to pay attention, Duncan. Is this the man from the cliff?"

"No." This game was dumb. He didn't want to play anymore. "Number six. Number six."

Madeline slid another piece of paper onto the table. It was only a picture. But kind of scary. He didn't want to touch it. "He's a fisherman."

His face was not very nice. He looked dirty. At the same time, he made Duncan think about Temperance. She could tell him if this man meant danger. Under his breath, he hummed, "She sells seashells by the…"

"Duncan?" Daddy touched his arm. "Is this the man?"

"No, no, no." With the tip of his finger, he pushed the picture away. "Number seven."

A mean face stared up at him from the table. "A bad man. He's very bad."

"Is he the one?"

In the back of his head, he heard a loud thud. A hammer. "He hurts people. Sharks eat little kids. Don't go near the seashore."

He saw big waves splash on the rocks. *Danger.* He needed to get away.

"It's okay, buddy." Daddy patted his back. "Did this man grab you?"

"Upstairs." He nodded. "In my bedroom."

Danger. He jumped off his chair and ran toward the kitchen. Alma was standing in front of him. He ran right into her.

She held him so he wouldn't fall down. She hugged him, and he felt warm inside. She didn't say anything, but he knew what she was thinking.

He patted her cheek. "I can't be your little boy, Alma. I already have a mommy."

"I know."

He liked her puffy hair. "We can be friends."

"I'd like that, Duncan." He stepped away from her and turned around. Daddy was right behind him. "We're all friends."

"You did good," Daddy said.

Duncan raised his hand. "High five."

There was only one person in this room who he hadn't hugged. Madeline. He could tell that she felt left out, and that made him sad.

He marched over to her, and she squatted down so her eyes were even with his. Pretty eyes.

He kissed her forehead above her glasses. She smelled like flowers. "I like you best of all."

"Thank you, Duncan."

He hugged her for a long time. She was cozy. They would be friends forever and ever and ever and ever.

But he felt something else. A shiver. He stepped back. "You must be very careful."

"I will."

"Danger, Madeline. Danger."

LATER THAT NIGHT while Blake was putting Duncan to bed, Madeline sat behind his desk in his studio. She still felt a pleasant glow from when Duncan had hugged her. His sweet little kiss on her forehead ranked as one of the most precious moments in her life. She had been waiting for such a long time for him to allow her to touch him and cuddle him. Now, she truly felt like a member of the family.

Yet, Duncan's warning about danger wasn't a message she wanted to hear. Flipping through their collection of mug shots, she tried to decide which of these men presented a threat. Duncan hadn't sensed any danger from his T-ball coach. He'd paused on the photo of Perry Wells. Something about Perry worried him but didn't frighten him.

The next photo was Lucy's boyfriend, Alex Gibson—a handsome, rugged man. When Duncan had looked at his face, he seemed disturbed then started humming the seashell song. In a way, that made sense because Alex was a fisherman. At the T-ball game, Alex had argued with Helen Fisher. He wanted the lighthouse to be rebuilt so the curse would be ended. A superstitious man. But was he dangerous?

Certainly not as scary as Joe Curtis. Duncan's negative reaction to the cop was unmistakably clear. Perhaps Curtis hadn't touched the boy when he stood on the cliffs, but he seemed to represent the greatest danger. She hadn't seen him since she'd warned him off with a bluff. Was that enough to keep him away from the Manor?

When Blake entered the studio, he came around the

desk and lightly kissed her cheek. "Let's go upstairs. I have something to show you."

A combination of instinct and passion told her to follow him up the stairs to the bedroom. To follow anywhere he wanted to go. But she couldn't let go of her suspicions. Holding up the photo of Curtis, she said, "This is the bad guy. Duncan thought so."

"Duncan didn't directly identify Curtis as the man who grabbed him." He unfastened the clip holding her hair up in a high ponytail. Her thick, heavy curls cascaded around her shoulders. "Let it go, Madeline. There's nothing we can do."

She looked away from him, remembering the big, muscle-bound cop aiming at her with his cocked finger. "I can't forget. He's dangerous."

"But he's not the one under arrest." He pulled out the photo of Perry Wells. "Duncan might have a psychic feeling. And you might have a hunch. But Lagios needed evidence to take the mayor into custody."

"What kind of evidence?" she asked.

"He practically confessed to me, and there are other people he could have talked to. Plus, there are the facts—Perry admitted to being the last person to see Teddy alive. The police found incriminating papers at his house."

What if the police were wrong? It wouldn't be the first time an innocent man had been accused of murder. "Wasn't your Homeland Security contact going to send you more information about Curtis?"

He went around the desk to the fax machine near the door and picked up a single sheet of paper. For a moment, Blake read in silence. "Damn."

"What is it?"

"The photograph of Joe Curtis on file with the Raven's

Cliff police department doesn't match the records from the LAPD. He faked his credentials."

Though wary, she asked, "Who is he?"

"My contact at Homeland Security ran his real photo through a system designed to recognize facial features. He found a match with a man who's on the official terrorist watch list. He works for an organization called the GFF, Global Freedom Front." When he met her gaze, his jaw was tense. "The man we know as Joe Curtis is an assassin."

Icy dread shivered down her spine as she thought of an assassin walking among them, passing as a policeman, someone to be trusted and accepted. A perfect disguise. "What should we do?"

"It's out of our hands. Homeland Security already got in touch with the local cops. And they're sending federal agents." He reached for the phone. "I'm calling Lagios."

She fidgeted behind the desk while Blake made his phone call. A professional assassin? It didn't make sense. What was a terrorist doing in Raven's Cliff? What could possibly have drawn him to this quiet little fishing village? Madeline was fairly sure that he didn't come here for the ambience or the trinkets.

Blake hung up the phone and turned to her. From his worried expression, she deduced that he didn't have good news. "Curtis is still at large."

"Maybe he's making a run for it," she said hopefully. "I hope he's running fast and far away from us."

"For now, Lagios is keeping his identity a secret, hoping they can find him before he bolts."

"So Curtis doesn't know the police are after him."

"Not yet."

"What if he comes here?"

Blake nodded. "I mentioned that possibility to Lagios, and he promised to send a couple of cops out here to keep an eye on things."

She shook her head. "I can't believe this is happening."

"It's all under control."

As she leaned her cheek against his shoulder, Madeline did her best to believe him. The danger would pass, and they'd be free from fear. Soon, she hoped. "Why would a terrorist come to Raven's Cliff?"

"Fisher Labs," he murmured. "That seems to be the only link with this little town and the wider world. Fisher Labs and Teddy's research."

"That formula he created."

"A nutrient that mutated the fish and caused an epidemic," Blake said. "In the hands of terrorists, Teddy's formula could cause a global outbreak."

That outcome was too horrifying to imagine. Though she nuzzled more tightly in his arms, her stomach plummeted. "It feels like I'm on a roller coaster. Every time I start feeling happy, I go into a tailspin."

"Come upstairs with me, Madeline. I have something to show you that will make you feel better."

The only thing to soothe her jangled nerves would be to see Joe Curtis being dragged off in handcuffs. But she appreciated Blake's effort.

At the top of the staircase, he led her past Duncan's room where the door was carefully locked. He stopped outside the forbidden room where he'd been working for the past couple of days.

"Your secret project," she said.

"Curious?"

"A bit."

He pushed open the door and turned on the light. "I call it the Madeline Room."

The red velvet curtains were the first thing to catch her eye. Then the antique white four-poster, also with red bed-covers. "It's red, like my dress."

"Scarlet is your color."

Beneath the crown moldings, an incredible mural deco-rated the wall nearest the closet. The style matched the other formal landscape paintings in the house, paying great attention to detail. But the colors for this painting were vivid—the strong blues and greens of a forest splashed with brilliant yellow and purple wildflowers. In their midst stood a woman in a crimson dress with long black hair flowing down her back. "Is that me?"

"It's why I call it the Madeline Room."

"You painted this?"

He shrugged. "I studied art before I got into architecture."

The breadth of his talent awed and amazed her. Reaching toward the wall, she traced the branches of the trees and each petal of the flowers. His painting made her feel as beautiful as a work of art. "This is the best present anyone has ever given me."

Stepping up behind her, he wrapped his arms around her waist. "Nothing I give you could ever equal what you've done for me. And for Duncan."

She rested in his embrace, almost forgetting the danger that swirled around them. An assassin. A terrorist. She hoped their police guards would get here soon.

Turning, she kissed his cheek and smiled. "Much as I adore being in your arms, I want to take a closer look at the Madeline Room."

Slowly, she paced around the perimeter, exploring the

exquisite details. All of the furniture was antique white, painted with a delicate primrose pattern that looked charmingly old-fashioned and very familiar.

"My ficus." She recognized the design. "This is the same design that's on the pot holding my ficus."

"Your family heirloom."

"Not that it's worth anything, but it's special to me. Let's bring it in here."

"My thought exactly."

They hurried down the hall, treading quietly so they wouldn't wake Duncan. Blake lifted the plant in its pretty container and carried it.

Anxious to see this finishing touch, she crowded through the door beside him. She bumped his elbow. He tripped. Before either of them could catch their balance, the urn holding the ficus crashed to the floor.

The primrose pottery broke into shards.

She knelt and picked one up. "It's lucky you painted a duplicate so I won't forget what this looked like."

"Sorry," he said. "This urn was important to you."

"A reminder of the past." Her regrets were minimal. The time had come to forget about her childhood in foster care—to break with her lingering sadness and repression. "I'd rather think about the future."

Picking through the shards and dirt, Blake found a zippered satchel. "What's this?"

"I have no idea."

He unfastened the zipper and poured a glittering array of cut diamonds into his hand. The sparkle took her breath away. Seven hundred thousand dollars' worth of jewels.

Marty must have stashed them in the pot, knowing that she'd never leave it behind.

When she reached toward the shimmering jewels, Blake pulled his hand back. His hazel eyes darkened with rage. "How could you do this to me? To Duncan?"

"Do what?"

"I trusted you. I accepted your teary-eyed confession about how your black-sheep brother used you."

"It was the truth."

"I'm not naive, Madeline. I can see what you are. Your brother's accomplice. You came here to hide out from the Boston police."

Shocked by his accusation, she sat back on her heels. "I knew nothing about this."

"You showed up here with nothing but your clothes, a couple of boxes and this ficus. Don't expect me to believe that was a coincidence."

"I didn't know. Really, Blake. Marty told Alma that the jewels were with me, but I had no—"

"Alma was in on this?"

He stood abruptly. His passion for her had turned to cold rage—the same outraged, overprotective fury she'd seen in him when she first arrived at the Manor. From experience, she knew there was no reasoning with him when he was in this mood. "Think what you want."

"I'll be turning this loot over to the police as soon as they get here. You might want to work on your story."

Unfolding herself from the floor, she stood tall. "I'll tell the truth."

"That your brother stole the jewels and they just happened to end up in your possession?" He scoffed. "I want you out of here. Tomorrow morning. And Alma, too."

He strode from the room, leaving her alone.

How could he be so quick to judge? Yes, the circumstances looked bad, but he ought to know by now that she wasn't a bad person.

A sob caught in her throat as she looked at the mural he'd painted for her. Another dip on the emotional roller coaster. With Blake, she experienced the highest highs and the most abject lows.

She trudged down the hall to her bedroom and closed the door. Pain washed over her. And remorse. Even though she hadn't done anything wrong, she felt guilty.

Perhaps it was better to find out now that his affections were fickle. A simple twist of fate had transformed Blake from a romantic lover into a tyrant. How could she have ever thought she was in love with him?

Then she heard the tap on her door.

He'd changed his mind.

He was coming to apologize.

She threw open the door. A cloth covered her mouth. She couldn't breathe. Everything went black.

Chapter Twenty

Behind the closed door of his studio office, Blake stared through the window into the night. Raindrops rattled against the windowpanes in a furious staccato. How could he have been so wrong about Madeline? He had believed her, trusted her. Maybe even loved her.

And she had used him. Used his home as a hideout. Everything about her was a lie. Her sweetness. Her common sense. Her passion. All lies.

Anger surged through him. How could she have done this to him? He'd opened his heart to Madeline. For the first time since Kathleen's death, he felt like there was a reason to get out of bed in the morning. With Madeline, he'd found hope—a reason to start looking forward instead of living in the past. She'd changed him...and betrayed him.

How could she have done this to Duncan? His son would be brokenhearted when she left. Somehow, Blake had to find a way to explain to Duncan that his beloved teacher was nothing but a thief, a criminal. It didn't seem possible.

But it was true.

Returning to his desk, he unzipped the pouch and spilled the diamonds across the surface. Here was proof, undeniable proof.

Where the hell were those cops Lagios promised to send? As soon as they got here, Blake intended to turn over the diamonds and point them toward Madeline. They could take her into custody, ship her back to Boston. She'd get what she deserved.

Pain cut through his anger. How could he do this to her? How could he stand by and watch while she was arrested, marched off in handcuffs? Not Madeline. Not the woman he loved. He wanted to shelter and protect her, wanted a future with her.

That hope was dead.

He gathered the gems in his hand. As he closed his fist, a strange heat shot up his arm, igniting a stream of fire that pulsed through his veins and arteries. He was consumed by sensation. Inside his rib cage, his heart pounded. Each heavy beat echoed louder than the last.

What was happening to him? He had to fight. Be strong. But he couldn't resist.

His knees folded and he dropped into his desk chair, too weak to stand. The room began to whirl. The light from his desk lamp blurred into jagged lightning bolts outside the window. Spinning faster and faster, he couldn't breathe.

He closed his eyes. Everything went still, as if he'd entered the eye of a hurricane. He was floating, detached, unaware of bodily sensation.

Behind his eyelids, he saw a scene being played out. It was unreal, dreamlike. Yet every detail came through with crystal clarity. A clock on the wall. A purse on the table. Madeline's purse. A man he didn't recognize held the pouch. As if from far away, he heard Madeline's voice. "Marty, is that you?"

The stranger replied, "Be right there, sis."

He dug into the dirt beside the ficus, buried the pouch. Blake could hear his thoughts. *She'll never leave this pot behind. I'll get the stones later.*

In a jolt, Blake returned to his studio. Everything was exactly as it had been. The rain still slashed at the window. The desk lamp shone on the gems.

There was no rational explanation for what had just occurred, but he knew that he had seen the truth. He'd seen the past. Marty had hidden the gems without telling Madeline.

Blake had experienced a vision. The realization stunned him. Just like his son, he'd been thrown into an altered state of consciousness. All these years, he'd denied the possibility of psychic awareness. He hadn't understood why Duncan wore gloves to ward off these feelings.

Now he knew. He and his son were alike. Hypersensitive. They saw things that other people didn't know about.

Slowly, Blake rose from his chair. His legs were still weak, but his heartbeat had steadied. His breathing was normal. He felt a lightness—a purity of thought he'd never known.

Madeline was innocent. She'd been duped by her conniving brother.

Blake never should have doubted her, should have trusted the inherent instinct that told him she was a good person, worthy of trust, worthy of love.

At the edge of his desk, he saw the barrette she used to clip her hair into a high ponytail. Earlier tonight, he'd unfastened the tortoiseshell barrette, allowing her curly black hair to cascade. *I'm sorry, Madeline.*

He picked it up. In an instant, his head was spinning. Another vision crashed into his mind.

He felt her terror. She was unable to move. Her wrists and ankles were bound with rope.

Through her eyes, he saw the dark walls of the cave.

Through her ears, he heard the roaring surf.

A necklace of shells lay on the sand beside her.

She had only minutes left before that necklace was placed around her neck and tightened, choking off her breath.

LYING ON her back on the cold wet sand, Madeline blinked slowly. The insides of her eyelids felt scratchy and crusted as if she'd been crying for days. She could barely see. Her glasses were gone. But she knew where she was. The caves. She could smell the ocean and hear the waves. Must be close to the mouth of the cave.

Another blink. Her vision cleared. The dim light of an electric torch glowed against the stone walls.

How had she gotten here? She struggled to sit up but couldn't. *I can't move.* Her lungs ached as if a huge, heavy hand pressed down upon her chest.

Concentrating, she tried to lift her arm. Only a slight twitch. Looking down, she saw that her wrists were tied together. She had to get up. Had to get away.

Another effort. Nothing. She was paralyzed.

"You're awake."

The face of Joe Curtis swam into focus. She struggled to speak but could only manage a groan.

"It would have been better," he said, "if you'd stayed unconscious."

Why? What was he going to do?

"When they autopsy your body, they'll find the same

mix of drugs that were in the other victims. I've got all the details right." His heavy shoulders shrugged. A casual gesture. "That's the good thing about using a cop's identity. I know the details of the Seaside Strangler's procedure. There's no way I'll be blamed for this murder."

He didn't know his cover had been blown. He didn't know that Lagios and the rest of the Raven's Cliff police force were searching for him.

If she'd been able to speak, she could have told him. There was no need to murder her. His time would be better spent running away.

He unfastened the rope binding her ankles. "I knew you were bluffing about being psychic. But that kid? When he looked at me, it was like he saw inside. I can't take the chance that he told you. Did he?"

He looked into her eyes. There was no way she could respond.

"Doesn't matter," he said. "After you're out of the way, it won't be hard to get to the kid. Maybe he'll have a tragic fall from the cliffs."

Desperately, she tried to shake her head, to signal to Curtis that he didn't need to go after Duncan.

She managed a tiny movement. The resulting pain caused her to wince. It was as though her entire body had fallen asleep. She had to wake up.

He stood, looming over her. "Your legs are untied. Go ahead. Try to run."

She exerted a fierce effort. Couldn't move. Not an inch. Her toes tingled painfully, like a thousand needles being stabbed into her feet.

Sensation was returning to her body. If she could feel, she could move. And she had to get away, had to protect Duncan.

"Nothing personal," Curtis said as he untied her hands. "But I have to strip you. The Strangler dresses his victims in white. Like virgins. That's not you. Is it, Madeline?"

She tried to protest but could only make an unintelligible noise.

"I know about you and Blake," he said. "I've been keeping an eye on the Manor. It's easy to slip in and out through an unlocked window. Tonight, I went through that secret passage. Pretty nifty."

He unbuttoned her shirt.

Hoping to distract him, she managed to blurt a single word. "Teddy."

"You want to know if I killed Teddy?" Roughly, he pushed the fabric off her shoulders. "Hell, yes. The little traitor deserved to die. He was supposed to be manufacturing that fish nutrient, the one that caused the epidemic. Hell of a thing, huh? That prissy little scientist was trying to cure world hunger. Instead, he came up with an efficient weapon for biological warfare. In the right hands—our hands—that weapon can control the world."

As he lifted her torso and took off her shirt, the prickling beneath her skin became an aching throb. A shudder went through her.

He dropped her back onto the sand. There was nothing sexual about the way he removed her clothing. Stripping her was just part of his job.

"Assassin," she said.

He eyed her curiously. "Did you say assassin?"

She blinked her eyes as if to nod.

"You're wrong about that, lady. I believe in what I'm doing. I'm a soldier for the cause."

Madeline knew she'd struck a chord. Forcing the breath through her lips, she repeated the word. "Assassin."

"You don't get it. The people I work for paid hundreds of thousands of dollars to Teddy Fisher. He was supposed to deliver. All of a sudden, he grew a conscience. He didn't want us to poison the world's food supply. Not that we were going to kill everybody."

"Why?"

"Some populations would have to go. Those who are a drain on the world's resources. The poor. The sick." Another shrug. "For most of those people, death is a welcome cure."

In his voice, she heard the insane logic of a fanatic. Joe Curtis was a true believer. What was the name of his group? Global Freedom Front. GFF.

"When I saw that Teddy had destroyed every speck of the nutrient, I tried to get him to tell me the formula, tried to beat it out of him with a hammer. He wouldn't talk."

In the end, she thought, Teddy Fisher had been a hero. He'd stood up to Joe Curtis. And he'd died in the effort.

She couldn't allow that same fate to befall her. She had to find the strength to move.

Efficiently, Curtis unbuttoned her jeans and tugged the wet fabric down her legs.

Sprawled on the sand in her bra and panties, she'd never been more vulnerable. Or more determined. She wasn't going to die. Not here. Not now.

She had to survive. All her life, she'd kept quiet, never stood up for herself. She hid behind her glasses, faded into the background like a quiet little wallflower. Not anymore. She was a woman who could wear a red dress. A fighter.

She wouldn't give up. *It's not my time to die.* She had

to live, to convince Blake of her innocence. She would have a life with him. And with Duncan.

Clumsily, Curtis pulled the flowing white gown over her head and down her body. The muscles in her shoulder tightened.

With every second that passed, she grew stronger. Her hand flexed. She made a fist.

ON THE BEACH, Blake saw the glow from the mouth of the cave. He knew Madeline was in there. *He knew.* His senses were heightened as never before.

Though he could have waited until the cops arrived, he didn't have that much time. He'd grabbed his handgun, told Alma where he was headed and instructed her to send the reinforcements in this direction.

The rush of the surf against the rocky shore covered the sound of his footsteps as he approached. A small dinghy had been pulled onto the sand. A garland of flowers draped across the bow. A signature of the Seaside Strangler.

His heart wrenched when he saw Madeline lying on the sand in a white dress. The huge form of Joe Curtis leaned over her. He placed the seashell necklace around her throat.

No time left. Blake stepped around the edge of the cave and aimed his gun. He was only ten feet away from them. "Back off."

Curtis looked up. "Come to rescue your girlfriend?"

"Get away from her. I'll shoot."

"Here's your problem," Curtis said. "I could snap her neck in one second."

Not as fast as a bullet. Blake aimed at the center of his

chest. A massive target. "Give it up, Curtis. The cops are on the way. They know all about you and the GFF."

"What?"

"Information from Homeland Security. They identified you from the terrorist watch list."

Curtis stood. He yanked Madeline's limp body in front of him, using her as a shield. There was no chance for Blake to get a clear shot; he couldn't take the chance of hitting Madeline.

Curtis pulled his own gun. Before he could take aim, Madeline reacted. Her arm flung wildly. She stabbed at the big man's face, clawed his eyes.

With a cry, Curtis dropped her.

Blake fired. Three shots in rapid succession. At least two were direct hits.

Curtis staggered backward but didn't go down. He lowered his gun, aimed at Madeline.

Blake lunged. Before Curtis could pull the trigger, he tackled the big man and they both went down. Blood poured from the wounds in his chest, soaking them both.

Blake grabbed for his arm, slammed his wrist against the rocks. Curtis dropped the gun. For an instant, he lay still, and Blake thought he'd won.

Then Curtis surged to his feet. He threw Blake off him and staggered toward the dinghy. With the strength of a wounded beast, he shoved the boat into the surf. The waves churned against his calves.

Blake didn't give a damn if he got away. As long as Madeline was safe, he didn't care.

Curtis whirled. From inside his jacket, he pulled another gun. His huge hand shook as he took aim.

From behind his back, Blake heard a shot. Then another.

Curtis fell.

Blake turned and saw Madeline with his gun in her hand. Unsteady on her feet, she wavered.

He ran to her, enclosed her in his arms. She was ice-cold, nearly frozen. All the strength left her body as she collapsed against him.

From down the beach, he heard the police arriving.

"You're going to be all right," he said, as much to reassure himself as her. "It's over."

She murmured, "How did you find me?"

"I saw what was happening. It was a vision. Like Duncan has."

One corner of her mouth twitched as if she was trying to smile. "Runs in the family."

They were all a little bit psychic, a little bit crazy. "I had another vision about you and Marty and the diamonds. I know you were telling me the truth. I never should have doubted you."

Her luminous eyes gazed into his face. Her wet hair streamed across her forehead. The murderous shell necklace encircled her slender throat, a reminder of how close he'd come to losing her forever. "I love you, Madeline."

Her lips moved. She struggled to speak.

"Does this mean…" she gasped for breath "…that I'm not fired?"

She would never leave his side again. Madeline was the woman he meant to spend the rest of his life with.

SEVERAL DAYS LATER, Madeline stood in the yard outside the Manor and kept an eye on Duncan, who practiced hitting balls off the tee. His friend Annie would be here any minute for a playdate.

When Duncan connected with the ball for a solid hit, she waved to him and called out, "Good one."

Sunlight glittered on the huge sapphire in her engagement ring. The stone was spectacular, as blue as the sea. After Marty's crime, it didn't seem right to have a diamond. Poor Marty! After she'd turned in the stolen gems to the police and Alma gave her statement, he couldn't deny his guilt. With good behavior, he might be paroled from prison in eight years.

Though Alma had been charged for withholding evidence, she got off with a fine and probation, partly because both Blake and Madeline had testified as character witnesses. Alma was still with them in Raven's Cliff, doing her job as a housekeeper with renewed commitment.

Blake came through the front door and joined her. His arm fit so neatly around her waist. His kiss on her cheek was sweet and sexy at the same time.

"I just got off the phone with Perry Wells," he said.

Though Perry had been acquitted of murder charges when Joe Curtis had confessed to killing Teddy Fisher, the scandals hadn't gone away. Perry resigned his office in disgrace because of the sleazy agreements he'd made with Teddy. The only point that the good people of Raven's Cliff agreed upon was for renovations on Beacon Manor and the lighthouse to continue, using the money Teddy left in escrow.

"How's Perry?" she asked.

"Desperate for cash. He reduced the price on that house he owns. He wants to sell for about half of what it's worth."

"I like the house." More specifically, she liked the idea of having a residence in Raven's Cliff—a place they could always come back to after Blake's assignments took them to more exotic locales. "But it would be wrong to take advantage of Perry's distress."

He gave her a squeeze. "Don't worry, I'm not going to cheat anybody. Even though it would be a solid fiscal move."

"Good business," she said. "Bad karma."

"He started babbling about how there's a new lead on his daughter. He still thinks Camille is alive."

"Could be. After she blew off the cliff, her body was never found." Glancing toward the yard, she saw Duncan marching toward the trees.

"Hey, buddy," his father called out. "Don't go far."

"Okay." Duncan waved. "Only to the trees and back."

Blake whispered in her ear, "While Duncan is busy with his little friend, we could have a playdate of our own."

Delighted, she whispered back, "I'll meet you in the Madeline Room."

"Wear your red dress."

And nothing else but a lacy thong and a sapphire engagement ring. She grinned. Every day with Blake was a playdate.

Duncan looked back over his shoulder. Daddy was right next to Madeline, hugging her. He was always hugging her and kissing her. They were in love.

Duncan was glad. He liked Madeline.

Counting every step, he walked across the grass to the trees. Real quiet, he said, "She sells seashells."

"Here I am," Temperance said.

"I have another friend," he said. "I don't want you to be jealous. Her name is Annie."

"Very well," she said. "If ever you wish to speak with me, I shall be here."

He had a question for her. The big scary man with hammer hands was gone, but Duncan knew he wasn't the person who'd grabbed his shoulder on the cliff. "Is there more danger?"

"Not for you. Not for the moment."

"Who was the man on the cliff?"

She rolled her eyes. "I told you before. Nicholas Sterling, the lighthouse keeper's grandson. And he never meant to hurt you. He was pulling you away from the edge."

"But everybody says Nicholas Sterling is dead."

"Is he?"

He heard a car honk and heard it pull up in the driveway. Annie hopped out. He waved to her, then turned back. "Goodbye, Temperance."

She was already gone.

* * * * *

This book couldn't have been written without
the patient support of my son, Officer Joseph Sharpe
(mistakes are mine, not his), and is dedicated, with love,
to his wonderful daughter, Carmen Amelia Sharpe.

ALICE SHARPE

THE LAWMAN'S SECRET SON

Harlequin Mills & Boon ™

INTRIGUE ™

First Published 2008
First Australian Paperback Edition 2008
ISBN 978 0 733 58885 3

Published by
Harlequin Mills & Boon®
Level 5
15 Help Street
CHATSWOOD NSW 2067
AUSTRALIA

Printed and bound in Australia by
McPherson's Printing Group

ABOUT THE AUTHOR

Alice Sharpe met her husband-to-be on a cold, foggy beach in Northern California. One year later they were married. Their union has survived the rearing of two children, a handful of earthquakes registering over 6.5, numerous cats and a few special dogs, the latest of which is a yellow Lab named Annie Rose. Alice and her husband now live in a small rural town in Oregon, where she devotes the majority of her time to pursuing her second love, writing.

Alice loves to hear from readers. You can write her at P.O. Box 755, Brownsville, OR 97327. SASE for reply is appreciated.

CAST OF CHARACTERS

Brady Skye—The oldest son of alcoholic parents, this ex-cop has lost both the career and the woman he loves. Now someone's out to take something even more precious—but they'll have to kill Brady first.

Lara Kirk—Brokenhearted, she left when Brady rejected her. Now she's back with a secret capable of destroying them all.

Tom James—Will Brady's old partner let his temper be the death of him?

Chief Dixon—The chief's decades-long hatred of Brady's father has now spilled over onto Brady.

Billy Armstrong—Brady is almost positive the boy drew a gun. Most think it never existed. Billy's death throws Brady's and Lara's lives into a tailspin.

Bill Armstrong—Billy's father's lust for revenge is pushing him over the edge of sanity. He swears to ruin Brady as well as anyone Brady loves.

Jason Briggs—This teenager must be silenced.

Roberta Beaton—The querulous old woman will pay a price for her curiosity.

Karen Wylie—A rebellious teenager with dreams of becoming a movie star.

Nicole Stevens—She's positive something horrible has happened to Karen Wylie. And she may know what.

Charles Skye—Brady's father has been lost in a bottle for thirty years.

Garrett Skye—Brady's younger brother has become a bodyguard for a casino comptroller and his attorney wife. This decision to make more money so he can gain custody of his toddler daughter is about to blow up in his face.

Prologue

Officer Brady Skye scanned the dark, empty road. Parked on a side street, he waited for his shift to end, using the dashboard light to attend to last-minute paperwork. He checked his watch—a quarter of midnight and still hot outside. Well, that was August for you.

He checked his watch again a minute later and smiled at himself. Talk about being anxious. But in fifteen minutes, he'd be off duty for two weeks and in fifteen hours, he'd stand at the altar with Lara Kirk.

Again.

He had to admit he'd been confused when Lara suggested they elope a week before the wedding. Why would she want to ruin her big day?

Her smile had been wistful when she replied, *"My big day? You mean my mother's big day. This wedding is turning into the social event of the year, Brady, it's not about you and me anymore. I want to go to a justice of the peace. I want to get married, just the two of us, the way we wanted. Then we'll come back and do it Mom's way."*

The memory of that private, secret ceremony and the night that followed made Brady all the more anxious to put this shift to bed. He would make her the happiest woman in the world. Things would be perfect. He'd make them perfect.

The squad car radio burst into life at that moment. Brady leaned forward, adjusting the volume. He caught little more than *blue sedan, dented right front fender* before a car matching the description sped past. He reported his location and that he had the vehicle in sight, rattling off the license-plate number as he trailed behind.

Apparently noticing Brady's flashing lights, the sedan accelerated. It made a series of turns, brake lights flashing through intersections. Brady followed, but not too close. They weren't going to get very far and he didn't want to push them into doing something stupid.

More information came in over the radio as the sedan made a wide turn toward the river. *Car stolen, two suspects, both minors, unarmed, alleged to have lifted beer from the all-night store up on Breezeway...*

Brady and his brother, Garrett, had grown up in Riverport, Oregon, not far from this very neighborhood. Unless the kid driving that sedan had a trick up his sleeve, he'd soon dead-end against the gate securing the old Evergreen Timber loading dock.

But the gate was old, the chain connecting the two sides weak with rust. With barely a pause, the sedan busted through the gate and kept going, careening back and forth as it skidded toward the waterfront and the Columbia River beyond.

Dumb kids. Lifting a couple of cases of beer was nothing to die for, even if they'd compounded the offense by stealing a car. Brady backed off as his buddy and soon-to-be best man, Tom James, chimed in he was seconds away from lending backup.

A collision with a stack of oil drums saved the car from plunging into the river. With a series of thuds, the sedan came to a grinding halt in the middle of the pile, heavy drums rolling and bumping into each other with dull heavy clunks. An overhead light illuminated the scene. Brady stopped his car and exited, rushing forward as the welcome sound of a waning siren announced Tom's arrival.

A few empty beer cans fell to the ground as the driver and passenger doors opened. Two kids got out of the car. The passenger looked familiar, hardly unusual given Riverport's modest population of under five thousand. The driver, closest to Brady, stumbled once before taking off across the torn concrete, leaping over oil drums with surprising agility.

"Hey," Brady yelled as he pursued the driver, leaving the passenger to Tom who he'd heard come up behind him. Within a hundred yards, Brady caught up with the kid and wrestled him to the ground. He avoided a few drunken punches and a torrent of swearwords as he flipped him onto his stomach and cuffed him. He pulled the boy to his feet and marched him back to the squad car where he found no sign of Tom or the passenger.

"If you're smart, this will be the last night you ever get drunk," Brady said.

The kid swore at him again.

Once the driver was safely secured in the backseat, Brady turned his attention to Tom and the other teen, following their raised voices. The ground became trickier as the pool of light dispersed. Rambling blackberry vines had sprung up between the cracked concrete pads and snagged his pants as he ran. He got out his flashlight and flicked it on.

A movement caught Brady's eye. Two figures, six or seven feet apart, facing each other a scant foot or so from the edge of the wharf, the river a shimmering ribbon behind them. Tom, a barrel-chested man who had played football when young, was heaving after the run. He'd lost his hat in the chase and his balding dome glistened with sweat. The boy, only half Tom's size, appeared posed for flight. The kid yelled something was his fault as Tom's low voice droned on.

Brady hung back, giving Tom a chance to calm the kid with his usual aplomb. He had a way with kids though some in the department thought him too lenient. Nevertheless, Tom usually got his point across. The kid grew quiet. Good old Tom and his silver tongue.

Brady swung his flashlight down before switching it off. In the last instant before the beam died, he caught a glimpse of the boy reaching behind his back, his pale arm stark against his dark T-shirt, then the glint of light off metal as a gun emerged from beneath the shirt. It all happened in slow motion, time suspended—

A torrent of training flooded Brady's brain as he pulled his Glock. Tom was a microsecond away from taking a bullet in the gut and he obviously didn't know it. In that instant, Brady, without options, fired.

For a few seconds, the echo of the gunshot was the only sound in the world. The kid, bathed in shadows, flew to the ground.

The shot thundered again and again in Brady's head. He couldn't feel his hand still gripped around his gun. He saw Tom kneel beside the boy, his body mercifully blocking Brady's view for a brief moment, saw Tom's jaw work as he looked over his shoulder and yelled something, saw him yank his cell phone from his pocket and start punching in numbers.

The place would be swarming with help within minutes.

Brady, finally able to move, walked toward Tom and the still shape of the fallen boy. He'd lost his flashlight, he couldn't feel his feet, he still held the gun and it weighed a million pounds. He stopped short.

Tom's flashlight illuminated the scene. His florid face had taken on green undertones. "It's the Armstrong boy," he said. "He's dead."

Brady's heart sank like a rock to the very bottom of the sea. No wonder the kid had looked familiar. The Armstrong family had lost their only other child, a sixteen-year-old girl, a few weeks before. This kid was a year behind her in school. Billy, that was his name. Brady had gone to school with Bill Armstrong Senior.

His voice low as though afraid of being overheard, Tom said, "What in the hell happened?"

"He was going to shoot you," Brady said. *Wasn't it obvious?*

Tom shone a light at Billy's empty hands, flung toward the river. The boy's silver watchband shimmered on his wrist. "With what?"

Brady made himself concentrate past the roaring inside his head. "He pulled a gun out of his waistband in the back. There wasn't time to do anything but react."

"Are you sure? I mean, the light is tricky—"

"He pulled a gun." Brady tried to muster more confidence than he felt. He had seen a gun, hadn't he? *Oh, God...*

Tom's voice sounded just as dazed. "I was trying to talk some sense into him. You must have heard him, ranting and raving, blaming himself for his sister's suicide, blaming the cops—"

"I thought you had him calmed down, but when I lowered my flashlight, I saw him reach—"

"All right, Brady, all right. If you say there was a gun, there was a gun."

Brady wasn't any more convinced by Tom's words than by his own thoughts. If there'd been a gun, where was it now? If he'd made a mistake, how would he ever live with himself?

Tom pushed his hat back on his high forehead and added, "This is going to hit his parents hard. And Chief Dixon. A thing like this looks bad for the department and he's been waiting for you to mess up."

Like my father, Brady thought. He couldn't wrap his mind around any of that, not now, not so soon. Distant sirens announced the imminent arrival of the troops. The supervisor, an ambulance, the M.E. The place would soon be crawling with professionals.

"Lara, too," Tom added as though it just occurred to him. "I bet she got to know Billy and Sara down at the teen center."

Brady shook his head. He couldn't think. Wait, sure, she'd mentioned these kids along with a dozen others...

Tom suddenly seemed to grasp the impact of his comments. He said, "Damn, I'm sorry, Brady. Don't worry, if there was a gun, we'll find it. You saved my life. I won't forget it."

Brady's gaze shifted to the river rushing only a few feet from where the boy had fallen. If Billy Armstrong's gun had flown into the water as Billy took the bullet, it was possible they would never find it.

And in the back of his mind, a voice. Slurred like his

Alice Sharpe

father's voice, thick with booze. *What if there wasn*
gun, you moron? What if you gunned down an unarmed
kid? What then?

Chapter One

The minute Lara drove over the bridge into Riverport, she knew coming back was a big mistake. It didn't matter how many times she told herself it was only for a couple of days, the feeling persisted. There was too much history here.

She turned on Ferry Street, passing the teen center without looking at it. Next came the bank and the hardware store. A red light at the corner of Ferry and Oak caught her as it always had. She kept her eyes on the road until the light turned green.

Her mother's big old Victorian sat perched on an acre of manicured gardens on the outskirts of town. Most of Riverport's other big old houses were gone, their land cut up and sold off to contractors for subdivisions. The mansion had been updated over the years—a solarium on the back, the kitchen expanded—until now it was quite a showpiece.

Lara had grown up in the house and it was with a surge of familiarity, if not homecoming, that she turned into the driveway. Her mother wasn't actually in residence as she'd left for an Alaskan cruise just a few days before. Myra, her mother's housekeeper, must have been waiting, though, for Lara had barely set the parking brake when the garage door rolled upward. Lara restarted the car and drove into the enclosure, sighing with relief when the doors closed behind her. She glanced into the backseat, then heard Myra coming through the side door that connected the house with the garage.

"Miss Lara," Myra called as Lara got out of the car. She approached with a big smile. "Your poor mother will just die when she learns she missed your visit. Here, let me help you."

Myra Halifax had worked for Lara's mother forever. A woman in her sixties with gray permed curls, she was built with a low center of gravity and formidable for-bearance. That trait was a plus when it came to dealing with Lara's high-strung mother.

Lara returned the smile. She couldn't return the sentiment.

An hour later, she'd emptied the car and spent several moments upstairs settling into her old bedroom. Restless and uneasy, she decided something cold to drink and a friendly chat with the housekeeper might ward off her growing sense of foreboding.

She was one step into the kitchen when the doorbell rang. The shrill interruption came as a surprise. With her mother gone and her own presence in Riverport more or less a secret, company was unexpected and unwanted.

"I'll send whoever it is away," Myra said as she bustled past Lara into the foyer.

Lara hung back. There was a sense of destiny in the air, of colliding worlds. An overwhelming desire to race out the back swept through her and yet she stood off to the side as Myra impatiently flung open the door.

"You!" Myra said, and even though Lara couldn't see who stood on the front-porch step, she *knew*. Myra added, "What do you want?"

There was a pause during which Lara stopped breathing. Her heartbeat drummed in her head.

And then his voice.

"I need to speak to Mrs. Kirk."

"Mrs. Kirk is away for several weeks." Myra started to close the door.

Lara saw the hand that caught it. *His hand.* "Maybe you can help me."

Myra sputtered a little before saying, "I don't see how—"

"I need to get in touch with Lara," he cut in. "I have to talk to her. Warn her. All I need is her address or a telephone number."

Was it possible he didn't know she was at this house? It seemed so unlikely. No, someone must have seen her drive by, someone must have alerted him.

What else had they reported?

"I won't give you her phone number," Myra announced. "You broke her heart once and I won't stand by while you do it again."

Lara grabbed the edge of the door and opened it wider. "It's okay," she told Myra who stood her ground, glowering at their guest. Staring up into two very dark eyes, she added, "Hello, Brady."

For a second he didn't answer. For a second he looked as dumbstruck as she felt and she knew in that instant that he hadn't expected to find her here, that she was as much a surprise to him as he was to her.

That moment gave her a second to absorb his changed appearance. The thinner face, the longer hair, the hollows in his cheeks, the deep, deep tan, the solid muscles under the worn T-shirt, the dusty-looking jeans. What had happened to Mr. Press and Fold, Mr. Perfect Haircut, Mr. By the Book?

This Brady looked younger, rangier, cagier, sexier.

"I'm glad you're here," she said, which was an out-and-out lie. Sure, she'd planned on seeing him while she was in Riverport, of course, but not quite so soon, and not here at her mother's house. She'd spent three long hours in the car rehearsing her what-comes-next speech and now drew a total blank.

She hadn't taken one factor into account. She hadn't considered the impact of seeing him face-to-face. The months of tears that had cleared her head apparently hadn't cleared her heart. Yet.

"I'll just be a minute or two, Myra," she said with a backward glance. "You'll take care—"

"Of course," Myra huffed as Lara stepped onto her mother's broad porch and softly closed the door behind her.

"I was going to call you later," she told Brady.

Before he could answer, a car drove by, slowing down as the driver craned his neck to see who stood outside the Kirk house. Brady said, "Let's walk around back so we don't give the whole town something to talk about."

Lara suspected it was too late for that. She'd recognized Frank Duncan leaning forward, eyes wide. The hardware store would be abuzz within minutes. But she led the way around the back just the same, toward the riverside garden where they couldn't be overheard through the open windows.

The back sloped down to the river, which flowed by at a leisurely pace this late in the summer. Lara stopped by a grouping of wrought-iron patio furniture arranged on a brick island, surrounded by a sea of flowers. Too nervous to sit, she stood in back of a heavily scrolled chair, gripping the metal for support. Brady leaned against the edge of the old brick barbecue, linking his arms across his chest. He'd always been fit, but had his shoulders and arms always bulged with so many muscles?

"I didn't know you were in Riverport," he said.

"I've been here less than an hour." She tried not to stare at him but her traitorous gaze strayed his way every chance it got.

"How have you been?" he said.

She shook her head, unable to bear the thought of small talk.

"You look good," he added, his gaze taking her in from head to toe. She hadn't changed out of her traveling clothes, the white shorts and white halter top felt suddenly too revealing.

She whispered, "It's too late, Brady. I didn't come back for this."

His eyes flashed, then he smiled, kind of, his lips doing all the work, his eyes not playing along. "Oh? Then why did you come back? Explain it to me."

"Don't use that tone with me. You're the one who called everything off."

"And you're the one who left."

"You sent me packing like a kid. I was hurt at first but I'm over it now."

No reaction showed on his face. He was quiet for a long moment before saying, "Listen, Lara. Things between us ended kind of abruptly."

She met his gaze.

"Okay, okay, it's all my fault. I know that." He threw up both hands. "I admit it. I take full responsibility. I couldn't give you a whole man—"

"So you gave me nothing," she said, pushing herself away from the chair and walking toward the river and the abandoned dock her father had built twenty years before.

"I was a wreck—" he said from right behind her.

She jumped at the nearness of his voice. "Of course you were," she said, memories of the night flooding back. His stunned expression, his self-incrimination, the reality of the last few hours circling them like a cyclone, lifting them off their feet, tossing them around before flinging them back to earth a hundred miles from where they'd been.

She pushed it all away. "This is pointless. Let's skip the postmortem on our very short marriage. You told Myra you needed to warn me. Warn me about what?"

His voice, pitched low and combined with the mysterious intensity of his dark gaze, made Lara's knees go weak as he said, "I expected divorce papers by now."

"I have a lawyer working on them."

"For a year?"

"I haven't wanted anyone to know—"

"'Anyone' being your mother."

"Does it matter? I'm sorry I haven't moved fast enough for you. I'll get to it right away." The truth was the papers were ready. They were upstairs, in her suitcase. But she couldn't give them to Brady without an explanation. There were things he needed to know, things they needed to work out. But not now, not in her mother's garden, not when she needed to get back inside the house.

"The only reason it matters is Bill Armstrong," Brady said.

"Billy's father? Why—"

"Since the internal investigation found reasonable cause for the shooting, he's threatening a civil suit against me. I guess I don't blame him."

She waited.

With a bitter twist to his lips, he added, "They never found the gun and trust me, they looked. Armstrong insists his boy didn't have access to a handgun and wouldn't have carried one if he did. I still swear I saw one. It's a stalemate."

"But the river…" she began, something more niggling at the back of her mind. But what?

"Yeah. I know. It could be buried in three feet of silt and muck, it could be halfway to the ocean by now. Who knows?"

"Mr. Armstrong won't win."

"He'll have the sympathy of the jury. He lost both his kids within a month. And you know what the name Skye is worth around here."

"You are not your father," she said. She'd said it before, but it never seemed to sink in.

His laugh was sudden and without mirth. "You've always been naive. Maybe it comes from being born with a silver spoon in your mouth."

"And you've been afraid you'll turn into your father. It's not written that you will be a drunk and a loser."

"Ah, darling, it's the family tradition," he said, his voice low and silky and taunting. "My dad, my brother—"

I will not rise to the bait, she told herself and stood there with her mouth closed.

He finally added, "Anyway, it's not me I'm worried about."

"Maybe you should."

Frowning, he said, "What does that mean?"

"What's happened to you? When did you stop caring?"

"Stop caring about what? What are you talking about?"

"Your appearance, for instance. I can't believe the department lets you wear your hair that long."

"I'm not a policeman anymore, Lara. That part of my life is over. I thought you knew that."

She could hardly fathom such a thing. Brady had always wanted to be a cop. "Then what do you do?"

"I work construction like I did in college."

That explained the muscles. "But you were exonerated, weren't you? Why didn't you go back? Was it Chief Dixon?"

He shrugged and looked away.

"Brady," she said, touching his wrist. Big mistake. Sensory recognition traveled through her system like a lightning bolt, erasing the last three hundred sixty-three days in the blink of an eye. She drew her hand away at once. "You wouldn't have shot the boy if you hadn't had to," she said, her voice gentle. "You saved Tom's life."

He looked straight into her eyes and her heart quivered in her chest. She did not want to feel anything for him, let alone the tumultuous combination of lost love and resentment currently ricocheting inside her body like a wild bullet. Her mother had warned her a man with Brady's past could never really love anyone. Lara hadn't believed it until that night when he'd proved it to her.

He said, "I have nothing to lose. But you do."

"Me? Oh, you mean money. You think Bill Armstrong is going to come after my family's money."

"If he finds you're legally my wife, yes. If he finds a way to stick it to me or anyone I care—cared—about, yes, I do. Our marriage is a matter of public record. All he has to do is look. Maybe you ought to light a fire under your lawyer."

She closed her eyes, trying to imagine her mother's reaction to someone suing Brady and walking off with the Kirk fortune.

"It's not the civil suit I'm worried about," Brady added. "It's Armstrong himself. He's gone half-crazy since losing Billy. If he finds out about you—"

"Why would he even think about me?" she said, looking at Brady again, but her mind's eye casting a different image. Both of the Armstrong kids had come into the teen center on occasion. First Sara, Billy's delicate sixteen-year-old sister, then Billy and his pal, Jason Briggs, both a year younger. When Sara took a whole bottle of her grandmother's sleeping pills, it had stunned the community and it had devastated Billy.

The senior Armstrong had come into the teen center looking for answers no one could give him. Grief and anger had battled in his feverish eyes and she'd felt horrible for him. And truth be known, a little afraid of him, too.

And then, three weeks later, Billy died.

Good Lord, no wonder Brady looked haunted.

But she couldn't offer him what he needed. Maybe another woman could, someday, one who knew how to crack through his defenses or live with them. But not her. She said, "I've been gone a year, Brady. I'll leave again in a few days. As far as anybody in Riverport knows, I'm just the girl you didn't marry."

He looked down at his feet then back at her, his gaze unfathomable. How could she have ever thought she knew him better than she knew herself? He was a stranger. She glanced at her watch. Almost three o'clock. "I have to get back inside."

His eyebrows raised in query. Before he could ask a question she wasn't prepared to answer, she told him something she hadn't planned to. "I have a meeting this evening with Jason Briggs."

As she'd known it would, this news diverted his curiosity. "What does *he* want?"

"I guess he wants to talk."

"Why does the boy who convinced Billy Armstrong that stealing a car and a half case of beer was a good idea want to talk to you?"

She shrugged. "He got out of juvenile detention earlier this week and apparently went straight to the teen center. My replacement called me up in Seattle where I live now, and I called Jason. He asked if I was going to be around Riverport soon because he needed to talk."

"And so you drove all the way back here to talk with a delinquent sixteen-year-old boy."

"Among other things," she hedged. "But, yes. There was something in his voice."

"What do you mean?"

"He sounded nervous."

"Jason Briggs hasn't, to my knowledge, told anyone anything about that night except to try to blame everything on Billy."

She almost smiled. Brady was acting like what

Brady really was. A cop. How could he not see that? She said, "I won't know what's troubling him until I talk to him."

"Yeah. Okay, I'll go with you. This may be a break."

"No, you won't go with me," she said firmly.

"Where are you meeting him?"

"Like I'm going to tell you?"

"You don't know what he has in mind."

"And neither do you," she said. With a warning glance, she added, "Come back later tonight. If Jason says anything I can pass along to you, I will."

"I don't like you going alone."

She stared at him until he had the grace to drop his gaze. "I'll call my lawyer tomorrow. We'll have this sham of a marriage annulled."

One minute he was staring at her as she talked and the next he'd closed the three feet between them and grabbed her arms. The energy that surged directly into her bloodstream almost knocked her off her feet. Her heart banged against her ribs.

He dipped his head so low his deep dark brown eyes burned into hers. "Can a marriage consummated the way ours was *be* annulled?"

"Brady…"

"Don't you remember our wedding night? Don't you remember what we did—"

She shrugged herself away from him. Sex had never been the issue. "You'd better go now."

Seconds ticked by in absolute silence before he finally moved. He paused at her elbow. "I'll be back at nine o'clock."

"Make it ten," she said.

He nodded once before striding away. She stood in

the garden for several moments, staring out at the old dock, waiting until she heard the roar of his motorcycle and knew it was safe to move.

Then she walked back inside the house, head high, eyes mostly unseeing. She'd shed her last tear for Brady months before. She was over him.

Chapter Two

Good Neighbors was a nonprofit organization utilizing volunteer workers to build low-income housing. Brady was one of the few paid employees. It was his job to assign and approve projects. He was also in charge of contracting jobs too big for the volunteers to handle alone.

The man who had donated the property had been truly generous as it wasn't a tiny city lot but a small parcel backed by the river. Eventually there would be additional houses built on the property. Brady hoped to have a hand in all of them.

After visiting with Lara, Brady couldn't keep his mind on anything. The sun baked his bare back as he sat on the plywood roof, banging in a slew of nails. They'd run out of ammo for the nail gun and he'd sent everyone else home for the day.

Had Lara really come back to Riverport just to talk to Jason Briggs? What was the boy up to? He'd been in and out of trouble most of his young life and Brady would bet money a few months in detention hadn't changed that. Brady knew the type, his own brother, Garrett, was a carbon copy.

For a second, Brady thought about Garrett and wondered where he lived now and what he was up to. Last he'd heard, Garrett was out of the army. Brady hoped that gig had helped his little brother get his head screwed on straight, but he wouldn't count on it. Garrett was more like their father than Brady was. The same reckless streak ran through both of them.

A bitter smile never touched his lips as that thought hit home. Could Garrett have done any worse with his life than Brady had? Had he killed a fifteen-year-old boy? Had he destroyed his one chance for a happy marriage with a woman who outclassed him in every way possible? Had he abandoned the only job he ever truly wanted and cemented his reputation as another worthless Skye, all because the thought of carrying a gun—and possibly making another mistake—made him queasy?

Unless Garrett had turned into a serial killer, he was probably doing as well if not better than his responsible big brother.

Brady missed a nail head twice and laid the hammer aside. Staring out at the river, he faced the fact he wasn't going to get much more done here today. He picked up his tools and scrambled down the ladder. He'd just finished storing the equipment in the on-site storage shed when an SUV pulled up alongside his Harley.

Brady yanked on his T-shirt as the dust settled around the SUV. The window slid down to reveal Tom James, flush face toying with a smile.

Twice divorced, Tom was five or six years older than Brady, creeping up on forty. His former partner was also shorter than Brady, heavier, big chested with very short black hair ringing a bald spot.

"Have I got news for you," Tom said.

Brady leaned against Tom's vehicle. It was brand new and the fact he could afford it after the cleaning his last ex-wife and her lawyer accomplished, spoke to the fact that Tom was banking on his future promotion within the Riverport Police Department.

And no reason he shouldn't. Brady was just damn thankful the Armstrong shooting hadn't destroyed Tom's reputation on the force as well as his own.

"Let me guess," Brady said.

Tom laughed. "You won't guess this. I got it hot from Carlson's Hardware Store."

"Lara is back in town, staying at her mother's house while her mother is on a cruise."

Tom's round face fell. "Someone told you."

"I saw Lara. I spoke with her."

Tom nodded, all humor gone now. He knew what the last year had cost Brady. He said, "How was it?"

"About how you'd expect."

Tom nodded. "What did she come back for?"

"She's meeting Jason Briggs tonight."

"Really," Tom said, eyes narrowing. "I heard he got out of juvie. What's she meeting him for?"

"He wanted to talk to her. Maybe you could keep your eyes open tonight just in case there's trouble."

"Where are they meeting? What time?"

"Don't know, she won't say."

"You going to tail her?"

Brady shook his head. "She'd kill me if she found out I was butting into her business."

"So?"

"So, she's right."

"But you want me to keep an eye out," Tom said, a smile pulling at his lips.

Brady looked away.

"Don't worry, buddy, I'll mention it to Chief Dixon, too. He can tell anyone else he sees fit."

Brady bit his tongue at this suggestion but said nothing as Tom drove off. He just hoped Lara never got wind that half the Riverport police force would soon know—thanks to him—that she had a meeting with Jason Briggs.

The thought occurred to Brady as he climbed on the Harley that Jason's driver's license had been yanked. Using a little deduction, that meant Lara would probably meet him in town. Like maybe at the teen center or the diner or even Lara's mother's house. He toyed with doing a little research but let the idea go.

Lara had made it clear she didn't want him in her face. Tom was going to keep a sharp eye peeled just in case. That was enough.

He got to his place about five o'clock and ate a tuna sandwich while standing at the counter. It was a new place, about as nondescript as they come. He'd changed just about everything in the last year, including his residence. The old place had reminded him too much of Lara.

At first, after the shooting, he'd toyed around with leaving Riverport himself. Without his job on the force, without Lara, what was there to stay for? But then the Good Neighbors job came along and he admitted to himself that, for good or bad, Riverport was home. Garrett could move around the country all he wanted—Brady would stay here.

After dinner, he usually went back to the Good Neighbors house to map out the next day's activities. No reason not to do so again tonight. He couldn't sit in the

impersonal apartment longing for a life he no longer had.
He was too restless to read or watch television. If he
couldn't settle down at work, he'd take the Harley out
to the river and use an evening swim to work out his
anxiety.

He and Lara used to do that, most of the time on the
spur of the moment after a movie or dinner out. He
could still picture her in the scraps of satin and lace she
called underwear, swimming in the river, honey-blond
hair mingling with the darkening water, the summer
smell of blackberries, the taste of her skin. She wore
summer the way some women wore diamonds...

He'd go anyway. Despite all that.

It took him two hours to plan the next day's work and
finish up a few odd jobs. It was nearing nine o'clock
by the time he started home. He went the long way in
order to avoid the Kirk house. He wasn't due there for
over an hour and he didn't want Lara catching sight of
him and accusing him of spying.

He was driving down Main Street near the west end
of town, undecided about the swim, when he spotted
Tom talking to what appeared to be a high-school girl
standing beside a little blue car. She'd probably been
caught speeding. As usual, when Tom put on the charm,
a scared kid relaxed. Brady knew he wouldn't give her
a ticket, he'd cut her some slack. Back in the day, Brady
had actually talked to Tom about his live-and-let-live
take on citing minors, questioning whether he was
actually doing a kid much good by not holding them
accountable for minor offenses. Tom had laughed him
off.

And again, that ache of no longer belonging. He
missed being out on the street, helping people, looking

for miscreants, figuring things out. Sure, he was still alive, he still walked and talked and worked and occasionally, even laughed. But it all seemed brittle and hollow. His life, abandoned.

Not wanting to talk to Tom again, he took a side street that led to the industrial side of town. There was a smattering of bars along the street. No doubt his father was holding up a stool at the River Rat or the Crosshairs. Brady avoided even looking in the open doors.

That's when he caught sight of a guy on a bicycle who looked familiar. Of course. Hair shorter, body a little bigger, but that was Jason Briggs.

For one long second, options flashed through Brady's mind. Turn around and go the other way, pull over to the curb, find a cold drink and do nothing or…

Brady slowed way down, giving Jason a good lead. He waited until Jason had cleared the edge of town and disappeared around a corner before taking off, hanging back, trailing him but not close.

What was the harm of trailing Jason if Lara never knew?

It looked as though the kid was headed for the river. Maybe he just wanted a swim. Maybe Brady would join him—if Lara wasn't there. Who knows what Jason might talk about while paddling around the river on a summer evening?

Traffic was light, so following Jason took skill. Brady left lots of room between them, uneasy with the inevitable times Jason disappeared around a curve. But Brady knew this road and there was only one place it really went—to the river. Unless the kid was headed over the bridge and on up to St. George.

Brady came around the latest hairpin curve to find

the road ahead empty. This was where it branched, straight across the bridge, or an abrupt right on the south side of the river. The bridge had two cars on it but no bikes. That left the southern road and it appeared empty. Brady concluded Jason had ridden his bike into the turnout on this side of the bridge.

So, he wasn't going to swim. The bank there was too steep, the river too deep thanks to the proximity of the bridge excavation. There was a far better spot just a quarter of a mile downstream where the river made a wide turn.

As the noisy motorcycle would ruin a stealthy approach, Brady steered the Harley behind a few trees, took off his helmet and started walking.

He found Jason still astride his bike, feet planted on the ground, facing the road. Waiting. He was wearing earphones attached to an iPod in his pocket. He was a lanky, fair-haired kid with shifty eyes, dressed in baggy shorts and flip-flops. Brady remembered the punches he'd thrown the night of the shooting, and his own advice to Jason: stop drinking. Well, they didn't serve adult beverages in juvenile detention, so hopefully a little time away from temptation had been good for him.

Brady ducked behind some very dense Oregon grape bushes. He scooted along until an abandoned wooden pavilion provided cover from the road and the parking area. The downside of this position was he couldn't see the road. The upside was twofold—he could, by contorting a bit, see the clearing and no one could see him.

Ten long minutes later, he heard an engine. Jason must have seen a car. He took off the earphones and got off his bike, pushing it near a picnic table where he leaned it against one of the benches. At last, a silver car with Washington plates drove slowly into the clearing.

Brady saw Lara behind the wheel. She parked the car facing the river embankment and rolled down her window. Jason walked toward Lara with his head down.

Brady tensed. He could imagine no reason Jason Briggs would hurt Lara, but his walking up to her like that made him nervous.

They spoke for a few seconds and Jason started around the back of the car. Lara's window slid back into place. Had she seen the Harley? Was she going to drive Jason to a different spot?

But Jason got inside the car and turned in the seat to face Lara. Brady could tell she hadn't turned the engine off. Probably wanted to keep the air-conditioning running.

He watched them talk for a couple of minutes, then became aware of an idling engine out on the road. Before he could finish wondering what Lara and Jason would do when another car rolled into the parking lot, a shot blasted the evening stillness.

An instant later, a muffled scream hit Brady like a gust from a tornado. It came from Lara's car. There was a perfect round hole in her back window. Jason had slumped forward. Lara leaned toward him. Brady started moving. Another shot. Some idiot was out on the road, shooting at Lara's car.

Before he could scramble from behind the pavilion, Lara put the car into gear and gunned the engine into a broad turn to escape. It appeared Jason fell against her during the turn. Another shot. She grabbed her arm. The car lurched forward. Brady watched helplessly as it hung on the embankment for a second before heading for the river.

As he ran toward the quickly disappearing car, he

heard an engine rev and tires squeal out on the road. No doubt thinking his mission accomplished, the gunman had fled. Every cop-related fiber of Brady's body quaked at the thought of the gunman getting away.

He got to the embankment in time to see Lara's car fly over a strip of boulders, its tailpipe clanging as the car launched into the river, a geyser of water spraying as it landed like a whale doing a belly flop, and quickly sank from view.

Chapter Three

Jason's limp body pinned Lara's foot against the accelerator pedal. Blood from the wound on her right arm dripped on his white T-shirt as she tried to push him away.

Oh, God, he was hurt, she didn't want to hurt him further, but the car was racing toward the river.

A final push and he slumped the other direction. She moved her foot and the racing engine slowed, but it was too late. The car hit the rocks skirting the river's edge and launched itself into the water. Her last act before she hit the river was to pound the electric window button. The window slid down six inches before water washed over the hood and the engine died. Within an instant, water covered the windshield and the vehicle sank to the bottom of the river as cold water gushed through the window.

"Jason!" she screamed.

He mumbled something as the water seemed to revive him for a moment. It was too dark to see much. "Jason, we're sinking. I'm going to try to get us out of this. Hold on."

A million images flashed through her mind as she

searched frantically for something heavy enough to break a window. *Her purse, no. Sandals, a small flashlight. Nothing heavy. No big tire iron.*

A million images. Brady. Nathan. Her mother. A million regrets, a million sorrows, all racing like electronic bleeps through her brain, like a movie reel moving too fast for images. And all the while she searched for a tool that would break the window and save their lives, and all the time she searched, she knew no such tool existed within the passenger cabin of her new car.

The water was up to their waists now and still gushing. She wished she'd not lowered the window or had thought to do it sooner though twin streams also spurt from the bullet holes in the back window. Her actions had more or less set them up for certain death. No one knew they were there but the person who shot them. He or she wasn't coming to their rescue.

She should have told Brady! She should have told her mother's housekeeper. She should have told someone.

How long would it take for anyone to notice she was gone. Nathan would first, of course, and then Myra, but neither of them would tell the one person who could help.

Brady. She should have told Brady.

She held Jason's head up for him as he seemed to have slipped back into unconsciousness and the water was above her shoulders. He would die without the terror. Lucky him.

A banging on the window behind her head caused Lara to gulp river water and she coughed. A rock. Someone was using a big rock to pound on the rear window. She immediately shoved Jason through the middle of the car, between the two front seats into the back, the water making it easier to move him, struggling to keep his face up, his nose above water. He ran into the seat and sputtered as she lost hold of him. She felt around in a panic until she caught hold of his hair and hauled him back to the surface. He gagged. At least he was still alive.

There was only a small pocket of air against the ceiling of the car now. The rock pounding sounded hollow until suddenly the window shattered into a thousand little cubes of glass. Hands reached inside. She shoved Jason toward them, praying the car hadn't sunk too deep, that their savior would get Jason to the surface before he gulped too much water and drowned.

As Jason's feet disappeared, Lara pushed herself through the seats. Her sandal strap caught on the gearshift and she wasted precious seconds yanking it off her foot. Hands appeared again, reaching toward her. She reached out. They grabbed her. A feeling of safety shot through her body as the hands pulled her free of the car. Her rescuer put an arm around her waist and swam to the surface, towing her along.

She emerged into the warm night air coughing and choking. Arms lifted her from her feet and carried her up the steep embankment, laying her down on the grass beside Jason, who was being tended by an older woman Lara had never seen before. A gray car was parked a few feet away, the driver's door wide open. A beeping sound indicated the keys were still in the ignition.

Lara coughed up a half gallon of water before looking up at the man who had saved her.

Dripping wet, hair streaming down his brown face,

clothes molded against his powerful body, expression unfathomable.

Brady.

Somewhere in her heart of hearts, she'd known it was him. "Why are you here?" she sputtered.

"It's a long story," he said, leaving her side to kneel beside Jason. "This lady saw your car go into the river as she crossed the bridge. She called an ambulance on her cell phone." He put his fingers against Jason's throat. Even from where Lara sat, she could see the spreading red stain on Jason's chest and she groaned.

"His breathing is shallow, he's going into shock," Brady said. Addressing the Good Samaritan, he added, "Do you have a blanket in your car, something to keep him warm?"

"I'll look," she said, struggling to her feet.

"He's lost a lot of blood," Brady said as he propped the boy's feet atop a rock. Lara took Jason's limp hand. He felt so cold.

Brady was in the act of stripping off his wet T-shirt, when the woman hurried from her car carrying a blue blanket. He rung out his shirt before wadding it up and placing it on Jason's wound. The muscles under his wet skin rippled with effort.

"It's the dog throw," the flustered woman said as she pushed the blanket toward Brady. "It's probably hairy—"

"It's fine," Brady said, tucking the blanket around the wet boy. "Can you take over for me? Can you keep pressure on his wound?"

"Of course." The woman did as Brady asked before looking up at him with frightened eyes. "This is a gunshot, isn't it?"

"Yes."

"And the girl?"

Now that survival wasn't foremost on her mind, Lara realized she felt not only light-headed, but her arm throbbed. She looked down to find new blood seeping into the wet cloth, making a pink watercolor of her blouse.

Brady took her good hand, pulling her to her feet. She stumbled against him and he caught her, his grip tight.

"You okay?"

No, she wasn't okay. She wasn't okay at all. She'd come close to dying. She'd come close to leaving secrets untold. She had to bite back tears as she said, "You know about the shooting?"

"Yeah."

"I don't understand. How did you get here?"

"Put some pressure on your arm," he said evasively. "Better yet, keep it elevated." He looked toward the road. "I hear a siren. Let's hope they had the good sense to alert the police."

OVERLAID ON THE IMAGE of Jason's unconscious body being loaded into the ambulance as red and blue police lights flashed in the dark was the old replay of the same thing being done to Billy Armstrong.

Two boys out for a joyride. One dead, the other hovering near death.

And now Lara.

Along with the police, two ambulances had responded. The ambulance carrying Jason took off almost immediately. The other stood waiting for Lara. Brady watched as Lara greeted one of the EMT guys like an old, lost friend. They'd probably gone to school together. It struck Brady that Lara had walked away from her whole life—her family, her friends, her job—when she walked away from him.

Ran away. And what choice did you give her?

"I have to talk to you," she told him, pausing as a medic guided her to the ambulance.

"Did Jason have a chance to say anything to you?" he asked.

She cradled her wounded arm with her good hand. Sympathy, the last thing he wanted from her, flooded her eyes. She said, "He was just getting settled when it happened. The only person he had a chance to mention was his girlfriend, the Wylie girl. I guess she broke up with him."

"That's all?"

"Yeah. I'm sorry." She lowered her voice and added, "I need to talk to you about something even more important. I could have died tonight. I would have died if you hadn't magically appeared."

"Not magically," he said, gazing into her green eyes. The flashing lights cast revolving colors across her hair and face. Her eyes glistened.

So many memories. Of holding her, kissing her, making love to her. She had been his and he'd lost her.

"There's something I have to tell you," she repeated.

"Me, too. I didn't just happened to be here tonight."

She shook her head. "I don't care. I'll wait for you at the hospital. Come get me when you can."

"Just tell me now—"

"Not now," she said. He felt his throat close as she walked away. His last glimpse was of her eyes before the ambulance doors shut and the vehicle charged back to town.

Tom hadn't arrived yet, but his new partner, a young

guy named Hastings, took Brady's statement, russet eyebrows arching when Brady described the gunfire.

"Two shots," Brady said. "Maybe three."

"But you didn't see the vehicle?"

"No."

"Show me again where you were standing when the shots started."

Brady walked Hastings through the whole thing, using flashlights. Tow trucks had arrived and the underwater recovery of the vehicle had begun. Hastings left as another squad car tore into the clearing and Tom emerged, tugging on his hat. Hastings and Tom spoke for a few seconds, then Tom came to stand beside Brady.

"I'd like to get to the hospital," Brady said.

Tom nodded. "Soon. But hell, Brady, what were you doing out here? Did you follow Lara?"

"Actually, I followed Jason Briggs. I saw him riding his bike."

"You followed Jason? With what?"

"The Harley. It's parked down the road, behind some trees."

"Let me get this straight. You shadowed the kid out of town, then hid your motorcycle and continued on foot? Why?"

Brady shrugged. "Because the Harley is noisy and I didn't want Jason to know I was following him."

"He never saw you?"

"I don't think so."

"And when you got here—"

"I stayed out of sight."

"How long did he and Lara talk before the attack? Did he say anything about Billy having a gun?"

"He didn't have time. They only talked for a minute

or two. She said he never got past mentioning his girl-friend. A girl named Wylie."

"What about her?"

"I guess she broke up with Jason. You'll have to ask Lara."

"And you didn't see the gunman or his vehicle?"

"No."

"This doesn't look so good," Tom said, pushing his hat back on his head.

Brady's eyes narrowed as he said, "Just what are you suggesting, Tom?"

"Nothing. Nothing. But you've got to admit it looks bad."

"Why?"

"The first day you find out Jason Briggs is home you follow him. The next thing anyone knows, the boy is as good as dead. And you're on scene."

"Are you saying I shot Jason Briggs?"

"I'm saying it looks like you could have shot the boy. He was the only other one in the car with Billy Arm-strong that night. He's fresh out of juvie. If he knew something maybe you didn't want him telling, he might confide in his old counselor—"

"I am this close to giving you a black eye," Brady growled, his fist bunched into a knot.

Tom shook his head. "I know you didn't do this, pal. No matter how you felt about Jason, you would never have jeopardized Lara. But Chief Dixon is going to ask these questions."

"I don't have anything against Jason. Did you tell Dixon about Jason wanting to talk to Lara?"

Tom thought for a second. "I guess so. At the brief-ing. Sure."

"And how many others?"

"I don't know. Half a dozen."

"Any way for Bill Armstrong to have heard the news?"

Tom thought again for a second before saying, "His ex-brother-in-law works in dispatch so I guess it's possible. What are you getting at?"

"I don't know what I'm getting at." Brady took a steadying breath. "How do we know Lara wasn't the real victim?"

"Why would anyone want to shoot her?"

"I don't know. Ask Bill Armstrong where he was tonight."

"Don't start on that. Bill Armstrong wouldn't shoot Jason Briggs."

"Wouldn't he? Your scenario of my not wanting Jason to tell Lara something might also pertain to Armstrong. Maybe there's something Billy told Jason that Armstrong doesn't want Jason telling Lara. Or maybe he just wants to hurt Lara to get back at me."

"Is something going on between you two?"

"No," Brady said. "But he doesn't know that."

Tom looked unconvinced. "We'll talk again tomorrow."

HOW DID YOU FIND a madman when you had no clues? Jason could have made new enemies in juvenile detention, he could have tempted old enemies who heard he was back in town and saw him riding his bike off on his own. Like Brady had. Was he sure there hadn't been a third party trailing him while he trailed Jason? Had he even thought to look?

No, and yet somehow Brady didn't believe that was

the answer. He thought it was as simple as someone not wanting Jason Briggs talking to Lara Kirk.

Why?

Or maybe someone wanted Lara dead and was a lousy shot.

Twenty minutes after leaving the clearing, he entered the emergency-room doors for the first time in almost a year, nodding at the nurse behind the desk as his still-soggy boots squeaked with every step. In lieu of a shirt, which he'd donated to help stem Jason's bleeding, he wore an old jacket he carried on the bike. It was too hot a garment for August.

"Hey, Brady. Long time no see."

"How you doing, Tammy? I'm here to check on Lara Kirk and Jason Briggs."

She frowned for a second. About his own age, she looked ten years older, probably because she smoked like a fiend when no one was watching. Brady had caught her outside a few times and used to tease her about it.

"Ms. Kirk was treated for a superficial gunshot wound in her right arm and was released an hour ago. The Briggs boy is in surgery. It's touch and go."

"I thought Ms. Kirk was going to wait for me," Brady mused aloud, unsure what to do now.

"She got a call and left."

Brady thanked her briskly and took off. Who had called her? Why? What was important enough for her to leave the hospital when she'd made a point of telling him to meet her there? Was it possible she didn't understand the importance of the fact that Jason Briggs wasn't the only one who had been shot tonight?

He got as far as the Harley before feeling a hulking

presence behind him. He turned abruptly and immediately recognized Bill Armstrong emerging from between parked cars.

Armstrong was about the same size as Brady though a couple of years older. He'd been a mechanic since graduating from high school. Married his high-school sweetheart. As far as Brady knew, he'd been doing okay for himself and his family until his daughter committed suicide and a few weeks later, his son died.

Thanks to Brady.

Now word was that Bill Armstrong had taken to drinking, his wife had threatened to leave him and his job was in peril.

"I heard you almost killed another kid tonight," Armstrong said, coming to a halt six feet away from Brady. The overhead lights illuminated the thatch of sandy hair that continued around his face in a trimmed beard.

"You heard wrong," Brady said. He didn't want to waste time with Armstrong, but he didn't want to turn his back on him, either.

"I heard Jason Briggs got shot and that you were there."

Brady waited.

"That little gal who left when you murdered my son is back in Riverport."

"Who told you that?"

He tapped his forehead with a finger. "I just know. Maybe it would have been better for her if she'd stayed away."

Brady advanced a few steps. "She was a counselor to your kids," he said. "She tried to help them. She's an innocent in all this."

Armstrong backed down a little. He looked in the direction of his shoes as he said, "Do you suppose she'd miss you if some concerned citizen took it in his mind to eliminate a public menace?"

Brady's gut tightened. His decision to stop carrying a gun suddenly seemed shortsighted.

"I don't, either," Armstrong said. "But killing you is too easy." His voice caught. "I want you to know what it's like to lose someone you love," Armstrong continued, his eyes moist now. "If you had a son it would be perfect. An eye for an eye. Poetic justice."

"Where were you tonight?" Brady said softly.

Ignoring the question, Armstrong said, "You don't know what it's like to lose a kid."

With total sincerity, Brady said, "I've told you a dozen times how sorry I am about your son. I had no choice. There was no time. He pulled a gun."

Please, God, let that be true...

For a second, Armstrong looked ready to throw his weight at Brady. And then he rocked back on his heels and steadied himself by grabbing the hood of the closest car.

Brady picked his helmet up off the seat. "Stay away from Lara Kirk and Jason Briggs," he said.

Armstrong shook his head. He took a deep breath and glared at Brady. "You're not a cop anymore, Skye. You're a washed-up has-been just like your old man. Maybe the other cops let you off the hook for murdering my kid, but I won't. You'll pay for what you did to me and mine."

"I know," Brady said. "You're going to take me for every dime I have."

The smile that broke Armstrong's face was worse than his sneer. "That'll be a start. We'll see where it ends."

Brady got on the bike and started the engine.

Was Armstrong a grieving man, more bark than bite, or was Brady's gut feeling Lara was in terrible danger more than his guilty conscience at work?

At any rate, he wasn't going to leave her alone tonight. He'd swing by his place and grab a toothbrush and some dry shoes and clothes. Trade the Harley for his truck in case they needed to go somewhere. Like it or not, she had a guard tonight.

WHAT WAS KEEPING Brady?

Lara stood by the front windows, freshly showered, wearing old sweats she'd found in a bottom drawer. She was still cold even though she knew it was a warm night, summer at its apex. When she closed her eyes, the cold river flooded her head.

Before the night was over she would tell Brady what she'd come back to Riverport to tell him.

She'd wanted to tell him forever.

The sitting room, as her mother called the room to the left of the foyer, was typical Victorian with very high ceilings and tall, stately windows. A rose and ivory Oriental carpet, its silk soft against Lara's bare feet, covered the hardwood floor.

"Lara?" Lara turned at the sound of the housekeeper's voice. "Everything is quiet upstairs," Myra added. "I think I'll turn in."

"Of course. Thanks for your help today. I don't know what I would have done without you."

"I wouldn't have missed it for the world. I'm just glad I didn't go on that cruise with your mother like she wanted. I did that once a couple of years ago and if you don't mind my saying, it wasn't much of a vacation for me."

Lara nodded. She could imagine. As Myra left the room, a pair of headlights pulled up in front of the house. Lara recognized Brady's green truck parked under the streetlight and she left the room, headed for the front door, suddenly aware her feet tingled and her palms felt sweaty. She took a deep breath as she pulled open the door.

He looked up as he took the last few steps. He'd obviously taken a shower and changed clothes and in the porch light, dressed in black jeans and a gray Henley, he looked lean, capable and focused.

She stood aside and he entered the house. He paused in the foyer, his gaze traveling up the broad, curved staircase as though looking for an invading army. Then his eyes met hers.

"You left the hospital."

"Myra called. She was having trouble—"

"What kind of trouble?" He covered the few steps between them and caught her arm. She recoiled and he dropped his hand.

"I'm sorry. I forgot about your wound."

"It's okay. There's a huge bandage on it. The doctor said there might be a scar but there was no permanent damage."

"Good. What kind of trouble did the housekeeper have?"

She looked away for a second, then back at him. "It didn't have anything to do with tonight, Brady, honest. I found a cab outside the hospital and took it home. Myra had to pay the man. I'd forgotten I no longer have a purse or a wallet. Do you know how Jason is doing?"

"I called from my place. He's out of surgery, but it's still touch and go."

She nodded. Touch and go. "Poor kid."

They each stared at the floor for a moment, then spoke at the same time.

She said, "Let's go sit down—"

And he said, "I'm staying here tonight—"

They both stopped talking, he turned his hand palm up as if to give her a turn first. She repeated herself. He sat down on the second from bottom step and patted the space next to him.

Lara understood that he felt uncomfortable in her mother's house and was reluctant to stray too far inside.

"You're nervous," he said.

She nodded.

"I want you to know I didn't follow you out to the river. You told me not to come, but I happened to see Jason riding his bike and—"

She put her hand on his arm and he met her eyes. "You saved my life. You saved Jason. How could you think I would resent you being there?"

"Well, you're nervous."

"Not about that."

"And you're angry with me."

"Oh, Brady. It's been a long year." Tears stung the back of her nose and she struggled to keep them out of her eyes and her voice. Though they didn't fall, the emotion behind them must have showed, because he covered her hand with his.

His face was very close. She could smell soap and aftershave and toothpaste. She stared at his lips. Flames licked her groin.

And just like that, their lips drifted together, inevitably, touching in a way that was at once familiar and bittersweet. These lips she'd thought she'd never touch again. Soft and warm with the power of life behind them.

But not for her. Not ever again.

She drew away and took a shaky breath.

"I'm sorry," he said.

"It's me. My emotions are all over the map."

"I won't let it happen again," he added. "I promise you."

She nodded.

"What do you want to tell me?" His hand had slipped from hers.

She bit her lip and finally decided how she should share her news. "Come with me," she said, standing. He stood as well and seemed startled when she led him up the stairs. Was he remembering the first time they'd climbed these stairs together, two and a half years ago when her mother had taken off for the Aegean Sea and Lara had used the opportunity to show him the room in which she'd grown up?

Things like that were impossible when her mom was in the house for the simple reason her mother didn't like Brady. She was one of those people Brady talked about, one of those who based their opinion of him on his family name. To Lara's mother, Brady was and always would be, "One of those worthless Skye boys." Slightly less troublesome than the younger boy, Garrett, but not to be trusted just the same.

She led Brady into her old bedroom. The light was low, the bed was covered in white eyelet just as it had been years before when she lived at home with her mother. Knowing she was coming, Myra had filled vases with roses from the garden and placed them around the room. Their fragrance perfumed the air.

"This is why I rushed home from the hospital," she said softly.

His brow furrowed as he looked at the bed, which suddenly seemed to glow with remembered passion. She moved aside so he could see what occupied the far corner.

So he could see the crib.

"Myra needed help getting Nathan to sleep," she said.

She watched his face as realization dawned. It was like watching the sunrise. He glanced at her and she nodded once, sniffing back tears before they could glisten in her eyes.

He moved toward the crib like a sleepwalker and stood staring down at the slumbering infant within.

Chapter Four

"He was conceived on our wedding night," Lara said. "His name is Nathan."

He had a son?

Just like that? One moment alone in the world, the next moment, a son?

Very slowly, he lowered his hand until the backs of his fingers grazed the baby's round cheek. How could skin be that soft? The baby tucked one tiny fist close to his chin. A bubble blew at his lips and then he made a sudden face, a frown, and scrunched up his tiny body before relaxing again, hands flung to the side.

His son. *Nathan.*

"You named him after your father," he whispered.

"Yes."

Brady kept his gaze glued to the infant because he didn't trust himself to look at Lara. Men usually had a few months to prepare themselves for fatherhood. Time to get used to the idea of a baby, to merge the dreamy possibilities of the future with the uncertainties of the past. Time to reckon.

But she'd deprived him of this.

She hadn't trusted him with the knowledge he was

to become a father. She'd gone through pregnancy and birth and the first three months of his child's life alone rather than trust him.

She's here now, a small voice whispered in the back of his mind. *They're both here now.*

He wasn't ready to listen. He shoved his hands in his pockets as he turned to face her.

Their eyes locked for a heartbeat before she lowered her gaze. "I'm sorry, Brady," she said so softly it might have been his imagination. "I was frightened."

That made it better? Now she not only didn't trust him and didn't like him, she was afraid of him?

"Later," he forced himself to say. He needed time to think.

"I just want you to know I didn't know I was pregnant when I first went away, and when I found out—"

He held up a hand to still her.

The baby made a little noise and Lara leaned over, her shoulder brushing Brady's arm. She grabbed her own arm, wincing, and he remembered her injury and how close he'd come to losing her. Good God, if she'd died tonight, would anyone have bothered to tell him about Nathan?

"Will you lift him for me?" she said, glancing up at him. "Or shall I call Myra?"

Brady blinked a time or two. "I can do it."

"It's easy, just make sure you support his head," she said.

And so he lifted his son for the first time, careful to put one hand behind the little guy's heavy head. The baby kicked and squirmed and Brady held on tight, terrified he'd drop him.

"Relax," Lara said. "You're doing fine."

"What do I do now?"

"Just comfort him, Brady. Hold him closer. Don't be afraid."

He pulled Nathan against his chest, one hand all but covering the small boy's back. He tried making soft noises and bouncing a little. One or the other of these tactics apparently worked because the baby settled down. Brady tipped him away from his chest for a moment, anxious to really look at these few pounds of humanity that had instantly redefined his life.

His throat tightened as he took in every amazing inch of his son's face. The dark orbs as he opened one eye, then the other. The very small nose, the tip of a tiny tongue. What struck him was the baby's total dependence. *Was he ready for this?*

He was still trying to work out his complicated relationship with his own father. What did he know about being a father to an innocent child? How could he teach what he'd never learned?

"Did you hear that?" Lara said, and he opened his eyes abruptly, yanked back from his thoughts.

"Did I hear what?"

"A noise downstairs. Maybe it was Myra."

"I'll go take a look," Brady said.

The door flew open at that moment. The housekeeper, dressed in a voluminous green robe, took one look at them standing by the crib and crossed the room in a half-dozen sturdy steps. "Give me the little lamb," she crooned. Brady looked at Lara, who nodded. Reluctantly, he handed the child over, amazed at how empty his hands and arms suddenly felt.

"I was downstairs in my room," Myra said, expertly wrapping Nathan in a blanket. "I heard breaking glass.

When I went to look, I found the window in the sitting room with a hole—"

Brady left without hearing the rest, taking the stairs two at a time. Armstrong had known Lara was back in town—did he also know about Nathan? He'd talked about an eye for an eye...

"The sitting room is to the right," Lara said. She'd followed him down the stairs. There was no color in her face and her eyes were wide. He moved into the formal Victorian sitting room lit only by a glass-shaded table lamp. Shards of glass lay on the table and carpet and a rock with a paper tied around it had tumbled to a stop on the floor in front of the table.

Myra, still holding Nathan, arrived in the doorway as Lara leaned down to pick up the rock. Brady grabbed her hand. He looked around the room until he spied a small lace doily draped over the armrest of a floral love seat. Using a corner of the doily, he picked up the rock and slipped the paper from beneath the rubber band.

"What does it say?" Lara asked, her voice little more than a whisper.

He angled the paper toward the light. A few words had been cut from a magazine and glued in place. "'Go home before it's too late,'" he read.

"Mrs. Kirk will have a fit when she hears someone broke her window," Myra fumed. She held Nathan against her polyester-covered bosom as though protecting him from the hounds of hell. "What is the world coming to? And that note can't be directed at Lara. It must mean you, Mr. Skye. What trouble have you brought—"

"Get a paper bag big enough for the rock and the note, will you please?" Brady interrupted.

Myra looked from him to Lara. "That's a good idea,"

Lara said, holding out her good arm. Myra very gently placed Nathan in Lara's embrace before leaving the room. Lara's eyes glistened in the dim light as she rested her cheek atop Nathan's fuzzy head.

Brady looked down at his shoes, not trusting his voice. What a sight the two of them made. His wife and his baby son. Her beauty, his innocence, elicited a cavalcade of emotions.

How had things gotten to this point? How had he so thoroughly screwed up?

How had he lost them?

He finally managed to say, "Someone wants you to leave Riverport," and looked at Lara again. She'd closed her eyes as though she couldn't stand to face another moment of this interminable night. She surprised him as she often did. Opening her eyes and pinning him with her gaze, she said, "That's too bad. I'm not going anywhere until I'm damn good and ready."

"Listen to me, Lara. This isn't just about you and me anymore, it's about Nathan now, too. Let me stay the night. Let me—"

"Okay."

"No argument?" he asked, surprised she was agreeing so readily.

"No argument. I'm not a complete idiot. But who would do something like this?" She moved a few inches closer to him and he took comfort that she still found his presence reassuring. "You said Bill Armstrong would try to get back at you. Do you think it was him?"

"I don't know," he hedged. Of course he thought it was Armstrong. But the thought of giving Lara more ammunition to feed the fear behind her eyes just seemed cruel to him.

"Are you going to give the rock and the note to the police?"

"You should give them to the police and report this incident, but I doubt anything will come of it. Maybe Tom could talk to Armstrong, that might help."

"Maybe I could talk to Mr. Armstrong."

Brady looked from Nathan's yawn to Lara's eyes. "No. Absolutely not. The man isn't thinking clearly. Please, stay away from him." He touched Nathan's tiny fist. "Think of this little guy."

She instantly bristled. "I seldom think of anyone else," she said.

He counted to ten under his breath, biting back the words that would just drive them further apart. But whose fault was it she felt alone in parenthood? Sure as hell wasn't his, he hadn't had a choice.

Sure you did. You sent her away.

She yawned, which destroyed the haughty look she'd affected. His defenses immediately fell. "Maybe you should try to get some sleep."

She nodded as she gathered the baby closer. He fought off the desire to wrap his arms around them both. What would he give for an invitation to join her in her bed?

A right arm? A left leg? How about a heart?

"Good night, Brady."

"Good night."

She left as Myra entered, pausing just a second to ask Myra to get Brady a pillow and blanket and anything else he needed for the night. To Brady, it appeared Myra vacillated between delight that he wasn't going back to Lara's room and distress he would still be under the same roof.

Myra crossed the room and handed him the paper bag. He dropped in the rock and the note.

"What do you need for tonight?" Myra snapped. Her constant antagonism was beginning to wear a little thin.

"Not a thing," he told her, relieved when she bustled off, muttering to herself under her breath.

LARA HAD THOUGHT she'd have a terrible time getting to sleep. She'd assumed unconsciousness would bring back those few moments in the submerged car. Plus, the burning pain in her arm made finding a good position to rest almost impossible.

But fall asleep she did and so deeply that she didn't wake until the first light filtered through the bedroom window. As Nathan usually provided the morning get-out-of-bed alarm, she immediately got up and crossed the room to the crib, holding her injured arm against her side. The throbbing started the moment she stood.

"Hey, sleepyhead," she crooned as she approached, her blue nightgown silky against her legs.

The crib was empty. She turned so abruptly she almost tripped on her own feet. Within a few seconds, she'd sprinted through her bedroom door and halfway down the stairs. "Myra," she called, growing more and more frantic at the still, watchful feeling of the house. A million what-ifs? darted through her head.

Myra appeared from the direction of the kitchen, a dishrag in her hand, a finger against her lips. Lara caught herself on the last step. Myra nodded toward the study on the opposite side of the foyer from the sitting room.

Brady sat in the one man-size chair her mother had in the house. Nathan lay against his chest, his father's big hands clutched around his tummy, his head tipped over to one side, like Brady's. They were both sound asleep.

With a jolt that shook her deep inside, Lara stared at the two of them. This was what had been missing for the past three months: the two of them together.

Her husband, Nathan's father. This was the picture that hadn't been taken and tacked in the baby book, the image she'd never dared to contemplate.

"They were down here when I got up this morning," Myra said. "I left well enough alone. I hope that's okay."

"Of course it's okay," Lara said, her heartbeat erratic as she fought a groundswell of inappropriate feelings. Father and son...

"You can't trust him," Myra said very softly. "He's just like his father—"

"No," Lara said succinctly. "No, Myra, he is not just like his father. And more importantly, he is Nathan's daddy. Brady and I aren't together anymore, but that doesn't mean you can be rude to him. If that's too much to ask of you, I'll go to a motel."

"Now, Miss—"

Lara rubbed her forehead. The beginnings of a headache pulsed behind her eyes. "I'm sorry. I shouldn't snap at you. This is more your house than it is mine."

"If he's good enough for you, well, then..." Myra's voice faded as though she couldn't bear to complete the phrase. She cast a raised eyebrow at Lara's scanty nightgown and added, "If you want to get dressed, I'll start breakfast."

"Thanks," Lara said.

She went back upstairs and dressed. Myra appeared

after a few minutes, Nathan in her arms, her face set in yet another frown. "That man took over the cooking," she said.

"He has a way with fried potatoes," Lara said as she started diapering Nathan.

Myra shooed her away. "I'll take care of the angel, you take care of the devil in the kitchen," she snapped.

Lara couldn't help but laugh.

Brady knew exactly how she liked the potatoes, crispy and redolent with onion. He executed their preparation perfectly. They sat across the informal kitchen table from each other without saying much. The trouble wasn't a lack of conversational material, Lara reflected as she buttered her toast. The trouble was there was too much that needed to be said.

The domesticity of sharing a meal, especially breakfast, at a small table in a room filled with homey smells, was daunting. It reminded Lara of other days, of other dreams. A half-dozen times she opened her mouth and closed it without speaking. She owed him an explanation, she knew that, but where to start, how to justify her actions? They'd made sense at the time. Now she wasn't so sure.

"I called the hospital," Brady said.

She looked up. "How's Jason?"

He laid down his fork and picked up the coffee mug. "He's still alive but unconscious. The police have stationed a guard at the boy's door. They want you to come by this morning, to the station, I mean. You need to give them a statement about last night. So do I."

"Okay. It's good about the guard, though, right?"

"It'll keep whoever shot him from finishing the job." He took a swallow of Myra's hair-on-your-chest brew and added, "You might as well know I don't intend to sit around waiting for something else to happen."

"Good. What's step one?"

"Ask questions. Ruffle feathers, starting with Bill Armstrong."

"Is it smart for you to talk to him yourself?"

"Probably not. I don't want to egg him on. I'll get Tom to have a chat with him. And then I intend to question Jason's old girlfriend. Maybe he told her whatever it was he was going to tell you last night. If Armstrong is losing control, the sooner he's stopped, the better."

"I still don't know what he hoped to gain by throwing that rock and making idle threats."

"Maybe they weren't idle threats. Anyway, even though the note had to be thought out ahead of time because of the way it was constructed, I don't think Armstrong really has a plan, I think he's just reacting to everything as it happens." He put the cup down and added, "Do you know this Wylie girl?"

"From the teen center, you mean? I think so. I think she hung out with Jason's sister. There was a small group of girls from the same neighborhood who used to come in together."

Myra stepped into the kitchen. "The little darling went back to sleep," she said. "I swear, Miss Lara, that baby is perfect."

"Even though he's a Skye?" Brady asked with a little of the old glint in his dark eyes.

Lara shot him a warning look.

"As far as I'm concerned, he's a Kirk," Myra said, banging a few pots in the sink.

Attempting to defuse a potential bomb, Lara addressed the surly housekeeper. She'd known the woman wouldn't be able to keep her antagonism at bay. "Do you know the Wylie girl's first name?"

"The older one or the younger one?"

"The one who's sixteen or seventeen?"

"Seventeen. Her name is Karen. The older one is married and lives in Portland. The mother takes in sewing at her house."

"I'm going to drop the note off with Tom and then go talk to Karen Wylie," Brady said, pushing his plate away. "It's summer vacation, maybe she's helping her mother."

"If Myra will watch Nathan for a little while, I'll go with you," Lara said. Maybe alone in a car, Brady and she could begin the delicate business of coming to grips with shared parenthood.

"The girl might feel more comfortable talking to you," Brady said. "But I have to go by work first and make sure everyone is on target."

"Good thing we're getting an early start."

Myra, scraping plates into the sink, looked over her shoulder. "After Nathan's nap, I'll put him in that fancy stroller you brought and we'll go next door to meet my friend, Barb. That would be okay, wouldn't it, Miss Lara?"

Lara could see that Brady was about to come up with a reason that wouldn't be okay, so she quickly jumped in with an answer. "That would be fine."

Brady glowered.

THEY ARRIVED at the Good Neighbors house at the same time as the supply truck filled with used brick. Brady spent a few minutes signing papers and double-checking job assignments before informing his foreman he'd be back later.

The drive out to Tom's place was full of starts and stops conversation wise. Brady could tell Lara was trying to find a way to talk to him about Nathan. He couldn't think of one thing she had to say that he wanted to hear, at least not about how she'd hidden her pregnancy and his baby from him. Not right now.

He'd lingered outside Lara's room most of the night, sitting in an uncomfortable chair so he wouldn't fall asleep. When he'd heard the baby fussing, he'd tiptoed into the room and plucked him from the crib, carrying him down the stairs, anxious for just a few moments alone with the little guy before he was forced to wake Lara to take care of needs Brady wasn't sure how to fill.

But Nathan hadn't kept fussing, he'd calmed right down and been wide awake. There in the study, his knees drawn up to make a lap, Brady had spent the better part of an hour interacting with his son. Eventually, they'd both fallen asleep in the chair. Brady hadn't woken until Lara's voice invaded his dreams.

He'd heard her defending him to the housekeeper. He'd kept his eyes closed, but her words had been comforting. She'd defended him and he didn't want her ruining it now by trotting out a bunch of lame excuses. So he switched on the radio and kept his eyes on the road and eventually she gave up trying to be heard over the country-western station. Fine with him.

Tom lived in a small house at the end of a long driveway. The house, painted white twenty years earlier, was dingy now. There was no garage but there was a large shop that Kenny used to work on cars.

The new red SUV was parked in front of the house. Lara stayed in the truck as Brady knocked on the door. Tom didn't answer, which didn't surprise Brady. He knew from his own shift work that Tom had worked most of the night and would probably sleep away most of the morning.

Brady made a cursory check of the shop just to make sure Tom wasn't out pulling an all-nighter on one of his projects. He saw a dark sedan with the engine hood open and a small car under a tarp, but no Tom. He was halfway back to the truck when the house door opened a crack and Tom looked out.

Brady veered toward the house. Tom, opening the door a few inches, called, "Thought I heard someone pounding on my door."

"Sorry about that," Brady said.

"You been out at the shop?"

"Yeah. Looks like you've got several projects going on out there."

"I like to keep busy."

"What's under the tarp?"

"I'm putting in a new clutch for Caroline," he said, rolling his eyes, his usual reaction when referring to his ex-wife. "Her warranty just ran out. The damn woman drives like a maniac. What brings you out here?"

Brady told him about the night before and his suspicions about who was behind the incident.

"Damn fool," Tom said around a yawn.

"I was going to talk to him—"

Tom shook his head. "Absolutely not. Stay away from Bill Armstrong."

"That's why I'm here," Brady said, jaw clenched. "To ask you to talk to him." His temper was right at the edge, and whether it was there because of lack of sleep or Tom's attitude or tension over Lara, he didn't know.

"Just you stay away from him. After following the

Briggs kid last night, all you need to do is to get in Bill Armstrong's face today. Dixon would love that. Leave it to me. Get Lara to take the rock and note to the station and report the incident so it's on record just in case. And Dixon is expecting you to come in and talk to him."

"I know."

They drove back into town in more silence. Brady made a quick stop to get the glass to fix Lara's mother's window, then parked at the station. They separated at the door. Brady cooled his heels for thirty minutes before Dixon had time to talk to him.

In his fifties, Chief Dixon was as tall as Brady but twenty-five pounds lighter. He sported a beak nose, dangerous little black eyes, thin lips and teeth stained by tobacco.

"Sit down, Skye," Dixon said, using his smoldering cigarette to point at the empty chair across his desk.

Brady leaned against the wall. "This is fine."

Dixon got to his feet, thumbed open a file on his desk, scanned the pages and closed the file. "What were you doing following Jason Briggs?"

Brady repeated his story in as much detail as possible. He knew Dixon had already read the reports and nothing he said was new. The fact he'd spent so many hours less than a year ago standing in this office having similar conversations with Dixon about Billy Armstrong just made the situation all the more uncomfortable.

Dixon led him through his story another time or two. "You're sure you weren't jealous?" Dixon finally said.

"Of what?"

"Of this kid spilling his guts to Lara Kirk instead of you."

"Jealous enough to shoot him and leave her and him both to drown?"

Dixon puffed on his cigarette and didn't blink.

Brady finally said, "No. I wasn't jealous. And I don't carry a gun around, you know that."

Dixon stubbed his cigarette out with Smokey the Bear thoroughness. "Yesterday you told Tom James to watch out for the Kirk woman and the Briggs boy. That was smart. But last night you got creative and put yourself on the scene of an attempted murder. That was dumb, even for you."

Brady pushed himself away from the wall. "If I hadn't 'gotten creative' as you say, you'd have a double homicide on your hands. Two dead bodies instead of two wounded ones. You do know that, right?"

Dixon sprang to his feet and leaned over his desk. "The Riverport Police Department doesn't need help from people like you, *Mr.* Skye."

"People like me," Brady mused. "Oh, you mean people who rescue other people from certain death?"

"What I mean is civilians. Stay away from everyone involved in this case, because it seems a little peculiar you were on hand on two separate occasions when two kids took a bullet. Any more little coincidences and I'll have you sitting in my jail. It wouldn't be the first time I entertained a Skye."

What could you say to that? "What about Bill Armstrong? Has anyone asked him where he was last night?"

"That's none of your business."

Knowing there was nothing to be learned from Dixon, Brady left the office. He was annoyed with himself for letting Dixon goad him into bragging. When he'd first become aware Dixon didn't like him, he'd tried to figure out why. Talk about hitting your head against a brick wall. All he knew was his father and Dixon had a history of sorts and loathed one another.

Apparently, Dixon had taken that hatred and passed it along to his nemesis's sons. There was no way to fight an unreasonable hatred like that, especially when it was your boss. You learned to live with it. After Brady quit, he'd heard tales Dixon took the department out to celebrate.

Lara waited in the lobby and just looking at her did a lot to calm the raging-lava flow in his gut. She carried a plastic bag through which he could see her soggy handbag and one ruined sandal.

"How was Dixon?" she asked once they were back inside the truck.

"Charming as always. Warned me to stay away from everyone connected to the case."

"Will you?"

He flashed her a smile. "Hell, no."

"He hates you."

"And my father."

She touched his arm after checking a few numbers jotted on a paper. "That must be the Wylie house. The yellow one."

Brady pulled up in front of a tiny square tract house. A narrow driveway and a converted garage ran along the east side. A sign over the door of the garage read, Lucinda's Alterations and Original Designs. Another sign announced the place was open for business.

The converted work space was small and cluttered with bolts of fabric, piles of clothing and other sewing paraphernalia. A large worktable held an industrial-looking sewing machine, behind which sat a woman, facing the door. She looked up as they entered, smiled warmly, finished sewing something, snapped the threads and stood. In her mid-forties, her face was thin, her eyes a grayish-blue. Blond hair streaked with silver fell in loose waves.

She stepped out from behind the machine. "Can I help you?"

"Mrs. Wylie?"

"Call me Lucinda," she said. "Everyone does."

Brady introduced Lara and then himself. By now, he knew he should be used to the way people looked twice when he gave his name. Face it, in this town his name would always be linked with Billy Armstrong's death.

But the truth was, he wasn't used to it and Lucinda Wylie's renewed spark of interest as she apparently figured out where she'd heard his name before made him squirm inside his skin. Staying in Riverport was a constant lesson in humility.

"If it's okay with you, we'd like to talk to Karen," Lara said.

Lucinda Wylie's eyes narrowed. "Why?"

"I used to work at the teen center," Lara said. "I knew Sara Armstrong and your daughter and a couple of the other girls."

Lucinda produced a tissue from her apron pocket and dabbed at her eyes. "That was so tragic about Sara. She was such a sweetheart. And her folks. Her mother is a saint, poor woman, and Bill Armstrong is all bluster on the outside and such a sweetheart underneath. The kids all love that man. He used to be like a father to Karen and my older daughter, Joanie. My husband's been gone ten years and, well, Bill was just wonderful with them. To lose Sara like he and Sandra did and then Billy—"

Too late she seemed to realize she was talking in front of the man who had killed Billy. Her gaze shifted uncomfortably in Brady's direction, then down to her feet.

Brady did his best not to look as confused as he felt. In his head, Armstrong didn't fit the teddy-bear image Lucinda described.

"I talked to Jason Briggs for a few minutes last night," Lara said.

Lucinda's brow wrinkled. "Then he's out of detention?"

"Just barely. He had something he wanted to tell me. He mentioned your daughter's name."

Lucinda shook her head. "Karen broke up with Jason while he was in juvie. Frankly, I was glad she did. I thought he was a bad influence on her. Now, I don't know."

"Before he could tell Lara what he wanted, someone took a shot at him," Brady said.

Lucinda gasped. "I didn't know that. Is he okay?"

"He's in the hospital."

Lucinda seemed to shrink. "You don't think Karen had anything to do with—"

"No, of course not," Lara assured her. "I was just hoping Jason might have told Karen why he wanted to see me. Is it okay with you if Brady and I talk to her for a few moments? You're welcome to be present—"

A sharp bark of humorless laughter escaped Lucinda's lips. Her hand flew to cover her mouth. "Okay with me? Karen does what she wants when she wants. She has a job down at the pharmacy. She'll talk to you if she feels like it. Otherwise, wild horses won't be able to drag a word out of her."

"Has she always been—"

"Difficult? Touchy? Secretive?" Lucinda interrupted. "Not always. After Jason got in trouble she kind of changed. After he went to juvie. She hasn't seen him since he got out."

"Are you sure?" Brady asked.

Lucinda's smile was bittersweet. "The only thing I'm sure of is that Karen's headed for trouble if she doesn't straighten herself out. Go ahead, try talking to her. She takes a lunch break about eleven-thirty."

Chapter Five

While Lara fed the baby, Brady fixed the window in the sitting room. He could hear Lara singing to Nathan. The song was a little nursery tune he vaguely recalled and he wondered if his mother had ever sung it to him.

She was gone now, so he'd never know. But even if she hadn't died, it would be a lost cause to ask her. His childhood memories had been soaked up by gin two dozen years before.

If this was the kind of baggage a little song dug up, Brady reflected as he tapped the glass into place, no wonder Lara had hidden her pregnancy from him.

Within an hour, they were both ready to catch Karen Wylie before her break. This time Lara chatted nonstop during the drive, flicking off the radio when he turned it on. To his relief, she seemed more interested in talking about Lucinda Wylie than their current mess.

"That poor woman is in over her head," Lara said as Brady parallel parked a few doors down from the drugstore. He immediately spied Tom's red SUV parked a few spots down and next to it, Bill Armstrong's black truck.

"She's lost control of her kid, that's for sure," Brady

said. What he wanted to do was march down the block and confront Bill Armstrong. His feet fairly itched with the desire to take him that direction. It went against every grain in his body to leave his problems to someone else to fix, even Tom. And doing what Dixon wanted always felt wrong.

But he didn't. His better sense had driven him to involve Tom and he would behave himself. The situation was just so damn frustrating.

"What are you looking at?" Lara asked as her gaze followed his.

"That black truck belongs to Bill Armstrong. Tom is apparently meeting with him. I'm sorry, I lost the thread of what you were saying."

"I was feeling sorry for Lucinda Wylie. Her daughter appears to be running wild."

"Just like my brother did," Brady said, looking at Lara. The truth was, the sight of her was no more comforting than the sight of Armstrong's truck. He was as powerless to touch her as he was Armstrong. "The difference is my parents didn't care when Garrett went off the deep end," he added.

"But *you* did," Lara said softly.

"Someone had to bail him out of trouble."

"And so it was you."

"Who else was there?"

"Have you heard from Garrett since, well, in the last year?"

"Not a word. Which one of us should quiz Karen?"

Lara opened her door but looked back at him. "Let's play it by ear."

Karen, a shorter, rounder version of her mother, stood behind a counter ringing up greeting cards for a woman with two little boys clinging to her legs. As soon as the mother and children left, Brady and Lara approached her. Karen met his gaze and immediately looked around the store as though making sure the pharmacist wasn't watching.

"You recognize me, don't you?" Brady asked.

She nodded. She had a plump, pretty face with pink pouty lips and hair bleached to platinum with black roots.

"I'd like to ask you a few questions," Brady said.

The girl looked from him to Lara and back again. "You ain't a cop no more," she said while biting her chewed-off thumbnail. "I don't have to answer your questions."

"No, you don't. That's true. Did you know your boyfriend, Jason Briggs, was—"

She stopped gnawing on her nail. "Jason ain't my boyfriend. We broke up months ago."

"I'm sorry, I meant to say your ex-boyfriend," Brady said calmly.

She shrugged. She wore a tight pink camisole under her pharmacy coat and a heart suspended on a silver chain. Brady suspected Lucinda Wylie was right to worry about her youngest daughter.

"How about we treat you to lunch?" Lara said.

"I ain't going to lunch. I'm on a diet."

"We really do need to ask you a few questions about Jason. You know he's in the hospital, don't you?"

Her heavily made-up eyes widened. "What happened to him? I saw him riding his bike yesterday. He looked okay."

"Someone shot him last night," Brady said.

The girl's knuckles turned white as she gripped the counter harder. "I didn't know. Is he going to be okay?"

"I hope so," Brady said. "But right now his condition is serious."

The front door opened to admit three people. One was a teenage boy who greeted Karen by name, the others were an older couple who made their way to the back of the store to the prescription counter.

"I gotta get back to work now," Karen said. "If Mr. Jones sees me standing around talking, he'll fire me. You guys should leave."

"It'll only take a second. Did Jason talk to you after he got out of detention?"

She shrugged. "Kind of. So what?"

Lara's voice was matter-of-fact as she said, "Did he mention he was going to see me last night?"

Karen shrugged again. "Maybe."

"Did he tell you why?"

The boy approached the counter, his gaze glued to Karen. She flashed him a million-watt smile and turned back to Lara. "I told you, I got to work now."

"How about we meet you after work?" Lara asked. "We'll buy you a cold drink next door. We'll only take five minutes of your time."

The teen put a pack of gum on the counter and pushed it toward Karen.

"Okay, whatever," Karen said, her eyes now on the boy.

"What time?" Brady asked.

"Three o'clock," she said. "I'll meet you next door."

"We'll be there," Lara said.

MYRA HAD ALREADY DONE the dishes, given the baby a bath and put on a load of laundry, so there wasn't much for Lara to do. Living this way was a far cry from her life up in Seattle where nothing got done unless she did it. It did lend insight as to why her mother traveled so much, however. With Myra taking care of the home front it was either travel or join clubs, and her mother wasn't one for community service.

With no chores to do, Lara called the hospital and got a very terse reply to her question about Jason's condition. "No change," is what the nurse on duty said. It was clear that was all she would say.

Lara spent the next hour on the phone with the towing and insurance companies. The car was less than a month old and was a complete write-off. Good thing she had a great policy. She was assured a rental would be delivered later that day, which she could use until she bought a replacement.

Money was never much of an issue for Lara seeing as she had inherited a sizable trust from her father when she turned twenty-one. Her mother had hinted the trust was the main reason Brady had wanted to marry her. Lara had always known that wasn't true. Men like Brady didn't live off their women.

Since Brady had taken off to check in on his construction project, Lara settled Nathan on a blanket under the tall trees in the side yard. It was so hot she stripped him down to his diaper and he reacted as he usually did to little or no clothes by kicking his legs. She leaned over him and talked nonsense, delighting in his drooly smiles as he grabbed fistfuls of her hair and squealed with delight.

She finally lay back on the blanket and closed her eyes. Her arm throbbed in time with her heartbeat.

How much longer should she stay in Riverport?

It had been less than twenty-four hours since she'd

shared news of Nathan's existence with Brady. How could she now even think of taking him three hours away? But how could she stay in Riverport and live this close to the daily temptation of Brady Skye?

She'd been worried he would misread her coming back to town as an attempt at reconciliation. That couldn't happen, she wouldn't allow it to happen. Feelings didn't matter at times, and one of those times was when trying to make a long-term decision that impacted an innocent child. Brady couldn't even hold a real conversation with her. His instinct to avoid confrontation had him turning up the radio and changing the subject every time she tried to broach their very real problems.

He thought he was protecting her, but it felt like isolation.

She understood where he was coming from. He'd grown up holding everyone in his family together by the sheer force of his will. He'd presented his family's public face to the world and even though it hadn't fooled anyone, he'd kept it up long after his family fell apart.

But her role now was tricky. Tricky to remain impassive when her heart leaped in her chest if he looked at her a certain way. Tricky to stand close to him without leaning, tricky to be near him, to share Nathan without entertaining foolish dreams.

She sat up abruptly and hugged her knees as she studied her drowsy son. She'd told herself she was enough for him, she would be his world, he would be hers. And now she admitted the fallacy of this conclusion. Nathan had a father. And Brady wasn't the kind of man to settle for infrequent visits.

Which, face it, was the real reason she'd put this off for so long. She'd been waiting until she felt strong enough to face Brady and not fold.

Brady, Brady, Brady. She was suddenly very annoyed with the direction her thoughts always seemed to drift.

Better she should keep her mind on the bullet last night. On the broken window and the threat. Better she should remember someone had tried to kill Jason and had left her and the boy to drown. Why? What could Jason possibly have to say to her that deserved this kind of reaction and from whom? There had to be a reason.

Was Brady right? Was the culprit Bill Armstrong? Again, why?

Jason had been safely kept in detention since the accident. He'd only been out for a day or two when he was shot. Had that been Bill Armstrong's first opportunity to get at the boy he blamed for his son's death?

But Bill didn't blame Jason. According to Brady, he blamed Brady. He wanted to get back at Brady. And Brady was spending time with Lara. He'd shown up at the house minutes after she arrived in town yesterday and his truck had been parked outside last night when the rock sailed through the window. Maybe the bullets had been intended for her and not Jason. Maybe Jason was just a hapless bystander.

Her gaze traveled from the small dock built out over the river, to the heavily shaded gardens to the nearby road. At that moment, a black truck passed, going so slowly it had three cars backed up behind it.

Bill Armstrong drove a black truck.

So did dozens of other Riverport citizens.

Nevertheless, a chill ran down Lara's spine. The yard no longer felt like a sanctuary. She carefully scooped up Nathan. Holding him close to her chest, she hurried back inside while the black truck and its stream of followers continued down the road.

THEY SLID into a booth at exactly five minutes before three. At ten minutes after the hour, they faced the fact that Karen Wylie wasn't coming.

"Why would she skip out on us?" Lara asked, pushing away her untouched ice tea. They'd been discussing all the things Lara had thought about out in the yard—well, most of the things. She'd left out the personal stuff.

And she'd left out being spooked by a black truck. That was just too embarrassing to admit.

Brady drained his glass and put a five on the table. "Let's go find out."

They walked next door to find an older woman standing at the counter. While Brady looked around the pharmacy, Lara waited in line. The woman was a contemporary of Lara's mother, a woman in her fifties with bright red hair. She claimed she didn't have the slightest idea where Karen went, just that she'd been called in on her day off.

Brady was in the back, talking to the pharmacist. Hayden Jones had been filling prescriptions since before Lara was born. She started to make her way back as Brady shook Hayden's hand and met her midway. Taking her elbow, he guided her out onto the sidewalk. "Karen quit," he said, leaning down to talk close to her ear. He must have felt her startled response, for he pulled her against the building so pedestrians could pass them by.

Her response had been twofold. The news Karen was gone and the proximity of Brady's lips to her ear.

"She quit? Did Mr. Jones say why?"

"No. He said he saw her talking to us earlier today. After we left, she used the phone and then ten minutes later she told him she was quitting and proved it by walking out the door."

"Yet when we were there, she was worried talking to us might get her fired."

"Let's go talk to her mother."

This time the silence in the truck was fraught with an underlying tension that had nothing to do with their personal situation. For the second time that day, they entered the converted garage. As before, Lucinda Wylie looked up from her sewing machine. This time her smile of welcome faded a little when she saw who it was.

"She won't talk to you, huh? Well, don't look at me. I already told you I can't get her to do a damn thing she doesn't want to do."

"Is she here?" Lara asked. "Is she inside the house?"

"She's at work," Lucinda said, eyes narrowing. "Didn't you go there to talk to her?"

"She was kind of evasive. She finally agreed to meet us after work at three o'clock."

"That's news to me," Lucinda said as her gaze darted to the wall clock. It was almost four.

"She didn't show up," Brady said. "Hayden Jones said she left work before noon. In fact, she quit."

Lucinda immediately stood up, irritation erasing her weariness. "She quit? I can't believe she'd quit after everything I went through to get her hired on down there." She marched determinedly out from behind the sewing machine and across the room, opening the door with a vengeance. She crossed the driveway and climbed the two stairs to the backdoor of her small house, disappearing inside without a backward glance at Lara or Brady. The screen door slammed in her wake.

"She's not here," Lucinda said a moment later as she stared through the screen.

Brady crossed the driveway. "Can you tell if she came home after she left work?" he asked.

"Come in while I look," Lucinda said.

They stood in the neat, tiny kitchen while Lucinda opened a closet door and then went down a short hall. She reappeared in a moment. "She's been home. Her smock is on her floor as usual."

"Anything missing?" Brady asked. "A suitcase, clothes, money?"

"She doesn't have any money," Lucinda said, but as she spoke, she crossed to the closet and opened it again, this time taking out her handbag. She opened her wallet and groaned. "She took the hundred dollars I had in here for groceries."

"Look for her suitcase," Brady urged.

Muttering under her breath, Lucinda disappeared down the hall again. She came back a few minutes later empty handed. "The suitcase is gone. So are some of her clothes. Where did she go?"

"There was a boy in the pharmacy she seemed to know," Lara said. "About her age, tall and kind of skinny."

"You just described half the boys in this town," Lucinda said.

"Did she leave a note?" Brady asked.

Lucinda checked the chalkboard by the refrigerator. "This is where we always leave notes to one another. There's nothing here."

"Call her friends," Brady urged. "If you can't track her down, call the police. She's underage, get them to keep an eye out for her. I'll drive around and see what I can find."

"What did you two say to her?" Lucinda demanded.

"Just what we talked about with you," Lara said. "She was working and she didn't want to talk."

"But she ran away right after you spoke with her, isn't that what you said?"

"After she made a phone call," Brady answered.

Lucinda narrowed her eyes. "She hasn't been the same since Billy Armstrong was killed and Jason went away." This time, she uttered the comments without flinching, meeting Brady's gaze head-on as though challenging him to contradict her. Brady said nothing. Lara had to bite her lip to keep from leaping to his defense.

"Start calling around," Brady said. "I'll leave you my cell number."

THOUGH LARA HAD WANTED to come with him, Brady had convinced her that her place was at her mother's house with Nathan. He knew she was worried about Karen and what role their questions had played in her decision to bolt. Hell, so was he.

For a second, he just sat and stared at nothing. What was happening? How much danger was Lara really in? And Nathan? Wasn't any danger too much?

He wondered how Tom's talk with Armstrong had gone. Had Armstrong admitted anything, like cutting little words out of magazines and gluing them to paper?

Though it was almost an hour before the start of his shift, Tom's SUV was parked at the station. No way was

Brady going to risk running into Chief Dixon or anyone else for that matter. He'd talk to Tom later.

For an hour, he drove up and down every street in Riverport, looking for a bleached-blond teenager carrying a suitcase. Eventually, drenched with sweat and out of sorts, he pulled to the curb and stared at the street.

Why had Karen Wylie taken her mother's money and run out without even leaving a note? A suitcase implied an extended absence. Maybe she was taking a trip. The only way out of Riverport, besides private transportation, was by bus. Could she have taken the afternoon bus out of town?

Brady drove to the station, a narrow building sandwiched between other narrow buildings. The place only opened up when a bus arrived or departed. Brady lucked out. A bus had just pulled up outside and two or three passengers were disembarking, their wilted expressions reflecting the change from the air-conditioning inside the bus to the hundred-degree sidewalk temperature outside.

He went through the glass door into a room furnished in old plastic chairs and little else. A man who looked a decade beyond retirement age glanced up from his seat behind the grille at the ticket counter. Marking his place in a paperback book with a gnarled finger, he said, "Next bus to the coast leaves in ten minutes."

"When did the last bus leave?"

"That would be the twelve-fifteen, going the other direction to Portland. Say, aren't you that cop who was in the paper last year? Brady something. Skye. Brady Skye. I knew your granddad."

Brady trotted out one of his leftover police-issue smiles. His grandfather had been an upstanding member of the community, or so the community had thought. In truth, he'd been a gambler. Addiction ran heavy in the Skye family. It was why Brady never bought himself a beer or a lottery ticket. He hoped Garrett had the brains to do the same.

"I'm wondering if a girl purchased a ticket. Using cash, probably. Seventeen, bleached hair—"

"Looked twenty-five?" the old man interrupted.

Brady nodded.

"She sure did."

"Was she alone?"

"She was the one and only passenger, period," he said.

"Was the bus full?"

The old man shrugged. "Couldn't say. I never went out and looked. No one got off in Riverport."

"Did she buy a ticket all the way to Portland?"

"Yeah. 'Course, the bus stops at St. George and Scottsdell first."

Brady looked at the posted time schedule and then the wall clock. The bus had disgorged its Portland passengers a half hour before.

His thoughts were all over the place as he left the station. Now came the unpleasant task of telling Lucinda Wylie her daughter had left Riverport on a bus bound for Portland.

The question was, who was she running from? Or who was she running to? And, just as important, did her running away have anything to do with Jason Briggs's shooting? In other words, did Karen have anything to do with Jason's shooting or did she know who did?

He looked up just in time to see Bill Armstrong's black truck turn the near corner.

Chapter Six

"You scared her off somehow," Lucinda Wylie said for the fourth time, each repetition louder and more strident than the one before. "You find her."

Once again, Lara looked up and down the lazy evening street as she said, "Lucinda, come inside my mother's house and let me make you a cup of tea or pour you a glass of wine. Something. I don't know when Brady will be back. I don't like standing out here."

And she didn't. But Lucinda didn't even seem to hear her, she was too caught up in her own angst. Lara couldn't shake the feeling someone was watching. She'd been feeling that way all afternoon, ever since she allowed herself to get spooked by the black truck that had passed the house slowly. Even after she reminded herself Mr. Crowley lived a few doors down and always drove his black truck as though he was leading a funeral procession, the feeling had lingered.

Anxiety had nothing to do with rationale.

She repeated, "Please, come inside to wait."

"No, thank you," Lucinda said crisply. "The police

said they don't know if Karen got off the bus in Portland or somewhere before that. They said she left of her own free will and it's not a crime."

She'd said all this before, too. Lara fought the desire to yank the woman into the foyer or slam the door in her face. Instead, she tried to remember some of her counseling training. This woman needed help.

Before she could decide what to do next, Lucinda was off and running again. "The driver made a head count after each stop, but he has a schedule to keep, they said, so he would just keep going even if not everyone who was supposed to get on the bus didn't get on. If he did make note of someone not getting back on the bus, it would go to the bus line's head office in Arizona somewhere and it could take days—"

Lara grabbed Lucinda's hand. The woman was on the verge of hysteria. Lara said, "The police know Karen left. Eventually they'll look for her. Come inside and wait for Brady."

Both women turned as Brady's green truck rolled to a stop behind the new rental the leasing company had delivered an hour before. Thank heavens, Lara thought, sighing with relief. Even Lucinda looked hopeful.

It was seven o'clock, the night was warm and sticky, and as Brady walked across the lawn, he looked preoccupied. Lara felt a jab behind her ribs. The simple fact was her pleasure at seeing him surpassed just wanting him to deal with Lucinda Wylie.

He perked up a little when he met Lara's gaze and she chided herself. No matter how she struggled to keep her emotions to herself, she knew there were times he sensed exactly how she felt. It had always been like that between them and until a day ago, it hadn't mattered, at least not to her. She'd never kept secrets from Brady.

Okay, not true. She'd kept a whopper, but not while living in the same town with him.

"Have you heard from Karen?" he asked, turning his attention to Lucinda as he jogged the last few feet.

Lucinda, lips compressed into a straight line, said, "I'll tell you what I told her. You two scared my kid into leaving town, you find her and bring her back."

To Lara's amazement, Brady said, "I'll try."

Lara opened her mouth to protest, but one look at Brady convinced her otherwise. Who was she to ask him not to go? He felt responsible for the teen's abrupt departure from Riverport. So did she.

Lucinda said, "Oh, thank you, thank you. I was going to ask Bill Armstrong to go but he's not home. I don't know who else to ask." She began repeating what the police had told her and Brady listened as though he didn't know their procedures by heart.

"I'll go to St. George and Scottsdell and look around," Brady said. "Once the police figure out Karen was Jason Briggs's old girlfriend, I have a feeling their interest in her whereabouts will pick up and they'll try harder to find her. Until then, I'll do what I can, but I'm not promising anything."

Lucinda visually bit back tears. "I know she didn't hurt anyone."

Brady walked Lucinda to her car and came back to Lara shaking his head. She took his hand and pulled him inside the quiet house. Nathan was asleep, Myra was on watch. She sighed as the door shut behind them, glad to get behind a closed door.

"Where have you been?" she asked.

A smile chased away a little of his fatigue. "Were you worried about me?"

It was on the tip of her tongue to deny it, but she nodded instead.

"What's wrong?" he said, narrowing his eyes. "Something has you spooked. Was it Lucinda?"

"She's been out there threatening things for the past half hour."

"She's worried—"

"I know. I'm worried, too. Plus, there's this feeling I have. I don't know." Her voice trailed off.

He said, "What feeling? What aren't you telling me?"

"It's nothing. Just a feeling that someone is watching. Waiting."

"Did you see anyone?"

"Not really. I told you, it's just a feeling." She touched her bandaged arm. "I got spooked, is all."

"Maybe I shouldn't leave tonight."

"No, you should go. We have to try to help Lucinda and Karen. The thought of that kid out there alone makes me sick. She thinks she's so grown up."

"I know."

Anxious to get things back on an even keel before he left, she said, "What did you do this afternoon?"

"I asked around. Found out about the bus, told the cops. The police have asked the St. George, Scottsdell and Portland cops to keep an eye out for Karen, but it's a long shot. It's anyone's guess at this point if she got off the bus between here and the city and drove off with someone she went to meet, or went all the way to Portland and disappeared into the crowds there."

"Maybe she was going to meet someone who lives in St. George or Scottsdell."

"Maybe, but that means she wasted a lot of money on a ticket she didn't plan to use."

"Maybe the point was to throw her mother off."

"Maybe."

"Why are you going tonight? What do you hope to accomplish?"

"Frankly, I can't think what else to do." He stared at her a second before adding, "I'd like to have a few minutes with Nathan first. He and I kind of started getting to know one another during the night. Is it okay if I go find him?"

"You don't have to ask me if it's okay if you visit with your own son," she said.

"I wasn't sure."

They stood face-to-face in the cool foyer. She studied his face with an impersonal eye. Yesterday, after an absence of a year, he'd seemed a stranger to her. Today he was familiar again, the last year seemed to have passed in a haze.

He came a step closer, banishing the concept of semidetachment. "Last night I promised I wouldn't kiss you again," he whispered. "Now I wish I hadn't made that promise." His fingertips brushed her thighs as he touched her hands. Could he feel the little sparks that passed between them?

"I miss you, Lara, and damn it, you miss me, too, don't you?"

"That's not the point," she said.

"That's not the point? Our need for each other isn't the point?"

"No."

"You're going to have to explain that to me."

She didn't know how to explain it, not when it was

taking every ounce of willpower she had to stay on her feet and not melt into his arms.

The big clock right behind Lara ticked away the seconds. She forced herself to say, "Eventually, we have to have a real conversation about Nathan. We have to figure out how to share him."

"Share him without sharing each other, you mean."

"Don't make this harder than it already is, Brady."

He swallowed hard. "Okay. Your rules."

"I tried to tell you yesterday that I didn't come here to get back together. I came to correct the wrong I made. When you stop being so angry with me, we'll talk."

They both became aware of footsteps on the stairs and turned to find Myra descending, carrying Nathan. The baby's cheeks were flushed from sleep. His fist, crammed into his mouth, muffled the little whimpering sounds he made when he woke up hungry.

Brady said, "Hey, little man, what's wrong?"

At the sound of his father's voice, Nathan's grumblings disappeared.

Brady held out his hands and Nathan kicked his feet in anticipation.

Myra stepped off the stairs, glanced at Lara, and relented. Brady gently took the baby. Myra traveled on toward the kitchen, casting a surly frown over one shoulder.

Brady made a face at Nathan and the baby laughed.

"That's the first time he's ever done that," she said, kissing Nathan's bare foot.

"Laughed? Well, maybe some of his good taste will rub off on his momma." He snuggled Nathan, who gurgled again, a deep sound that for pure joy rivaled any sound Lara had ever heard. Brady was a natural.

She'd wondered, of course. She'd heard the horror stories of his youth, she knew how he'd struggled with two drunks as parents and a brother running out of control. But watching him now she decided there must have been some good years, too. Years when he and Garrett were babies and their parents weren't so dysfunctional.

Or was it all Brady, did it all come from his instincts, his heart, his love?

Clutching the baby firmly in his big hands, he held him a few inches over his own head and then lowered him close enough to kiss, and all the while he talked. He told the baby about his day, about the conversations he'd held with various people, about his plans for the evening, including Lara in the proceedings with occasional glances and comments about Mommy.

Brady had gone from lover to father in the beat of a heart. It was disconcerting.

And just the kind of thing Lara knew she had to steel herself against. It was no secret to her that she still found Brady Skye beguiling. That she still lusted after him and dreamed about him, and wished a hundred times a day he wanted a woman to share his life with, the good and the bad, and not packed away in tissue paper.

"Humor me and stay away from the windows tonight," Brady said as he finally handed back a cooing Nathan. As soon as Lara touched him, the baby started whimpering again, his hunger reawakened. She held him very close as though the sweet nearness of him could protect her from both his father's charms and his scary warnings.

Brady's eyes met hers as he added, "Don't wait up."

THE DRIVE WAS a fool's errand and was made as much to get away from the entanglements in his personal life as it was with any real hope he'd find Karen Wylie.

He drove slowly through both small towns and then on to Portland where he checked out the bus station and hoped to hell the kid was off the black streets.

On the drive back to Riverport, he organized his thoughts into a string of events. Jason, out of detention, calls Lara. Lara comes back to town to speak with the boy. Someone shoots Jason and wings Lara. Armstrong makes threats, reveals he knows Lara's back in town. The rock, the threat. A very brief talk with Jason's ex-girlfriend. The girlfriend makes a call, steals money from her mother and bolts.

Why?

The most likely reason—Karen Wylie knew something about the shooting that made her nervous.

He thought again about her reaction upon learning Jason had been shot. Damn, he'd bet money her reaction had been genuine. She'd looked and acted stunned.

So, did someone think she knew something?

Or did she think she knew who was responsible and she was afraid of them?

There were too many variables. He wasn't sure.

It was two in the morning when he drove back into Riverport. There was really no reason to detour past the Kirk house as Tom had said they'd have someone drive by it every hour or so. He did anyway.

Lara had apparently pulled the rental car into her mother's garage. All the lights were off. Brady glanced down the side street and kept going. He circled the block and parked. He got out of his truck. He wore black jeans, a black T-shirt. He closed the door quietly and walked down the alley, eyes and ears adjusting, blending into the dark.

He wasn't sure why he was out here skulking around, just that there was no better way to find someone where they shouldn't be than by being there yourself. He stood in the cross street on a stretch of black pavement. There was no traffic. Nothing moved in the heavy air. No sounds, not even a dog or the nearby river.

As he watched, a light flicked on somewhere on the second floor. He took out his cell phone and dialed Lara.

She answered on the second ring. "Brady?"

"Yeah, it's me."

"Where are you?"

"Outside. No, don't draw back the curtain. Are you okay?"

"I'm fine."

"Is Nathan right there with you?"

"Yes. In fact, he's in bed with me. I think I have you to thank for his sudden desire for middle of the night tête-à-têtes."

"How about the housekeeper?"

"I heard her use the bathroom a little while ago. Brady, what's going on?"

Brady rubbed between his eyes. He stared at the house and the grounds for what seemed a week. Nothing moved. He finally said, "Give Nathan a kiss for me and try to get some sleep. I'll talk to you tomorrow."

"Brady?"

"It's okay. Honest." He clicked off the phone. As he slipped it into his pocket, he heard an engine rev. Bright lights shone all around him.

He turned to find a vehicle approaching with the speed of a tornado. He barely had time to jump to the side. The roar behind him convinced him to keep going. The vehicle jumped the curb. Brady kept running, not daring to look back, diving into the hedge in front of the neighbor's house. The headlights blinded him as the vehicle missed him and the bushes by inches. Brady pushed himself up off the ground. He'd fallen against a water spigot and banged his elbow. His right knee had apparently hit the edge of a brick as the denim was torn and bloody. He peered through the leaves in time to see two red taillights disappearing down the street.

He sat up, fighting to catch his breath. Lights flicked on in the house in whose hedge he squatted. After a few moments, the porch light came on and the door opened. Pajama bottoms and slippers shuffled into view. After a minute or two, the homeowner stepped back into the house, slammed the door and pushed the dead bolt home. Brady waited until the lights went off again before finally moving out of the hedge. Limping, he made his way across the street.

Lara opened the door before he could knock. He fell into her arms.

WAKING UP in Lara's bed wasn't the treat Brady knew it could be. Of course, the fact she wasn't in bed beside him might have something to do with that. She entered the room and sat down on the bed, flopping a paper bag on the floor.

"How do you feel this morning?"

Thinking of the way she'd so gently sponged off and bandaged his wounds the night before, the way her eyes had softened as she'd tucked him between her sheets, he said, "Hopeful."

"I thought you said you didn't find out a trace of Karen last night."

He stared at her a second and let it be. "I didn't. What's in the bag?"

"I used your keys to go to your place. You needed clean clothes," she said. "Then I went to the store and bought a new car seat for Nathan."

"You went out alone? After what happened to me in front of your house last night?"

"Yes. And I returned to tell the tale. Stop being so damn protective."

"How'd you know where I live?"

"I drove out to the house you're working on first and asked your foreman. He didn't know, so I called Tom and he told me."

"You didn't say anything about last night to Tom—"

"You asked me not to, so I didn't. I still think you should tell him."

"And explain why I was standing in the middle of the street in the middle of the night? No, thanks. I didn't see what kind of car or truck tried to run me down."

"Maybe there are tracks on the neighbor's lawn—"

"No," he repeated. "It could have been some plastered kid."

She narrowed her eyes. "You know it wasn't some kid."

"No, sweetheart, I don't know it wasn't some kid. Okay, it was probably Armstrong, but there's no way to know for sure."

"I give up. By the way, your foreman said he can handle things at the house today."

"Where's Nathan?"

"With Myra. If you get dressed quickly, I'll let you come with him and me to St. George and Scottsdell. I agree with you, there's no point trying Portland. It's too big. Let the police handle it."

He'd made the mistake of telling her he wanted to go back to the smaller towns at the same time of day the bus went through. It now appeared she'd commandeered the trip. He glanced at the bedside clock. Past eleven. He hadn't slept this late in years.

As Lara stood up, he threw back the covers. She didn't flinch despite the fact he wore nothing but his boxer shorts. Of course, it wasn't as though she hadn't seen him in a lot less than that.

"I think I should go alone," he said, pulling his jeans gingerly over the bandage covering his knee and getting to his feet to button them. Besides his knee, there were a few other scrapes on his legs and some blossoming bruises, but all in all, not as bad as he'd feared. "You and Nathan will be safer here—"

"Knock it off," she said, meeting his gaze straight on.

How could she resist him? That's what bugged him. Standing there so close one tiny nudge would have them touching, the energy between them so vibrant it burned away her flimsy dress. The memories so hot they sizzled.

She walked to the door and looked back over her shoulder. "You have fifteen minutes until breakfast is ready."

And then she was gone.

Chapter Seven

Thanks to the twisty river road, the bus never got up to speed. As Nathan dozed off in the back, secure in his brand-new baby seat, they discussed the right way to go about things. Lara finally admitted it made sense that one of them stay with Nathan and the car while the other scouted the area around each stop.

Brady's hope was that someone from the day before would be around today and that this someone might have noticed Karen Wylie. The police would talk to the bus driver when they located him, and eventually they'd do what Brady was doing, but Brady had a gut feeling time was of the essence.

The St. George stop was a coffee shop. After learning from the driver that he hadn't driven this route the day before, Brady followed the one departing passenger into the restaurant. The solitary waitress had been on duty the day before, but she didn't remember anyone getting off the bus. Brady talked to the busboy and even the cook, then he went outside as the bus pulled away from the curb.

He walked across the street and talked to the guy at the gas station, then into a small store where the clerk barely looked up from her magazine to answer a few questions. Outside again, he looked up and down the deserted street and couldn't think of anything else to do.

They caught up with the bus again five miles outside of St. George and followed it into Scottsdell where it stopped at a station even smaller than the one in Riverport. Nathan had woken up and was hungry, so while Lara nursed him, Brady got out of the car.

The driver had the baggage compartment open for the two passengers disembarking and the three catching the bus. Brady looked around to see who he might question. He'd start with the bead shop next to the station.

The woman in the bead store hadn't noticed the bus the day before for the simple fact she'd been closed. He tried a couple of other stores, back on the hot sidewalk a few minutes later. The bus was pulling away from the curb again and Brady was batting zero.

He spied a man standing on the far corner holding a sign. He approached, a few bills in his hand.

The sign said, "Out of gas, please help me get home to San Francisco."

"So, you're stranded here in Scottsdell, huh?" Brady said, stopping in front of the young man. He had longish brown hair and wore clothes the thrift shops would turn away. He smelled like old smoke, beer and culverts.

Looking at the money in Brady's hand, the man said, "I don't really have a car. But you're right, I am stuck."

Brady hadn't expected honesty. He handed over the money, which was pocketed with a mumbled thanks.

Brady finally said, "Were you standing out here yesterday?"

"And the day before that."

"Did you notice the bus come in?"

"You a cop?"

"Not anymore."

"Anyone in trouble?"

Brady shrugged. "Not really. A kid ran off and the mother is worried. That's all."

"A girl about nineteen or twenty?"

Brady's heart kicked up a few beats. "Close enough."

"Bleached hair."

"That's the one."

"I noticed her."

"Can you tell me what she did?"

The man narrowed his eyes. "She's in no trouble?"

"Not yet."

"She got off the bus carrying a little suitcase. I noticed it because she hadn't stowed it in the luggage compartment like the other lady who got off. The girl looked around, crossed the street and nodded at me."

"Did she say anything?"

"Nope. She waited on the next corner till the bus took off."

"And—"

"She stood there."

"For how long?"

"Don't know. Awhile. Then she started walking down toward the river."

"Did you watch her?"

"Yeah. There wasn't a lot else going on. I watched her until she got down near that warehouse."

Brady shaded his eyes. He could just see the dilapidated fence surrounding a large, low building. Vines baked to a brittle brown still clung to the fence.

"I looked away 'cause a car came up and a guy gave me a ten. By the time I looked back, the girl was gone."

"What do you mean, gone?"

"I couldn't see her anymore. I figured she caught a ride or something."

"And you didn't see her again."

"Nope. Listen, I don't want to get the kid in trouble. I say live and let live."

"And that's why I'm looking for her," Brady said.

As he walked back to the car, he wondered what had prompted him to spin the man's comment the way he had. Was he really afraid for Karen Wylie's life?

The answer was yes. In his years as a cop he'd learned to listen to his instincts and his instincts now were screaming at him to pin down this kid's location.

He looked up from these unsettling thoughts to find Lara had gotten out of the car with Nathan. She was perched against the hood, shaded by an old walnut tree. She held the baby close. He couldn't hear anything, but from the way her lips moved and her body swayed, he could tell she was singing to the baby.

The sight of the two of them caused a tiny fist to squeeze a drop of blood out of his heart.

"Karen got off the bus here and walked down near that warehouse," he told her, reaching for Nathan. She handed him the baby, who gurgled at Brady. "Let's walk down there and take a look," he added.

The three of them made their way five or six blocks down to the warehouse. Despite the heat and Brady's concern for Karen Wylie, that walk was one of the better walks Brady had ever taken. He loved the way Lara's stride matched his and he loved the soft weight of his son cradled in his arms. In a perfect world, they could have just kept walking, forever, maybe. That would have been fine with him.

They found a locked-up building plastered with several No Trespassing signs. Most of the windows appeared to be broken. The grounds were surrounded by a fence from which hung a very old-looking padlock.

Brady looked in a 360-degree circle, hoping to find someone else who might have seen Karen.

"How about that house across the street?" Lara said.

The Craftsman-style house looked as old as the warehouse. As they crossed the street, the door opened and an elderly woman wearing baggy hose and very large eyeglasses stepped onto her porch. "I saw you up there talking to that bum," she said by way of greeting. "He's been there all week. By now he could have bought a car with all the money suckers like you hand over."

Lara kind of froze in her tracks. Brady grinned. The woman was a snoop. Cops loved snoops. It made their jobs so much easier. He said, "I was asking him about a teenage girl who got off the bus yesterday about this time."

"That floozy. I saw her standing over there across the street until she walked off with that man."

"Did you see who she walked off with?" Brady said.

"Of course I did. Big man. Like you. Blue jacket with yellow doodads on it."

"Doodads?"

Her hands fluttered around the sleeves. "Doodads. Insignias maybe."

"Like military?"

"Maybe," she said, and for the first time, Brady noticed the thickness of her lenses and wondered how good her eyesight really was. "Did you recognize the man?"

"I never saw his face. He must have come up to her while I was looking away. By the time I saw them, they was walking the other direction."

"Could you tell how old he was?"

"He was wearing a cap and he never looked my way. He didn't walk like an old man. The two of them wandered off down that street over there."

"Is there anything else you can recall? A car—"

"A black truck?" Lara finished.

"My phone rang right then. That old fool Agnes was on the line. Claimed she caught her mailman peeking through her window. Last week it was the UPS man. Like they have nothing better to do than catch Agnes in her bloomers."

Brady thanked the woman and they walked back to the car, then drove down the street she had indicated. The houses quickly gave way to vacant lots.

"Dead end," Brady said.

"What now?"

"I'll tell Tom. Maybe he can talk to the Scottsdell sheriff."

"Won't Tom tell Dixon and won't Dixon come unglued you got in the middle of his investigation?" Lara asked as she looked over the seat to check on Nathan.

"Probably. Ask me if I care. They could have been here first if they thought it was important."

"I have a bad feeling about Karen Wylie," Lara said, settling back into the leather seat and frowning.

"I think she ran off with a new boyfriend," Brady said, glancing at Lara.

But the truth was, he had a bad feeling about the kid, too.

IT WAS WITH profound relief Lara watched Brady drive away to talk to Lucinda Wylie. When she'd learned Lara and Nathan would be gone all day, Myra had taken the day off and was even planning to spend the night with her sister. The house was all hers, Lara thought, hers and Nathan's.

She bathed her adorable son, laughed with him, fed him, then lay down beside him on her bed. After a few rousing games of patty-cake and a few kisses on his round tummy, Nathan's dark eyes—eyes like his father's minus about two hundred degrees of intensity—started to close.

As she silently watched slumber overtake him, she was stunned to feel tears burning behind her nose. No way was she going to lie there and blubber. Over what? What did she have to cry about? Karen's disappearance had been more or less explained. Brady, while still un-communicative about their personal situation, was acting friendly enough. There was absolutely nothing to cry about.

How about the fact that you're losing a husband, that you are choosing to deny Nathan a chance to grow up in the same house with his father?

No. She'd already spent those tears. She pinched her nose and sat up, taking a few deep breaths in the bargain.

After she tucked Nathan into his crib, she washed her face, turned on the baby monitor, grabbed the handheld receiver and went downstairs.

What she needed was a project. Like sweeping a floor or starting dinner. Something normal with a be-ginning, middle and end.

As her foot hit the polished wood floor of the foyer,

a knock sounded on the front door and she opened it quickly, without thinking, not wanting the visitor to grow impatient and ring the doorbell and risk waking Nathan.

She didn't recognize the man at first. Hand on the doorknob, she stood facing him for the count of ten, taking in little about his appearance past his eyes and a scraggly sandy beard that ringed his gaunt face.

He said, "You're Lara Kirk."

She placed him at the sound of his voice. "Bill Armstrong," she said, recalling the day he'd come into the teen center, soon after his daughter died.

Just like Brady, Armstrong had changed in the past year, but in Armstrong, the change appeared to start and end in his eyes. Where before they'd burned with confusion and grief, they now seemed oddly flat.

"You remember me," he said.

"Of course I do." The big house loomed around her. The privacy she'd enjoyed a minute earlier now threatened to trap her. Hoping to hurry him along, she made her voice crisp. "What can I do for you, Mr. Armstrong?"

"I want to talk to Skye."

"He's not here," she said. "Try his house."

"He's not there. Everyone knows you two have taken up again. Everyone knows he's been living over here."

"That's not true," she said clearly. "But when I see him, I'll tell him you stopped by." She started to close the door. He caught the edge and met her gaze.

"What were you two doing in Scottsdell?"

She froze. "How—"

"I saw you," he said.

Once again she tried to close the door and once again he stopped her.

Annoyance tinged with alarm caused her to blurt out, "We talked to a woman in Scottsdell. She told us she saw a man about your size walking with a teenage girl who's gone missing. So, Mr. Armstrong, let's turn your question around. What were you doing in Scottsdell?"

"Following Skye," he said. "What girl?"

She shook her head. At that moment, a noise erupted from the monitor receiver still clasped in her left hand. Nathan's amplified cries jarred Lara down to her bones.

Bill Armstrong's gaze darted to the monitor and back to her face. She immediately clicked it off.

"Don't look so nervous," he said with a smile that ratcheted up her unease. "I know you have a baby."

Nathan's cries wafted down the stairs behind her. "I have to go—"

He held up both hands as though disowning his previous attempts to detain her. "I know you and Skye are married. I found out about it at the courthouse. And now I know you came back to town with his kid. How about that? He kills my son and a year later, he has one of his own." He lowered his voice to a whisper. "Now, I ask you, is that fair?"

His voice and the sudden passion in his eyes terrified her. It came to Lara that he was teetering on the edge of control. She took an instinctive step back, her spine tingling with alarm.

"Has Skye started carrying a gun again, do you know? I understand killing my boy kind of shook him up and he stopped packing. Hard to believe he's willing to leave you and his kid with no protection, but I guess that's how it is with some men."

"What are you saying?" she snapped, anger replacing some of the fear. "Are you threatening us?"

"'Course not," Armstrong said. "I know you got shot a couple of nights ago, that's all. The night Jason Briggs was hurt. How are you feeling by the way? Is your arm mending okay?"

This time she managed to slam the door in his face and click the lock. She stared down the hall toward the kitchen. Had Myra locked that door when she left?

Should she call Brady? Should she pack Nathan into her rental car and leave town?

As she stood in the foyer, racked with fear and indecision, Nathan's cries grew increasingly pathetic.

She had to make a decision. Any decision.

No, she had to make the *right* decision.

BRADY DROVE AWAY from the Wylie house. His growing sense of unease hadn't been soothed by Lucinda Wylie's near hysteria.

He'd been a father for less than two days, at least as far as knowing about it went. He'd spent precious few moments with his son. The child couldn't speak and yet already, Brady found his thoughts straying to him over and over again.

All this newfound understanding made Bill Armstrong's loss all the more real to Brady. No wonder a year wasn't enough time to mitigate the pain. How much time would be enough? A thousand years? A million?

He headed out to the Good Neighbors house. His foreman was excellent, but there were some big decisions coming up that needed Brady's input. He and the foremen settled on a couple of sturdy wooden chairs out back under the trees, the river gurgling nearby, while they ironed out details for the coming week. When that was done, Brady got back in his truck and paused, unsure what to do next. Go back to Lara's house?

No. He suspected she'd want to hash out visiting rights and financial aid, and he suspected that would lead to talk of the inevitable divorce.

He couldn't face it, not right now. Maybe never.

He'd taken a cursory look at Lara's neighbor's front yard before they drove to Scottsdell that morning. He'd found no clues as to who had tried to run him down the night before. It hadn't rained in two and a half months and the neighbor wasn't big on sprinklers, hence he'd found no tire imprints even if he had the resources to take a cast and compare them to Armstrong's truck. A few broken branches didn't point any helpful fingers, either. And the neighbor, who'd come outside to see what Brady was doing, hadn't seen a thing the night before, just heard the engine.

Brady headed home.

The phone inside the house started ringing as he inserted the key in the lock. It hardly ever rang, there were times when he wondered why he even kept a landline. Concerned it might be Lara with a problem, he snatched it off the base on the fifth ring.

A male voice, deeper than Brady remembered, hearty, full of life. "Hey, big brother!"

Brady dropped his keys on the counter and hooked a stool with the toe of his boot, pulling it close. Over the last decade, Garrett had called for one reason and one reason only: he needed help. Perching on the edge of the stool, Brady said, "I can't believe my ears."

"Yeah, I know, it's been a while."

"How are you? Where are you?"

"Actually, I'm in Reno."

Brady frowned as he said, "Why Reno?" *Please, not for the gambling,* Brady added to himself. He'd never known Garrett to be a gambler, but he hadn't heard from his younger brother for three years and three years was enough time for all sorts of bad habits to emerge. Gambling meant debt, which no doubt explained this call.

Garrett said, "I got married a couple of years ago."

"No kidding."

A slight pause was followed by, "It didn't work out. Tiffany decided she wanted to be a showgirl. She moved to Reno so I followed."

"You followed a woman?" Brady said. "That doesn't sound like you."

Garrett's voice took on an edge of sarcasm as he said, "Yeah, right. I'm the one who usually leaves, is that what you're saying?"

Brady didn't answer. He'd been thinking exactly that. Garrett's unwritten manifesto was simple: get involved with someone, make a mess of it, leave. Run away. Let someone else pick up the pieces. Avoid pain. *Like you have room to talk?* his subconscious whispered.

Garrett added, "I didn't follow Shelly. I followed Megan."

"Ah."

"Megan is my daughter, Brady. A two-year-old doll. Tiffany is using my child support to subsidize her new dream job while my little girl spends her time with a grandmother who isn't too thrilled about being a babysitter. I was working at a casino, trying to put something away to fight for full custody, when the comptroller slash bigwig VP hired me to be a body-guard for his wife. The money is a lot better."

Brady could hardly believe his ears. Garrett sounded mature and focused. He said, "That sounds great." He mentally reviewed his finances, wondering how much Garrett would ask for, how much he could spare.

"Brady?"

"Yeah, I'm here. Listen, how much do you need?" He hadn't meant it to come out quite so abruptly.

"What do you mean?"

"Money to tide you over."

Icy silence followed by, "I guess I earned that."

Brady, realizing his gaffe, said, "Hey, I'm sorry. I just figured—"

"It's okay. I've lost count of how many times you've bailed me out of trouble over the years. But not any-more. The reason I'm calling is because of Dad."

"What about him?"

"I've been trying to reach him for three days but he doesn't answer his phone."

"He's probably on a bender."

"Spoken like the cop you've always been even before you put on that uniform," Garrett said. When Brady didn't respond, Garrett added, "Last time I spoke to him was a month ago and he swore he'd quit. When did you see him?"

Marveling that Garrett would actually believe their father after all the broken promises, Brady admitted it had been a couple of months. He didn't include the in-formation that the sighting had been at a distance, him walking down the street, glancing through the open door of one of the riverside taverns, their father sprawled at the bar, a half-empty shot glass in front of him.

"Will you go by his house?" Garrett asked. "Today?"
One more pointless thing to do. "Sure."

"And call me back at this number?"

"Yes."

He wrote down his brother's number and soon after hung up. He snagged the keys again and opened the door.

Lara stood on the step, Nathan in her arms. Brady was so shocked to find her standing there with one hand raised to knock that for a long count, he just stared at her.

Lowering her hand, she spoke without looking at his face. "I have to talk to you."

There was that tone of voice again. Determined, tense. She was getting ready to tell him she was leaving town and they had to talk *now*.

"I have to drive over to my father's house," he said, relieved he had a legitimate excuse for leaving. "Garrett called. He's worried Dad hasn't answered the phone in a few days. I told him I'd call him back, so I better go. We'll hook up later—"

"I'll drive you," she said.

"You don't want to go to my father's house—"

She met his gaze. "Yes, I do. I..." She shook her head and looked away. His heart lurched with concern.

"What's happened since we got back from Scottsdell?" he said, keeping his hands to himself though his instinct was to grab her. "Something is wrong."

"It's nothing. Well, maybe it's something. I don't know. I'm not sure what to do."

He ached to wrap his arms around her. "Just tell me."

"Let's take care of your father first. We've got so much to discuss. But not like this."

"You could wait here."

"No. I want to go with you."

"We'll take your car," he said, adding, "I'll drive."

LARA KNEW where Brady grew up, she'd driven by the house a time or two when they first met. She also knew he very seldom, if ever, went back to that house. She'd run into his father a time or two, but he hadn't been part of the formal wedding plans, he hadn't attended the rehearsal dinner or the shower or any of the other social activities preceding the "big day." The big day that never happened.

Caught up in these thoughts, she glanced over at Brady. He had one of the world's truly great profiles. Strong, well-defined features, lips bordering on chiseled, cheekbones angular, the dark slash of his brows framing the incredible depths of his eyes. He looked preoccupied. Did he care more about his father than he was willing to admit, even to himself?

She tucked her hands beneath her thighs to quell the rampant desire to slide her fingers across the seat, to rest her hand on his thigh as she'd done in the past. Her body longed to bend beneath his. Erotic thoughts hit her fast and hard, leaving her rattled. Maybe the fear Bill Armstrong had awakened with his insinuations caused this pounding desire to have sex with the one man she knew would move the world to protect Nathan.

Was that what she was feeling? Some kind of primal instinct to mate with her protector, to bond him to her and her child?

"How was Garrett?" she asked. She had to get her mind away from Brady's face and body and the magic of his hands, the safety of his arms. She couldn't talk about Bill Armstrong right that moment, this wasn't the time, it could wait until the trip back. Surely Brady's younger brother provided a safe alternate conversation.

He shrugged before saying, "He actually seemed more together than I've ever heard him sound. Maybe he's finally growing up."

"Why do you say that?"

He spared her a quick glance. "He didn't call because he needed bailing out of anything. He's either getting a divorce or already has one, I'm not sure which."

"I didn't know he was married," she said, though of course she wouldn't have known. Garrett had left Riverport after high-school graduation and according to Brady, never looked back.

"And he has a two-year-old daughter."

She smiled. "Really? What did he say when you told him you have a son?"

He cast her another quick look before mumbling, "I don't think I mentioned Nathan."

Narrowing her eyes, she said, "Did you tell him about us? About me?"

"What about you?" he said, staring straight ahead. "That you married me or that you're leaving me?"

"Either one."

"No."

"About the shooting? About quitting the force?"

"No," he said.

She sensed his hackles rising. It was okay to free her hands now, the intense longing to touch him had passed.

Brady's attention was drawn out the side window for a moment and Lara followed his gaze to see a police car parked behind a blue compact. Tom James was leaning down, looking in the window, talking to the driver, a kid Lara vaguely recognized from the teen center days. Tom looked up in time to notice them and nodded slightly as he kept talking to the kid.

"Someone is going to have a lot of explaining to do tonight when they get home and their parents find out they got a ticket," Lara said.

"If they get a ticket. Tom believes in second chances." He glanced at her as he said that.

Did he want a second chance, is that what he was saying? Could she afford to give him one? Could she afford the devastation in her own life if he failed to change? Could she go through all that again?

He turned into a driveway of a very nondescript house whose curtains were drawn. The plants in the front had dried up and died. He parked the car and pulled the parking brake, then turned to face her.

"What do you expect out of me?"

"I don't expect anything," she said in a soft voice, with a backward glance at Nathan asleep in his car seat.

Brady looked at the slumbering baby, too, and lowered his voice. "Yes, you do. You're obviously annoyed I didn't tell Garrett about you and Nathan. On the other hand, you can't wait to leave town and take my boy away from me. Plus, one of these days, you'll find someone new and give Nathan a brand-new stepfather and I'm supposed to brag about this mess to my long-lost brother? I'm supposed to feel good about all this?"

She couldn't bear to meet his gaze, to meet his pain. Every single thing he said was true.

"The trouble is, you don't talk to anyone about anything," she finally murmured. "You set impossible goals of perfection for yourself. You don't trust anyone to love you despite—"

He held up a hand. "Please, honey, no therapy. Not right now. You haven't said what you came to say. Get it over with."

"What do you mean?"

"You're leaving, right?"

"Yes."

"And yet that doesn't explain why you looked so spooked a few minutes ago."

She bit her lip. "I know it doesn't. Brady, do you still have a gun?"

He stared at her for a count of ten. "Yes," he finally said.

"Is it true you don't carry it?"

"I'm a civilian," he said. "How many civilians do you know who carry guns?"

She looked down at her hands as he heaved a sigh. If she kept annoying him like this, he'd stop trying to get close to her.

"Listen," he said, "I've got to go in there and find out what's going on. Stay here and wait."

"I'll go with you—"

"Please, Lara, just stay here. Let me handle this."

And there it was in a nutshell. He wanted to "handle" his father, he wanted to "handle" her. He just didn't know how to do both at the same time. She said, "I could help, Brady."

"No," he said, casting her a miserable look. He walked across the dead grass and knocked on the door. After a minute or two, he tried the handle. The door opened and Brady disappeared inside the house, the door closing behind him.

So, true to form, he'd tucked her away in the car while he saw to his father. That was his standard operating plan: this person and problem here, that person and problem there, never mix them up, don't chance things getting out of control.

A movement on the street behind her caught her attention and she turned in time to see a black truck pull up against the curb across the street. The driver turned and stared through his back window.

Bill Armstrong!

How had he known to come here?

Two nights before, she'd sat in a car with Jason Briggs as a bullet tore through the rear window. Her arm, as though prodded by the memory of the second bullet, the one that had torn into her flesh, throbbed anew. Her face went clammy, her mouth dry. With shaking fingers, she unbuckled her seat belt and got out of the car, unable to even contemplate sitting there like a clay pigeon at a shooting range. She opened the rear door and fumbled with the seat belt holding Nathan's carrier in place, then swooped it and him up. She walked across the dry grass, resisting the urge to glance across the street, opened the front door without knocking and walked straight into the shelter of the house.

And into chaos. An unbelievable clutter of newspapers, bottles, cans, plates of half-eaten food and discarded clothing covered every horizontal surface. It looked as though the house had vomited its contents onto itself.

Plus, the smell. Rotting food. Unwashed bodies. Sickness. It hit her like a fist.

Was this how Brady and Garrett had grown up? In a sty like this? No wonder Brady valued order.

She stopped in her tracks and called, "Brady?"

He stepped out of a bedroom down the hall and

walked toward her. Her stomach unclenched an iota at the solid, real sight of him.

"What's wrong?" he said as he picked his way through the debris.

She stared at his face for a moment. At the despair in his eyes. The sudden stoop of his square shoulders.

"Lara? What's wrong?"

"Nothing," she said, scrambling for a plausible excuse for showing up in a house where it was clear she wasn't wanted.

"It got hot in the car and I thought maybe I could help in here. I'm a trained counselor, remember. I can help you and your father open a dialogue about—"

"He's not here," Brady interrupted, hitching his hands on his waist and surveying the mess. "I don't know," he added. "Maybe he's buried under all this crap. Let's get out of here." His gaze dropped to Nathan, his voice grew tender. He took the carrier from her. "Asleep or not, I don't want the little guy exposed to this filth."

They stepped out onto the porch together. Lara's gaze darted across the street. Bill Armstrong was gone.

As Brady closed and locked the door, a police car pulled in behind her rental.

Chapter Eight

As Tom got out of the car, Brady glanced up and down the street. Not a single neighbor peered around an open door or through an unshuttered window. Apparently the arrival of a police unit at 322 Court Way didn't arouse much curiosity anymore.

"What's up?" Brady asked.

Tom smiled at Lara and tickled Nathan's cheek. Glancing back at Brady, he said, "A call just came over the radio. The owner of the River Rat reported a disturbance. Chief Dixon was on his way home and took the call. I saw you pass a minute ago and figured you were driving over here. Do you want to go down there with me?"

"Why would I—"

"It's your dad."

Brady took a deep breath. He glanced at Lara, his gaze fell to Nathan.

"Don't worry about us," Lara said. Did her voice tremble? He glanced into her eyes but she looked away again. What was going on?

"Are you sure you're okay?" he asked her.

"Of course," she added brightly, reaching for Nathan's carrier. "I'll catch up with you later."

Tom tapped his watch. "If you're coming…"

"Yeah, okay, I won't be long, Lara."

His conscience whispered to him as Lara walked toward the rental. *You're relieved fate has once again intervened to cut short the farewell conversation.* When had he become such a coward?

"You going back to your mother's house?" he called.

She turned, met his gaze and shrugged.

"You won't leave town," he said.

"Not tonight," she said. "Go. Don't worry."

He settled into the passenger seat and Tom wasted no time backing out of the driveway and speeding off.

It was the first time since the night he shot Billy Armstrong that Brady had been inside a squad car. The memories it brought back choked him with regret. For the millionth time, he wished Billy and Jason Briggs had chosen the next night to swipe a car and steal beer. By then, he would have been honeymooning on a beach in Hawaii. Billy would probably still be alive, Brady and Lara would be living as man and wife, Jason might not be laid out in the hospital.

"You happen to know how the Briggs boy is doing?" Brady asked Tom as he turned onto River Front Street.

"The same. Still in a coma, not talking, but I doubt he knows who plugged him."

"How about you guys? Do the cops have any leads? Tire tracks, bullet casings, witnesses?"

"The doctor dug a 30–08 out of the boy. That bullet could have come out of any deer rifle in the county or from an assault weapon. We're looking for stolen. No witnesses besides you."

"Did Bill Armstrong have an alibi?"

"Not much of one. Said he was driving around. Chief Dixon said he saw him."

"Dixon saw him, huh? I don't suppose Armstrong admitted stopping by the Kirk house to lob a rock through the parlor window?"

"Claimed he didn't know what I was talking about. I'll keep an eye on him."

It was on the tip of his tongue to tell Tom about the incident in front of the Kirk house early that morning, the one that had him dodging into a hedge, but what was the point? Instead he said, "How about Karen Wylie?"

"How about her? A runaway. I guess her mom's been calling Chief Dixon. Does he have you to thank for that?"

"Probably. I talked to a couple of people in Scotts-dell today. A homeless guy saw her get off the bus with a suitcase, a cranky old woman who lives across the street from the old warehouse down the street saw her walking away with a man about my size."

"Oh, brother, I hope the chief doesn't get wind of that. He'd love to pin all this on you."

"Tom, I'm not that unusual a size. Bill Armstrong is as tall as I am. A little heavier maybe. For that matter, so are you and Dixon and the guy at the gas station. Besides, why would I run off with a seventeen-year-old kid?"

Tom spared him a wry glance. "Seventeen isn't a kid, Brady. You have an alibi for yesterday afternoon?"

"I was driving around Riverport trying to find the girl. Her mother was coming apart."

Tom shook his head. "You get any names from these witnesses?"

"No. The woman won't be hard to find. The guy was standing on a corner across from the bus station holding a sign begging for gas money for a car he doesn't have. He might be gone by now."

"I'll write this up when I get to the station. Might as well have someone go out and question those two tomorrow," Tom said as he slowed down. The chief's unmarked car was parked in front of the River Rat. As Brady got out of the car, he steeled himself for what was coming.

The River Rat was no stranger to drunks or cops. Built fifty years earlier and mucked out every decade or so, it defied health codes. It was the kind of place for serious drinkers, no party-going yuppies need apply.

A call squawked on the squad car radio. As Tom moved to take it, Brady said, "If you have to go, don't worry, I'll get him home in a cab."

Tom nodded as he leaned in and grabbed the mike.

This early on an August evening, the joint was blessedly free of crowds. Besides the bartender, Chief Dixon and Brady's father, there were just two bleary-eyed older guys down at the end of the bar.

Brady's father sat on a stool, weathering Dixon's hissed remonstrations. It was hard to believe this wasted man had once fought in Korea, had once driven a logging truck, had wooed and won the heart of a beautiful woman.

Charles Skye. Hair graying and sparse body, too thin in places and too thick in others. Clothes that needed washing, face that needed shaving, expression slack. The kind of man more at home in a gutter than on a sidewalk.

The kind of man for whom Brady had always felt little more than contempt.

But watching Dixon berate his father aroused a curious sensation in the pit of Brady's stomach. Forced to name it, he'd have to go with *pity*. For the first time he felt pity for his old man.

Unnoticed by Dixon or his father, Brady caught the proprietor's eye and leaned across the bar. Harry Pie was about the same age as the other two men, and like them had spent his life in Riverport. "My father was causing trouble?" Brady asked.

Harry shook his shaved head. "No. Couple of punks came in and started giving him grief. They left as soon as I called the cops. Your dad didn't do nothing but sit there and take it. I expected him to throw a few punches, but not tonight."

Ignoring Dixon's glare, Brady approached his father. "Come on, Dad," he said, laying a hand on the older man's shoulder. "Time to call it a night."

His father looked up at him with eyes diluted by years of vodka transfusions.

Chief Dixon turned his belligerence on Brady. "I'm damn tired of you getting in my face, Skye."

"Running into you isn't my idea of a good time, either," Brady said.

"I heard about you going to Scottsdell today."

How had he heard that quickly? It implied a tail of some kind. Brady said, "It was a nice day for a drive."

"Listen to me. The Wylie girl ran off, clear and simple. Now you got her mother all riled up, calling us, demanding we find her kid and haul her home. You know it doesn't work like that."

Ah, Karen Wylie's mother had demanded action. Brady said, "I don't know how it works. Like you keep telling me, I'm not a cop."

"And don't you forget it. Now, get your old man out of here before I throw his ass in jail."

Brady's father didn't appear interested in the conversation. He'd stopped looking at Brady and instead studied the empty shot glass on the counter as though desire could fill it.

Brady gently pulled his father to his feet. He looked over his old man's head and said, "What did he ever do to you, Dixon? Why do you hate him?"

Dixon chewed on his cheek for a second. Brady would have bet a bundle the man was dying for a cigarette.

With a barman's nose for gossip, Harry Pie moseyed along the bar until he stood opposite them. Pretending to wipe down the counter with a damp rag, he said, "Didn't your Dad ever tell you about your mother?"

Dixon cast Harry an if-looks-can-kill frown and said, "Never you mind, Harry."

Brady's dad looked up. "Theresa?" he said, glancing around as though her ghost might have stopped in for a nightcap.

"Don't you even say her name," Dixon spat.

Theresa Skye had died driving drunk twelve years earlier. Brady didn't even know Dixon knew his mother past recognizing her as Charlie Skye's wife. It stunned him to hear Dixon's distress at hearing Charles Skye speak her name.

Dixon glared at Brady and added, "Get your old man sober. Keep him that way."

Sure, Brady thought. *That'll happen.*

As Dixon stomped out of the place, Harry Pie wiped a nonexistent spot from the bar and said, "Dix, Charlie, Theresa and I all went to school together. Did you know that?"

"I guess," Brady said. He tried to move his father a step closer to the door. The man was thin as a reed but oddly bottom heavy, as though all his weight had pooled in his feet.

"Theresa married Dix right out of high school," Harry added. Brady stopped trying to budge his dad and looked at Harry.

"What did you say?"

"Your dad went away to join the navy. When he got home, Theresa left Dix and married Charlie. Dix never got over it."

Stunned, Brady mumbled, "My mother was once married to Chief Dixon?"

"'Course, he wasn't a chief then," Harry said, rubbing a spot on the bar with his cloth. "Dix couldn't go into the service because of some sleepwalking thing. I guess he propositioned a thirteen-year-old girl down the block, leastwise, that was the rumor going around, so Theresa threw him out and married Charlie. I think Dix is working on wife number three now. Anyway, it was all very hush-hush."

"Chief Dixon propositioned a kid?"

"That's what your dad said a long time ago. I don't have any way of knowing if it's the truth or not. I can't believe no one ever told you about this."

Brady looked at his father's face. His old man blinked and trotted out a belch. Again, Brady felt a twinge of pity.

He didn't try to explain to Harry Pie that by the time Brady was old enough to care about things like his parents' pasts, both had been lost in a bottle.

APPARENTLY, CHARLES SKYE had been more aware of what happened at the bar than he'd let on.

"Dix is a jerk," he said in a garbled, slurred voice as Brady shoveled him into a taxi. Charlie Skye had lost his license years ago and usually staggered home under his own steam or caught a ride. When Brady first became a cop, he'd actually tried to be at the bar at closing time so he could give his father a lift. That had ended when his father socked him in the eye and told him to mind his own business.

"Yeah," Brady said, giving the driver his father's address.

"Thought he owned Theresa," the older man continued, pulling at his pants as he spoke as though the cloth burned his skin. "Even after she left. Tried to get her back."

"I didn't know they were married," Brady said.

His father grew very still. He finally looked up at Brady and mumbled, "You were the good one. You were the one who answered the door."

The one who kept the cops and the neighbors and the school officials away, Brady thought to himself.

I was the enabler in my family. I was the glue.

Well, what choice had he had? Someone had to see that there was food around and that bills got paid and Garrett didn't rot in detention after ditching classes day after day.

"Your brother got in trouble all the time," Brady's father said, his voice lower now and close to a snore. He jerked and flung a hand up and said, "Where's Theresa?"

"Dead," Brady said. They'd had this conversation, like all the others, a hundred times, a thousand times. "She's gone, Dad."

"Dix's a jerk," his father repeated, bookending his conversation, and then his chin slumped onto his bony chest.

Brady managed to pay the driver and wrangle his father into the house where he deposited him on a semiclean chair while he went into the bedroom, changed the sheets and started the shower. A half hour later, his dad tucked in bed and dead to the world, he called Garrett.

"Sorry to take so long getting back to you," he said.

"Dad down on River Front Street?"

"Yeah. He's home now. Listen, Garrett. There are some things I need to get cleared away up here and then I thought I might come down your way and visit you in Reno. It's been a while since we really talked."

What had caused him to say that? *Lara.* She'd gotten under his skin. He filled the silence by adding, "If this isn't a good time—"

"I think it's a great idea," Garrett said. "I've been thinking of coming up that way, myself. I'd like to show Riverport to Megan."

"Let's give it a few weeks and talk again," Brady suggested. "We'll figure out who goes where."

Brady worked off the tight feeling in his chest by scouring his father's house, loading the dishwasher and dumping empty bottles into the recycling bin. He hadn't revealed their mother's first marriage to Garrett. That was news better left for a face-to-face meeting. And they hadn't talked about treatment plans for their dad because they'd been down that road a dozen times before.

He knew Garrett understood, as he did, that there would be no long-term help until Charles Skye really wanted it. Down deep. Down in his gut. Down where he kept his pain. If alcoholism was a disease, then it had to be fought like one and not surrendered to. Until then, he might sober up for a few days or even weeks, he might swear to turn his life around, but sooner or later he'd seek refuge where he knew he could find it.

At three-thirty in the morning, Brady found his father's car keys and went out to the garage to see if the old sedan still ran. Wonder of wonders, it turned over at the first try. He drove himself home and as he walked to his apartment around in the back, he happened to see a car parked at the end of the row behind his neighbor's piano-delivery truck. Lara's rental, Nathan's car seat abandoned in the backseat.

He walked quickly around to his door only to discover a broken pane of glass by the lock, patched now with a piece of wood pounded into place with a dozen nails from the inside. That explained how she got in. The door was now locked again and he opened it.

The apartment was pitch-black. He hit the switch on the wall. Nothing happened. Odd, and considering everything, a tad alarming. He stepped inside. Before he could turn the light on, he ran into a pile of pots and pans that clanged and rattled to the floor as he scrambled to catch them.

What was going on?

Why had Lara set a trap and why didn't the noise of it clamoring to the ground bring her scampering into the room? He tried the light switch, but nothing happened. Using the tiny flashlight on his key ring, he stepped around the mess. The fuse box was in the kitchen. Only the switch for the entry lights had been thrown and he reset it.

He found her on his bed. Not only on his bed, but on his side of the bed. Fully clothed, stretched out on top of the sheet, all legs and blond hair and delicate tan, as smooth as a centerfold and a hundred times more appealing because she had once been his.

And would be again.

Standing there, staring at her in the weak light of his tiny flashlight, he made a promise to himself and to her.

And to his son, who had apparently kicked aside a blue baby blanket and now wore nothing but a diaper. He lay beside her, occupying an amazing amount of real estate smack in the middle of the mattress. His small, half-clad body looked so impossibly vulnerable that Brady's heart all but stopped beating. He flicked on a lamp and turned off the flashlight.

He moved to rouse Lara but stopped himself. She must be exhausted. How else to explain being nervous enough to set a trap but sleepy enough to nod off and miss the sound of it springing? Was there any reason to wake her now?

Maybe he should ease her farther down on the bed, cover her though the room was warm. She'd be more comfortable without her shoes—

Which would mean he'd have to cup her smooth, bare calves in his hands, unstrap her sandals. He'd have to lift her shoulders, reposition her head. He could almost feel the silky strands of her hair sliding between his fingers...

No, he wouldn't touch her. He wouldn't torture himself.

He rubbed the bridge of his nose with thumb and forefinger. His leg hurt where he'd gouged his knee the night before. His heart felt heavy and way too big for his chest. He turned around and stared at Lara and Nathan as the seconds ticked off on the alarm clock.

Was there any danger in just catching a few hours' sleep before finding out what was going on?

He walked to his dresser. His keys, with the flashlight attached, were still in his hand. He found the right key and used it to open the locked drawer on top.

The Glock seemed to glow in its holster. He stared at it, even reached for it. But his fingers stopped short of touching the damn thing, and he shut and locked the drawer again. He left the lamp burning on the dresser, then headed to the closet for a blanket and pillow. He'd settle for a few hours on the sofa.

Wait. This was his house, his wife, his child, his bed. For what was left of the night, they could all just share. He stripped down to his boxers and slipped beneath the sheet on Nathan's far side.

His weight hitting the mattress jostled Lara. She sat bolt upright with a gasp, eyes flying open. Grabbing her chest with her hand, relief flooded her face as he whispered her name.

Tears glistened in her eyes, but they didn't fall. He'd noticed the new Lara didn't cry.

Nathan whimpered, then relaxed once again into sleep. Lara pulled the baby blanket up around the baby's frail shoulders as Brady rolled onto his side and watched her.

What had she done with the ring he'd given her? She didn't need the money, so he knew she wouldn't have sold or hawked it, not yet at least, not until she remarried, maybe, and his ring became a memory of a marriage she wanted to forget.

Her ring, her husband.

"How's your father?" she said at last.

"Sleeping it off. Why are you here, Lara? Why did you break in and booby-trap the front hall? What happened today?"

"Bill Armstrong came to see me."

He took a deep breath and started to roll off the bed.

She reached across Nathan and caught his arm, snapping her hand back at once. "No," she said softly.

He stared at her. "Why the hell not?"

"He didn't really do anything."

"That's why you came here earlier today," he said. "You were afraid but you didn't tell me. You wouldn't tell me."

"I guess I thought you had other things on your mind. And then Bill drove by your father's place. I just got spooked. So after you left with Tom, I decided to come here because Myra was staying with her sister for the night, and I couldn't stand the thought of being in my mother's big house alone."

"And you haven't seen Armstrong since he drove by my father's place?"

"No. He said he came to your apartment earlier in the day, but I got the feeling he didn't think you lived here anymore so I thought it might be safe. I'm sorry about your door and the pans—"

"Don't," he said, his gut twisting at the thought of her fear. He'd put her off, he'd left her. He'd been relieved to have an excuse to avoid confrontation.

"I'm the one who's sorry," he said.

"I looked for your gun."

He kept a smile to himself as he said, "You were going to shoot Bill Armstrong?"

"If I had to," she said.

"You don't know how to shoot. You would never let me teach you anything more than how to click off the safety."

They stared at each other. He wasn't sure what she was feeling. He was suffering a major case of guilt and inadequacy.

She finally yawned and rubbed her temple, then slipped back down in the bed, resettling her head on the pillow. "Can we finish talking about this in the morning? I'm so tired I hurt."

"It is morning."

"You're here now," she whispered as her eyes drifted shut.

He stared at her a few moments longer, memories of making love to her stampeding through his head, galloping south where they wreaked havoc on his libido.

He lay awake for a long time.

Chapter Nine

As Nathan slept the next morning, Lara sat cross-legged on her side of the bed. Brady propped his shoulders against the headboard. She told him everything she could remember about Bill Armstrong's visit the day before. He listened with his usual intensity, reading between the lines, his expression growing increasingly murderous.

Eventually, Nathan woke up and they moved to Brady's small kitchen. He cleaned up the pots and pans while she fed the baby.

In retrospect, her behavior the night before seemed way over the top. How had she allowed herself to get so spooked?

Flat, dead eyes floated in front of her. Oh, yeah. That's how.

Brady finally sat down, ignoring the folded newspaper at his elbow and playing at eating cold cereal. She knew he was upset and was trying to figure out what he should do next. He threw occasional glances at her and Nathan, his expression so tender it almost hurt.

How could something that at times seemed so right, at other times seem so wrong? How could she change him?

You can't, you fool. The cost of loving Brady Skye is

*allowing him to set the limits. Allowing him to keep
things to himself, to brood when he needs to, to let him
draw lines around everything and everyone and keep it
all separate and safe. Can you spend your life like that?*

No. And that meant getting out of Brady's apartment where the fantasy of them being a family tore
at her heart.

When Nathan started cooing, she handed him to
Brady's outstretched hands and poured them both more
coffee. She'd brought no clean clothes so there was
nothing to do after breakfast but go back to her mother's
house. She said, "Brady, about this divorce."

He looked up at her, his expression frozen.

"Now that you know about Nathan, we can go ahead
with the proceedings."

"Lucky us," he said.

She ignored his remark. "I don't really want to move
back to Riverport, at least not right now, but on the other
hand, I do want you to be part of Nathan's life."

"Just not part of yours."

"Brady, please. Don't make this harder—"

"Sorry," he said, casting her a dark look, the kind that
despite its surliness reminded her what it was like to be
pulled into his demanding arms, his gentleness tinged
with need, his giving, his taking, all of it wrapped up
in the heart-stopping power that surged through his
body into hers like a freight train.

"I see no reason to make this easy," he added.

"What do you mean?"

"I don't want you to leave."

"That's what I'm trying to say. I'll move back unless
you want to move north."

"You mean up to Seattle?"

"Yes. I imagine they need cops up that way the same way—"

"No."

"Brady—"

"I won't carry a gun again," he said. "But all this is a moot point because I have decided to win you back."

She heard Nathan cry. Naps were like that sometimes—they could be ten minutes or two hours, you just never knew. She got to her feet and stared down at Brady. "We've been through this."

"Just give me a few more days," he said. "There's a lot at stake here, you know."

"But it's pointless."

"Shall I go get Nathan or do you want to get him?"

He was putting her off—again. She walked quickly down the hall. Nathan lay on Brady's bed, halfhearted cries alternating with hiccups. She picked him up, threw a clean diaper over her shoulder to catch spit-ups and soothed him, walking back down the hall, determined to come to some conclusion with Brady.

Her new cell phone rang as she entered the kitchen again. Brady turned from the sink where he'd been rinsing out his bowl and reached out for Nathan, plopping down in his chair as Lara dug in her bag for her cell phone. She didn't recognize the displayed number except that it was local.

"Hello?" she said as she leaned against the counter.

"Is this Miss Kirk?" a young female voice asked.

"Yes, it is."

"My name is Nicole. Nicole Stevens. Do you remember me?"

A vague image of a small girl with waist-length glistening black hair floated into Lara's mind. "Did you used to come into the teen center?"

The relief in the girl's voice was audible. "Yeah, I did. I was a friend of Sara Armstrong's."

And Karen Wylie. The three of them had hung out together. Lara glanced at Brady who had caught her tone of voice and was looking at her. Lara said, "I remember. How are you?"

"Okay. I guess. I was wondering if I could talk to you."

"Of course you can talk to me," Lara said, her gaze linked to Brady's. "What can I do for you?"

"I am also a friend of Karen Wylie's, Miss Kirk." The girl lowered her voice. "Karen ran away day before yesterday. Her mom said you talked to her before she left."

"Yes, I did."

"That's why I want to talk to you. But not on the phone. Will you meet me tomorrow?"

"How about today?"

"No." The voice got even softer. "I'm off work today and I have...plans."

"Okay. How about the coffee shop?"

"No. Someplace more private."

"You mean someplace with fewer people?" Lara said, her mind immediately leaping to Jason Briggs's call a few days earlier. Hadn't he made the same request? But this time she'd have Brady with her. No reason to tell Nicole that, but Lara sure as hell wasn't going alone. "Like where?" she added.

"I babysit a couple of kids. They like to go to the park, to that new play-structure thing, do you know what I'm talking about?"

"Yes," Lara said.

"There's a bench off to the side."

"Okay. What time?"

"Three-thirty?"

"Okay." Lara paused for a second before adding, "Karen's mom told me you and Karen used to like to go to Sara's house. She said Sara's father was like a dad to all you guys."

Nicole didn't respond, but Brady's eyebrows shot up his forehead.

"Yeah, I guess," Nicole said after several seconds. Her voice held a new edge of wariness.

Afraid she was in the process of scaring Nicole off, Lara said, "I was just thinking how nice it was you were all so close."

Strained silence.

"Sara was a sweet girl," Lara added.

Finally, a soft, "Miss Kirk, let's keep the meeting just between us, okay?"

A chill ran up Lara's spine. "Sure."

Nicole disconnected.

"What was that all about?" Brady asked.

Lara set the phone down and returned to her seat across from Brady. She fooled around with her mug of cold coffee before saying, "You're going to think I'm nuts, but there's something odd going on. I had a lot of time to think yesterday, you know. I mean, does Bill Armstrong strike you as the cuddly father-figure type?"

"No," Brady said, using the diaper to wipe a trickle of drool from Nathan's chin.

"Me, neither."

"But Armstrong's had a horrible year."

"True. I'm just going to say this. I don't have any proof, it's just a thought but it won't go away."

"Go for it."

"What if Bill Armstrong is a child molester?"

Brady's forehead furrowed. "How did you ever reach that conclusion?"

"Bear with me. First his daughter kills herself without leaving a note. That seems odd. Teenage girls like drama, and if she had something horrible enough in her life to kill herself over, I think she would have left a suicide note. No, before you ask, I don't know what the statistics are, but I did know Sara. She changed right before her death. She got quiet and introspective and started writing long poems. What would cause her to kill herself without a note?"

"Her desire to protect someone?"

"Yes. Like her mother. Like, if her father was molesting her. I wish I knew if she died a virgin."

"She didn't," Brady said. "I saw the autopsy report."

"There you go."

"Honey, lots of sixteen-year-old girls have sex with their boyfriends."

"Right. I just don't recall Sara having a boyfriend. Okay, let's move on to Karen Wylie. Her mother went on and on about Karen's relationship with Bill Armstrong."

"So, obviously he was molesting her, too?"

"Don't laugh at me."

"I'm not laughing."

"And now a third girl wants a private conversation. And when I mentioned Bill Armstrong's name, she grew guarded."

Brady laid Nathan over his lap and gently burped him. "So?"

"So maybe Bill Armstrong met Karen Wylie in Scottsdell."

"Then drove back here in time to threaten you at your mother's house?"

"Maybe he stashed Karen in a motel somewhere. Maybe we need to figure out a way to get to her before it's too late."

"Too late?" He picked Nathan up and cradled him against his broad shoulder, doing all these baby things with an ease that amazed Lara.

"One girl is dead. One is gone," she said. "Another one is on the phone, afraid. She wants to talk to me. So did Jason Briggs. Jason is in the hospital. Doesn't that sound suspicious to you?"

"Yes," he admitted, patting Nathan's back. The baby squirmed and fussed. Brady got to his feet and paced the small room, a movement that quieted Nathan for about ten seconds. "But there's nothing here that is vaguely related to evidence."

"If Bill Armstrong thought news of his perversions were about to be spread, he'd panic. He'd probably do anything to make sure the other girls didn't talk. He'd be ruined—"

"Have you seen him?" Brady said. "He's already ruined."

She smiled. "Are you defending Bill Armstrong?"

He handed her Nathan. "Take your son, he doesn't want me, he wants you. And no, I'm not defending Bill Armstrong."

He sat back down and picked up the local paper, snapping it open. His gaze fell to the headlines as Lara checked Nathan's diaper, then he sat up straighter and slammed the table with an open hand.

The baby, momentarily startled by the gesture, stopped fussing.

"Look," he said, sliding the paper across the table.

A picture of a house fire occupied the space above the fold. The headline screamed, One Life Lost in Scottsdell Inferno.

"This is terrible," Lara mumbled. House fires had always terrified her. She supposed that came from growing up in a three-story Victorian with a mother who thought fire alarms were "ugly."

"Open up the front page," Brady said.

Lara snapped the paper open, which further startled Nathan, who renewed his cries. As she raised him to her shoulder and soothed him, she glanced at the second photo and read, "'Longtime Scottsdell resident, Mrs. Roberta Beaton, wife of late mayor Roscoe Beaton, died in a fire last night that burned her home to the ground.'"

The picture showed the feisty woman they'd spoken to the day before.

"I KILLED HER," Lara said. She'd finally gotten Nathan down for another morning nap and now stood in Brady's living room feeling as though the earth had dropped out from under her feet.

"Of course you didn't," Brady said.

She sat down on the ottoman. "You don't understand. When Bill Armstrong began threatening me, I lashed out. I told him we spoke with a witness who spotted him with Karen Wylie. I was trying to unnerve him. I didn't tell you before because it's embarrassing he got such a rise out of me."

Brady sat down in the chair opposite her. "What did he say?"

"Nothing. No, wait, I didn't mention Karen by name. He asked me what girl I was talking about."

"So we don't know if he followed us there or was already in town—"

"Visiting Karen wherever he stashed her."

Brady ran a hand through his hair. "This is all supposition. And stop blaming yourself. You didn't even know Roberta Beaton's name. You couldn't have told Armstrong which woman you meant."

"If he saw us in Scottsdell, maybe he saw us talking to Mrs. Beaton. It wouldn't take a genius to put two and two together."

Brady was quiet for a second before he said, "You're not the only one who mentioned her. I told Tom. He said he'd inform the detective in charge of Jason's shooting, just in case these things dovetail down the line. That means the whole department—including Bill Armstrong's bother-in-law who works dispatch—knew we'd talked to the woman across from the boarded-up warehouse. Plus, I wouldn't be surprised if Dixon talked to Armstrong."

Lara buried her face in her hands. She couldn't imagine that spunky woman burned to death.

Brady's phone rang. He took the call, uttering very few words before hanging up and returning to Lara. He reached for her hands and pulled her to her feet.

She went into his arms without quibbling. She needed his strength, his big solid body so warm and so real in a world that suddenly seemed full of shadows. His breath on the back of her neck was comforting, his heart beating so close to hers, a balm.

He held her for a long time, their bodies melding together where they touched. She knew allowing this contact was cruel to both of them. It would be so much easier to hate him than to love him.

Would he break his promise and kiss her? She could save him the decision by initiating the kiss herself. Was she ready to do that?

Why? Because she wanted to live with him as his wife or because she felt wretched and scared and wanted the comfort he offered? Being on the taking end of easy comfort always came with a price. Was she prepared to pay it?

She said, "Who was on the phone?"

"Tom," he said, his exhaled breath brushing her ear, sending deep quivering sensations pulsing through her body. She made herself put some distance between them.

He looked down at her with an expression she knew. He had remembered making love to her. He had hoped it would happen again. Hell, despite knowing better, so had she.

He took a deep breath. "The preliminary finding is that the fire was started by Roberta Beaton's kerosene heater igniting a stack of old newspapers. Apparently the old lady never threw anything away. The Scottsdell Police Department said they've been anticipating a tragedy at that address for a decade or more."

"It's all so convenient," Lara said.

"And coincidental," Brady murmured. "I have to go talk to Armstrong. He has to know to stay away from you and Nathan."

"Can't the police—"

"You said he wanted to talk to me yesterday, so I'll go talk to him."

"And if he's behind everything that's happened?"

"You mean Jason's gunshot wound and Karen Wylie's leaving home?"

She nodded.

"He'll continue to come apart at the seams," Brady said. "Sooner or later he'll implode. I just want to make sure he doesn't do it anywhere around you or Nathan."

THE ARMSTRONG HOUSE was only two blocks from the Wylie house. Sandra Armstrong opened the door before Brady even knocked and stood there with no expression on her face. She looked to be about his age with light brown eyes and matching straight hair pulled back with a clip. She wore jean shorts and a white tank, bare feet.

He'd seen her at the inquest into her son's death but not since. Brady wished with all his heart he hadn't come to this house. He'd expected to find Bill. For some reason, he hadn't counted on Sandra.

"He's not here," she said.

He backed away. "I'm sorry I bothered you."

She stared at him for a long time as though on the verge of saying something. He waited as all sorts of things happened behind her eyes.

"My husband's vendetta is tearing him apart," she finally said.

Brady said, "I know."

"He blames you for everything."

Brady knew that, too.

"But that doesn't mean he should be wanting to hurt you in the same way you hurt him."

Brady stopped his retreat and advanced a step. "Do you mean by hurting my son?"

"Hurting your boy won't bring ours back."

"Is he trying to hurt my boy?" Brady said softly.

"He talks about it. It scares me."

It scared her! It was all he could do to keep his voice even as he said, "Maybe if your husband and I could sit down and talk—"

"He won't sit down with you. You killed our Billy."

"I had no choice, Mrs. Armstrong. Please believe me. There was no other option."

"There's always an option," she said, and quietly closed the door.

Always an option? Was she right? As he drove to Lara's house he thought back to the night he shot Billy Armstrong and tried to figure out what else he could have done.

Tom's gun was still in its holster. He'd been talking to Billy about his sister, Sara, trying to calm Billy down. Billy was the one who went off the deep end and reached for a weapon. Billy had upped the stakes. It was just a case of protecting the innocent and in that case, Billy had not been the innocent.

Billy or Tom.

Brady had done what he had to do, what he was sworn to do. And now he would have to live with it and with the fact that there was no proof the boy had ever had a gun, that what Brady had seen wasn't the flash of his watchband distorted by his own fear.

It didn't matter. It was over and he would have to live with it.

But should Nathan have to live with it, too?

LARA STOOD in the doorway of her old bedroom as Brady paced back and forth.

"You have to go," he said. "No argument. Now."

Lara had left Nathan downstairs with Myra. The look the housekeeper had thrown Brady as he dragged Lara up the stairs to pack was one of mixed emotions that still played in Lara's mind. Delight they were arguing, sadness Lara and Nathan seemed to be leaving.

She said, "I'm not going anywhere, Brady."

He dragged her suitcase out of her closet and threw it on the bed. "Yes, you are. You're going to pack up all your stuff and you're going to leave Riverport right now. You're not going to come back. Get your mother to visit you up in Seattle."

"I have to be here to talk to Nicole. Have you forgotten about her?"

"I'll talk to her—"

"She called *me*, Brady. I have to go."

"I don't care about this Nicole, Lara. I care about you and Nathan. I want you both out of Riverport as of yesterday. Just go."

"I thought you were going to win me back," she said, still standing in the doorway. As odd as it seemed, his anxiety had dampened hers.

"Change of plans. Where are the divorce papers? I'll sign them right now."

Was it possible his declaration of the morning had actually reawakened a spark of hope in her heart? She wasn't sure except that it currently seemed in danger of being extinguished, and how could that be if it had never existed in the first place?

Had she made the decision to risk everything without ever acknowledging that decision to herself? She said, "No."

He was piling baby clothes and diapers into the

suitcase. He stopped for a second and looked up at her. "Have you listened to a thing I've said?"

"Yes. Bill Armstrong's wife believes he's on the verge of hurting Nathan." Speaking the words out loud made her stomach churn. She quickly added, "You want us out of town right now."

"That's right," he said, opening the dresser drawer and scooping up a handful of her underwear without giving any indication he saw what he held. "You understand. Now, pack. Please."

"No."

"Why not?" he barked, a satiny pink thong trailing down his arm.

"We're safer here with you to protect us."

"That's very flattering and totally wrong," he said, glancing twice at the underwear as he added it to the growing pile in the suitcase.

"If Armstrong is determined to hurt Nathan, do you really think taking him a hundred miles north will make a difference? You have to figure this out and while you do, Nathan and I will be safe in this big fortress of a house with you standing guard."

"But—"

"And why are you suddenly willing to sign the divorce papers?"

"I want you to get Nathan away from here," he said slowly, as though worried he might have said everything too fast before and she hadn't caught it. "I want you to raise him where everyone who looks at him won't judge him for being a Skye."

"Like your father," she said, gearing up for the old argument.

"No. Like me. I will always be the cop who killed

the unarmed kid. Long after they forget Billy Armstrong's name, they'll remember the name Skye. Long after my father's drunken ways are just a memory, my contribution to the disgrace of bearing the Skye name will still burn bright. Change Nathan's name to Kirk. Get him out of here."

"You could leave Riverport," she said.

He shook his head. "I can't even think about that until this matter is resolved."

She stepped into the room, closed the door, and on second thought locked it. She did not want Myra barging in. She walked to the far side of the bed and sat down next to the suitcase. Patting the mattress on her other side, she said, "Sit down."

He sat beside her but not before glancing at his watch.

"Do you love Nathan?" she asked.

He studied her face for a long time before narrowing his eyes. "You know I do."

"Yes. And your love is what is going to keep him safe. Until this threat is over, until Bill Armstrong stops acting crazy and gets some help, we need to stay together. My taking Nathan away might well escalate things. I can't leave knowing that."

And I can't leave you to bear the brunt of his revenge alone, she added to herself.

He took a deep breath before saying, "You talk about love as though it's some kind of armor."

"Isn't it?" she said, and without thinking, reached up to brush a few dark strands of hair off his forehead. He caught her hand, moved it to his mouth. His lips pressed against the pads of her fingers, sending echoes of passion throughout her body.

"People lose the ones they love all the time," Brady said, his warm breath caressing her palm. "Love can't protect against evil."

"I know," she said, closing her eyes. What was happening? She felt hot and cold at the same time. Felt at peace and yet frightened. Felt like running away and like staying.

She could hear the creaks of the old house as Myra moved around in the kitchen. Brady inched closer; desire resonated in the tiny space between them.

His free hand traveled around her back, his fingers ran lightly under her waistband, down near her tailbone, brushing the rounded curves of her buttocks. It was time to move away from him. It was time to think clearly.

Instead, she arched closer.

Chapter Ten

Her minimal surrender was not lost on Brady whose life force seemed to double in the blink of his deep, dark eyes. She could feel his focus shift from their argument onto her as a woman. His silent realization of the changing stakes was so strong it instantly charged the atmosphere in the room.

She'd always known he regarded her as his. His love, his woman, his wife. Being the center of such desire was hypnotic and she had to guard against it. But her body knew his passion was equaled only by his enthusiasm, and inside she could feel the beginning of the end to reason.

Her heart banged against her ribs as his lips moved close to hers. "Remember your promise," she whispered, as if throwing out a life preserver and hoping one of them had the good sense to grab it.

"I promised I wouldn't kiss you again," he murmured in his sexy, low grumble that skated on the edge of every nerve ending in her back. His hot breath bathed her neck, then he tenderly sucked on her earlobe, sending long-dormant hormones into overdrive.

Maybe just a kiss. Just one. What could it hurt? She

put her hand on his chin and closed her eyes as she guided his mouth to hers.

He turned his face at the last moment, and her lips landed on his cheek. Okay, he had a lot more willpower than she had. Who would have thought that in the end what would save her from her traitorous body would be his common sense?

"I made no promises about not making love to you," he added.

Walk away…

"Come here," he said, sliding off the bed onto his knees, pulling her along so that she landed next to him, on the luxurious carpet.

"What are we doing?" she said very softly.

"What do you think we're doing?" he said, tugging his T-shirt off over his head, exposing his finely toned chest. Without even thinking about it, her fingers sprang to touch him, to stroke his muscles, to delight in the fiery heat of his bronzed skin.

"We shouldn't—" she said, even as her hands dipped down his chest and over his flat belly, brushing the buttons on his jeans and the obvious arousal straining beneath the denim.

He unbuttoned her blouse very slowly, never taking his eyes off her face. Her bra was a front-hooking type and he unhooked it, freeing her breasts, catching the hot mounds in his hands, his gaze dipping, his eyes feverish and hungry.

He licked his lips. The sight of his tongue flicking across his lips made her delirious. "Beautiful," he whispered. "So beautiful."

Maybe one last time, she told herself as he lowered his head to her breasts. The next thing she knew, he was running his tongue over each nipple and she knew she was lost.

"I have to have you," he said, pressing her so close it was hard to breathe but who needed to breathe, when the sensations came one on top of the other like ripples, building inside as his lips touched her neck and ears and face. She felt herself dampen in anticipation, her lust for him overriding every single thought process but one.

"Make love to me," she murmured pulling him down atop of her.

He kissed her everywhere but her mouth as he undressed her. She'd never made love with him without exchanging a hundred deep, wet kisses that built with the urgency of their passion. But try as she might to trap his face and claim his mouth, he avoided her. At first she thought it was due to that stupid promise and then she caught the glint in his eyes.

He was playing with her.

And she could tell that as soon as he knew she knew, the game stopped. He very slowly lowered his face, millimeter by millimeter, until his lips hovered right above hers, forcing her to reach around his neck and pull him the last inch, crushing their mouths together in a kiss that started in the mouth and instantly traveled everywhere else in her body. His tongue plunged inside her, and to Lara it was as though she absorbed him into herself.

From that moment, everything happened so fast it made her dizzy. Off came the rest of his clothes as they frantically clung to each other, discarding the past as they beat down the door on the present. It was as though the stored-up passion of the past year burst through a dam and swept down a valley, taking them with it, hurtling them against each other in an act as old as time and as new as daybreak.

Until they collapsed against one another, spent, and yet more desirous than ever. If things had been different, Lara would have coaxed him off the floor and between her sheets and done the whole thing again.

So why did this have the feeling of a goodbye?

As though reading her thoughts, he pulled her back into his arms. This time, his kiss was slow and thorough, an almost tender kiss that existed as it was, in the moment it happened.

Afterward, the bittersweet taste of farewell lingered on her lips.

BRADY SPENT the late afternoon returning his father's car to the garage and checking to see if his old man was still out like a light. Surprise, surprise, the house was empty, his dad was gone, no doubt back to River Front Street. For a microsecond, he toyed with the idea of going to fetch him, but in the end, hiked back to his own place and reclaimed his truck. He spent the next couple of hours at the Good Neighbors house, overseeing a few small projects.

It was nearing seven by the time he drove back to the Kirk house. He'd hoped to find Lara packing, but of course she wasn't. The woman was stubborn beyond belief. He had to think of a way to convey the growing conviction in his gut that there was a noose tightening around them.

It was kind of the same feeling he used to get when he was a kid and his parents got into one of their knock-down, drag-out drunken fights. He could remember lying in the top bunk, knowing Garrett was listening to everything, too, trying to figure out how he could make his parents stop, how he could make them see their behavior was hard on his little brother.

And feeling just about as helpless as he did now, when he couldn't find the right words.

After dinner, he moved to the desk, writing down what he knew about the missing Karen Wylie, the wounded Jason Briggs and a wild card named Nicole, a second teenager who wanted to talk to Lara in private.

It all amounted to a lot of nothing and a few maybes. He called Tom and asked if he knew anything about Jason's condition. No change. What must the kid's parents be going through? First, their boy had been part of robbery and car theft that left his best friend dead, followed by months in detention, followed by a gunshot wound less than two days after being released.

He asked Tom if the investigation into the shooting was progressing and got a terse yes. It's police business was the unspoken message.

Brady's gaze wandered to Lara. She sat in the big chair, Nathan on her lap, playing some game with him that involved kissing toes and fingers. She must have felt him looking at her, for she glanced up and met his gaze. Her smoldering eyes made him contemplate getting to his feet.

Myra came into the room, taking care of that urge. "I have the world's worst headache," she told Lara. "Mind if I take something for it and turn in early?"

"Of course not."

She shot Brady a surly parting look that seemed to say, "I know what you're up to, buddy." There was no doubt she sensed the change in the dynamics between

Lara and Brady since they'd argued their way up the stairs and descended smiling at each other.

Lara's voice interrupted his thoughts. "Are you staying here tonight?" she said.

He looked up from his doodling. "I'm staying if you are. I thought that was kind of obvious."

She got to her feet and he saw that Nathan had fallen asleep in her arms. "We're going to bed."

"I'll be along shortly."

She stared at him as she bit her bottom lip. "There's a guest room next to mine," she finally said.

"Good to know. I plan on sleeping with you."

"I—"

"Put Nathan down and come back. I'll wait."

She disappeared up the stairs. Brady tore the doodling paper into little pieces and put them in the trash, then he stood and paced until he heard her footsteps on the stairs.

He turned as she came into the room. "Nothing changed because of this afternoon," he said.

She started picking up baby paraphernalia in what appeared to be a bid not to have to look at him as she said, "I'm so glad to hear you say that. I was worried you might think we're back together."

Her words thundered between them. She glanced up and met his eyes.

He said, "I meant that you and Nathan are still in danger."

"I see," she said softly.

"Tell me what you meant."

She tucked a stuffed bear under one arm as she folded a baby blanket against her chest. Her voice was brisk as she said, "Fabulous sex doesn't change our basic issues."

He took two steps and grabbed her hands, sending

the blanket to the floor again. "Stop talking like a damn counselor."

"That's what I am!"

"Not with me."

"I see. It's okay for your cop persona to exist off-hours but I have to modify what I am?"

What was she talking about? He said, "I do not have a cop persona."

"Give me a break."

"Why did you have sex with me?" he said.

"That's a stupid question."

"Humor me. Never mind, for once, I'll play counselor. For two days you've been trying to get me to sign divorce papers. You've been trying to talk about child support and visitation and joint custody and all the rest of that crap because you couldn't wait to get out of Riverport. And then I finally tell you to go, I'll sign whatever paper you want, just leave so you'll be away from whatever is happening here, and all of a sudden, you won't go."

"That's not how—"

"Yes it is. That's exactly how it happened. You won't go because I want you to go."

"What's that got do with our making love?"

"I don't know," he grumbled. "Maybe you were just trying to distract me."

"Oh, brother." Twisting her hands from his grip, she added, "You better stick with being a cop or building houses or whatever it is you do now, because you're not going to be the next Freud."

"I don't want to be the next Freud. I just want to be the man you can't live without. I just want to be your husband."

She looked straight into his eyes and said, "That's what you had. That's what you sent away when the going got tough."

He had nothing to say to that because her words hit him square where he lived.

"I'm trying to protect you," he said.

"A year ago you tried to protect me from the fallout of the Armstrong shooting. Yesterday you didn't want me to see your family home, you tried to protect me from your past. Now you're trying to protect me from Bill Armstrong's vengeance. You don't know how to include me, Brady. How to include a wife. You love me but you don't know how to be married. I guess after seeing the way you grew up I understand a little—"

"The way I grew up?" he said, because he had to say something, he couldn't just stand there. With a gesture that included the mansion in which they stood, he said, "Look at the way *you* were raised. Do you think you have any more of a grasp on reality than I do?"

"At least my parents allowed *me* to be the child," she said softly.

He stared hard at her, loving her but hating her, too. Hating the emotions she could force on him, hating the power she had to get inside him. Finally, he lowered his gaze and she left the room, climbing the stairs to her childhood bedroom by herself.

He wanted to leave that mausoleum of a house in the worst way possible. He opened the front door and looked out onto the dark, empty street. How could he leave his family unprotected? But how could he stand to sit still? He dug a blanket out of the hall closet and emptied his pockets, then stared at the chair.

A moment later, he was locking the front door

behind him. Hands shoved in pockets, he took off down the dark sidewalk, forcing himself to turn at the corner and make a circle and then a larger one and another, the Kirk house always the hub even when he went blocks without actually seeing it. After more than an hour, he finally started back to the house.

No amount of walking would erase the sound of Lara's voice in his head: *At least my parents allowed* me *to be the child.*

It had been a ridiculous thing for her to say. He'd been a child....

No, he hadn't.

That's why her words stung. She was right and he knew it. What he didn't know was how to fix it.

He approached the big house with his head down, determined to stand guard outside, swearing to himself he would never go inside the place again. He glanced up as he stopped on the porch. His mouth went dry.

An orange glow in the sitting-room window danced and flickered. Fire!

He fumbled in his pocket for his keys, banging on the door and yelling as he did so. He finally found the keys and shoved the right one into the lock, pushed open the door and stepped into the foyer, looking toward the sitting room.

Flames leaped up the draperies, traveling toward him even as he watched, using the carpets for fuel. He reached for the phone on the small table by the grandfather clock and found the line dead. Grabbing from the floor the baby blanket Lara had dropped an hour or so before, he covered his nose and mouth and took off up the stairs, taking them two at a time.

The second floor was smokier than the first and he coughed as he ran down the hall to Lara's room, surprised to find the end of the hall a wall of fire.

Her door was closed and locked. He raised a leg and kicked the door in, doing his best to shut it afterward, but it was no use, he'd shattered the frame. Lara sat up upon his entry. She'd fallen asleep with the bedside lamp on and it miraculously still worked. Her expression went from surprised to horrified with her first conscious breath of smoke-laden air.

She immediately started coughing and he pulled her from the bed. "Get some shoes on. Hurry," he said as he ran to the crib where he picked up Nathan. Ignoring the baby's startled cries, Brady wrapped him in layers of baby sheets and blankets, tucking up loose ends as fast as he could. Lara was at his side by then, wearing nothing but a T-shirt, underpants and slippers. He handed Nathan to her then guided her back across the room to the door.

The flames had traveled down the hall, again fueled by expensive carpets laid over hardwood floors. "Fire in the kitchen must be coming up the old dumbwaiter," Lara said.

"We'll make a run for the stairs," Brady said, until he remembered the fire in the sitting room downstairs and wondered if those flames had managed to climb the stairs yet. If they had, would he be leading his family into an inferno?

"The solarium roof," Lara said, turning and running back to her window. He took a moment to push a dresser in front of the broken door, hoping to stop the flames for as long as possible. Both Lara and Nathan were coughing by the time he got to the window.

It was the old-fashioned double-hung kind and she was struggling with one arm to get the bottom panel raised. "Keep the baby down near the floor, honey, under the smoke," he said, and she dropped immediately. He worked on the window until he got it far enough open to kick out the screen. The fire would seek this new outlet soon, he could already see flames licking the edge of the door.

Lara pulled on his jeans and he knelt, coughing into the baby blanket he'd somehow managed to keep hold of. "The solarium juts out from the back of the house," she said. "It's about a ten-foot drop to the roof."

"You go first. I'll drop Nathan to you."

"No, you go—"

He grabbed her by the arm, took Nathan, laid him on the floor by their feet and lifted her to the window. "Hurry," he said.

Her gaze slid from the door to his eyes. "I love you," she said.

"I love you, too. Now, climb out. Perch on the sill, take my hands, I'll lower you as far as I can, then you'll have to drop."

She immediately climbed into the window and leveraged herself outside. He gripped her hands and she used her feet to rappel against the outside wall until his arms were stretched tight, her weight dragging him farther out the window.

"Let go," she called, and he dropped her. He heard a thud a second later. She yelled she was okay.

The lamp snapped off as electricity to the house was lost. Brady picked up Nathan and tightened the swaddling around his struggling body, the baby's cries bruising his heart. Over and over, Brady prayed that his son would make it through this night, and he kissed the tear-stained cheeks.

The flaw in their plan showed itself when Brady held Nathan outside the window and found he couldn't really see Lara's exact location. How could he drop his son if he couldn't see?

And then, like a miracle, a brief flash of light from the ground scanned the side of the house and he caught a glimpse of Lara standing right beneath his position. A second later the light flickered off, but now Brady knew where Lara was.

"Here he comes," he called, and dropped his son.

A second later, broken words floated up to him, reaching his ears like music. "I...I caught...him." And this was followed by some very healthy baby bellows.

He was on the verge of making the jump himself when movement in the yard caught his attention. A man ran beneath the weak light affixed to the end of the small dock out by the river. The dock light was apparently on its own circuit. The man hurried along the dock and disappeared over the side. A second later, a boat detached itself and was lost on the dark water.

"Brady!" Lara screamed.

"I'm coming."

"What about Myra?"

He jumped, landing on his feet and hands, his bad knee buckling under him, pitching him forward. He caught himself a few inches from the edge of the roof.

"What about Myra?" Lara said again, grabbing his arm, her voice barely audible over the sound of the fire and her son's wailing.

"I'll go get her. Where exactly is her room?"

"On the other side of the kitchen."

They used the wisteria trellis nailed against the solarium wall to get to the ground, both of them pausing for a second to look at the house, both of them stunned with how far the fire had spread. It appeared to have started in three or four places at once.

He took Lara's arm and they ran around the solarium to the kitchen where flames glowed through the windows.

"Myra's room is on the other side," Lara said.

"Go to a neighbor's house. Make sure the fire department's been called. I'll get her out."

"You shouldn't go back in—"

"Go," he urged, pushing her away.

She ran from him as he stuck the baby blanket in a birdbath and used the kettle barbecue like a battering ram to break the window into the laundry that adjoined the kitchen.

The wet blanket went around his shoulders, over his head. The laundry was filled with smoke. The kitchen fire wasn't as bad as it had seemed from the outside, and he was able to dash through.

A narrow door on the far side of the counter, back in an alcove he'd never noticed before, had to be Myra's door. There were flames in front of the door. He grabbed a kitchen chair and banged it against the door, hoping the noise would wake the woman. Using his wet blanket, he grabbed the knob and wrenched the door open, running into a room so filled with smoke it was hard to take a breath.

He'd have one chance at this, he knew. If she'd staggered out of bed and fallen in a corner, he'd never find her in time. He dashed to the bed and threw back the covers.

Light from the fire showed him the shape of a woman in the bed. He grabbed her shoulders, but she didn't stir. He didn't dare take time to assess her condition, and leaning down, lifted her over his shoulder in a fireman's hold. He ran back the way he'd come, through the flames and the smoke, through the kitchen into the laundry room and out the backdoor.

He heard sirens in the distance. Man, he loved that sound.

He got Myra as far away from the house as he could, out near the flowers under the trees, and lowered her to the grass. She looked at him with dazed eyes, and then she, too, began coughing.

He waited until she caught her breath and checked her pulse. Her color was returning to normal.

"Where am I?" she said as she seemed to see him for the first time. She sputtered, "Who are—oh my goodness, is that you, Brady? What happened?"

Brady stepped aside so she could see past him to the now towering inferno.

"Lara and the baby—"

"They're safe. I want to go find them. Will you be okay?"

"Yes."

He ran toward the house until he saw a figure jog around the corner. Lara's voice screamed, "Brady! Brady!"

He yelled as he moved toward her. "Get away from there!" He was afraid she'd be cut if the windows blew.

She turned in his direction. He could see the outline of her slender body, thanks to the burning house behind her, but he couldn't see her face. She started running toward him, covering the distance in a very short time, long bare legs flashing in the light of the blaze.

He caught her in his arms.

THE FIREFIGHTERS COULDN'T stop talking about the chances of two house fires in two days, even if they were in separate towns and nineteen miles apart. What were the chances?

Pretty good, Brady thought. If an arsonist wanted to get rid of two people in two different places, two fires might just do the job.

"I have to leave for a while," he told Lara.

She'd reclaimed Nathan from the neighbor she'd left him with while she came to look for Brady and was now standing near the ambulance crew and Myra.

"Do you have to?"

"Yes."

"Myra's sister offered to take us all in for the night. She's on her way over." She looked down at herself and added, her voice kind of awestruck, "I don't have any clothes."

One of the firefighters had given her a blue blanket that she had draped over her scantily clad body and over Nathan, too. The little guy had fallen asleep again.

Brady cupped the back of Lara's head and kissed her forehead, his heart aching with the things he wanted to say to her. "I'll be back soon."

"The police—"

"That's why I have to get out of here right now, before they start asking questions."

She looked up at him, her eyes watering still from the smoke. "You know who did this, don't you?"

"Yes."

"Was it Armstrong?"

"Yes. I saw him out by the dock. He left in a boat."

"Why don't you wait until Tom—"

"No," Brady said. "Not this time."

"Take your gun," she said.

Chapter Eleven

Brady didn't need a gun. He was mad enough to take Bill Armstrong apart with his bare hands. A gun would just get in the way.

Too late he realized his truck keys were in the burned-up house along with his cell phone and wallet. He ran the mile to his place in record time. He kept the Harley key hidden on the bike and within seconds of hitting his parking lot, roared off into the night without a helmet, as that was locked inside his apartment.

All the lights were on at the Armstrong house despite the fact it was two-thirty in the morning. Brady left the Harley a couple doors down. No need to announce his arrival.

He kept to the shadows as he moved quickly through the yard. He was sure Tom or another Riverport cop would arrive any minute and he wanted a few moments alone with Armstrong before that happened.

In the end, he was left with a decision: knock on the door or break it down. One or the other. If he barged in, he was likely to be blown away by a shotgun wielded either by a crazy Bill Armstrong or his terrified wife. No jury in the world would blame either one of them.

He knocked.

The door opened at once. His heart lurched in anticipation, but it was Sandra who peered through the crack at him, not Bill.

"What's happened?" she said, her hand bunching her robe up near her throat, her knuckles shiny white.

"Do you know where your husband is, Mrs. Armstrong?"

She stared at him so long he wasn't sure she was going to answer. She finally said, "He's gone." As if to prove he wasn't there, she opened the door wider and stepped aside.

He entered the house warily, though he had a hard time believing Sandra Armstrong would purposefully set him up for murder.

The room was lit to the point of glaring brightness, obliterating any dark corners, revealing every secret. Immaculately kept to the point of starkness, the only ornaments, and there were literally dozens of them, were framed pictures of two good-looking brunette kids, one girl and one boy, no more than a year or so apart in age. The pictures were a chronicle of their lives, starting with a small toddler sitting by a baby lying on a blanket, up to the same children as teenagers dressed for a dance or a party, standing side by side, looking kind of impatient at having to pose and yet vibrant and alive.

He was standing in the middle of a shrine dedicated to the memory of Bill and Sandra Armstrong's children, one dead by her own hand, the other gunned down by Brady Skye.

"What happened to you?" Sandra Armstrong gasped. He caught his reflection on the blank television screen. Six-foot-one-inch of soot-covered male who looked angry and crushed at the same time.

"Someone set my wife's mother's house on fire tonight, Mrs. Armstrong."

She clutched her robe up high, under her chin again. Her pale skin seemed to drain of even more color. Her eyes went wide with shock and pain and he once again wished he was anywhere but standing in front of her.

What would learning of her husband's actions of the last few days do to her? What would happen to her if Lara's theory was right and she discovered her husband had molested their daughter and her girlfriends?

"I need to talk to Bill," he said.

"He didn't do it," she protested. "He wouldn't—"

"He was there, Mrs. Armstrong. I saw him."

She staggered and he grabbed her elbows, guiding her to a chair. She sat down stiffly. He perched on the edge of another chair to face her eye to eye.

"I can understand why you and your husband hate me," he said. "I don't blame you. But your husband either tried to kill my family tonight or he knows who did. I have to talk to him."

She stared at him for another of those interminable minutes before she finally muttered, "He came home late. He'd been drinking. He was talking to himself. I tried to get him to go to bed but he wouldn't do it. Instead he went out to the garage and banged around out there for a long time. I finally went to see what he was doing. He was...he was loading the truck."

"Loading the truck?"

"I thought maybe he was going to go camping or something. I thought it might be a good idea if he left town for a few days and stopped obsessing about your son. He loaded his skiff in the back. Fishing, I thought.

The outboard motor came next and then two or three fuel cans—"

He stopped her. "Fuel cans? Why so many?"

This time her stare challenged him to connect the dots.

"And then he left," she mumbled.

"And you haven't seen him since then?"

Another pause as she searched his eyes. "He came back less than an hour ago. He smelled like, like smoke."

"You have to tell me where he is now, Mrs. Armstrong. He has to be stopped."

"He left again," she said. "He didn't tell me where he was going or when he was coming back."

There wasn't a doubt in Brady's mind Armstrong had shined that light on the burning house, which meant he knew Lara, at least, had escaped. He got to his feet in a hurry. He had to get back to Lara and Nathan.

Sandra Armstrong caught his arm at the door. Her wide eyes seemed to swallow him. "Please," she said. "Please, you have to help Bill."

"I'll try," he said, anxious to get going.

But it was obvious there was something else she needed to say and he made himself stand there for the few seconds it took her to add, "He took a rifle with him."

TOM WAS WALKING UP the sidewalk as Brady left the Armstrong house.

"Lara wouldn't tell me where you went, but I figured it was over here," he said, hitching his hands on his belt. "You left the scene of a crime."

"I have to go," he said, not stopping to talk.

Tom called, "Wait a second."

Brady paused and looked back over his shoulder.

"I'm in a hurry. Lara took Nathan over to the house-keeper's sister's house. I have to get over there."

"The fire investigator will be here in a few hours," Tom interrupted. "The place reeks of gasoline fumes. There were several fires started. Do you have any reason to suspect Bill Armstrong?" He nodded toward the house. "Is he in there?"

"No," Brady said, but knew he had to explain. He hurriedly told Tom what he'd seen that night and the conversation he'd just had with Sandra Armstrong.

Tom shook his head. "Dixon isn't going to like you coming over here—"

"I don't care what Dixon does or doesn't like," Brady said. "He's not my boss, he's yours."

"And you're my partner."

"I *was* your partner."

"I'm just telling you to stay out of my way. Is that too much to ask?"

Brady leveled a stare at his ex-partner. "Bill Armstrong tried to kill my wife and son tonight. Now he's out there somewhere with a gun. So the answer to your question is yes. Asking me to leave everything to you is asking too much." And with that he took off down the sidewalk to reclaim the Harley.

Once on his bike, he realized he had no idea where Myra's sister lived or even what her name was. He returned to the Kirk house where he found firefighters putting out the last of the blaze. Tom's new partner, the Hastings kid Brady had first met the night Lara's car went into the river, was attempting to keep the small crowd of onlookers—mostly neighbors, it seemed—at a safe distance. Brady recognized the local newspaper reporter and gave him a wide berth.

What would Lara's mother think of him now that he'd been indirectly responsible for the destruction of her home? He hoped she kept up her insurance payments.

One of the firefighters was an old friend and called out to Brady. He passed along a message from Lara, giving him Myra's sister's address. Brady rode the Harley to the woman's house, which turned out to be less than a mile from his place, and spent hours standing guard, filthy and tired but strangely wide awake. When Bill Armstrong failed to appear by daybreak, Brady went back to his apartment, roused the manager for a spare key and took a shower.

He guessed it was up to the police to find Armstrong. His job was to keep Lara and Nathan safe.

LARA HAPPILY TOOK OFF the robe Myra's sister, Gretchen, had loaned her and changed into the sweatpants and T-shirt Brady had brought her from his apartment. The clothes were a little big, but they smelled like him and that was comforting.

She exited the bathroom to find Brady sitting on the guest bed next to Nathan, who wore diapers fashioned from kitchen towels and nothing else. The baby was clean and pink again, declared healthy by the EMTs. And he was safe, at least for the moment.

"I need to do some shopping," Lara said, leaning over to kiss Nathan's bare tummy.

Brady pulled her onto his lap and nuzzled her neck. She closed her eyes for a second and relaxed in his arms. She owed him her life and that of her son. He'd even risked himself to save Myra.

But in the end, it didn't change the basic facts of their differences.

He finally said, "You don't have credit cards or cash. I'll go with you."

"I'll pay you back—"

He tightened his grip around her waist and interrupted her. "I want you to know I won't ask you to leave Riverport again. You were right. Until Armstrong is behind bars, you and Nathan belong right here. We'll talk about what comes next later. I'll stop pressuring you."

She drew back a few inches and narrowed her eyes. "Who the heck are you and what have you done with Brady Skye?"

He laughed at her lame joke and she took a deep breath.

"I know we're lucky to be alive," she said. "I'm thankful for that, I really am. But when I think of my mother's house I just want to cry. How am I ever going to explain all this to her?"

"Maybe if you let her hold Nathan as you tell her, she'll keep her priorities straight."

"I know that. But her whole life went up in flames. My childhood, too. That counts for something."

He opened his mouth to answer, but the words died on his lips. He'd been about to say, *Be grateful you had a childhood to lose.*

He wouldn't say it. He couldn't. Besides, she didn't need an argument, she was just telling him that she'd lost something important.

"She'll understand," he said, hoping it was the truth. "If she's honest, she'll realize her dislike of fire alarms could have resulted in your deaths."

"I hope that decision doesn't void her policy." With a sigh, she added, "I guess there's nothing I can do about any of it now."

"I guess not."

MOST OF THE DAY was taken up with replacing the clothing and accessories lost in the fire and calling credit-card companies and anyone else they could think of who needed to know their identification had been destroyed.

After shopping, they spoke to countless officials, including Chief Dixon, who kept staring at Nathan whom Brady held. *Let him say one word about "Another Skye," and I'll punch him into next week,* Brady thought, but Dixon reserved his comments for the fire. Tom had been right. Dixon was irked that Brady had gone to Armstrong's house after they escaped the blaze and told him so. Brady ignored him.

The truth was, the whole department knew Brady had placed Bill Armstrong at the scene. It was also common knowledge Armstrong was coming unglued. The fact he was now running around town with a gun had everyone on edge.

"Chief Dixon said they think it was Bill who shot Jason. He said they've gone to his house and looked for guns."

Brady imagined how that intrusion must have felt to Sandra Armstrong. If he could find Bill, maybe he would ease some of her pain. He owed her that much. Lara glanced at her new watch and added, "It's getting late. Let's take Nathan back to Myra and go talk to Nicole."

"Do you think she and Gretchen can keep Nathan safe?"

"Are you kidding? Gretchen is armed to the teeth. She stayed up all last night patrolling the house while Myra, Nathan and I slept."

"I didn't see her," Brady said skeptically, "and I was outside."

"Maybe you didn't see her, honey, but she saw you."

AFTER THE FLOOD a few years earlier, the city of River-port had applied for and received a grant from the state to rebuild their city park. Walkways and fences had been constructed almost immediately, but it had taken until the year before for the new playground to take shape. Everyone agreed it had been worth waiting for, however, as it was a modern structure that combined slides, rock-wall climbers, sliding poles and bridges within the illusion of a ship.

They parked with a few other cars and walked across the grass where two kids braved the ninety-degree heat to play on the adjoining swings. A lone adult-size figure stood to the side, yelling at one of the children to stop swinging the other so high. The one close to orbit screamed at the top of his lungs.

Lara barely recognized Nicole from the few times she'd seen her at the teen center in the company of her friends. Her long, shiny black hair was short now, spiky, with bright pink and blue tips. Her hair wasn't the only thing that had changed. The kid had grown three inches and developed a curvy figure. She wore a gauzy navy blouse emblazoned with golden swirls, cutoffs and strappy sandals.

"Nicole?" Lara said when they were a few feet away.

The girl turned. She smiled when she saw Lara, though the smile faltered as they got closer and she seemed to realize the tall man trailing Lara was actually with her.

"This is my friend Brady," Lara said. She could almost feel Brady wince when she called him her friend.

"I know who he is," Nicole said. "I saw his picture in the paper. He killed Sara's little brother."

Lara didn't dare turn around and look at Brady whose whole body she imagined had tensed. Instead, she jumped into the ensuing silence with, "Brady is more than a friend, he's also an ex-cop, as you seem to know. Let's sit down, okay?"

The girl said, "I won't talk in front of him."

Brady took a look around the park as though searching for snipers. With a start, Lara realized that's exactly what he was doing. Looking for Bill Armstrong. And that's why they'd taken the circuitous route to the park. He'd been checking for a tail. He said, "I'm going to go sit right over there and check out the water fountain, Lara. Call if you need me."

Lara and Nicole both watched Brady walk across the playground. Nicole said, "He should be in jail."

Lara motioned at the bench and they sat down. Staring at the kids who were now scooting up and down the ladders and slides, she said, "Brady Skye is a very decent, honorable man who pays every day of his life for being forced to shoot Sara's brother. But right now, we're both trying to figure out what Jason Briggs wanted to tell me. Do you know?"

Nicole answered the question with one of her own. "I heard about the fire at the Kirk mansion. Do they know who did it?"

"We think the same man who started the fire has been hanging around a lot, making threats."

Shouting erupted from the play equipment. Nicole stood abruptly, took a few steps forward and said, "Sammy, you stop that or I'll tell your mother."

Sammy was tugging the other kid down the slide by

his hair. Both the children started laughing as they slapped at each other. They ignored Nicole.

Nicole sat down again and faced Lara, looking younger than before. "I'm never having kids. Never."

Lara said, "You said you wanted to talk to me about Karen Wylie."

"She called me. You know, the day you guys came into the pharmacy and talked to her. She called me after u left. You spooked her. She told me she was going o go away with her boyfriend, that they were going to et married. She said it was his idea."

"Her boyfriend?" No one had mentioned a boyfriend t ough they all now knew she'd met up with a man in S cottsdell.

"But she was lying," Nicole added.

"How do you know?"

"Because the man she thought was her boyfriend is n body's boyfriend," she said, her voice suddenly s fter. "That's not how he...operates."

"And how do you know this?"

She glanced quickly at Lara and away again. "I just do. He and I...it doesn't matter. Anyway, he's still in town."

Nicole looked around as she spoke, as though wa ching for someone. Her nerves got to Lara, who lowered her voice, too. "Who is this man?"

Nicole stared at the kids. They were at each other aga n. "I can't tell you."

"Nicole—"

" can't. I won't."

"Then why did you want to talk to me?"

She shrugged one thin shoulder. "I kind of like Mrs. Wyli . I know she's worried. I'm just telling you that Kare didn't run away with a boyfriend, that's all."

"Then why did she go?"

"Because she's stupid about guys. She thinks she's going to be a movie star. The girl is stupid." Nicole stared into the distance and then added, "And *he's* mean."

"This man?"

"Yes."

"In what way?"

She shook her head so hard the colored tips looked like confetti. "I'm not going to say any more."

"You're afraid of him."

Nicole nodded. "He's got a lot of power."

"I have to have a name. The police will want to talk to you."

She stood abruptly, ready to bolt.

"Listen," Lara said, standing beside her. "I know you girls spent a lot of time at the Armstrong house when Sara was still alive. I know he befriended you. Is it Bill Armstrong?"

Nicole bit her lip.

"I can help if you'll confide in me. There are laws against hurting people."

Nicole met Lara's gaze and laughed.

Brady strode across the playground. "Everything okay?"

"I don't know," Lara said, and paraphrased what Nicole had told her. Nicole wouldn't meet Brady's gaze.

"Call your mother," he urged. "Get her to come over here—"

"I can't," Nicole said. "This is the boys' afternoon to be at the park. I have to watch them."

"Bill Armstrong is running around with a gun,"

Brady said. "Take the boys back to their parents' house and stay there until your own mother comes home."

A few minutes later, Nicole piled the kids into her tiny blue car and drove off. A sticker on the rear window read, Riverport High School honor student.

Lara said, "I blew that. She tried to reach out and I blew it."

Brady's voice sounded speculative as he said, "I keep thinking I've seen her before."

"Has she ever been in trouble with the cops?"

"I don't know."

"Maybe—"

Both Lara and Brady had replaced their phones earlier in the day and now Brady's rang, interrupting Lara. He answered it quickly, surprised to hear Myra's voice, though her attitude toward him had undergone a decided thaw since he'd rescued her from the fire.

"The hospital is trying to get hold of Lara," Myra said. "They called the police who called Gretchen who called me, but I can't find the phone number Lara gave me, but I could find yours."

Lara called the hospital and after identifying herself, listened with growing attention. "I'll be right there," she said at last and, clicking off the phone, touched Brady's arm. "Jason Briggs is conscious and he's asking for me."

THEY ARRIVED at the hospital to find a guard on Jason's door. Chief Dixon was also standing close by and he barred Brady's admittance. "The kid wants to talk to Ms. Kirk," Dixon said. "He didn't say nothing about you."

"Have you found Bill Armstrong yet?" Brady

asked in a low voice Lara recognized as his voice of massive control.

"No," Dixon said. "But we will."

Lara said, "How long has Jason been conscious?"

"Not long. We've had a guard on his door since the first night. Only his doctors and parents have been allowed in. His parents are on their way over, so if I were you, I'd get in there. I'm sending in a police officer, too, to take notes of what he says. The doctors say you can have five minutes, no more."

Leaving the two men to glare at one another, Lara entered the room quietly. Jason Briggs, last seen unconscious lying on the grass, didn't look a lot better lying in the hospital bed. Almost as pale as his sheets, his black hair stark against his skin, hospital apparatus blipped and beeped all around him.

A nurse stepped to one side to allow Lara to lean close. Lara whispered, "Jason?"

The boy's eyes fluttered open as though he'd been waiting for her. His breathing sounded labored.

"Hey, Jason," Lara said. He looked so young and vulnerable, and for a second, she flashed on the moment she'd lost hold of him in the car as it filled with water, the frantic grabbing for his hair to pull him back to the surface...

"Ms. Kirk," Jason whispered.

"I'm here."

His eyes closed and she felt a stab of disappointment. She glanced at the police officer, who shrugged. As she started to straighten, Jason's eyes opened again. "Ms. Kirk?"

She put her hand on his shoulder. "Yes, Jason, I'm still here."

"It was…fossil…blue," Jason said. "Billy…"

Fossil? What did that mean?

"The Colt…"

Billy, blue fossils, colt—the memory came back with a flash. Billy and Jason at the teen center, an overheard conversation about an old Colt revolver…

Aware the officer was writing down everything Billy said, Lara's heart all but stopped beating as she murmured, "Are you talking about a gun, Jason? Did Billy Armstrong have a gun the night he was shot?"

"His grandpa's," Jason whispered.

Lara felt like smacking herself. The knowledge of the gun had been niggling at her memory since she returned to Riverport and talked to Brady that first afternoon. "I understand," she said, aching to tell Brady. She waited patiently as Jason's eyes drifted shut, but once again, when she moved, he rallied. "Karen?"

"Karen? You mean Karen Wylie?"

Jason nodded. "Talk…to…her."

"I'm sorry," Lara said softly. "She's…well, out of town."

He grew restless as he reached up and grabbed Lara's wrist. His grip was amazingly strong. "No," he said.

Karen's name was all Jason had managed to say before someone shot him. She'd been on his mind since he got out of juvie. Lara said, "What is it about Karen?"

His hand slid from her wrist. "Naked," he said, licking dry lips. His voice was so soft both Lara and the attending officer leaned in closer to hear.

"Karen was naked?"

He nodded again.

"I don't understand—"

He whispered, "Bad pictures."

He was fading in and out. The nurse who had been standing cleared her throat. Lara said, "Jason, one more thing. Did Billy's father ever—"

"Ms. Kirk," Chief Dixon said sternly from the doorway.

"I'm coming," she told him. The officer stopped writing and took a step toward the door.

Jason said, "Mr. Armstr—"

"Ms. Kirk?"

Lara glanced up at Dixon, annoyed beyond endurance. "Please, just give me a moment!" She looked back down at Jason, but his eyes had shut again, and this time when she gently touched his shoulder there was no response.

The nurse examined him quickly. "He's just asleep," she said after a moment. "You'd better go now."

Lara looked around at the officer who had been taking notes. "Did you hear what he said about the gun?"

He grinned. "Every word."

Lara walked past Dixon, out into the hall, walked right up to Brady and took his hands.

"Billy Armstrong had a gun the night he died," she said. "He was carrying an old Colt with blue-fossil grips. I actually remember hearing the boys talk about it a week or so before the shooting. They were practically drooling. I think Billy stole it from his grandmother's house. I doubt she ever knew it was gone."

"Then he wasn't unarmed?" Brady said softly.

"No."

"I did see him pull a gun?" he said, his voice reflecting the growing wonder of this discovery.

"You must have, because a gun like that never showed up in the investigation, did it?"

"No, and they tore the place apart. The car, too."

"The gun fell into the river."

His eyes glistened as he put his arms around her, lifted her off her feet and buried his head against her neck.

Chapter Twelve

"Jason also tried to say something about Billy's father," Lara said as they drove back to Myra's house. "That damn Chief Dixon interrupted and Jason fell asleep before he could finish his thought."

"Dixon has impeccably bad timing," Brady said. They were driving his truck. As disappointing as it was that Lara hadn't heard what the boy had to say about Bill Armstrong, Brady was still riding high on the euphoria of knowing Billy had had a gun.

He hadn't shot an unarmed kid. He felt twenty years younger, twenty pounds lighter, the day appeared twenty times brighter. "What do you think he was trying to say about Karen?"

"The naked-picture thing? I have no idea."

"We'll ask Armstrong, if we ever find him."

There were two police units parked in front of Gretchen's house. Tom James and Chief Dixon stood outside talking to Myra. The housekeeper looked up as Brady slowed the truck. She'd been crying.

"Something's wrong," Lara said, fumbling with the door handle. Brady was outside and around to her side in a flash. Together they ran across the grass.

In that ten seconds, Brady died a thousand deaths. He shouldn't have left Nathan unguarded. He should have stayed with the baby instead of going with Lara to the hospital. He should have insisted they all stay together.

Myra burst into new tears when she saw Lara but it was Brady to whom she turned, almost collapsing in his arms. "He tried to take the little dear," she cried.

Lara's gasp seemed to suck in a gallon of air. Brady immediately put an arm around her.

"He tried? Who tried?"

"Armstrong," Tom said.

Myra's watery eyes searched Lara's face as she added, "I only left him on the porch alone for a moment, I swear. The breeze comes through that way and it's so much cooler. He was asleep in his new car seat. I cracked the door and went back inside for iced tea. I shouldn't have left him, this is all my fault. I just went away for a moment. When I came back, there was Bill Armstrong, big as you please, walking out the door with the baby still in his car seat."

Lara grabbed Myra's arm. "But he didn't actually hurt Nathan, right? Nathan is okay, isn't he?"

"I threw my iced tea at Bill! He dropped the seat—"

Lara's hands flew to her mouth.

"It didn't hurt the baby, the little lamb never even woke up! He's inside with Gretchen, right as rain."

Lara took off at a run toward the house, Myra on her heels.

Tom cleared his throat and looked at Brady. "Apparently, the housekeeper's scream alerted the other lady, who attacked Armstrong with a dust mop. He ran off after that and they called us."

Dixon added, "We've got everyone and their brother looking for him. He can't have gone far."

Brady clenched his jaw. He'd been trying for days to get the department to take the threat of Armstrong seriously and now they were stuck playing catch-up. Icy-hot fury flamed in his gut, but he swallowed hard and directed his anger where it belonged—at Bill Armstrong. The man was out of control, capable of anything.

Not with my son...

"The lab boys will be here any minute," Dixon said, sparing Brady an uneasy half glance. "I'll get a patrol car out here, too, until we find Armstrong. Tom, I want you on the street with the others."

Tom touched his gun, his eyes blazing as he looked at Brady. "You stay here with Lara, buddy, she needs you. I'll find the bastard."

"That's right," Dixon said. "This is a job for professionals."

Tom strode off to his car. Dixon produced a pack from his pocket and tapped out a cigarette. He looked up at Brady as he lit it and said, "I know the Briggs kid said the Armstrong boy had a gun."

"Yeah," Brady said.

Putting the cigarette to his lips, he inhaled deeply. "It doesn't change a thing," he said as he exhaled a cloud of smoke. "We're better off without you."

Brady met Dixon's gaze and said, "At least I don't go around making passes at little girls."

Dixon snatched the cigarette from his lips, threw it to the sidewalk and stomped it out. "Where did you—"

"Hear about your first marriage? Hear why my mother divorced you?"

Dixon finally sputtered, "The kid I supposedly propositioned was a few months shy of seventeen. She did the propositioning, by the way. I married her after the divorce."

"I heard she was thirteen."

"Your father won Theresa and then he destroyed her. I guess he showed me."

Brady didn't blink.

Dixon cast him one more baleful glance before turning on his heels. Brady jogged to the house as the chief drove off. Lara, holding Nathan, looked up at him and smiled as he opened the door. Brady was across the room in two steps, gathering his wife and son in a huge embrace.

They were his salvation. They were the reason he wouldn't turn out like his father or Chief Dixon.

There was a loud knock on the door. Gretchen appeared from the kitchen and admitted the lab guys. Casting Lara and Brady an apologetic smile, she disappeared into the house to show them the way to the porch, which they would process.

As soon as the swinging door closed behind them, Brady leaned down and claimed Lara's lips. He kissed her with relief, joy, fear, anger—it was all part and parcel of being alive. He wanted her in the worst way possible, not for an hour or a few stolen moments. He wanted her forever. And he wanted her to want him.

"I should have left when you asked me to," she said, searching his face. "Now I'm afraid to go. He's out there. I can feel his eyes on the back of my neck. I can feel his hatred. He'll never quit until he's hurt Nathan."

"I won't let that happen," Brady said. "It's gone on far too long as it is. I'll take care of it."

"But Tom—"

The memory of Tom's fingers dancing near his gun as he vowed to find Bill Armstrong surfaced in Brady's mind. He said, "If Tom finds Armstrong first he's likely to do something impulsive. I've got to stop him before he sabotages himself. Chief Dixon said he'd send a patrol car over. As soon as it comes, I'm going to go find Armstrong and put an end to this."

She stared at him a long moment before finally nodding. "Okay."

He caught her hand and held it against his chest. "I'm so sorry I wasn't vigilant enough."

"Oh, Brady, listen to us," she said. "I'm to blame, you're to blame. What difference does it make?"

It made a lot of difference to Brady. He kissed her again. "I'm crazy in love with you," he whispered against her lips. "I've never loved another woman. I never will." It was on the tip of his tongue to promise to become the man she wanted, open and happy-go-lucky and willing to examine every dark corner of his subconscious. But the words wouldn't come.

As he kissed Nathan's forehead, she whispered, "Be careful."

A PATROL OFFICER Brady didn't recognize arrived a few minutes later and Brady left. He drove to his apartment and let himself in with his new house key. It took him a couple of minutes to find his backup key for the dresser drawer, but once he did, he reached for the Glock without hesitation.

He strapped on his holster and despite everything, hoped he'd find a way through the ensuing hours to bring in Armstrong without drawing the gun.

As he got into his truck again, he tried to clear his

head and organize his thoughts. Bill Armstrong was coming apart. He was acting on impulse, striking out. Where would he go between strikes? Where would he feel safe?

Okay, maybe not safe. Where would he feel connected, where would he feel some kind of comfort? Somewhere apart from his wife's consuming grief. Someplace private and meaningful.

At the graveyard where his two kids had been buried side by side?

Think, Brady. Where would you go if you were Bill Armstrong? What if the need for revenge ate up every available brain synapse? What if the past felt twice as real as the present, the past was all you had left besides hate? Where would you go to think up your next idea to hurt the man who killed your son?

And then he knew.

HE DROVE to the old Evergreen Timber-mill site, his heartbeat accelerating when he found the chain and lock securing the repaired gate had been sawed apart and looped through the fence again so it would appear linked to all but a careful observer.

He left the truck parked down the block and let himself in through the gate. The afternoon had faded to evening, the hot, oppressive air weighed down on him as he walked, memories of a year ago dogged his heels.

He reached the place where Jason had wrecked the car and the two boys had sprung from it like rats leaving a downed ship. Armstrong's truck was parked almost in the same spot, the back empty now.

And parked beside it, a police unit. Tom's car.

He should have known Tom would have reached the same conclusion he had. He made a quick examination of both vehicles then took off to the right, veering toward the river, following the invisible path he'd traveled a year before.

He stopped when he got close to the spot Billy Armstrong's life had ended. A feeling of déjà vu struck as he heard an Armstrong voice raised in anger, but this time it belonged to the father instead of the son. It came from behind a nearby stack of abandoned railroad ties.

He moved in that direction, balancing stealth with the burning need to see what was going on. Was Tom with Armstrong? He strained for the sound of another voice, but Armstrong's ramblings obliterated everything, even the sound of the river rushing by.

Armstrong's words grew more distinct. "Voices, voices," he cried. "Day and night, voices, bad voices telling me what to do, a son for a son, retribution will be mine!"

The words froze Brady's heart, but not his step. Crazy people did crazy things. Where was Tom? Had Armstrong already turned the tables on him? Was Tom still alive?

Moving a few steps, Brady peered carefully around the pile and saw Armstrong standing near the edge of the wharf. The man was as gray as the river at twilight. Even his sandy hair and beard had faded, though that was no doubt a trick of light.

Armstrong began pacing back and forth near the edge, mumbling one moment, shouting another, stabbing at thin air. He didn't appear to be armed, though a rifle lay a few feet away.

Brady couldn't see Tom, but the sound of his friend's

voice finally filled a lull in Armstrong's ramblings. "You've done too many evil things, you've caused too much pain," Tom said.

Brady took a deep breath. Tom was still alive.

"I know, it's true," Armstrong said, all but crying now. Brady shifted his position and managed to see Tom through a crack in the railroad ties. He stood a good twenty yards away, florid face flushed a shade darker than usual. He stood with his feet planted out to either side, arm extended, gun in hand, pointed at Armstrong.

Worse, the tension that boiled in Tom's body seemed to cause a disturbance in the air around him. He looked like a cartoon bomb, fuse lit, ready to explode.

Undoubtedly, Tom had called in his position and his sighting of Armstrong's truck, which meant the police would arrive within minutes. Should Brady stand by and wait or should he try to defuse the situation himself?

Armstrong began shouting again, and this time Tom's voice was raised, too. Brady made the only decision that made sense to him. He slowly stepped around the ties, the Glock in its holster, his hands spread out to the sides.

Both of the other men immediately looked at him.

Armstrong took a step in his direction. He said, "Your son. A son for a son. No, no. Protect the—"

But that was all, for in the next instant, Tom fired his gun. The bullet hit Armstrong, who had twisted away at the last moment, in the shoulder, and he staggered backward, grabbing out for a piling to steady himself. Brady yelled as Tom fired again and Armstrong disappeared over the side of the wharf, the sound of him splashing into the river reverberating along the wharf, riding on the tail of gunfire.

"What the hell?" Brady yelled, oblivious to anything but a searing sense of unreality. Tom had just plugged Armstrong and was running to the wharf's edge, gun still drawn.

"Put that damn thing away!" Brady yelled as he ran to join Tom.

"I had to do it," Tom said. "You saw."

"Saw what?" Brady snapped as he scanned the rippled surface of the gray water. "Saw you shoot an unarmed man? Radio for help. Hurry, he might just be wounded." He looked around the wharf for something to use to throw to Armstrong should he surface. There wasn't a thing.

"I don't believe you," Tom shouted, gun waving. "Armstrong tried to kill your wife and your son. You know how it works, he would have pled insanity. Sooner or later, he would have come after your family again. I did it for you."

Brady repeated, "Put the gun away." He thought he saw Armstrong surface, but then what he thought was a head disappeared and he wasn't sure. "What you did was shoot a defenseless man," he told Tom. "Get some help out here or I will."

"I covered for you last year," Tom said, sounding aggrieved. Nevertheless, he tucked his revolver into its holster.

Brady, still searching the river, said, "Jason Briggs woke up today and told everyone Billy had a gun the night you and he argued. And I never asked you to cover for me, you know that."

"Jason woke up? He talked?"

"A little. Wait a second. Over there!" Brady yelled as a head popped up out of the water, this time for sure. Armstrong was obviously hurt, but he was just as obviously alive. "He's wounded, Tom. He's crazy and wounded and he's going to drown if you don't do something now. You can save him. We'll figure the rest out later."

"I can't swim," Tom said as they watched Armstrong battle the current with increasingly futile strokes. "What have I done? Oh my God, what have I done?"

Brady was already yanking off his boots. He dropped his cell phone and gun onto the wharf. He zeroed in on Armstrong's position and dived into the river.

The water was surprisingly cold, but the late-summer current wasn't as strong as he'd feared. He allowed that current to sweep him along until he got close enough to Armstrong to take strong strokes in his direction. The current grew weaker and he made good time. He paused to look around. Armstrong had found a small, partially submerged log, which was helping keep him afloat, but he looked ready to let it go and slip under the surface.

"Think of your wife," Brady hollered, swimming faster.

Armstrong's eyes seemed to refocus. Brady got close enough to see the ripped cloth of his left shoulder and the torn flesh beneath. He grabbed hold of Armstrong, anticipating trouble when he told the man to let go of the water-soaked log, but Armstrong did as asked, depending on Brady now. The nearer shore was too industrial. Brady could see no way out of the water over there, so he headed back the way he'd come. Flashing lights meant the police had arrived. Police meant able hands to help him get Armstrong back on the wharf and hopefully to a waiting ambulance.

He tried not to think of Tom as he swam, but his former partner's words haunted him. Tom had done something terrible out of misplaced loyalty. Brady was saving Armstrong as much for Tom's sake as for Armstrong's.

Help came long before he reached the wharf in the form of two officers with a flotation device. Brady left Armstrong with them and swam to the wharf, climbing the rusted metal ladder placed there decades ago as a safety measure for dockworkers.

He found his boots, keys and cell phone where he'd left them, but there was no sign of his gun. He looked around for Tom, but couldn't see him. Tom's partner, Hastings, stood watching the rescue operation, so he approached him.

"Where's Tom?" he asked as he pulled his boots on over his soaking-wet socks.

"I haven't seen him," Hastings said. "His unit isn't here."

"It's out by Armstrong's truck," Brady said.

"No, it isn't. Are you the one who fired the shots?"

"Wait a second, Tom called you—"

"The call came from some guy who heard gunfire. An ambulance is on the way."

Brady stared at Hastings as he tried to make sense of what he was hearing. Tom had found Armstrong's truck but hadn't reported it? He'd gone off on foot in pursuit without alerting backup?

"Is that Bill Armstrong out there in the river?" Hastings said.

"Yeah." What was going through Tom's head?

"Hey, where are you going? You can't leave!" Hastings called as Brady walked away.

Brady didn't respond.

AFTER LOOKING THROUGH the peephole, Lara opened the door to Tom James. His eyes were very bright in his flushed face. He looked as though he'd just run a marathon. Her heart jerked into overdrive. "Is Brady okay?"

"He's fine, he's fine," Tom said.

She glanced across the street where the police officer sat in her patrol car and waved as Tom stepped inside the house.

Tom said, "Officer Alcott knows I'm here. I've come to take you to Brady."

"Why? What do you mean, take me to him? You said he was okay."

"Calm down. Truth is, he saved me from myself this evening. I collared Armstrong down by the river and there was a tussle, no one hurt badly, you understand, but Brady went into the river after Armstrong. Your husband is quite the hero."

Lara studied Tom's eyes. It crossed her mind that he might not appreciate his nonpolice ex-partner stealing some of his thunder. As for herself, she didn't care who caught Bill Armstrong, just that he was caught. She could take a deep breath now, the first in many days.

"Myra ran down to the store, but Gretchen is in the kitchen. I need to tell her I'm leaving," she said over her shoulder as she walked to the blanket she'd spread on the carpeted floor. Nathan lay atop the blanket, kicking bare legs and smiling up at her. She kneeled down to pick him up.

"I'll tell her," Tom said as he disappeared into the kitchen. Lara heard his voice and Gretchen's. She stood with Nathan in her arms, scooping up the diaper bag and the new car seat.

"All set?" Tom asked as he walked back through the kitchen door. Gretchen called out a goodbye.

"All set. But you still haven't told me where we're going to meet Brady."

"Procedure sends everyone who goes into the river over to the hospital, so we'll catch up with him there," Tom said as he took the car seat from Lara. He tickled Nathan's chin and winked at the baby before turning back to Lara. "Don't look so worried, it's just routine. Your husband is fine."

"Thank heavens this is over."

"Exactly," he said, opening the door. "By the way, Brady told me Jason Briggs woke up today."

"Yes. The boy confirmed Billy had a gun with him the night you and Brady chased him. Isn't that a relief?"

"You bet," Tom said, taking her arm. "We're kind of in a hurry," he added as he escorted her across the lawn to his unit.

Lara waved at Officer Alcott as she left, anticipating the moment she saw Brady and they knew this was all behind them. And afterward?

Fear and panic had pushed them together. There had been moments when she knew where her destiny lay, moments without confusion, when everything seemed clear. The only question was—could it last?

BRADY SWITCHED OFF his headlights as he turned onto Tom's long, straight driveway. Through the trees, he saw lights on in the house but no sign of Tom's SUV parked out front. Still, unsure what his friend's state of mind might be at the moment, he decided on a quiet approach and rolled to a stop after turning the engine off.

So, what was he doing here? Had he come to arrest his ex-partner for shooting an unarmed man? He couldn't arrest anyone, Tom had stolen his gun for some crazy reason and besides, he wasn't a cop.

Lara was right. He was a cop, with or without a badge, that's how he thought. That's who and what he was. And right now, he was more a cop than Tom. He retrieved the flashlight from the glove box and got out of the truck.

On his way to the door, he decided to hell with the quiet approach. If Tom was inside he could just answer his door and a whole boatload of questions, too. He'd taken justice into his own hands tonight and sooner or later he'd have to face the music. What was he thinking shooting Armstrong? They needed answers from the man. They needed to know why he shot Jason Briggs and if he burned down Mrs. Beaton's house with her in it and maybe most importantly, what he was guilty of when it came to Karen Wylie.

Repeated banging on the door accomplished nothing. Brady stalked across the yard. He used the flashlight to peer through the window into the dark workshop. There were two cars in evidence, but neither of them was Tom's SUV. The tarp was missing off the small car Brady assumed belonged to Tom's ex-wife. The other car was a dark sedan, about as nondescript as a car could get. Brady had first seen it a few days before with the engine hood up.

He stepped away from the shop then paused. He

turned back and shined the light through the window again. The smaller car looked like the one Nicole Stevens had been driving earlier that day.

It couldn't be. It was the same size as the car he'd seen under the tarp, the one Tom had sworn he was working on for his ex, Caroline. Brady tried every available angle and couldn't see the rear window. The metallic Riverport High School honor-student sticker was all he could think of to connect this car with Nicole.

Why did he want to connect it to Nicole?

Another memory surfaced. He finally remembered where he'd seen Nicole before. Standing on the sidewalk in front of a blue car, talking to Tom. Hair was different, though. Lighter, fluffier. When? Think. In the evening. Not long ago. The night someone shot Jason Briggs.

His brain felt as if it had been caught in a fog for days, if not months. He'd been so focused on his own problems, on Lara and Nathan and then Bill Armstrong's threats that he hadn't thought clearly about other things. What else had he missed?

Okay, so maybe Tom was working on the girl's car for her in his spare time. Or maybe he'd lied about it being his wife's car because he was embarrassed to admit he was screwing around with a seventeen-year-old kid.

"Tom, you pathetic loser," Brady said. He shone the light on the other car now. His light froze on the trunk, which was slightly ajar. The sleeve of a dark blue garment with gold decorations trailed from inside.

Nicole had worn such a garment earlier that day.

Good Lord, was Tom involved with Nicole? Were there two separate issues here: Armstrong's revenge and Tom's lechery?

He had to look at that garment and he had to see the back of the blue car. There was only one window in the shop and a brand-new lock on the door, which meant he would have to break the window to get inside. There would be no way to cover up a broken window.

Wait, there was an additional room attached to the back of the shop. Tom's climate-controlled gun room. Brady couldn't remember if it sported its own door, but if it did, maybe the lock would be older and easier to break. There were also the two big doors through which Tom drove cars into the shop.

Brady set off, keeping close to the perimeter. He passed a row of three steel barrels and an old engine block before coming across the double shop doors. Shining his light over them, he could see they were locked from the inside. He skirted new construction to get to the extension that housed the gun room. No doors, no windows, no nothing.

So, did he walk away?

Hell, no.

But first things first. He knew by now the police would be looking for him. Tom might have gone to turn himself in. Someone would undoubtedly get in touch with Lara, who would then worry. He took out his phone and punched in her number. Her phone rang once then switched to her answering machine and he left a brief message. He called information and got Myra's sister's number then placed that call. Myra answered.

"Lara left with the police," she said. "I wasn't here but Gretchen was. She said one of the officers told her they were going to meet you at the hospital."

Brady frowned. "Which officer?"

He heard Myra ask Gretchen the question. She came back on the line a second later and said, "She doesn't know. A man was all she said."

Brady said, "Did she take Nathan with her?"

"Of course. I don't think you'll be prying the little dear away from her anytime soon."

"You're right," Brady said. "Okay, I'll meet her at the hospital in a little while. I have something to do first."

Using the long-handled flashlight, Brady smashed the shop window. He used the flashlight again to clear the jagged pieces of glass away, then pulled a wheelbarrow close to the window and used it to climb through to the top of the workbench on the other side. Mindful that Tom could show up at any moment, he resisted turning on the bright work lights and made his way to the blue car.

The metallic sticker was right where it had been at three o'clock that afternoon. So, where was Nicole Stevens?

That led him to the trunk of the sedan where he flipped up the trunk and extracted the garment.

A wave of relief flooded him as he realized it wasn't Nicole's blue blouse but Tom's old letterman jacket from college. It, too, was dark blue though a heavier material. The gold decorations were merit badges for three different sports. Just an old jacket. What had he been thinking, casting Tom as some sort of villain?

The jacket felt stiff and was stained dark in places, as though it had been used to absorb a fair amount of some liquid. Brady flashed the light into the trunk, where he found the carpeted floor also stained. A corner had been pried loose as though Tom was preparing to replace the carpet. The light glittered off something small and silver in the middle of the stain.

Setting the jacket aside, Brady picked up the little ornament he now recognized as a pendant shaped like a heart, filled with a light pink shell-like stone.

Once again he had the feeling he should remember something, this time about the little heart. And once again he was stymied. He could see it lying on skin. Not Nicole, she hadn't been wearing a heart bracelet or necklace—and it hit him then with a jolt. Not Nicole. *Karen.*

Karen Wylie had been wearing a necklace when they talked with her at the drugstore. A necklace with a small silver heart. He turned the silver pendant in his hand. This heart. And now the heart was in a trunk stained with something dark...

He fought the conclusion his brain raced toward. It couldn't be blood. That would mean Tom—

Mrs. Beaton wore really thick glasses. From a distance, would Tom letterman's jacket look like a uniform? Would the sports patches look like insignias of some kind? Had Tom been the one to meet Karen and lead her off?

He deposited the jacket on the workbench and searched the shop until he remembered seeing a half-empty water bottle in Nicole's car. He fetched the bottle and poured a little on the stain. A tiny river of red pooled on the piece of sheet metal under the jacket.

His stomach lurched.

Not proof, but together with everything else...

Messing around with girls didn't mean murder. So what was Karen Wylie's necklace doing in the questionably bloody trunk of a car Brady had never seen before? What was Nicole's car doing in Tom's shop?

Okay, so Tom was involved with teenagers. Maybe he did go meet Karen. Maybe as they were driving into Portland, they ran over a dog. Maybe Tom used his jacket to pick up the injured, bleeding animal. Maybe Karen helped. They might have put it in the trunk. Karen's necklace could have caught and broke when they took the dog out at the vet's.

Maybe it wasn't even Tom's car. Brady searched until he found Tom's insurance card on the visor. Okay, it was Tom's car, but the scenario, while not plausible, was surely possible enough to cut his ex-partner a little slack. Wasn't it?

His phone rang. Lara's number glowed on the screen, but the voice that answered his greeting wasn't hers.

It was Tom's.

Chapter Thirteen

"I know you're at my house," Tom said.

Brady flinched, wondering if Tom used a hidden surveillance camera. And then the choice of Tom's words struck him. He'd said house, not shop. He must have seen Brady's truck parked outside the house. He said, "Why are you using Lara's phone? Where is she?"

"She's here with me. So is Nathan."

"Where exactly is 'here,' Tom? What's going on?"

"So, hero, did you save Bill Armstrong?"

"Yeah, I did. Listen, I haven't talked to the police yet. If you go to Dixon and explain how you got a little too anxious—"

Tom laughed. "You don't lie very well, partner."

Brady took a deep breath. All he had was a bunch of unanswered questions. He said, "How about you and I sit down and talk this through? Lara and Nathan don't need to be involved. We can figure something out."

"You're right. There are things we need to talk about. I underestimated your tenacity and your sheer stubbornness. You come to me, I'll just keep Lara and Nathan here as insurance."

"What the hell does that mean?" Brady snapped.

"Why did you leave the wharf, why did you take my gun?"

"Isn't it obvious?" Tom said.

Brady took a steadying breath. "Explain it to me."

"Not now, later. I want you to fill your truck with gas and drive out to that house you're building. You and I can talk. I'm not going to the police and I strongly suggest, for your family's sake, you don't either. Is that clear enough? Oh, and I wouldn't dawdle if I were you."

"Tom, man, don't throw away your life because of one mistake, don't—"

The phone went dead.

Brady swore as he punched off the phone. He rifled Tom's workbench looking for tools. He wasn't going to confront Tom unarmed, not after what he'd seen him do that day and the troubling evidence in the shop, and now he'd taken Lara and Nathan! He needed a gun. And if Tom hadn't changed things around, there was an arsenal behind the padlocked door in the back of the shop.

He found a chisel and a mallet. They would have to do. He sidled around the two cars and moved toward the back where he made short work of the padlock.

He swung the door inward and turned on the light as there was no reason to fear Tom coming back now.

And stopped dead in his tracks.

Tom had turned his gun room into a trophy room.

LARA TRIED to think of one smart decision she'd made in the last several days and couldn't come up with a thing.

Clutching a mercifully sleeping Nathan to her chest, she closed her eyes. She was sitting on the floor in the corner of a dark walk-in closet. It was stuffy, pitch-black and hot. Her lip throbbed. Even her arm hurt after a day of not bothering her at all.

Tom had her phone. He'd told her he was going to call Brady to come get her. She knew he was setting a trap for Brady, she just wasn't sure why.

After Tom picked her up, they'd driven out of town, away from people and buildings. He made up excuses for not going to the hospital. As Nathan grew increasingly fussy, she grew suspicious. How could she get herself and her frantic baby, strapped into his car seat and then into the backseat, out of the police car? All the locks were controlled by the driver. She'd tried to stay calm as she begged Tom to stop so she could comfort Nathan, but Tom had ignored her.

At last she realized they were going to his house. She'd been there once, with Brady, and even then she'd found it a remote and lonely place. The thought of visiting it at night with Tom acting the way he was made her queasy. How could she stop him?

He'd driven toward the house from a different approach. When his headlights swept over the yard before the driveway intersected the road, she'd caught sight of Brady's old truck and hope had soared in her heart like a Fourth of July rocket. It had died just as quickly.

Tom hadn't even slowed down, but he'd finally started talking, and the venom that came out of his mouth had stunned Lara down to her core. And terrified her. Tom blamed Brady for things Lara didn't even understand. He kept saying Brady wouldn't quit, Brady would keep pushing and pushing, Brady had ruined everything.

Brady would pay.

When Lara had tried to reason with him he'd spared

a hand from the wheel to backhand her across the face.
He'd split her lip open, but he'd also shut her up.

And then they finally stopped and he herded her into
the closet at gunpoint, taking her purse and her cell
phone in the bargain. Nathan had finally fallen asleep
at her breast and now lay against her, his forehead moist
against her neck, his breathing noisy from a nose
stuffed up from all the crying. She didn't know what
was coming next, only that Tom was off his rocker.

And she and Nathan were in mortal danger.

The door opened suddenly, blinding her with light.

"Tom," she said, throwing an arm up to ward off the
glare. Please—"

"Get up," he interrupted. "We're going to get ready
for Brady. I told you I'd call him to come get you." As
she stood up, he grabbed Nathan from her arms. The
baby awoke with a startled cry. Lara tried to take him
back. Tom pushed her away with the heel of his hand.
She stumbled backward into a wall, hitting her head,
causing stars to appear. He strode off with Nathan.

There was no handy shovel or two-by-four with
which to hit him over the back of the head. There was
nothing to do but stagger after him.

For now.

THE GUN ROOM HAD UNDERGONE a terrible transformation since the last time Brady had visited.

The guns were still there, kept now behind a locked
glass door in a cabinet designed to display them for best
effect. A computer had been added, the accompanying
desk pushed up against the west wall and littered with
electronic equipment including two printers and several
cameras.

What stole the show, however, were the dozens of photographs pinned to the walls, all depicting naked or nearly naked young women, some posed playfully, some engaged in sex acts, some in chains, some bound, eyes wide with real or feigned terror.

Jason Briggs had said he'd seen naked pictures of Karen Wylie. Brady took in a half-dozen different faces, including Karen's and Nicole's.

A picture above the desk was one of the more disturbing images. A female was bolted to the wall in shackles and chains. Her eyes were closed, bright red blood trailed from a slash across bare breasts.

Sara Armstrong.

There was a man in this photo as there were in a few of the others. He held a whip and wore a mask, but Brady knew it was Tom. Same build, same coloring, same tattoo on his left buttock. Brady strode across the room in three steps, tore the picture from the wall, wadded it up and threw it across the room. Taking a deep breath, he forced himself to leave everything else as it was.

He used the flashlight to break the glass in the gun cabinet. Tom fancied himself a connoisseur of handguns and there were several to choose from. Brady retrieved a Glock very much like his own. A .38 came next, a gun Brady often tucked into his boot. At the last minute, he also pulled a derringer from the case. Just like in the Old West, the derringer was small enough to palm. Even the .22 Magnum bullets were small, and though the shot would have to be damn near point-blank to cause deadly harm, in a pinch, it might come in handy. He grabbed Tom's dog tags off a hook inside the case. He found ammunition for all three weapons from a drawer below the case.

Inside an adjoining rifle case, he saw an AK–47. Would ballistic tests show that was the gun used to shoot Jason Briggs? Brady no longer had any doubts they would.

Among other things, he now suspected his former partner was a cold-blooded killer.

Brady turned toward the bare overhead lightbulb to load the guns, and that's when he saw a narrow door set in the corner. It was locked from the outside and needed a key. He recalled the new construction he'd seen when he walked around the building.

No time to satisfy idle curiosity…

And yet there was something about a door leading off a room like this that raised the hair on the back of Brady's neck. He took the time to hide the derringer and the .38, then used the revolver to shoot the padlock, making sure it was backed by the door frame first. The blast boomeranged around the enclosed room. Brady kicked in the door, ears still ringing.

A rumpled bed dominated the small space, covered with blue satin, stained and rumpled, backed by a pale yellow wall. Mirrors were positioned overhead and lights hung from the ceiling. A movie camera on a tripod pointed at the bed. The doors of the cupboards against the far wall stood ajar. Brady caught a glimpse of chains, whips, handcuffs, eyebolts.

As he stood there taking in the fact his ex-partner was running some kind of underage porno ring, he heard a noise coming from the far side of the bed. He crossed the room in a second.

A woman lay on the floor, stark naked, gagged and bound hand and foot, eyes wide with terror, features smeared with blood. It took a second for the brightly colored tips of her hair to register on Brady's brain. Nicole Stevens.

He stuck the Glock in the holster he still wore on his hip, grabbed the satin cover off the bed and draped it over her. Then he helped her onto the mattress. She began crying as he gently tugged the gag from her mouth.

"He'll come back, he said he would, we have to get out of here," she whispered, her words clipped like staccato notes. "Please, please, get me out of here, help me."

"He's not coming back," Brady said, taking out his pocketknife and hacking the tape binding her wrists. "Are you hurt?"

"Not too bad," she said through her tears. "I just want to go home, please."

Brady sawed at the tape around her ankles. If he called for emergency help, Tom might hear on the squad car radio and know the extent of what Brady had seen. He'd probably figure it out anyway when and if he saw all the guns, but there was no reason to alert him prematurely.

Brady couldn't leave Nicole, though, and he couldn't let her drive her car away even if he did know how to get the doors open, even if she was in any shape to drive. Like the pictures in the other room, the cars constituted evidence.

"Does Tom know where you live?" he asked as Nicole wrapped the spread tighter around herself and stood on wobbly legs.

"Yes. Where are my clothes?"

"I don't know. There isn't time to worry about them. Think of somewhere else I can take you. Somewhere between here and the south side of town." It seemed like hours had passed since the phone call, but when he checked his watch, he found only nine minutes had ticked by. Since he had no intention of putting gas in the truck, he was okay.

Nicole came up with the name of a friend who lived on the way to the Good Neighbors house. She started talking, her voice jittery at first, as soon as they were in the truck and moving away from Tom's place.

"He caught me in a DUI," she said, her gaze darting between Brady and the road ahead. "It wasn't the first time. He offered me a deal. All I had to do was have sex with him on camera. He said he filmed it for himself, you know, to look at later, but I heard him talking one day and I know he really sold it on the Internet. At first I said no, but then he told me how I would have a police record and how I wouldn't be able to get into college or anything and I thought of my parents, especially my dad, and well, eventually, I agreed."

Brady's hands tightened on the wheel. All those times he'd thought Tom was giving kids warnings instead of tickets, he'd actually been recruiting.

"When I got to his place, I saw pictures of Karen and Sara on the wall. I remembered a couple of months before Sara killed herself that she told me she'd been busted smoking dope at a party. She said she'd made a deal and it was going to be okay. And Karen thought she was going to be a damn movie star."

Brady took a corner fast. Nicole clutched the satin spread in one hand, the door handle in the other.

"After I talked to Ms. Kirk today, I decided I wasn't going to make any more movies," Nicole said, once again dissolving into tears. She finally added, "So I went over there to tell him I was quitting and that if he said a word about the DUI, I was going to tell the cops on him because Karen is gone and where is she? I think he knows."

"And that's when he started beating you," Brady said.

"He...he raped me, too," she mumbled. "And he filmed it all. The beating, the rape, me screaming. He liked it. He said he'd come back later and finish the job. When I heard you poking around and breaking things, I thought it was him. When that gun went off I almost died."

So, she'd put two and two together, which was more than Brady could take credit for. He'd been so wound up in his own troubles he hadn't seen what was going on with his old partner in his own backyard.

I hear voices, Armstrong had said over and over again. *Voices, telling me what to do.* And as soon as he'd seen Brady he'd mumbled something about trying to protect Nathan. In the next instant, Tom shot him. At that moment, Tom hadn't known about Jason Briggs waking up. If he was responsible for shooting Jason as well as corrupting Bill Armstrong, he might have thought he could still save himself.

Had Tom fired the shot out of anger as he claimed, or had he fired it to save his skin? Was it possible Tom had been feeding Bill Armstrong directions to hasten his mental disintegration? Had Armstrong started the fires thinking in some convoluted way he was exacting justice? Was it possible Armstrong had tried to take Nathan to protect him from Tom, not to harm him?

Hell, anything was possible. The world was upside down. Tom had forsaken his oath to serve and protect and become a child molester and Internet purveyor, Karen Wylie might well be dead, he'd beaten Nicole to a pulp, he'd shot a man in cold blood and now he'd kidnapped Lara and Nathan.

Brady pulled up in front of Nicole's friend's house with screeching brakes. "Go inside. Call the cops and tell them everything you know."

"I can't," she said, shivering despite the eighty-degree night.

"You have to. There's no hiding this. You have to face it."

"But I think he hurt Karen—"

"So do I. Call the police. Get them to go out to Tom's place. I'll take care of Tom."

For a second he paused. Should he have the girl tell them about the Good Neighbors house? And risk a horde of police showing up with sirens blaring?

No way.

He left in a hurry, senses heightened, ready for battle. There wasn't a doubt in his mind blood would be spilled that night. It was up to him to make sure not a drop of it was innocent.

LARA WAS in the dark again, only this time she was outside. A light suspended from a tree branch hung directly over her head, but remained unlit.

Tom had strapped Nathan back into his car seat and left him inside the house where his cries couldn't be heard. Then he'd gagged her and all but carried her toward the river where he'd thrown her into a heavy wooden chair. He'd bound her with tape and left her there.

It was a nightmare.

Tom was gunning for Brady, and Brady was on his way. She was bait, sitting out by the river, trussed up like a sacrificial goat, set to lure the man she loved to his death.

It was up to Brady. She closed her eyes for a second, then opened them wide. She'd just heard a sound.

Brady?

No. The shape illuminated by the sliver of moon revealed a man the same size as Brady, but it wasn't him. The gait was wrong, this man was heavier. Tom. He held something bulky, like Nathan's car seat. Straining for a sound from her baby, she heard nothing but footfalls traversing the rubble-strewn landscape.

And the thundering beat of her own heart.

BRADY STOPPED the truck long before turning onto River Road. It was a rural area, no nearby houses, not yet. They would come later. He pulled on the light jacket he kept behind the seat and got out of the truck.

It would take the police a few minutes to respond to Nicole's call. Dixon would be notified. He'd probably hurry out to Tom's place. The whole force would eventually end up out there. Miles from here. A good thirty minutes.

He took off at a trot, reaching the dark house within moments. If the squad car was at the house, it had been pulled inside the garage.

If all Tom wanted was a means of escape, then he'd have left in the squad car. He'd had lots of lead time. He didn't need to take Lara or Nathan, he didn't need Brady's truck. He could have disappeared into Portland within an hour or two.

Brady had had a little time to think as he drove. A couple of hours had passed between the shooting down at the wharf and Tom calling on Lara's phone. By the time he made that call, he'd already decided to involve Lara and Nathan, he'd already collected them.

Brady surmised Tom hadn't been sure what he wanted to do until he'd seen Brady's truck in his driveway and figured the game was up, there was no getting away, the police would be looking for him, he'd waited too long to make a clean escape. If all he wanted was hostages, he would have just taken Lara and Nathan. So what he wanted in addition to hostages was revenge.

The why was what Brady didn't know.

He snuck up under the front window and peeked inside the house. No lights, no movement. He had already taken the Glock out of the holster and held the weapon in his right hand. He moved silently to the door and found it unlatched. He pushed it open.

The house had an empty, silent-as-a-tomb feel to it. He moved through the rooms carefully. He found a baby blanket near the walk-in closet under the stairs and he stared at it for a count of ten, his heart in his throat. Then he continued a systematic search of the dark house until he got to the bedroom in the back. As he glanced out the window toward the river, a light came on.

Lara sat in a wooden chair under a work light hooked up to an electrical cord strung between the house and the river. She was bound and gagged, like Nicole, though mercifully, unlike Nicole, she hadn't been stripped and beaten. Her eyes looked terrified. Tears he'd actually wanted to see at one time now streamed down her face. There was no sign of Tom or Nathan.

He knelt down on the floor, took out his phone and punched in Chief Dixon's number. It was time to give Lara and Nathan an insurance policy in case he failed.

"Dixon here," was the prompt reply.

"Chief, this is Brady Skye. Listen carefully. I'm at a new construction at 555 River Circle. Tom James has my wife and son. I'm going in to get them." He hung up the phone before the questions could start and turned it off, leaving it on the bedroom floor.

It would take a half hour for Dixon to respond. If he was lucky. If Dixon didn't write the call off as a prank.

He wound his way back through the empty house to the sliding glass door at the back. The undeveloped yard appeared empty, though it was heavily shadowed.

So, Lara was the bait.

A movement behind her caught his attention. Tom, moving into the light, holding a baby seat in one hand, a gun pointed at the back of Lara's head with the other. The faint cries of an infant assaulted Brady's ears.

He hadn't outwitted Tom. Tom had anticipated what Brady would do, and now held all the cards.

"Come on out," Tom shouted. "We've been waiting for you."

For the first time in his life, Brady hoped Chief Dixon would show his face. He opened the door and stepped outside.

LARA DID HER BEST to stop crying as she watched Brady approach, so strong and capable looking in boots, jeans and a light jacket. She could communicate with nothing but her eyes and she tried, with her expression, to apologize for being so naive and stupid and endangering them all. And to tell him she loved him and trusted him and yet didn't expect him to be able to pull this particular hat out of this particular fire. The issues she'd had with the way Brady handled life now seemed insignificant. Great eleventh-hour insights.

Brady met her gaze once and then didn't look at her again. Thankfully, Nathan had grown quiet, though his stuffy breathing reached her ears every few seconds. She could tell by Brady's expression he was plotting and planning his next move.

"What the hell do you think you're doing?" Brady asked, coming to a stop a few feet away.

"Getting even," Tom said as he came around from her left. Her gaze immediately went to the baby whose eyes were closed, his cheeks flushed and damp. He'd apparently cried himself to sleep. Tom pointed the gun at the baby's head.

Lara gasped, though the sound was swallowed in the gag.

Brady took a step forward.

"Stop right there, partner. You know about Karen Wylie, don't you?"

Lara hadn't expected to hear Karen's name. Her gaze flew to Brady.

Brady said, "I'm guessing you killed her."

"It had to be done."

"I know about Nicole, too. So do the police."

"Then we'll make this short and sweet," Tom said. "Walk right over there and put all the hardware on the ground. That includes the .38 in your boot. My .38, right?"

"You know me too well," Brady said.

Tom laughed. "You're a predictable SOB. Now, do it slow and so I can see you. I have an itchy finger and this baby's skull looks kind of fragile."

Brady disarmed himself slowly, laying the Glock down first, then carefully extracting the .38 from his boot. Watching him, Lara died a little inside, not only for her chances and Nathan's but for Brady. He'd told her once he would never disarm himself for a gunman, that he'd prefer to take his chances. He was doing this for them. He was giving his life for them.

How it must irk him to surrender control. She felt new tears burn her nose and sting her eyes.

"Now, come free your wife's hands. And don't try to be a hero."

Brady walked up to Lara and started unwinding the tape. He looked at her once and smiled, then he looked at Tom. "Just tell me why," he said.

"You haven't figured it out?"

"Not all of it. I think I know what you've done, I just don't know why you're gunning for me."

"I hate to admit it, but I've been playing catch-up ever since you shot Billy Armstrong."

Brady took off the last of the tape, his fingers lingering on Lara's wrist for a moment, the touch tender, like a goodbye.

Tom yanked him by the back of the shirt. "That's enough." He threw a pair of handcuffs at Lara. "Turn around, let the little lady handcuff you. And do it right, honey, or your baby gets it."

Lara picked up the cuffs with numb fingers. Brady turned around, his hands behind his back. She looped the handcuffs on his wrists, trying to see if there was a way to make them loose enough for him to escape. But Tom yanked Brady around again and the cuffs clicked into place.

"Very nice," Tom said. With the gun now pointed at Brady, he handed Nathan to Lara, whose feet were still tied to one another and to the chair. She took the baby with a flood of relief and held him close as if she could protect him with her love.

Brady turned around and faced her, his eyes dark and consuming. Tom, the gun still in one hand, patted Brady down head to toe. Apparently convinced Brady was now harmless, he said, "Figured it out yet?"

"Most of it. I saw you talking to Nicole Stevens a

half hour before Jason Briggs was shot. How did you change cars so fast?"

"I didn't. I used to carry the AK-47 in the squad car trunk."

"You shot him from your squad car? That was taking a terrible chance."

"Maybe," Tom said smugly.

"I'm guessing you burned up that poor old woman in Scottsdell, too."

"Snoopy bitch. Who knows what she might have remembered the next day."

"Like seeing the sedan you drove the day you promised Karen Wylie you'd meet her bus in Scottsdell and whisk her away to Hollywood? It's her blood in the trunk, isn't it? Where'd you dump her body?"

"She's in one of the barrels behind my shop. One more time, partner. Have you figured out why?"

"Why you corrupted Bill Armstrong into starting the fires and lurking around and making threats? Why you kept me running all over the place, too worried to think straight?"

"And don't forget your dear old father. I hired a couple of punks to pick a fight. The old man has gotten soft."

Brady said, "All to protect your little movie empire, am I right?"

Tom laughed again. "Partly. It actually started with what Billy yelled at me down by the river the night you so kindly shot the brat."

"What he yelled? It was gobbledygook. He was upset about his sister's suicide. He was drunk."

"Not really. You know, you've been a major pain in the neck for a year now," Tom said.

"You were talking about Billy," Brady said softly. "What he told you—"

"He saw his sister's pictures on the Internet. He confronted her about it. The little tramp told Billy I was behind it."

"You were behind it," Brady repeated.

Tom shrugged. Lara saw Brady's gaze travel to the weapon in Tom's hand. His eyes grew steely. "Where'd you get that gun, partner?" he said.

Tom laughed. "Finally, you see the light."

"You took it off Billy's body. You knelt by him and you stole the gun because you were afraid I overheard him accuse you of driving his sister to kill herself."

"More than that. He figured out I forced her to take her grandma's pills. I had no choice. The girl started making noise about telling her father everything."

Lara twisted to see the weapon. She had to assume it was Billy's grandfather's .45-caliber Colt automatic. The gun the boys had found and lusted over. The gun Billy had taken with him the night he and Jason stole the beer and the car, the gun he'd had on him when providence delivered both him and Tom James to a lonely riverbank.

Brady said, "I shot the wrong person, didn't I? I should have let the kid plug you. You'd already murdered his sister, but at least Karen Wylie would still be alive. And Mrs. Beaton."

"Hindsight," Tom said, "is cheap."

"You set me up. You wanted to keep me so off balance I wouldn't stop to think about what I heard, so you stole the gun from his dead body."

"I was going to dump it later, but it's a beauty."

"And that's why you shot Jason, because you knew he knew about the gun and you figured he was going to tell Lara about it. What he was really trying to do was to get Lara to talk to Karen about posing nude. He'd seen her pictures, I guess while in juvie. And maybe Billy had told him about what you got his sister to do."

"They need to keep a better eye on the inmates' computer habits."

"And then you started feeding Bill Armstrong a bunch of lies and fueling his grief to escalate his threats, to keep me from thinking straight. And when he tried to tell me what was happening, you tried to kill him. And failed."

Tom shrugged again.

"I never heard what Billy said to you that night," Brady said. "I just heard Sara's name. Nothing else."

"I thought for sure you'd heard some of it. Well, no matter, it's all worked out okay."

Brady shook his head. "You call what you've done working out okay? The misery you've caused, the death and the destruction? And now you're stuck here in Riverport because you were too stupid or too vain to leave when you could, and all that is what you call working out okay?"

Tom's voice turned razor sharp. "I'm taking your wife and your kid and using them to get out of here and you're going to the bottom of the river with a bullet in your gut. So, yeah, after the pain in the neck you've been, it's all good."

Lara closed her eyes as Tom raised the gun.

She heard Brady say, "We've gone through a lot together, you and me, Tom. How about letting me say goodbye to my wife and son?"

Lara's eyes popped open. Tom seemed to consider the ramifications of Brady's request and finally said, "Sure, why not? Just make it quick."

Brady approached her, hands secured behind his back. Leaning down he brushed his lips against her cheek.

She managed with one hand to pull the gag from her mouth. "I love you," she said.

He leaned a little closer and looked tenderly at Nathan. Then he glanced back at her. "Dog tags," he said so softly she thought for sure she'd misunderstood. She met his gaze. His eyes bored into her. Dog tags? He wasn't wearing any she could see, but of course, he wore a zipped-up jacket—

In August?

As he kissed Nathan's forehead, she did the only thing she could think of. She moved her hand up under his jacket and shirt, and felt the skin-warmed steel of a small gun dangling from his neck. Her fingers curled around the grip and she yanked as he straightened up. The gun and chain slipped into her hand and she covered it with Nathan's blanket. She switched off the safety as he'd taught her to do years before.

"I love you," he said, giving her the time to slip her hand around the grip, his voice covering the sound of her pulling back the hammer. "No matter what, I love you." Turning, he stepped aside.

It was up to her. He'd given her the means, now she had to make it happen. With a steely determination she never knew she possessed, she pointed the tiny gun at Tom.

And fired.

"I WAS HOPING he would be in too big a hurry to pat down my chest," Brady said. "We got lucky. And you saved us."

Lara snuggled against his side. If she closed her eyes, she could still see Tom James laying at her feet, blood gushing out of the bullet hole in his chest. She kept her eyes wide open.

"He's going to make it," Brady said as though reading her mind. "Chief Dixon said he survived the surgery. He'll get a trial and hopefully, he'll rot in jail."

Her lips curved into a smile against the downy softness of her son's head. They were seated in Brady's living room, decompressing after hours of standing around in the dark. The TV played softly in the background, turned on to provide background noise as she worked to get Nathan to sleep, left on out of pure inertia.

Lara had spoken to her mother, who had aborted her trip upon learning of the fire that destroyed her house. She'd flown home and was now ensconced at the downtown hotel. Brady again seemed to read her mind as he said, "Let's have a wedding."

"We're already married," she said, looking up at him.

He hugged her tighter. "I feel as though we cheated your mother out of a wedding. If she still wants one, let's go through with it, the bigger and messier the better."

Lara laughed softly. "It might help her forget we burned down her house."

"For a while, anyway. Hey. Maybe she'll hire me to rebuild it for her."

Lara smiled again. She'd heard Chief Dixon offer Brady his old job back. She was betting money Brady would give up contracting and return to his true vocation before long, though she really didn't care what he did as long as it made him happy. She said, "You still haven't reached your father?" When he shook his head, she added, "The bars closed hours ago."

"I know."

"And Garrett?"

"He doesn't answer his phone, either."

She settled into the cushions. She knew daylight would bring at least one decision. Would they stay in Riverport or move to Seattle? The one thing they didn't have to decide was whether or not they were a family.

For Lara, that question had been answered hours before when she sat in a dark closet, anticipating Brady's arrival, knowing he was walking into a trap and she was powerless to save him. And knowing that if he died, so would she. He was her man just as she was his woman. There was no one else for either of them. There never would be.

It had been cinched when he gave up control of the situation and handed it to her. Thank heavens she'd come through.

She said, "Next time, *you* shoot the bad guy, okay?"

He kissed her tenderly. "Okay."

"Because I don't care for it."

"I know." He leaned his head against hers. They should go to bed, but neither of them had the energy to move. Her mind drifted until Brady's body suddenly stiffened, "Where's the remote?" he asked, a note of urgency in his voice. "I just saw Garrett's face on the news. Something about a bomb."

She dug for the remote and turned up the volume. The picture on the screen showed the face of an attractive woman with intelligent deep-set gray eyes. The announcer said "—over the sudden death of forty-one-year-old Reno attorney Elaine Greason."

"What's this got to do with Garrett?"

"I don't know."

"Greason was killed in a car bomb yesterday morning." A new picture filled the box above the newscaster's left shoulder. Lara drew in her breath as Brady jumped to his feet.

Garrett's picture seemed to fill the screen. The newscaster said, "Once again, police are looking for this man, Garrett Skye, Greason's bodyguard. Police caution Skye should be considered armed and dangerous."

As the news moved on to the next big story, Lara got to her feet, juggling Nathan and his blankets. Brady stared at the floor, a knot in his jaw.

She said, "Garrett wouldn't kill anyone—"

Brady turned to her. "Wouldn't he? What if someone paid him? He was desperate to get his little girl back. What if he saw this as his only way?"

"I can't believe that."

"But they said—"

She put her free arm around him. "Things aren't always as they seem. You'll help him, won't you?"

"Of course I will." He wrapped her in his arms.

They stood in silence for a long time, Lara's cheek pressed against his chest, his heartbeat drumming in her ear.

There would be bumps, there would be problems— what life came trouble free? But they would face everything, the good, the bad, all of it, together.

* * * * *

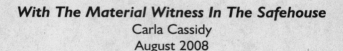